Dancing with Adam

Eva Headley

Contents

Prologue

"That's it, Fiona! Spin, keep going!"

Grinning as her father watched her dance, Fiona kept spinning around and around on her first pointe shoe, doing her very first pirouette. "Daddy, I'm doing it! Look, look!"

"I'm looking!" Her father chuckled, watching proudly from the sideline. "That's my girl."

Returning to fourth position, Fiona squealed happily at her father. "I did it! Oh, my gosh, I did it, daddy!"

"For sure, sweetpea," He stretched his arms out to her. "Come here, my beautiful girl."

Fiona ran into her father's arms and hugged him, almost crying with happiness. She clutched him tightly and felt him kiss the top of her head as he hugged her right back.

"I'm so proud of you, princess," He told and pecked her cheek. He drew back to look at his daughter with a face full of love written across his features. Fiona smiled brightly up at him. "You're gonna kick some ballerina butt at your audition tomorrow. Are you sure this is still what you want?"

Fiona nodded frantically. "I wanna be a ballerina! Just like Lizzi's mommy!"

"Alright, alright, it's your call," Her father sighed and then patted her on her arm. "I just don't want you breaking any of your beautiful bones. Your ma and me spent so much time making that letter to the stork about how we wanted you, so don't you go tripping over those perfect little feet of yours."

Fiona giggled and shook her head. "OK, I won't. Can I try one more pirouette, please, daddy?"

"Of course, baby. Try getting on your leg a little more this time, your foot was traveling. Or so this book says," Her father held up a book with a ballet slipper on the front. "I swear I'll be fluent in French by the time I finish this baddie. Anything for my little girl."

Fiona giggled and jumped back out onto the garage floor, taking fourth position again. Her dad sat down in his chair like before and crossed his arms over his chest, watching his daughter with a smile. She then set off into her second pirouette, spinning around on the floor.

"That's it, princess," Her father cheered. "That's good! Remember your leg. Keep staring at the star we drew on the wall. Don't lose focus, you're almost—ugh," He suddenly stopped in the middle of his sentence and choked on his words. His face started turning red. Fiona instantly stopped spinning and stared worriedly at him.

"Daddy?"

"Mmng," He choked out, just as his hand shot to his left arm and his eyes expanded. He stared straight at her. "Fi..."

"Daddy!" Fiona screamed as he fell off his chair and collapsed on the floor, his whole body rigid. "Daddy, what's happening! Daddy!"

His body strained for another two seconds, but then all of a sudden, he stopped moving. Fiona looked at her father in shock for moment, but then fell to her knees besides him and shook him.

"Daddy, wake up! Wake up, it isn't funny!" She cried. Why wasn't he moving? She didn't like his joke. "Daddy! Daddy, stop playing, I don't like it. Daddy! Please wake up, dad, please... p-please... please! daddy!"

Chapter 1

"**M**ove, move, move! Get out of the way!"

Jumping to the side when two people steering a shopping cart with a guy sitting in it came rolling wildly down the hall, howling with laughter, Fiona nearly fell backwards and landed on the floor had it not been for her quick reflex to catch on to the sill of the door to the studio she was glaring inside.

Loud music started thumping, just as a bunch of people spread aside for the shopping cart that came rolling in with uncontrolled speed. Everyone did like Fiona and stared with open mouthes as the two controlling the cart suddenly braked and had the guy sitting inside flying out with his limbs bashing about.

And then—just as Fiona waited to see the inevitable crash and hear the bones on the poor guy break—he landed on his hands and knees in a pose, just as the beat dropped.

Everyone in the studio took a synchronized step back as the guy lifted his head in tact with the beat. That's when Fiona realized it was all choreographed.

They all jumped at the next beat, striking a similar pose to the guy in the center, who clearly had a flair for the dramatic.

With soft, but wild chocolate brown hair, tan skin and a muscular built, fit for a dancer, he looked insanely good.

Everyone suddenly started doing a synchronized domino move where one started a move, then the next one copied it a fraction of a second later, then the next, and so on. The guy in the middle then stepped out and did a routine. He was fast, Fiona noted, watching him dance with a gaping mouth. His footwork was amazing. He twirled on the floor, did a headstand, a pose, then did a backflip, landed on his hands and struck another pose with his legs in the air.

Who the hell was this guy? Fiona wondered as she watched from the door.

Jumping back up again, the guy clapped his hands twice and then the rest of the crew begun dancing again, all of them jumping into the same pose as him. They danced out their routine, the guy in the middle appearing to be the crew leader, topping off everything they did with a move that was twice the more amazing.

The whole crew ended the routine off with doing a thing where the lead guy jumped up over a wall they had made with their bodies and landed on his feet, throwing his cap at the mirror with a grin. As the music snapped and ended, everyone broke out of formation and cheered and clapped. The guy at the front grinned as well and picked up his cap again, putting it back where it belonged. He bumped fists with a few of the guys and teased a couple of the girls with some booty-pinches. He then shifted his eyes to the door, still wearing his grin, and spotted Fiona.

She jumped as if having been stung, swung around and quickly headed on down the hall where she was supposed to be.

Watching them dance had been fun, but she could never in a million years do something like that, join a crew. They were so loud and extroverted. Not that that was a bad thing, it was just the exact opposite of what she was.

Looking down at her feet that were covered in her her warmup ballet slippers, she readjusted her tights that clung to her thin but muscular legs as she walked to the closed studio she had booked.

The DanceDec was a place that had dance studios for rent all year long, but over the last few months, the popularity had risen like crazy. Had it not been because Fiona had booked well ahead of time, she wouldn't have been able to dance this month. It would've ruined her.

Stepping inside studio 13, the one at the far end, located away from all the others, she closed the door and locked it, sliding the blindfolds down over the observation windows. She then dumped her duffle bag down by a chair that had a stereo on it and sat down on the floor, fishing out her phone. She plugged it in and hooked it up with some classical, soothing music. It started flowing through the speakers, calming her heartbeat down to normal again.

She then begun fishing out her rolling mat, her yoga mat and her stretch latex for warmups. She begun with her calfs, rolling them over the rolling mat, stretching out all her muscles. She then rolled her feet out, flexed her toes, then rolled again.

When her all muscles were stretched out properly, she moved to the barre and stepped into first position. She begun a simple warmup routine to get her body and muscles heated up and prepped for later.

Demi-plié, demi-plié, arabesque, grand battéman, back to first position. Switching to second position, she lifted to her toes, held her balance, then bent down to the floor so her fingertips touched the tip of her slipper. Then up again and do an exhale.

Warmups took almost half an hour which only gave her one hour to dance in. It wouldn't be long enough like always, but the money deposits along with the popularity had increased as well. An hour and a half was all she could afford.

Finally came the time where she switched her slippers out with pointe shoes.

As she rose to en pointe, she felt all the troubles that had weighed her shoulders down all week release. The noise from the hall faded out and all she heard was Beethoven's moonlight sonata play through the stereo. She begun moving across the floor, taking a step, rising to her toe, doing a simple arabesque. Her arms molded themselves to fit the music's sweet flow, gentle like a summer's breeze, but strong and supported as they should be.

She spun, twirled, chasséd across the floor, did a jump, then came to en pointe again and into fourth position, preparing for her fouettés.

But like always, instead of setting into the spin, she froze up. Her legs refused to move and instead her arms lowered and her heart sunk into her stomach. There it was. Right on cue.

As the tears pressed in the inner corners of her eyes, she held them back and tried to focus on her goal.

She could do this. She could do a fouetté. It wasn't a pirouette. She had to remind herself every time. Fouettés were harder, more dangerous, but still, they were just too close to pirouettes.

Stepping into fourth again, she took a deep breath and then another.

- And then she lifted to en pointe and spun.

And spun.

And spun.

She spun so fast, her spot on the wall started to blur. Her leg kicked out each time and caught more speed before it folded back in and allowed her to spin again. In the end, it was no longer her who was spinning, it was the world.

"Jeeeesus, you're making my head hurt," A humored voice suddenly broke through her spinning bubble.

Startled and horrified, Fiona lost her spot and her balance, tumbled out of control and out of course. Her mind was in a whirl; she couldn't sense where she was going, only knew that eventually she would hit the floor. And shatter.

But the floor never came. Instead a pair of arms caught her and tipped her over backwards, keeping one hand on her back, the other on her thigh, elevating her leg slightly.

Blinking up, the room still spinning, she looked into a pair of hazel-green eyes that shone down at her, a hint of amusement sparkling within them; It was the crew leader from before.

"Nailed it, baby," He smirked, his voice smooth and humored. "One more time from the top?"

Chapter 2

Fiona screeched up at the guy and jumped out of his arms the very next second. Her reaction caused him to let out a chuckle as she shuffled away like he had boy cooties.

"You okay there?" He asked her with a little grin and rose a bemused brow.

"How the hell did you get in?!" She exclaimed and wrapped her arms around herself. She could've sworn she had locked the door – she knew she had. Did he bust in or something? Wouldn't she have heard that?

"You do know that none of the locks here work, right?" He informed and shot a thumb over his back towards the door. "They're just for show. The only working locks you'll find are on the stalls to the girls bathroom."

"How do you know that?"

"Didn't you hear what I said? The only place you'll find a working lock is in the girls bathroom."

Fiona shook her head, but then instantly snapped out of it. "I had the blinds closed. Were you creeping on me?"

"Well, I was passing by and I glanced in through the cracks and saw you spinning like a fidget spinner, but then I saw your feet—"

"You were creeping on my feet?"

"—and then I noticed you were twisting your foot wrongly," He finished, and then to Fiona's surprise walked into the middle of the floor. Her eyes widened when he stepped into fourth position and held out his arms into a perfect arch. "You want to watch your foot when you go en pointe in your fouettés so that you don't travel, and more importantly, don't break your ankle."

Fiona took a quick step back when he then set off and made a clean fouetté, kicking his leg out and turning perfectly. He spun three perfect spins, then came back into fourth, ending as elegantly as he started.

"You dance ballet?" She asked. She hadn't expected that from the hiphop boy, but maybe that was presumptuous of her.

"I dance a little of everything." He grinned, then eyed her up and down. "But I don't think I've seen your tutu around here before. You new to the Dec?"

"No. I usually just dance in the evening." She averted her eyes to the floor. Why were they talking? She should be dancing, not talking with some random guy with a foot fetish.

"The evening?" He responded. "Little dangerous walking home that late, don't you think?"

"I grew up in Harlem, I know my way around."

"I grew up in Harlem too, but you don't see me walking the streets at night."

"You grew up in Harlem?" She asked and couldn't help the pinch of surprise in her voice.

He smirked slowly and crossed his arms. "What? Can't a gringo grow up in the hood? That's racist, baby."

She rolled her eyes and crossed her arms as well. "That wasn't what I was implying. I was just surprised."

"I'm full of surprises, baby girl. So, you wanna try that fouetté again?"

"What?" She blinked rapidly when he switched subject faster than she could spin. "The... fouetté?"

"Yeah, it'll only take a minute to teach," He said and took a step towards her. "It's really easy once you get the hang of it."

"Uh... no, thank you, I'm good," She declined and stepped back when he came closer. He stopped up and raised a brow.

"I don't bite, tutu. It really only takes a minute to learn, I'm not kiddin—"

"I said I'm fine!"

He slowly held up his hands. "Alright. Easy, tiger. I was just trying to help."

"I'm sorry." Before thinking too much about it, Fiona shot for her bag, gathered her things and rushed towards the door. She couldn't be here. She couldn't. "I'm so sorry."

She blew right past him, but managed to catch his baffled expression as she practically ran from the studio. Panic was chasing her and she couldn't get away fast enough—but that wasn't all that was chasing her she quickly discovered.

"Wait, whoa, why are you leaving?" The guy called behind her as he hustled down the stairs after her, following her all the way to the doors and out. "Did I do something wrong? Did I say someth—"

"I'm fine, please just leave me alone!" Fiona threw her bag over her shoulder and ran out on the street. It was a scalding hot day in New York. The heatwave that had attacked the city blanketed everyone in a coat of sweat. The air was humid to breathe, almost drinkable, and she felt the sun sting her dark skin even through her stockings. She stepped onto the curb and begun rushing down the pavement in her pointe shoes.

"Wait!" The guy said behind her again, still following her like a lost puppy. Or a stubborn stalker. "Can we just start over? I'm Adam. What about you?"

"If I answer, will you leave me alone?"

"No promises, but I'll let you run on me while I pretend my feelings aren't severely wounded."

Fiona felt her cheeks heat up. She feared it wasn't the sun's job.

"Fiona." She hurriedly breathed out and then set into a run, leaving Adam on the curb as she rushed away. He kept his promise and stayed behind, but she did hear him call after her one last time though.

"Nice meeting you, princess!"

As Fiona the next day walked into the DanceDec, she felt a spike of anxiety in her stomach when she laid eyes on all the other dancers who for some reason were sitting in a circle on the floor in the middle of the foyer. Music was booming loudly and they were all laughing, and now as Fiona shyly glanced their way, she noticed they were taking a break and eating a late lunch. That is, if you could even call what they ate food.

Pizza boxes and empty burger wrappers were spread out on the floor around them, along with crushed energy cans and plastic bottles of soda. Some of the dancers were still chewing on slices of pizza and picking at left-over fries while some were just lying or sitting on the floor, talking about and discussing choreography with each other. They all looked to be having a good time, eating their calorie bombs.

So of course it was no surprise that amongst the social circle, Fiona spotted Adam. He was sitting in an elegant crossed-legged position and was explaining something with his hands to two others who were laughing and shaking their heads. One of them threw a French fry at him which made him toss his head back with laughter.

Fiona lowered her head and continued walking straight past them, hoping she could pass by unnoticed – but of course she'd never had that kind of luck in her life.

"Hey, Fiona!" Adam's voice rung through the foyer and caused all the attention to land on her as she froze up. The prickle of at least a dozen eyes on her had her nearly throwing up on the spot. "Wanna join? There's still some pizza left!"

Fiona swallowed dryly and quickly shook her head without looking at them, then ran upstairs. She almost slammed the door to her studio, but the instant she was safe behind closed drapes, she felt the tension uncoil inside her. She let her bag drop to the floor, then dropped down herself, curling her arms around her knees to try and breathe.

Breathe. Exhale. Inhale. Breathe. A simple human task became so hard whenever that prickle of anxiety skated up and down her back and bit like a thousand small ants. She managed to somehow get her limbs to stop shaking, but her breath kept coming out erratic. Hopefully dancing would rectify that.

After another moment, she slowly begun her usual routine, but her mind just couldn't seem to focus. Her eyes kept flying to the door with the broken lock instead of the mirror where she should be looking. She couldn't help but think if someone was gonna burst in like yesterday. It locked her knees in fear. They couldn't see her dance. They just couldn't...

Just keep focus, she told herself when the fear settled in her stomach and threatened to spill out. You have to practice. You only have three more weeks left, so make them count.

With a deep breath, she willed herself to start the music after she had finished warmups, and then stepped out onto the floor, keeping one thought in her head; The purpose of all this mental torture. The reason she kept dancing when fear locked her up. As usual, as soon as the music began playing, the fear dissolved into thin air. Her limbs begun moving and her breath calmed down.

This was familiar. It was what she knew. It brought her body to peace and it blocked everything else out.

Just breathe.

Fiona danced through her piece. Several times. Her feet began aching in her pointe shoes, but it was a pain she had grown almost immune to. Her toes could be bleeding, blistering, falling off, and she wouldn't be able to tell. It was one thing to feel pain in your feet occasionally; it was another to have a constant pain in your chest whenever you didn't dance.

But just like yesterday, when she came to her pirouettes, she froze up. The same sensation locked in her throat as she went into fourth and felt her knees begin to buckle. The tears came, the anxiety, and then finally, the memories.

'F-Fiona...'

'Daddy?'

'Fi...'

'Daddy!'

"I told you, you need to get on your foot," A voice broke through her pain once again. Fiona let out a hiccup and turned around, quickly blinking the tears out of her eyes until the blurry image of Adam standing in the door again cleared up.

"What are you doing here again?" She angrily snapped, feeling the tremors go through her body. "You said you'd leave me alone."

"I said no promises," He reminded her and stepped inside again, uninvited. "And you were about to go and break your ankle. You gotta let me teach you, baby."

"I don't need any help," She bit back, wishing he would just go away. What was his problem anyway? "Just leave me alone."

"Do an arabesque," He said and crossed his arms, challengingly. He raised a brow when she just pursed her lips angrily. "What? Come on, just humor me."

Gritting her teeth, Fiona went en pointe and extended her leg out backwards, finding her balance. She then went down again, turning around to just catch Adam nodding.

"Just as I expected. You're not supporting your leg at all. If you did, then you would've been able to hold your arabesque for longer."

Who the hell did he think he was? Fiona growled to herself. A principal dancer? Purely from what she had seen yesterday with his crew, he had spent more years perfecting his head-spins than his pirouettes.

And they're still better than yours.

"I told you, I don't need your help," Fiona replied in a more than snappy voice. Adam pointedly ignored it and came further into the studio which only pissed her off more. "Do you mind?"

"Do you?" He shot back. "Just let me show you how to stay centered. If you keep doing what you're doing, you're gonna end up twisting your foot."

"I've been dancing like this for years, I haven't broken my foot yet."

"Yet," He strongly echoed and looked firmly at her. "You've been doing it wrong for years then. Why won't you just let me show you? It takes a minute. Come on."

Fiona pressed her lips tightly together. He really just wasn't backing down, was he? Why was he so stubborn?

Pot, kettle.

"It kills me to see someone dance in a way that could potentially damage something," Adam voiced, as if reading her mind. He looked at her for a moment and then put his hands on his hips. "If you're gonna do ballet for several more years, you might as well learn it now; No company is going to take you in if your footwork is sloppy."

Sloppy footwork? "Fine. Teach me then. You have exactly one minute." Before she ran out and never came back again.

Adam split his lips into a grin. "Hand me your foot."

"What?" Fiona blinked when he immediately crouched down in front of her and held out a hand. "Why?"

"Because I'm going to show you how to place it so your balance gets centered right up your leg. Just trust me," He said and smirked up at her. "Foot?"

Fiona took a deep breath. It was just her foot. Just that. It wasn't like he was dancing with her. He just needed her foot. Nothing more.

Nervously, she lifted her foot into the palm of his out-stretched hand. When she felt his warm palm close around her pointe shoe, her throat closed. 51 seconds.

"Alright, so the way you do it is like this," He explained and bent her foot skillfully, letting the tip of her shoe touch the floor. "It strains your ankle and—" He placed his thumb right below her ankle and pressed. Fiona felt something twitch inside her foot that made her leg shake, "—that's what happens. Instead, try this," He instructed and now bent her foot seemingly the same way, only he twisted it ever so slightly more inwards. "You flex your foot out too much, but by just turning it in an inch, like this—" He pressed the same spot as before, but this time, Fiona didn't feel any twitching. She blinked perplexed down at him. "—it releases the pressure on the ankle and sends the support straight up through your leg. Try putting some weight on it."

He completely let go of her foot and stood up, crossing his arms as Fiona tryingly stepped en pointe and felt as her feet carried her a lot easier.

"See?" Adam smiled. "Much better, right? Now try that arabesque again."

Blindly following his orders, Fiona let her other foot raise from the floor, lifting her leg up behind her in a small extension with a slight curve at the knee. She felt her toe lift all her weight, but it didn't hurt like it had before. The support went straight up her leg and lifted her easily as she extended her hands above her head.

"Nice," Adam noted and walked around her to observe her. "Tuck in your ribs a little, strengthen your core—there you go."

Fiona did as he told and felt herself centre completely. Dancing had never felt that easy.

- Until she suddenly felt a hand on her hip and another one smoothing up on her elevated leg.

Sucking in a gasp and almost losing her balance, she switched her eyes to the mirror and saw Adam right behind her, standing centered and supporting her leg like a pas de deux partner was supposed to. "Wh-what are you—"

"Focus," He said and lifted her leg ever so slightly, giving it the last extension it needed. Fiona's body tensed up and she felt herself burn where his hands delicately held her. "Keep your eyes on the mirror. You're losing your centre. Focus, Fiona."

Focus, Fiona.

In shock, Fiona couldn't think of anything else to do but to do as he said. She got on her leg again and felt as Adam lightly tightened his hold on her thigh, took a small step and then begun walking around her, spinning her elegantly.

Fiona couldn't breathe. The music was still playing and now they were turning. This now categorized what they were doing as dancing; Dancing together.

"Stop!" She immediately lowered her leg and went off pointe. She was out of Adam's arms before he could even blink.

"What happened?" Adam looked at her with a perplexed expression as Fiona raced up to her bag to pick it up. "You're running again now? Is that just your answer to everything?"

"It's none of your business," She breathlessly replied. Her pulse raced. Anxiety pumped through her body and made her dizzy. Focus. Breathe.

She slung her bag over her shoulder and bolted for the door, but before she could get there, Adam stepped up in front of her, looped an arm around her waist and spun her right back into the room. She almost stumbled again if it wasn't for his strong arm. She felt him grab her bag, snatching something that was apparently sticking out of it.

"What's this?" He asked and held out the brochure Fiona had picked up a few weeks ago, the one she slept with under her pillow like some absurd tooth-fairy wish. Her eyes widened as she saw him read the cursive text on the front. "The New York Ballet?"

"Give that back!" She raged and ripped it out of his hands, quickly stuffing it into her bag again and zipping it up.

"You're trying out for the open auditions?" He asked with a slightly amused grin, lifting his brow. "Seriously? You think you have a shot?"

"Get off my case!" She furiously replied. Who was he to judge? He'd caught her dancing twice. How could he determine whether or not she had a shot from just that? Just because he thought he was some sort of dance guru—

"I was just asking," He defended, raising his hands again. "I just wanted to know if you were auditioning or not. If you are, I think you're gonna be greatly disappointed. You're way technically limited. Have you ever danced anything but ballet?"

Question upon question. Why didn't he just poke her with a stick? They were complete strangers. She didn't owe him any answers.

"Go away," She spat, her words much harsher than the crumbling sensation that tumbled inside her. "Leave me alone, I don't want your help."

"The New York corps dances a lot more than just ballet, Fiona," He stated and walked up to her. "If you want even the slightest chance of getting in, then yeah, you sure as hell do want my help."

"How can you possibly help me? You're just a hiphop boy with a crew who happens to know a little ballet. That doesn't make you an expert." Now who was judging? Rage was whipping her up.

"You got that from Wiki?" He rightfully deadpanned at her. He then leveled with her. "I dance a lot more than just hiphop and ballet, Fiona. Like I said yesterday, I dabble with a little of everything. It's my passion. Just let me help you with yours."

"Why do you even care?" She loomed.

"Because I love dancing with black chicks."

She was so done here.

"I'm kidding," He chuckled when she tried to get past him again. He stepped in front of her once more. "I care because dancing means something to you, and here at the DanceDec we help each other. Even the ones who judge me by my cap."

She glanced up at his cap and saw him take it off and run a hand through his brown hair. He threw it away on the floor, then looked at her with a little smirk. "Good enough for the diva?"

Fiona rolled her eyes and looked away. "You're not the problem."

"Then what is?"

She was.

Ballet was as competitive as modeling, except it was fifty times harder. A model could get a dozen pictures taken and the photographer could pick the best one that would get showed to the public, whereas in ballet there were no stills. When you stepped onto that stage and danced, there wasn't room for mistakes or flaws, only sheer and utter perfection, bodily and technical. You had to be the best at everything and that included all types of dancing.

Fiona knew her chances of passing through the first rounds of the open auditions were bleak, but every time she had thought about signing up for a dance partner or instructor, fear had crippled her and she had chickened out.

Her father collapsing played before her eyes every single time she tried to spin, and that was when she was alone. Imagine how catastrophic it would go if she tried dancing with someone else judging her. Looking at her. Correcting her.

Looking at her right now was Adam, and his eyes weren't wavering as he waited for her answer. It scared the shit out of her. He was a complete stranger and he was volunteering for weeks of tutoring her to prepare her for an audition she'd probably end up blowing. What did he get out of it? She had practically been nothing but rude towards him since yesterday, yet here he still stood. What was his gain? Gratification?

"Look, let's just take a step back, alright?" He offered. "When's your audition?"

Fiona bit her lip. "Three weeks from today..."

"Three weeks? Shit." He scratched the back of his head and thought for a moment. He clearly hadn't counted on the audition being so close. "Alright, look, I can't perform miracles, but I can teach you all the basic stuff you need to know to get you through round one. We'll have to train every day, all day, after school, so no rest. After that, if you're still interested, I can keep coaching you through to the callbacks. What do you say?"

She was terrified. She wanted to run. She also knew this was the best kind of offer she would ever find, but could she do it? She wasn't worried about the three weeks of intense dancing, she was used to that. What concerned her was... could she dance through her fears?

"I..." She knew one day she'd have to get over them. If she got accepted into a company some day, God allow it, she couldn't be afraid to dance in a theatre with a packed audience.

"Sleep on it," Adam looked at her, watching the indecision in her eyes. "You'll be here tomorrow, right?"

"Yeah..."

"Give me your answer then. But decide fast," He opened the door to the studio and then paused in it, giving her a glance over his shoulder. "You need all the help you can get."

Chapter 3

As Fiona came home that evening and dumped her bag on the kitchen floor next to the dining table, she found her mom looking over her shoulder at her, giving her a smile. "Hey, honey. How was your day?"

Fiona crept into one of the chairs and pulled her leg up. "It was okay. Nothing special."

Her mom gave her a quick assessment from the stove where she was cooking dinner. "You look worn out. Are you hungry?"

"Yeah..." She fiddled a little with the cutlery on their minuscule dining table. "What's for dinner?"

"Roasted chicken with sweet potatoes, béarnaise sauce and a green salad."

"Sounds great." She offered her mom a small smile before she turned back to stirring the pot again. She then let out an exhale. Why did she always cook so calorie-fed food?

They ate together and talked about everything and nothing. Fiona listened to her mom tell her about the day she'd had at the diner she worked at while Fiona nibbled on the small piece of chicken she had selected and managed to eat one whole potato. She left the sauce untouched but dug into the salad, eating as much as she could. By the time her mom was done eating, Fiona had been done for 15 minutes.

"Thank you for dinner," She said as she washed her plate and cutlery clean and put them back in the cupboard and drawer where they belonged. "I'm gonna go take a shower and get started on my homework."

"Alright, hon. Call if you need help," Her mom said as Fiona picked up her bag and headed for her room. "No staying awake past 11pm. I'll be checking on you!"

"I won't." Fiona promised before she quickly closed the door to her room. Dumping her bag down again, she let out a shaky sigh and closed her eyes, simply just leaning back against the door for a moment.

Then she went into the bathroom.

She locked the door and turned on the shower before turning to the toilet and flipping the seat up. She crouched down on all fours and took a deep breath, then she closed her eyes and stuck a finger down her throat as far as it went.

Her dinner came up with an acid-like taste that burned her throat all the way. She retched two more times, then coughed and quickly hit the flusher. Leaning back on her feet, she closed the toilet lid again and raggedly breathed.

Inhale. Exhale. Inhale. Exhale.

The taste of vomit lingered in her mouth, but she was used to it by now. She slowly got up and grabbed her toothbrush. She scrubbed her mouth clean before stripping down and then finally stepped under the spray of the shower.

The calming effect of the water eased her tight muscles and made her relax at last. The day had been beyond what she could mentally handle, but somehow she had pulled through. She had no idea how.

After about half an hour of rinsing her skin and washing her hair, she stepped out and wrapped a towel around herself. Her frizzy curls would be a mess to tame, but oils always made it easier. She lotioned her skin and flossed her teeth to get anything she had missed, then stepped out of the bathroom and into her bedroom again.

Her school bag waited for her by the door.

With a sigh, she tiredly walked up to it and grabbed what she needed. She splayed out her homework on her bed and got to work.

Today had been hard. Tomorrow would be harder. She had no idea what she was going to do. She wanted this so badly, but the fear inside her locked her limbs and made it nigh impossible for her to see how it was going to be possible.

She just didn't want to disappoint herself... and even more so, disappoint her father.

The DanceDec was lively as always when Fiona jumped off the bus, straight from school, and walked inside. Her insides were churning and she had more than five times been close to getting off the bus, turning around and driving home instead.

She was scared. Adam was a sweet guy and maybe he really did just want to help her, but she didn't want to dig up her past, and that was exactly what would happen if she didn't pull her shit together and danced perfectly today. She couldn't show her weakness in her turns and she couldn't get stage fright when they started dancing together.

No room for flaws. No weakness. Only perfection.

Mustering up her courage, she swallowed her fears and walked in with her head lowered and her bottom lip skewered between her teeth. The other kids were jumping around to ten different kinds of music that blasted from separate studios, and the smell of sweat engulfed her as she took the stairs and walked up to studio 13, feeling her anxiety rise with each step she ascended.

Breathe. Focus. Breathe. Focus. She continued chanting it in her head until a voice suddenly pierced through it.

"You came."

Stopping up in her track just outside studio 13, Fiona slowly turned around and found Adam standing there in a pair of gray, loose-fitted slacks and a green top, sweat already shining vaguely on his arms. His forest green eyes were looking assessingly at her, a soft lift to his right eyebrow.

"Yeah," Fiona managed to get out. Her tongue felt dry like sandpaper. "I did."

Adam's lips slowly rose into a little smile. "I'm glad. So you accept my offer? Three weeks of tutoring?"

Not trusting her voice this time, she nodded stiffly. She couldn't look him in the eyes and instead stared at the floor, a spot right beyond his feet.

"Great. Then we better get started. Ain't got a moment to lose." With that, he walked up to her and opened studio 13, stepping inside. After a short moment of silently panicking again, she followed him. This was happening.

"So are you warmed up or do we need to stretch you out first?" He asked while going up to the stereo with his phone, plugging it in. Fiona's eyes saw him scroll through a long playlist, his lips pressing together concentratedly as if trying to decide.

"I'm stretched out," She nervously replied, feeling her fingers shake lightly. Breathe. Focus. "C-can we just get started?"

Adam glanced over his shoulder and eyed up her anxious expression. "You're stiff as a stick. You need to loosen up." A grin suddenly erupted on his face. "I've got just the thing!"

"I usually warm up to Beethoven," Fiona enlightened when he scrolled determinedly through his phone. He chuckled at her reply and shook his head.

"No Beethoven today, baby. I think I know what your jam is, though." He finally selected a track.

A song she had never heard before started playing through the stereo, but one thing was for certain; it certainly wasn't Beethoven.

Adam put down his phone and began walking up to her, smirking as the music thumped. Her eyes grew wide when he then wagged his finger at her, telling her to step onto the dance floor.

"That's... that's not my jam," She said as he begun dancing a little, still motioning her to come closer. She didn't move from her spot, only tried to listen to the lyrics of the song playing. The beat was impossible. Too fast. How were you supposed to dance to that?

"Come on, don't be chicken," He chuckled. His face was a picture of tease, eyes sparkling and lips pulled into a crooked grin. He came closer to her, tapping his feet to the beat. "I don't bite. Well, not unless you're into that."

She felt her lungs shrink. Her comfort zone was being squeezed uncomfortably tight when he kept coming closer, now suddenly standing right in front of her. "I... I..." Breathe. Focus. Breathe...

"Come on, you gotta move," He said, taking her hands and pulling her out onto the floor. Her body stiffened when he let his hands fall to her hips and forced them to twirl to the beat. "Loosen up. Just feel the music move you."

"I, no—I can't dance like that," She protested, her whole body stiffening up as he moved closer and ground his own hips against hers to help them along. It only resulted in him popping her personal bubble. "A-Adam, I can't—"

"Woah, look at you, red suits you," He suddenly chuckled and pinched her cheek. How the fuck could he see her blush? "Are you embarrassed? Come on, never danced with a guy before?"

Fiona's blood ran cold and her lips locked themselves. Admitting she'd never danced with a guy before was much worse than admitting she hadn't danced with anyone since her father.

"Snap, you haven't?!" Adam exclaimed and then laughed. "Well, let's change that, baby. Here, put your hands on my hips."

He took her hands and placed them on his own hips, locking her fingers around his hip bones before she could protest. Her lungs snapped completely shut. "A-A-Adam—"

"Now look at me and feel what I'm doing," He said and lifted her chin when she begun averting her eyes, feeling the room spin when she couldn't breathe. "Come on, look at my beautiful eyes. I promise you won't hate them."

"Adam, I don't want to dance—"

"Sorry, I don't understand those words," He said, giving her a grin. "Now, step back, step forth, right foot, left foot, right, left..."

He maneuvered her body, pressing his own against hers. When she felt his chest press against her own, that's when she shattered.

Pushing away from him and escaping his grip, she rushed to a corner while clutching herself, hyperventilating. Sobs escaped her lips and she felt her whole body trembling, going into a panic attack.

"Holy shit, Fee. I'm sorry, are you okay?" Adam instantly shut off the music and rushed to her side. He rubbed her back when she bent over forward, trying to breathe. "Shit, I didn't mean to scare you. I was just trying to get you out of your shell."

"I can't—" Fiona choked and whimpered when her knees buckled and refused to hold her up anymore. She nearly collapsed, but Adam swiftly caught her with a shocked expression before slowly pulling her down to the floor. He knelt down next to her and wrapped an arm around her.

"Breathe, Fee, I'm so sorry," His voice was so concerned. He continued rubbing her back, but now lifted her chin and forced her to turn her head. "Look at me, Fiona. Right here, look at me. Look."

She managed to flip her eyes up and find his green irises looking calmingly at her. They pierced her brown ones and exuded calmness as he took a deep breath. Fiona mirrored it involuntarily.

"That's it. We're breathing. In and out, like air does. In and out," He kept looking at her and breathing with her. "We're not dancing anymore, we're just sitting here like two human beings, turning oxygen into carbon dioxide. Fuck we're good at it. In and out. Keep going. Good job, Fee, you're an expert."

"Stop talking," She clapped a hand over his face when he began annoying her. She couldn't be sure as she looked away, but she thought she felt him smile against her palm. "This was a mistake... I can't do this."

Adam removed her hand and instead held it in his own, giving it a squeeze. "No, it wasn't. I just misjudged you. I just thought you were shy, not—"

"Not what?"

He pressed his lips together. "Afraid. What's holding you back when you dance? I see it in your eyes. You're scared of something."

"I'm not scared of anything."

"Then dance with me right now."

"No."

"Why not?"

"Because!" Fiona shouted and jumped to her feet again, pacing away from him. "Why do you have to stick your nose in my business? I told you, this was a mistake, I've changed my mind, I can't do this—"

"Whoa, hey, pump your breaks, don't curve me again," Adam said and stood as well when she was already aiming for her bag. "Fee, you can do this, I just need to come at you from a different angle. I can still teach you, I just—"

"How?" Fiona snapped, feeling the stubborn tears well up in her eyes. "How can you teach me when I can't dance with you?! Why do you even want to?"

"Do you trust me?" He said and leveled her with his eyes. They were sober and calm, no joking this time. "Say yes and I'll show you. Say no and walk out that door, throwing away your only chance at winning that scholarship."

Fiona's limbs froze up and her lips squeezed themselves tightly together. Anxiety still rush inside her veins, but will and persistence lodged in her mind.

Her father died teaching her how to dance. If she didn't do this... if she threw away a once in a lifetime opportunity when it appeared... she would be dishonoring his memory. She owed him to try, to not be scared and finish what he tried to do.

"How?" She croaked again, her voice breaking apart. "How..."

"Come here," He said and extended his hand, waiting for her to come closer. "Put on your pointe shoes. Don't think about anything, just trust me, alright?"

Gulping, she hesitantly took it. She then slowly dug her hand into her bag and found her pointe shoes. When she sat down to begin tying them on, he nodded and walked up to the door.

"I'll be right back. Don't move, okay?" He told.

Fiona stayed on the floor as he ran out, and focused on tightening her shoes. Three minutes passed where she stood up and rested her shoes against the linoleum, bending and stretching her feet. Then, the creak of the door sounded. She turned around and found Adam standing there, holding something in his hand; A yellow and blue school tie.

"Trust me on this, okay?" He said and came up to her, lifting the tie. "I won't drop you and I definitely won't let you fall."

"What are you gonna do with that?" She asked, already knowing the answer when he lifted it to her face.

"Turn around. Face the mirror," He said, and for some reason, she did. She saw his reflection lift the tie over her head, then bring it to her eyes where he began tying it behind her head. She closed her eyes and let the darkness descend. "This way you can't see me. You'll only hear the music. Don't focus on my touch, just focus on the rhythm and your steps, alright?"

Fiona felt as he tied the last knot. She could scarcely see the light dipping in from the ridge of her nose, but other than that, it was completely dark. She heard footsteps, then the sound of thumbs meeting a screen, then finally a small thud.

An enchanting sound poured through the system. A gentle piano and a soft set of violins created a melodious tune that instantly flowed through her body. Like a drug, her nerves calmed down and she exhaled, feeling the calmness wrap around her.

"Good," Adam's voice gently spoke. "Now dance, Fee. Don't go en pointe, just show me your steps."

It was scary, but Fiona somehow trusted his words and put her faith into his hands as she rose to the flats of her toes, not en pointe like he said. She felt his palms softly land on her waist, steadying her balance and keeping posture straight. Gulping, she tried to focus on the music like he said and took the first step.

Moving forward, she elevated her leg and instantly felt Adam's hand come to her thigh and support it. Her pulse spiked at the intimacy, but something felt different. The fact that she couldn't see him, couldn't see him see her... she hadn't really thought this would work, yet somehow it did. The music kept her lulled and her concentration sharpened on her steps rather than his touch. Breathe.

Feeling him turn her about ninety degrees, she lowered her leg and instead lifted it to en angle at her front. As her arm lifted above her head, she felt his finger twine with hers and steady her balance once again; he held her by her waist and kept her leveled on the ground as she set off.

"Nice and slow," His voice was a gentle whisper. Exhaling, Fiona turned her leg out and let herself spin, slowly. A simple turn, that was it. Her knee grazed his thigh as she came to her position again. Slowly lowering her leg and arms, Adam placed both hands on her hips.

"Sous-sus." She followed his command and let her feet cross on the floor. Rising to her toes, she exhaled and placed her hands on his, centering herself. With her point in the mirror being gone, every step felt shaky and scary.

But Adam had her back ever step of the way.

"Now grand battement," He held her firmly by her hips as her right leg lifted high and slowly lowered again. She could feel his stealth and confidence behind her seep into her, powering her own. It was weak, but it was something she had never felt before. Not since...

"You're doing good, Fee," He murmured close to her ear. "Don't lose focus."

Maybe he could read minds, or maybe he had notice the way her respiration had stopped for a few seconds. Just as she could feel his strength, he could sense her angst. Giving her hip a little squeeze, he centered her once again and made her slowly exhale.

"That's right. Breathing humans. That's us." God, even when he was annoying, his words somehow worked. The dumbness distracted her from the fear. "You think you're ready to dance with me yet?"

"I..." Was she? It seemed so soon. Sure, his little tie-trick may have worked, but she doubted she was just magically fixed now—even if his school colors were the colors of Ravenclaw.

"We'll take it nice and easy," He pulled the tie off her head and allowed her to regain her sight. Blinking in the sudden harsh light, she caught him walking up to his phone to change the music. "We'll stay in the classical. You know Romeo and Juliet?"

"Uh... yeah." Every ballet dancer worth her pointe shoes knew Romeo and Juliet.

"How about the Paris and Juliet pas de deux? The simplified version." He glanced over his shoulder when she remained mute. "Come on. Let's try it. We can stop if you start feeling the jitters."

Taking a deep breath, Fiona reminded herself again why she was doing this, putting herself through this torture. New York Ballet. Her father. Doing what she loved.

Exhaling, she opened her eyes and looked at Adam who stood by the soundsystem, awaiting her reply. "Okay."

A smile broke out on his lips. "Fuckin' A. Let's do this. From the arabesque."

The music started playing and Adam hurried up behind her. Fiona felt her heart beat rapidly in her chest as she realized this was really happening. She was about to dance with a boy. As she felt Adam move up behind her and take his place, her body nervously went into her own position. The blood was rushing in her ears so loudly she almost couldn't hear the music. Her eyes were pinned on the two of them in the mirror, seeing him stand perfectly behind her, waiting for their mark.

Three, two, one...

Fiona moved as her cue came and Adam moved right alongside her, supporting her arms. On cue with her cue, her anxiety blared up as well and made her legs shake as she lifted to her toes. Improper balance nearly threw her off until she heard something that suddenly distracted her.

– Adam was humming along to the music right behind her.

Not really sure how to react, Fiona frowned, blinked and kept dancing. Adam kept humming behind her, even going up into the high squeaks of the violin. It sounded awful. Somehow, she made it through the first few steps by listening to his annoying humming. The fact that it was right near her ear didn't help. Or did it?

As she started focusing her attention more on her annoyance to his humming, she forgot about the fact that she was supposed to be feeling anxious about this part. It was exactly like when you had a pain somewhere; if you hit yourself somewhere else, the other pain almost became redundant. Adam's humming was her pain. A pain in her goddamn ass.

Watching him grin at her irritated expression in the reflection of the mirror, he only kept humming and dancing with her. Her anxiety rose and fell throughout the whole routine, but to her unbelievable surprise, it mostly stayed dull. She couldn't believe it. Was an annoying distraction really all she had needed?

Before she knew it, the scene came to an end. She ended gracefully with her hands folded beautifully in the air while Adam slid to his knee on the floor in an elegant pose. As the music faded, she saw his grin evolve and turn into a full laugh. "Yeeeeah! That's what I'm talking about, baby! Woo!"

Slapping her straight across her butt, which was eye-height with his head, he jumped up and fist-bumped the air, just as Fiona screeched, mortified. Watching Adam do a sassy victory dance, she seriously started questioning if that was really his passion or just too much Adderall. Nobody was this hype. Were they?

"You did it, princess! You slayed the fucking beast all on your own!" He grinned, coming up to her. "How did it feel?"

To be honest, she was still in shock. She couldn't believe she had actually pulled through, but she guessed it had been a victory. And a good day. Who knew if tomorrow would go as well?

Holy shit, tomorrow. She really was committed to this, wasn't she?

"It felt... okay, I guess," She replied. It hadn't been as bad as she thought it would be. Sometimes, the mind built things up bigger than they really were... and sometimes it didn't.

"We should do it again straight away," He said, going back to his phone. "We can play around with a few different pieces today, but I think we did this one perfectly."

"You know a lot of classics?" Amidst all her own shock, Fiona had almost failed to notice how well he had danced as well. His technique was beautiful, very straight and on point. It made her wonder what his story was; how a ballet boy turned hip hop.

"Some," He scrolled through his playlist, finding another classical song. A slow smirk spread on his lips. "But I'm more into the newer stuff. Don't get me wrong, I love old school, but new jive works better with my style."

"What is your style?" Fiona asked, placing her hands on her hips.

He turned his eyes to her and flashed her that same little smirk. "You'll find out if you keep dancing with me."

God, he was annoying. Watching him grin, she sighed and then heard as the music of Swan Lake started pouring through the system. They really were going classic.

"Whenever you're ready," He put his phone down and started walking up to her.

"I'm ready. And could you try not to hum so loudly this time?" She bickered, only to annoy him back. She secretly didn't want him to stop.

Chuckling, he gripped her hips and leaned in to her ear. "I was trying so hard not to hum High School Musical."

Chapter 4

"So," Adam smugly smirked as Fiona stepped into the studio the next day. "It's day two and you haven't skipped town yet. Hashtag progress."

"You're still as annoying." She extracted a broad grin from him when she rolled her eyes. Did he ever stop smiling, seriously?

"And I'm gonna become even more annoying today, baby. No more ballet." He told with a smile. Fiona's heart stopped for a second but quickly restarted when he reminded her of why; "This training is about teaching you anything but that, so get warm and I'll be right back," He said and walked up to the door, his axe body spray wafting into Fiona's nostrils as he passed her. "Nature calls."

She gave a wooden nod, then took a deep breath and begun warming up like he told her to, stretching out her muscles and joints. She warmed up for a long time and had nearly forgotten about the time when she accidentally glanced up and saw it had been almost 20 minutes since Adam left.

She frowned, confused. Where the hell did he go? Did he have Indian food last night or something?

Getting up from where she was bending on the floor, she walked up to the door and had barely put her hand on the doorknob when her eyes caught something through the window. Coming out of the girls bathroom from down the hall, Adam had his arm slung around a girl who was fixing her messy hair. Her face looked flushed and her lips were gnawed, and Adam wore a small grin.

They stopped up in the hallway. Adam turned the girl towards himself and put his hands on her shoulder. They certainly seemed familiar with each other. Fiona saw him say something to her, holding a pause, then smirking and adding something more. Whatever he said made the girl blush and made him brush her cheek with his thumb, chuckling cheekily. He then leaned in and pecked the same cheek before giving her a hug and waving her off. Fiona instantly backed away from the door when he begun walking back.

She pretended to have seen nothing as he returned, walking in like nothing was off. "Sorry about that, something came up. You warm and ready?"

Fiona snorted lightly. Yeah she bet something came and it definitely went up. "Whatever..."

Adam frowned a little her way. "What's with the salt? What'd I do?"

Probably a lot of things with that girl. He better have washed his damn hands. "Nothing."

"This is a trap," He declared and stared at her with conspicuous eyes. "You say 'nothing' and I say 'alright', but the next thing I know, your knee is lodged between my legs and I'm singing gospel on the floor."

Fiona rolled her eyes. "It doesn't matter."

"My balls say otherwise."

"Look, what you do is none of my business, but you were the one who offered to help me," She stated, shortly. "If you're just gonna waste my time while you fool around with girls in the bathroo—"

"—whoa, whoa, wrong kind of jumps you're doing there," Adam interrupted and walked up to her. "You saw me with Ali?"

"I don't care what her name is, I care about dancing—"

"And I care about the folks around me," Adam cut her off again and crossed his arms. "And you just made a damn wrong assumption, Fee. I didn't ball her, Jesus. Not even close."

"It's none of my business," Fiona repeated and turned away from him, walking up to the barre. "Just keep your extra activities out of my—"

"That girl just got dumped by her boyfriend and she needed a shoulder to cry on," He spoke over her and walked after her, leaning up against the barre besides her. "She was bawling her eyes out, so I cheered her up. When we came out, I gave her a hug and told her to forget about that dick and told her to start looking at other dicks. I told her she could look at mine if she wanted to."

Fiona stared speechlessly. Who exactly was he? A saint that never left this building and just walked door to door, cheering up all of the crying girls? "Whatever, okay? Just... can we please get started?"

"Fine," He shook his head a little, but then suddenly gave her a slow grin. "You really thought I was doing her in the bathroom? Come on! Give me a little more credit than that," He laughed when she fought the urge to roll her eyes again. "And even if I did, I'd need a helluva' lot more time than just twenty minutes." Scratch that; she did roll her eyes again when he walked away with a wry wink.

Why couldn't he just be a normal gross teenage guy so she'd have a reason to snap at him? Oh, wait.

"Alright. Let's get started," He finally said, slapping his hands together. "You're comfortable with ballet, but you're not comfortable with anything that basically breaks your lines. That's our first challenge," He went up to the stereo and plugging his phone in. "We need to tear down that wall, Ms Gorbachev, and get you out of your little comfort zone; Get you back to your roots."

"My roots?"

Adam glanced over his shoulder and met her with a non-sensical glare. "Fiona, you are a gorgeous African American woman and I wanna see your black magic on this dance floor."

Fiona felt her body both heat- and freeze up at the same time when a fast beat song that was impossible to dance to suddenly boomed through the system. Why did he pick these songs? Why?

"No backing down today," He said and walked up to her, taking her hands. "You danced with me yesterday and we're gonna dance now. Move those hips and let me see those feet work. Channel your inner African Queen," He smirked, and then to Fiona's mortification, started shimmying his shoulders invitingly to the beat. "Come on, Feeeeeee... you know you want to."

Hell no. Fiona stepped back when he suddenly jumped onto the floor without further ado, bent his knees and then begun dancing full on African style. Something cool she swore she had seen one of Beyoncé's background dancers do in one of her music videos, but when Adam did it... it looked so fucking weird. It was impressive he could actually do it, she gave him that, but seeing his pale hip hop ass move around on the floor like that was just a downright sight to behold.

"Please stop... whatever you're doing," Fiona told him, seeing him shake his head with a laugh. "No, please stop. My eyes are about to bleed."

"Not gonna happen," He grinned, making a fool of himself by turning around and actually sticking his ass out at her. And then he fucking twerked. Please dear God make it stop, she prayed. "Show me yours and I promise I'll never show you mine again."

Fiona actually felt her face melt and covered her eyes when he kept popping his ass at her, laughing loudly at her reaction. He was making a fool of himself and he wasn't the least bit embarrassed. How could he not be? "Please, please, please stop."

Suddenly he turned back around again and grabbed her hand before she could move away. He yanked her to him and caught her against his chest, rolling his body towards hers. Fiona's heart immediately jumped up into her throat when he cupped her face and pinned her with his eyes. They were intense, but only on one thing.

"Move, Fee," He told her.

She shook her head. She couldn't dance like that. Not even with his stupid ass next to her. "I can't."

"Yes, you can. It's just a matter of confidence."

The thing she had none of? "I can't..."

"Hold up then." He abruptly untangled himself from her and walked up to the door. He opened it wide and stuck his head out, then startled her by hollering down the hall full blast; "RANI! KALO! CODE BLACK, I need some damn magic up in here! Where you at?!"

There came some whopping downstairs. Then rushed footsteps pounding the floor.

What the hell did he just do?

"Watch this," Adam grinned excitedly and wagged his eyebrows at her when she spotted two girls in loose fitting hip-hop slacks and oversized crop tops come grinning towards their studio. Adam rubbed his hands like a kid in a candy store and then chuckled when they burst in. "Kalo! My little coffee toffee!"

"Whatcha doing hollering in here for, gringo?" Kalo, one of the gorgeous girls said, coming up to Adam who laughed. "What'd ya need, boy?"

"This girl right here," He said and gestured to Fiona, "Needs to get her inner African Queen out. I don't think she actually knows what twerking is, and apparently my moves aren't good enough."

"Don't tell me ya skinny little ass tried twerking again?" She shook her head disapprovingly at him. "Boy, I thought we told you to never do that again. You look damn stupid. Step aside and watch how it's done. And you," She said and looked at Fiona who was in a frozen standstill. "You watch and learn. Jump in when you're ready. And if this puta tries to do the same, do us a favor and slap him. Never seen something so damn stupid in my life."

Adam threw his head back and guffawed, but then clapped to the beat when Rani and Kalo stepped onto the floor, swaying their curvy hips sexily. They then jumped into the song like that.

They moved and danced in perfect synchronization. They danced so coordinated and so rehearsed, Fiona could all but step back and stare. They brought it and they brought it good.

She heard a wolf whistle from her side and automatically turned her head to see Adam grinning at them, cheering them on. "That's what I'm fucking talking about! You see that? See the passion? The freestyle? The cake? That's what we're aiming for!"

Fiona simply just stared at them and their impossible moves. She had never moved like that in her life. Ballet was all about fine and clean lines. This... this was all over the place. She wasn't going to make a fool of herself trying to replicate it. "I can't do that. I c-can't..."

She suddenly felt Adam move up behind her, placing his hands on her hips. "Yes you can, Fee. It's all about the music. You gotta feel it, baby," His voice was right in her ear and sent shivers up and down her already alert body. His hands started moving her hips, making them sway from side to side. "Try it."

"Why couldn't you start me up with something easier?" She whispered, shaking her head and stopping his hands. She couldn't do this. She felt uncomfortable and ridiculous.

"Because we have three weeks, Fee," He replied. "There's no time for easy. You either go full out or not at all."

"You know they won't be dancing like this at the NY ballet."

"No, but they'll be wanting to see where you come from. You're from Harlem, Fiona. There's culture running through your veins," He said and let a finger slide down the vein in her neck. "I want you to release it and show me what you got."

Suppressing the surge of heat that traveled through her from his simple touch, she sucked in a breath and focused. "Are you suggesting that I cut?"

"I'm suggesting that you move. Starting with this." And before she could think, she felt a sharp smack on her ass. She practically jumped and let out a screech while Adam chuckled behind her.

"Get your hands off my damn ass," She yipped. That was twice he had slapped her butt within two days.

"Then get your ass on my dance floor," He moved and walked out on the dance floor, out to Kalo and Rani who were still dancing. In less than a second, he jumped into the rhythm with them and started dancing alongside them, doing the exact same routine. He moved confidently, the girls moving fearlessly beside him as well. Watching all three of them slay it African style, she stared astounded.

But suddenly, it didn't look so stupid.

Observing them for another couple of minutes, Fiona knew she would never feel confident enough to jump out beside them and try and attempt to do what they did. At least not today. This wasn't just about people seeing her dance, this was uncomfortableness on a whole new level. She needed more time to get used to this.

Catching her sunken expression, Adam jumped off the dance floor and came up to her. Cupping her face and turning her head up when she tried to look away, he caught her gaze. "Hey... don't lose hope on yourself. The moonwalk wasn't perfected in a day."

She didn't want to lose hope, but the feeling in her stomach wasn't the most uplifting right now. "Do you think... maybe we could... try it alone?"

He watched her for a moment, then gave her a smile. "Alright." Without any further explanation, he then turned to the two girls. "Hey, gumdrops. Could you give us the room again? We all know I look best not standing next to you two shimmy-shaking it."

The girls laughed and walked up to him and leaned in towards him, placing a kiss on either side of his face. "You owe us. Come find us when you're free."

Chuckling silently, he smacked them on their asses as they left, skipping out of the room with a bounce to their feet. Apparently his booty-slap was his signature. Turning back to her again, Adam then held his hands out, gesturing into the open and now empty studio.

"The stage is yours, Beyoncé."

Sighing, Fiona reluctantly joined him on the dance floor, gulping when he didn't waste a moment to walk up behind her and place his hands on her hips.

"Rhythm comes from the heart and I know you got that part down," He told, his lips moving to her ear like usual. She suppressed her shiver and closed her eyes. "I want you to channel it to the rest of your body. You need to feel it in the tips of your toes and every curve on your body before you can dance like a professional. Today, though, we just want you to channel your energy to your hips."

He patted her on her hip bone, then gripped it like he was going to assist her in a turn. Channel to the hips... breathe... "Alright..."

"Bend in your legs," He instructed. She did as he told. "Arch that ass out a bit and pop your chest. Then, place your hands on top of mine..." He waited until Fiona had taken a deep breath and timidly followed his last instruction; carefully placing her hands on top of his. They were warm and soft, yet calloused. "Now start grinding those hips like you mean it."

Guiding her hips to move, he molded them around in a slow, circular motion until she got the hang of it. The music had long ago stopped playing, and the silence and her shallow breath was making her very self-conscious about how close her rear was to his crotch. If he moved just a centimeter...

"Keep going," He encouraged, softening the grip he had on her when her hips started to move on their own. "You're doing it, Fee. Try picking up the pace a little."

She did, and the second she did, she felt him behind her. She gasped as she felt him start moving behind her, following her movements. When she started loosening up, yet tightening at the same time, he moved away and came up beside her.

"You're doing it!" He grinned, watching her move slowly, but definitely not uncoordinatedly. "I knew you were a natural! It's in your blood, baby. Let it out."

Fiona couldn't actually believe she was doing it. It felt boundary breaking, moving her hips so daringly. Ballet certainly wouldn't allow this. It wasn't about wiggling your ass, it was about keeping it tight and tucked in. Having to do the exact opposite right now... it felt weird.

But good weird.

A nervous sound passed her lips. A laugh? Beside her, Adam laughed too. He suddenly moved towards the stereo and put on the same song as before, letting her get used to the rhythm of that one. Now knowing how the song went, Fiona tried to envision what the two girls, Rani and Kalo, had done. They had moved around, kicked their feet somehow and made snake-like twists with their hands in the air, making it appear effortless and gorgeous. She wasn't about to go there yet.

Coming up beside her again, though, Adam was losing his cool and howling. He was grinning and moving in the same rhythm as her, matching her movements. Why did it suddenly look... hot? He was dancing with her, dancing like her ancestors, and suddenly... it didn't look ridiculous.

"C'mon, Fee! Kill it for me!" He started moving his arms, showing her again what Rani and Kalo had done. Nervously, she copied him to the best of her ability. He chuckled and nodded, watching her do it. "Hell, yeah! I'm seeing that magic! Fuck, keep going and you'll blind me, baby."

It was nerve wracking whenever he talked like that, watching her with that look and that smirk. It was blatant flirting, and yet all it did was make her feel... good? More assured of herself. The best part was, the way he did it wasn't in a crude or 'I-wanna-fuck-you-senseless' kinda way. There was nothing behind it, simply just... encouragement?

"That's it," He moved closer to her again, coming up behind her and placing his hands on her hips again. Her pulse instantly spiked up. "Keep going, keep moving your hips. Now try shifting your weight onto one foot and move the other back. Repeat with the other and then turn. Got it?"

Shakily nodding, Fiona figured she might as well try it before she lost her courage. Doing like he said, she shifted onto her left leg and moved her right one back, taking a step backwards. Adam did the same behind her. Repeating with the other leg, she was surprised how well he was able to coordinate with her, like instruments harmonizing. All that was left to do now was turn.

But, just as Fiona turned, his hand slid to her lower back, way too close to her rear. It distracted her and caused her to fall out of rhythm, messing up her turn. She swung around clumsily before Adam was ready, and that resulted in her knee landing in the one place she had been trying to avoid ever since they first started dancing together.

- His groin.

Screaming, she jumped back when Adam cursed out and fell to the floor, clutching his jewels. He had managed to break some of the impact before she got him too good, but still, her knee had definitely hit him. She cupped her mouth in horror and embarrassment as Adam crimped down on the floor, his face twisting. "Fuck!"

"I'm so sorry!" Fiona panicked, watching him curse some more and squeeze his eyes shut. "Oh my God, I'm so, so sorry!"

He blew out a hard breath. Then, he groaning, he tried to sit up. "I fucking knew it—my balls would pay for it."

"I didn't mean to do it!" She exclaimed. When he finally looked up and gave her a half-assed smile, she let out a frustrated sound. "You jackass!"

He chuckled hoarsely and shook his head again. "Fuck, that's gonna sting all day. You have heels for knees, Fee. Just thought you should know."

Glancing down at her knees by reflex, her eyes also dropped to his crotch where he slowly tried removing his hands. And that's when she saw it.

"You're not wearing a dancer's belt," She stated. Even through his loose track pants, she could tell that he wasn't wearing any protective underwear that could've helped... tug away the problem.

"They're uncomfortable as hell," He replied. He finally managed to stand up with another small groan, still slightly clutching himself. "And besides, all of this shouldn't be contained," He added and smirked as he gestured towards his crotch.

It became Fiona's turn to groan, and with an eye-roll, she turned away, suddenly less concerned about him as his humor seemed to have returned already. If a knock to the groin couldn't knock off his smirk, then what could?

"It's dangerous dancing without a dancer's belt. At least up close." She reprimanded. She might not have danced with an actual boy before him, but that didn't mean she didn't know the risks and safety procedures of doing so. "If we're going to keep dancing, you better start wearing one." She couldn't have him flapping all over the place as they progressed to twerking. Oh, God. Twerking.

"If I owned one, I would wear it," He chuckled, blowing out a breath. "But speaking of dancing, I might need a small break. Lunch?" He suggested with a ginger grin.

Sighing, Fiona walked up and turned the stereo off while Adam took a seat on one of the chairs up against the wall. He still looked a little pale, but somehow he was still smiling. Even so, Fiona knew she couldn't keep dancing with him if he didn't start protecting himself. Knowing herself, his junk wouldn't survive if he didn't.

- Yeah, she was definitely going to have to fix that.

Chapter 5

The next day when Fiona walked into the studio around 4pm, she found Adam already prepping their usual studio. She swore he never left that place. He smiled when he saw her come in, zipping off his hoodie and taking off his cap. "Hey, baby. You ready for another round? Did you remember to bring your inner dancing Queen?"

Oh, that wasn't all she had brought. "Yeah. And I brought you something as well."

"Yeah? Your ass?"

Dropping her bag, she ignored his smug smirk and dug her hand into its depth for just a moment before pulling something out. Throwing it towards Adam, he quickly caught it and then looked at it.

"You got me... a thong?" A slow, mischievous grin spread on his lips, and he then proceeded to hold up the square package and laugh. "Aw! Thank you, baby, you shouldn't have!"

"I really should," Fiona mumbled as she watched him open the package and pull out the skin-colored piece of clothing.

"And you even got the size right," He endearingly noted and held up the dancer's belt to his hips like a girl would a bikini bottom. "How'd you know?"

"I just eyeballed it—no!" She widened her eyes when she realized what she just said. "I didn't eyeball it—you! I-I—" But it was too late; The damage was way beyond done.

Adam threw his head back and howled with laughter as Fiona reddened up to a tomato, even with her dark skin tone. He kept laughing and wheezing hysterically while Fiona prayed the floor would open up and swallow her whole. This just wasn't happening.

When Adam finally caught his wind, he crouched forward and wiped an actual tear from his eye. "You've been eye-balling my junk, Fee? I thought you were the one who said no extra activiti—"

"Shut up!" She snapped and hid her burning cheeks. "You know that's not what I meant!" When he kept wheezing from laughter, she growled and turned away. "Just shut up and go put it on so we can get started. We're wasting time."

"Oh, I will go put it on. No ones ever bought me a thong be-fore," He laughed, shaking his head. "This is legit the greatest day of my life."

With that, he grabbed his bag and strode out, heading towards the girl's bathroom. He still couldn't stop laughing.

Fiona sighed and then proceeded to wait the couple of minutes it took for him to change. She was in the middle of stretching her leg against the barre when the door to the girl's bathroom suddenly burst open with a loud bang. Then...

"Oh, my God."

"FIRE IN THE HALL!"

Adam leaned back and bellowed through the hall so loudly it overpowered all the music coming from the other studios. Everyone stuck their heads out to see what the commotion was, looking up and down the hall until they spotted where the noise came from. Or rather who.

"WATCH OUT, HOMIES, BIG BALLER COMING THROUGH!"

- And with that, Adam proudly danced down the hall in a pair of tight black ballet leggings, showing off... literally everything.

Everyone in the DanceDec broke into a wild laughter that resounded through the entire building. Adam had no shame at all, but rather seemed to enjoy the attention. To really top it off, Fiona couldn't believe when she saw him bust into the iconic Gangnam style, riding the invisible air.

Who the hell was the boy and who let him out of the mental facility?

Finally coming towards her studio, he chuckled at the cat-calls and wolf whistles that came from behind him. Fiona was aware of her stunned face as he dramatically paused up in the doorway and posed like a hero, putting his hands on his hips.

"Well?" He looked expectantly at her with a shit-eating grin. "How do my balls look, Fiona?"

"You're absolutely, one-hundred percent crazy and a maniac, you know that, right?" She said, watching him cackle as he stepped in and shut the door, the music from the other studios resuming and people going back to their dancing now that the show was over.

"I'm just alive, baby," He replied, flashing her a grin as he teasingly shimmied his hips at her. "Can't you tell?"

And then it struck Fiona; The reason why she felt so comfortable around him, why his flirting only made her feel good. Could the answer have been right in front of her?

"Are you gay?" The words came from her mouth shockingly insensitive and bluntly before she could stop them. Gasping, she quickly covered her mouth, regretting how rude it had come out. "Oh, God, I-I'm sorry, I didn't mean to—" What if he was still in the closet? Although given his display just before, highly unlikely.

To her surprise, Adam only laughed again. "I'm gay because I just danced down the hall in a pair of tights?"

"No, but I mean... it's okay if you are," She voiced, hoping she hadn't screwed up. Confronting him on his sexual orientation was neither here nor there, and it certainly had nothing to do with their dance practice. In truth it didn't matter, so why had she asked?

"I'm not gay, Fiona." He sighed.

"Okay." She wasn't sure though. It would actually make so much sense if he was. Why everyone he slapped on the butt didn't get mad... why he was so... extra all the time. Not to stereotype, but it would just make more sense.

"I'm really not," He repeated when he perhaps read the disbelief on her face.

Fiona bit her lip. "It's just... I mean, you kinda give off that vibe, just a little. I mean, the way you don't care about humiliating yourself and all that... Isn't that part of the macho ego-package?" She could be all wrong, but she just assumed guys preferred to stay cool or something like that.

"Only package I'm carrying is the one you just put a string on," He chuckled and walked up to the stereo. He plugged in his phone and started scrolling through his music.

"So you don't care that some people might think you're gay?" Fiona asked, curiously. She had literally never met a guy like Adam before, so carefree and indifferent about people's opinions. She couldn't help but be curious.

"Why should I? There's nothing wrong with being gay, is there?" He lifted a brow and a little smirk when Fiona rolled her eyes. "I take it as a compliment, really. This body and this face is handsome enough to pick up another stud. I count my blessings."

"What about gay jokes then?" She challenged. She didn't understand why she suddenly got so interested in him - in his way of taking on life. She felt like she could ask him these questions without offending him. He was so... relaxed about it. He just did whatever he wanted, fuck the norms.

"What about them?" He asked and gave her an easy smile. "Alright, look. Being a male dancer, you automatically fall victim to every gay joke there is out there, so at the end of it, you just stop caring," He said, before turning back to his phone. "And yeah, I do make a fool of myself, but it makes people laugh, doesn't it?" His grin broadened. "Laughter is the best medicine. I'm comfortable with my sexuality, and I don't really care what people think, so I honestly couldn't care if what I do makes me look or sound gay. At the end of the day, I know what I like, and that's all that matters, right?"

"Right..." Again, Fiona was left speechless. Somehow, this boy had a way of making her speechless at least once a day, and it always left her thinking.

He was such a happy, positive and extroverted person, so full of life and laughter. Not many young people were that these days, or just people in general. It made her wonder... what had made him have this unique spirit and outlook on life?

"So," He said, giving her a grin and raising another brow. "Still wanna dance with me now that you know I'm not gay? I promise I won't grab you by the pussy."

The snort that passed Fiona's lips surprised her. It almost sounded like a laugh. Almost. Adam grinned back. "Whatever you say."

"Alright then!" He finally selected a song and it quickly started booming through the speakers; Of course it was another impossible beat. "Let's get started."

– And with that, he walked up behind her, slapped her butt and watched her squeal in horror as he laughed. Fiona flipped around, glaring at him. "Hey?!"

"Never promised I wouldn't grab the butt," He winked, but then laughed as Fiona pursed her lips sourly. Him and his damn butt-slaps.

They then got started on dancing, Fiona reluctantly letting Adam guide her through what he had planned for today's lesson.

Somehow through it all, she forgot to be scared.

Around 7pm, they had been dancing for 3 hours. At that point, Adam's stomach growls were growing louder than the music, which had forced them to stop to head down and grab something to eat.

"There's a bowling place right around the corner," He told as Fiona changed into her sneakers, suddenly feeling a change in the mood as she realized where he was going with this. "A couple of guys from the Dec were gonna go there and grab something to eat, maybe hit a few pins. You wanna come?"

This was new. This hadn't been what she had signed up for. Social scenes and going out with other young people... the teenage life... it wasn't her.

"Uh... no, thank you," She replied, averting her eyes and distracting herself by stuffing her things into her bag. "I should get going home."

"C'mon on, Fee," Adam stepped in front of her when she tried to walk out on him like she always did. Fleeing was always easier. "Come out with us tonight. Nobody says you need to talk to anyone. Just come out, grab a few slices, hear a few of my jokes, laugh at them when nobody else will, and then call it a night. What do you say?"

She suddenly realized she was scared again. Somehow, this had become scarier than dancing with a partner. This was... commitment. This was choosing to not be alone where it safest and where she couldn't hurt anyone... and where anyone couldn't hurt her. This was... this was...

Friendship.

"I promise I'll keep you safe," Adam said and stepped closer to her. Her eyes automatically flicked up and met his jungly green eyes, feeling captured for a moment. The air between them seemed to shift. "Please with extra cheese?"

She didn't understand why he wanted her company so much. Why he was even helping her... she didn't know who he was, but he wanted so desperately to help her move along from things he didn't even know about yet... and for some reason, she wanted to accept his help.

But that was too dangerous.

"Not tonight," She therefore said and pulled away. Her eyes turned down again and she hiked up in her bag. "Maybe some other time."

Before he could say anything more that would try and convince her, she skidded around him and headed for freedom.

She just couldn't yet.

At home, her mom had cooked a pasta carbonara dinner with garlic bread on the side. Fiona had tried to eat as much as she could, but the second it landed in her stomach, she had felt sick.

Not thirty minutes later, after saying goodnight to her mom, she had been in the bathroom with two fingers down her throat, forcing it up again.

With all the extra dancing she and Adam were doing, she knew she was burning more calories and in need of more energy if she had to keep doing what she was doing. The thing was, her body worked better when she pushed it harder, when she pushed it to its limits. She had made it this far, and it wasn't like she wasn't eating... she was just choosing which meals to keep down. It was also her body, so she could decide what to do with it. Even if other people didn't agree.

Right now, life was finally going her way; School was great, homelife was manageable, and dancing seemed to at last have turned into something more than just... dancing. She was moving forward, and everything was good.

And that's why she couldn't take any chances.

Flushing the toilet, Fiona stood up and grabbed her toothpaste, scrubbing the foul taste from her mouth.

Just 16 more days.

Chapter 6

As Fiona walked into the Dec after school, something was definitely wrong.

It was much more silent than usual, even with all the music blasting from the occupied studios, there was a different kind of quiet today. The other kids weren't lingering in the halls like they used to. It was odd...

Fiona went up to the counter to check if studio 13 was unlocked yet, the one her and Adam always booked, but found that it wasn't. The key was still there. And that's when she knew what was wrong.

Adam wasn't there.

Looking around with slight confusion, Fiona scanned the DanceDec for the sound of his unmistakable laugh and realized why it was so quiet. If Adam was there, all she had to do was find whichever room was the loudest or whichever group of people was the largest. That boy had a thing for being the center of attention... but there was no hoard of people gathered around somewhere to catch his contagious energy.

The doors behind her suddenly burst open. Fiona spun around, and to her surprise, saw a panting Adam come running in with his school and gym bags. He barely noticed her in his hurry, but then finally stopped when he spotted her standing there.

"Oh, hey!" He flashed her a quick smile. "Sorry I'm late, I missed my bus. Give me five minutes, I'll be right there! Go warm up!"

And with that, he bolted up the stairs and into the girls bathroom.

Despite his order, Fiona stayed put for another second. His tardiness suddenly wasn't what concerned her any longer, but rather something else.

The uniform he had been wearing when he had raced in.

As Fiona slowly started climbing the stairs and headed towards studio 13, the pieces started to click inside her head.

She knew that school tie had looked familiar—that day he had tied it around her eyes when he wanted her to dance blindly and trust him, she had thought something about it looked familiar, but she had been too nervous to connect the dots. Now, after seeing his full uniform, she knew.

She had just started warming up on the floor inside the studio when the door to the studio opened. Adam came in, still slightly winded, but now changed into his usual gray sweats and a black T-shirt. He gave her a smile as he walked past her, dumped his bag down and went straight for the stereo with his phone to plug it in. "Sorry about that. How far are we?"

Fiona looked at him. Again, she felt like it wasn't her place to ask, it didn't concern her, but she had to know; Only kids with a background wore that school tie.

"You go to McCuvey's?"

Adam halted up and slowly looked at the stereo. Then, turning his head slightly, he gave her a small smile. "Yeah."

So it was true. He was a criminal.

Every kid from the block knew that all thugs from around here ended up in one school after they got out of juvie. Unless they had rich parents that could get them into a better school, there was only one school that accepted all the rejects of the neighborhood and provided them with a uniform to make them feel part of something.

– And that's where the McCuvey-juvie necktie had gotten its name from.

"Does that change anything for you?" Adam voiced, after a moment where Fiona did nothing but stay silent. She was having a hard time processing the Adam that stood before her fitting the bill of a street thug.

"I... I don't think so," She said, but felt an uncertainty in her chest. How could he be a criminal? Adam? The hyper-active, always-happy smiling boy who brought sunshine with him wherever he went? Was it all just... an act?

Adam laid his phone down and slowly walked over to where she was stretching on the floor. He sat down and grabbed her foot and bent it and rolled it around to help her stretch. "It wasn't like that, Fee. I was in juvie, but it wasn't for a hardcore crime. You can ask me, you know. It's not a secret."

Fiona looked up. Most people preferred not to talk about their dark past, and if they did, they always did it with a somber look.

Adam was meeting her eyes with his jungly green ones, smiling a little with a crooked lip. He didn't seem like he was about to have a series of traumatic flashbacks. Instead he looked like he was open to discuss his delinquent past.

And maybe, that was the reason why Fiona took a deep breath and slowly asked.

"Why'd you do time?"

His smile stretched and he released a sigh. Letting go of her foot, he then joined her in the stretching.

"I was young and stupid. I was alone and I wanted to fit in, and everyone was either part of a gang or joining a gang. So, I joined a gang."

Fiona watched as he followed her lead when she stretched her legs out in a middle split. She leaned over forward on her elbows and pointed her toes, and so did he. "So you got busted while riding with a crew?"

He laughed and shook his head. "Naw. I almost wish it was something as cool-sounding as that, but it was much less fancy, I'm afraid. I was too energetic to be part of a gang, so they got me delivering products instead."

"A mule?" Fiona asked. She'd seen those kids around the block. They were easy to spot if you knew what to look for. In their world, it was the same as passing a test; showing that you were loyal and willing to do the hard work. Once you paid your dues, you were in—provided you didn't fuck up along the way.

Adam nodded. "I didn't know what I was carrying, only that my backpack had a padlock, and if the padlock was gone by the time I arrived at my destination, I would get a front window in my head. Considering the crew I hung with, that was an easy threat."

Shit, Fiona thought. She couldn't imagine him being a part of that – the smiling, positive fool in front of her trafficking drugs through town. Things must've been bad for him back then if he decided to join a gang. And that was even harder to imagine.

"So my job was to ride the merch to the dealers and ride back again with the money. It was an easy gig as long as I didn't open the bag," He told. "All I had to do was be one place, then another. Always the same route."

"So, what happened?"

"I got tagged," He shrugged. "Some cops started noticing my daily routines. They didn't have probable cause to stop me, though. I was a school-kid with a backpack, nothing out of the ordinary there, so they started following me instead. One day they flashed their lights at me to spook me and I shat a brick," He chuckled. "I tried to bike from them in my stupor, which was about the dumbest thing I could've done."

That much was true, Fiona thought. That was the golden rule; you didn't run from the cops if you were innocent. Only the guilty ran.

"Obviously they ended up catching me," Adam continued. "They caught me in an alley and busted me. I was in for three months."

"Three months?" Fiona slightly gaped.

"That's a low sentence," Adam pointed out. He shifted off his elbows and leaned towards one foot. "I had no priors and the cops took pity on me. I could've gotten away jail free if I wanted."

"So why didn't you?"

"There's one thing you don't do on the street, and that's rat," Adam finally stood up and rolled his shoulder blades around. "I didn't tell them anything, and it probably saved my life. Had I gotten out after being copped, the crew would've known I blabbed and then probably killed me. If I went to juvie, they knew I didn't flab my gums. I got out of that life the second after I got released on parole. Been dancing my problems away since," He finished with a grin.

Fiona was astounded. Even after all that, he had come back smarter and happier. She was sure he was making it sound easier than it really was, though – nothing ever went away that easily. Breaking from a community like that always had its fallouts.

"How long ago was this?"

"Five years. I was fourteen."

"Fourteen?!" She shouldn't have been surprised, but she still was. Most kids started getting into shit around that age, but again, it just didn't seem at all like Adam.

"That's right. You're hanging with an ex-con," He winked. He then walked back up to the stereo and shook his head. "That life is behind me now. I've walked a thousand miles and then some to get past it, and I made it to the other side. I'm all about this life now."

And just like that, happy music started blasting from the stereo as he pushed a button. Fiona sighed and rolled her eyes when like a switch, the Adam she knew was back again.

He started laughing and smirking when she watched him jerk his finger at her with an annoyed face, urging her to the dance floor.

"That's enough history for now," He said as she stood up reluctantly. "We're on a mission, remember? Today we're doing freestyle. Now, since you don't actually know any freestyle, I'm going to be teaching you some. Just a few basic moves—kind of like the ABC's of dancing."

"Right," Fiona sighed. Just once, she would've wished he didn't choose such an upbeat song, but something more mellow. But Adam and mellow didn't go together in a sentence.

And now, after knowing his past, maybe she knew why.

He had been through his dark times and he had no intentions of going back. Music, for whatever reason, had been his light, and it was through music that he had found himself. And dancing.

And as they started dancing and Adam begun teaching her the steps, Fiona couldn't help but think of what life he would've had today if he hadn't found his true passion.

And where she would be right this moment without him.

Fiona was wicking sweat like a window on a rainy day. Her skin shone with perspiration and her muscles ached and burned. They had been dancing for nearly three hours, non-stop.

"Five, six, seven, eight!" Adam clapped his hands in tact with the beat, standing besides her and doing the steps along with her. Fiona's eyes were pinned on the mirror in front of them, but she could tell Adam was looking straight at her. She was struggling with the steps, not because they were hard, but because she still didn't feel comfortable doing them. They didn't feel like her, didn't feel like ballet.

– But that was the whole point, as Adam had said.

"Again," Adam ordered when she finished the routine. She heaved out a breath and crutched forward on her knees. "Come on, Fee. One last time. Own them this time. And five, six, seven, eight..."

Fiona took a deep breath, but then bust out in the moves as Adam joined her. They did the steps together, Adam doing them like he had done them since in the womb. Fiona tried her best to copy his moves, but she still only saw a stiff, much more robotic version of herself in the mirror compared to Adam.

"Alright, that's enough," He blew out a breath and then nodded. "Good start. We'll pick it up again tomorrow and then start you up with some new routines as well. Great job, Fee."

Great job. For some reason, those words sounded like mockery in Fiona's ears. Or like the words you told a five year old when they handed you a badly drawn picture.

Fiona walked towards her gym bag without a word and sat down, reaching inside to get her water bottle. She pulled the cap and drank from it like she was parched, which she was. Behind her, she heard Adam unplug the music while breathing heavily.

Fiona stayed silent for a moment. It was day four of their training, yet she felt like she had done no progress so far. She had learned some baby steps within other genres than ballet, but how was she supposed to master them in just three weeks? Was she fooling herself here, thinking she even stood a chance?

Suddenly, there came a knock on the door. Fiona froze up, but Adam walked up and opened it, then grinned tiredly when he saw who was behind it. "My coffee toffee!"

"Hey," Kalo grinned back. She walked in and looked between them. "You ready? Are you finishing up?"

"Yeah, just give me a second," Adam walked up to his bags and then crouched down to Fiona. "You did a swell job today, Fee. You really did, just don't get too hung up in your head about the flow. Just let it happen. It'll come naturally in the end."

She glanced towards Kalo who was leaning in the doorway, looking into the mirror and fixing her hair. "Do you two have plans?"

Adam smiled. "Yeah. I'll see you tomorrow, though, right? No weekends off."

Fiona nodded silently. She then watched Adam get up, but not before giving her a pat on the shoulder and a good squeeze. "Get home safe, tutu."

Turning, he then walked up to Kalo who grinned and scrunched her nose when Adam tried to give her a bear hug. She said something about him being sweaty and stinky and not wanting to ruin her outfit. Adam laughed at that and instead followed her out, giving her ass a slap. As usual. They walked downstairs together, disappearing out of sight from Fiona who stayed behind in the studio.

Fiona sat silently on the floor, legs outstretched. She was absolutely drained and exhausted, but her heart and mind were still running hotter than her body.

What was she even doing here? Fiona looked around the big empty studio and watched the cracked walls and floors and the places where the large mirrors were broken.

Maybe all of this was stupid. Maybe Adam was wasting his time trying to teach her something that would never happen. Becoming a dancer was a one in a million dream come true. And that was if you were a natural – a prodigy. And there she was, struggling to make a few freestyle steps clash together not totally terribly – and failing.

Fiona lowered her eyes and felt the tears well up in her eyes. She pressed her lips tightly together and felt the weight on her heart.

She had wanted to be a dancer ever since she was little, so much so she had begged her dad to sign her up for lessons, even when they didn't have much money to spend. He finally caved when her heart wouldn't let go of the dream—he would've done anything for her, and he did. He cleaned out their old garage so she could have a space large enough to practice her pirouettes. He checked out books at the library, became her coach so she could improve every single day to reach her dream.

He did everything for her, yet all he ever truly wanted was to see his baby girl happy. He died for her happiness, and now his death felt like it had happened in vain.

A tear trickled down Fiona's chin. She quickly wiped it away and cupped her face, shaking away the thoughts.

She couldn't give up. She wouldn't. She refused to let her own fatigue stop her, refused to see an end to it, even if all hope felt lost. It wasn't over yet.

Blowing out a breath, Fiona slowly lifted her head and looked into the studio again.

God acted strange sometimes. He tested people and she had to believe this was her test. She had been on the cusp of giving up when he sent Adam to her... pushed him into her life. He could've chosen to walk away from her, she meant literally nothing to him in his life, but he still chose to help her. Why? She still didn't understand, still questioned his motives.

Sighing, Fiona slowly got up and walked to the center of the floor.

All these questions in her head weren't important. All that mattered now was how she spent her time and pushed herself towards her goal. Adam was going to help her with that, but in the end, she had to do it herself. She had to dance, she had to feel those steps... she had to make her own dream come true.

Closing her eyes, Fiona took a deep breath and then exhaled through her mouth. She faintly heard music playing from the other studios, the few kids who were still here. The Dec was open till 10pm, which left her two more hours to practice.

Feeling her muscles ache and twitch in protest, Fiona pushed out a hard breath and focused on the mirror.

She would make this happen for herself. For herself... and for her dad.

"And five, six, seven, eight..."

Chapter 7

Saturday meant longer days of practice. The Dec opened at 9 and Fiona arrived by bus at exactly 9.12am. She would've been there earlier, but she slept through her first alarm. She didn't get home till 10.30 last night, and didn't get to bed till almost midnight. Showering and explaining to her mom why she missed dinner had taken quite some time as well.

But now, the next morning, Fiona felt ready for another day of dancing. She walked into the Dec in her black tights and training bra with a loose blue shirt on top. The temperatures were getting scalding hot in New York, even right from the morning. The weather forecast said the heatwave would continue to rage the city for another good week or so. No signs of rainclouds anytime soon.

Which mean boiling hot days of practicing in a poorly air-conditioned dance studio.

As Fiona stepped into the foyer of the DanceDec, she was immediately met by a lively energy. A bunch of people were sitting in the usual circle on the floor in the foyer, talking, eating their breakfast and some even doing their school homework. The Dec was a home to a lot of the people that came there, amongst them no doubt Adam. He always seemed to be there, always chatting with people or always up to something or other. That boy had a fire up his ass.

That's why, as Fiona scanned the large circle, she wasn't surprised to find Adam sitting amongst them with some of the girls, laughing and talking. There were a few guys as well, one of them talking to the girl Fiona remembered Adam comforting after her boyfriend had broken up with her. She was grinning and touching his arm, and the guy seemed happy with the attention. Adam sat a few feet away from her, next to Kalo who sat right beside him on a wooden crate. Together, they were bent over a third girl's head of hair, weaving her afro into scalp braids.

"¿Por que no usas el vestido nuevo que compraste ayer?" Adam said, glancing at Kalo. "¿No te gusto?"

"No, no, es hermoso, lo tengo en mi bolsa para más tarde," She replied in fluent Spanish. "La fiesta de compromiso es esta noche, usaré mi vestido ahí."

"¿Para un hombre en especial?" Adam enquired with a grin.

"¿Puede ser?" Kalo grinned back and then innocently looked around as Adam broke into a grin.

"¿Oyé, por que?!" He laughed, then shook his head and looked back down at the braid he was making. "¿Por que no me quieres platicar de él? Quien se supone que es él? Necesito conocerlo y aprobarlo a él."

"¡Oyé! Gringo, tú no eres mi padre, por favor."

"¿Y entonces por que me llamas papí aqui?" He smirked.

"¡Oyé! Bastardo!" Kalo slapped his arm hard and shoved him away with a roll of her eyes, making Adam break into loud laughter.

It was that moment Adam happened to look up. He noticed Fiona standing there with a confused expression, then perked up and shot her a grin. "Hey, princess! Welcome to the party! You already know Kalo, and this is Deeva," He gestured to the girl sitting in front of them, getting her hair done. She looked up from under a thick mob of fro and gave her a smile as well. "You wanna be next in line? Kalo's gonna be braiding all day."

"It's community service in this weather," Kalo stated. She shook her head and grabbed another section of Deeva's hair, parting the sections up. "We out here already poofing like a poodle, this humidity ain't making things easier. You want me to do yours next? I'll hook you up soon as I'm done here."

"I'm good," Fiona replied. Her hair was always in a bun, that way it was never in her face when she was dancing.

She glanced at Adam again as he finished a braid, then stood up and grabbed his bag.

"Alright then. She might change her mind later," Adam leaned down and staged whispered to Kalo as he grabbed his bag. "If her weave ain't flying by the time we're done today, I'm quitting dancing on the spot."

Kalo snorted loudly. "That'll be the day."

Adam laughed and Fiona had to silently agree with Kalo. She had only known him for about a short week now, but even she knew that him quitting dancing would be like Hell freezing over. This kid would dance even if he had no legs.

Or dance floor. Or just floor in general. He would find a way to dance on the walls somehow.

"Watch it," Adam warned, pointing at her with a mischievous grin. He then looked at Fiona and jerked his head, waving her along as he headed up the stairs. "Come on then, tutu. Let's get those feet moving. Shit, we might just burn them off. It's like the floor is lava in New York. Actually, it's like the air is lava. I almost couldn't fall asleep last night, how about you? Can you sleep in hot weather or do you have a fan on?"

Fiona didn't get to reply as they walked inside studio 13, Adam unlocking it and dumping his bag down. He continued yapping on, asking one redundant question after another, so fast, she never even got the chance to answer. It was 9.20 in the damn morning and he was already flipped on to the highest. That meant a long day ahead.

"Okay chill out, would you?" Fiona finally had to break through when he was going on and on about how his cold showers had turned into arctic showers just to be able to survive this heat. "Jeez, you talk more than my grandma."

Adam grinned widely. "My grams says the same. She says I talk the ears off of her every night at dinner and don't stop to swallow my food. I tell her it's not my fault she cooks enchiladas on a regular basis. If she wants me to stop, stop feeding me the good stuff."

"You live with your grandma?" Fiona asked. Again, her curiosity got the better of her as Adam easily gave up another part of his personal life like it was normal trivia.

"Yeah," He plugged his phone into the stereo and started scrolling through it. It was so routine by now, Fiona automatically started stretching out on the floor. "I mean, she's not technically my grandma though. I don't know anyone in my family, but I call her grams because she's been taking care of me ever since I was little."

Fiona raised a confused brow. "What?" If she wasn't his grandma, then who was she? And did he just say... he didn't know anyone in his family?

"She's one of the old nuns back at the orphanage I grew up in. She adopted me when she retired from the church and raised me as her kid."

Fiona's jaw dropped before she could stop it. As Adam continued scrolling through his phone with a concentrated look, she tried to process the new shocking information he had just given her.

"You're... an orphan?"

Adam slowly turned his head and saw her reaction. He smiled. "Yeah. I told you I grew up in Harlem. Just not where."

Fiona closed her mouth and let it sink in. The more she learned about him, the more fascinated she got... and amazed.

He had had a rough childhood, yet here he was, the happiest person she had ever met, smiling and laughing so much, she was positive half of his abs came from that alone. But somehow, it just didn't add up to her.

"I'm sorry," She said, lowering her eyes to the floor and pretending to be focused on stretching her feet. "I didn't know."

"I have no secrets, princess. Unlike you, I'm an open book," When she looked up, he gave her a cheeky wink. "All you have to do is ask."

Fiona quickly dropped her gaze again when he kept looking at her with a challenging smirk. Like he was daring her to open up as well or ask him more. Talk.

But that would mean she was interested in him as more than just a dance partner.

"What are we dancing today?" Fiona asked and looked up, meeting him with a sober glance. He chuckled slowly, but then sighed.

"Tell me something first. I need you to answer me this, Fee."

She lifted her head again when Adam then walked up to her, eyes pinned on her face. Fiona swallowed nervously, watching his serious expression; An expression she hadn't seen on his face that often. He wore red shorts today, shorts resembling bathing shorts, and wore a loose black shirt with some sort of pressed-on logo. His brown hair was freed from his usual cap, which left his eyes to be that much more prominent. Eyes that were staring at her with resolve.

"What does dancing mean to you? Real dancing. When you step into this studio," He gestured into it with an open hand, showing her the dance floor, "When you're out there, what's going through your head? What's driving you when everything inside you hurts to the bone and you can't stay on your feet a second longer? What keeps you going?"

Fiona felt her skin prickle and her insides twisted at his questions. They were deep, invasive and poked a hole in all of her insecurities. All of her fears. He was asking her... why he was teaching her.

She took a deep breath. Everything inside her was suddenly in a turmoil, because nobody had ever asked her that question before. Not even herself.

"It's the only thing that makes sense in my life," She whispered, releasing a fragile truth from her heart she didn't know was real until she spoke it aloud. "I can't... if I don't dance daily... I feel like everything is going to fall apart. I can't... it's just something I have to do."

"And that makes it all worth it?" Adam asked. He was standing so close to her now, he could've reached out and touched her cheek if he wanted.

Fiona took another deep breath. It was all worth it. For her dad. "Yes."

Adam watched her for a long moment, but then slowly gave a nod. "Then show me that on the floor today. Own the steps I showed you yesterday," He took a step backwards, then another one, keeping his eyes on her. "You're not here to copy me or anyone else. You're not even here to impress me. You're here for you. So show me you're worth it, Fee."

The music started blasting with a kickstart and Fee snapped her eyes up. Adam stepped into the center of the floor and opened his arms, challenging her to join him. Timidly, she stepped forward, stepping onto the floor.

"Show me," He said, leaning down to her ear. "Show me, Fee. Move."

Fiona shut her eyes again and remember her thoughts from yesterday. No giving up. No being scared anymore. She had to do this.

Opening her eyes, Fiona glared up at Adam. He stared equally hard at her, still waiting for her to make the first move.

And then, she did.

She didn't count the beat in her head this time. Her feet moved on their own and recalled the steps he had taught her yesterday, the steps she had spent an extra two hours pushing herself through. Unlike yesterday, though, they came to her naturally, and as the beat changed, so did her moves.

Adam's lips slowly split as she danced, showing him the steps he had taught her – showed him how to own them. He nodded and then started moving his own body slowly to the rhythm. He let her lead the beat, but then as the pre-chorus came around, he spun around and took his place beside her, facing the mirror with her. And then, as the beat drop, they did the moves together in perfect sync.

Fiona let go of all of her thoughts and let the music just guide her. She didn't think too much about perfecting the steps, didn't think about how stupid she felt moving on the floor in weird, unclean lines.

Because she didn't. For the first time since they started this, Fiona didn't feel stupid dancing the steps, and as her eyes fell to Adam who was dancing next to her, caught up in the beat as well, for the first time she didn't feel insecure either. She felt...

Confident.

"Fucking SHIT!" Adam howled once the beat ended and took a run to slide across the floor on his knees. He grinned at the ceiling and threw both his fists into the air. "Fuck yeah, Fee! Fuck, you can't tell me that didn't feel like great sex! Goddamn, I knew you had it in you!"

He got up and turned around in time to catch Fiona blush and cover her mouth. For some reason she felt like crying and laughing at the same time. Her whole body was shaking, mostly from anxiety, but also from disbelief. She actually did it.

"Hey," He came up to her and offered her a winning smile. "You did it, Fee. Those better be happy tears I'm looking at."

Was she actually crying? She quickly wiped her eyes down. "Shut up. It's allergies. I have h-hay fever..."

"You have a fever alright, but it's not hay," Adam smirked, then turned and walked back to the stereo. "Let's keep going before you lose your nerve and I bust a nut from watching you own the floor. Same steps, new routine. Then I'm going to show you a few more steps. Tomorrow we spend half the day practicing true freestyle, then the other half we spend moving on to something slightly different. With me?"

Fiona dried the last of her tears and shook off the final jitters. "Let's do it."

Adam shot her a bright grin. "Fuckin' A."

Around 12 o'clock, Adam called for a lunch break. They all gathered downstairs, and after some convincing, Adam managed to drag her downstairs with them. Fiona still didn't feel completely comfortable in large crowds, but Adam promised the people down there wouldn't hassle her.

"I'll speak so much they can't get a word in edgewise," He grinned. After that, Fiona had sighed and reluctantly let him drag her downstairs to join the rest of the gang.

The DanceDec was for people of all age, race and background. That meant the crowd carried from young kids who spend their afternoon hanging out with their classmates, busting moves and learning from the older boys and girls who had been coming there for years, to elder people. Sometimes you'd see an adult or an actual dance instructor who came by ever so often to host an actual dance class. Sometimes seniors also dropped in for an evening of waltzing or ballroom dancing. Anyone with 30 bucks a month could rent a studio, but on weekends it was mostly kids of Fiona's own age that hung around the Dec.

"Lunch time!" Adam bellowed as soon as they entered the foyer, which seemed to be the official meeting spot. Everyone looked up and Adam was greeted with smiles, curses and hollers in both Spanish and English. The girls cooed him over and he quickly nodded Fiona along.

"Hey, snacks," He said as he took a seat on the floor, Fiona quietly taking one someone beside him/somewhat behind him. "What you got going on today? Something smells delicious and it's not you, Kalo."

Kalo shoved him with a laugh and muttered some Spanish curse words at him. "Oyé, puta. It's my ma's homemade chili. We had a cookout last night, the whole entire family came over. I ate so much food, I'm surprised I can fit into my shorts today."

"Yeah, I did notice your ass looked a little extra today. Want me to help you work that off?" Adam leaned in and smirked in her face.

Kalo shoved at him again and shook her head as Adam laughed. "You're lucky I didn't bring my chancla today, gringo."

"And you're lucky I didn't bring my belt."

"¡Oyé, pinche pendejo!"

Kalo slapped his arm and shoulder as Adam tipped over sideways with laughter. They then all dug out their packed lunches, Adam unwrapping a large deli sub filled to the brim with kebab, hot sauce and cheese with some lettuce and tomato sticking out here and there. The other girls had packed various things such as sandwiches, burger meals and bags of potato chips. They all passed them around like they were one big family.

Fiona herself had packed a modest salad. It was mostly lettuce, cucumber and a few canned beans she had rinsed and dried that morning. She had topped it with some more canned corn and a squeeze of lemon juice.

"Want some chips, Fee?" Adam turned to her when the bag had made it his way and he offered her a handful. Fiona shook her head politely declined. Fried olive oil, trans fats and high sodium. Not to forget the salt and starch. She would blow up like a popped tire.

"No, thanks."

Adam shrugged, but then happened to glance into her lunch box. He didn't comment, but instead turned back and pulled up another grin as Rani, one of the other girls he had danced with, said something funny.

Fiona fell in and out of their conversation. She focused on nibbling on her salad, keeping her eyes and head down to avoid accidentally catching someone's eyes. Eye contact usually led to conversations.

"This tango is killing me, man," Kalo suddenly groaned, shaking her head. "I don't know if it's Dimitri or me, but we keep messing up the end."

"Yeah? What's the problem?"

Her and Adam started going into a deep conversation about a tango Kalo was apparently rehearsing. What for, she didn't catch. Fiona finally gave up on trying to finish her lunch and popped the lid back on. Then, getting up, she grabbed her things.

Adam looked up. "You finished? I'll be right up, just go ahead."

Fiona gave a nod, but then left and walked up the stairs. She felt a weight drop off of her chest as she ventured back into the silence of the studio, away from all the others.

She didn't know why, but she had always felt like an outsider amongst people her age. She never seemed to fit into a category. The kids at her school all seemed to have their own thing going on, but none of them were as passionate about dancing as she was. She knew there was a cheerleading team, but the girls on the team were very outgoing and perky. She wasn't like that at all.

Everyone else had practically been friends since kindergarten or had known each other from the block somehow, which left Fee feeling outside again. She and her mom had moved from one side of Harlem to another side after her father died when they could no longer afford to live in their old house. They had sold most of what they owned and moved to a new neighborhood. Still, the streets somehow felt familiar – Harlem being her home.

But with no friends to share it with, she had kept from going outside and had focused on what was most important.

Sighing, Fiona peaked through the closed blinds and down into the foyer. All the kids were still down there, Adam howling with laughter as usual and the girls grinning, but turning their noses up at whatever he said.

Even in a place like this, she felt outside. The black kids here were all from the street and had way more cred than her. She felt too white to hang out with them, but too black to hang out with the white kids at her school. She was in between, her personality a split between growing up with a white mom and a black dad who died before she could adopt some of his confidence...

Looking at Adam, Fiona pressed her lips together. He was doing it like it was nothing. He had grown up in Harlem like her, had been through shit, and maybe that's why the street accepted him. Even if he was as white as they came.

Fiona turned away from the window and walked back into the center of the studio. At the end of the day, she knew it had nothing to do with color or creds. The problem was her; She just didn't know how to connect with people her own age. They were all immature and goofing around like they had no problems, or like they at least didn't exist, and took on a happy personality to cope with the fact that when all was said and done, they were all broken inside. And that's where she differed.

She couldn't forget her pain. Not when it haunted her with every literal step she took.

The door to the studio suddenly opened and Fiona looked up to see Adam coming in. He dumped his bag down by the wall and then looked back at her. His lips lifted in a little smile.

"Ready for more, princess?"

And wasn't that a loaded question.

Chapter 8

On Sundays, Fiona's mom dragged her to church. The service started at 9.15, which meant she couldn't make it to the studio until 10.30, at least. As much as she liked church, time was just too sparse for her these days. The second the sermon was done, Fiona had said goodbye to her mom and gotten on the first bus to the DanceDec.

Arriving late and still in her church dress and shoes, Fiona walked in and looked around, hoping to find Adam and apologize for being late. It was that morning that she had realized that she didn't have any way of contacting him – didn't even know his last name to look him up in the phone book. She had been so focused on dancing and keeping to herself, she hadn't even bothered to ask.

Then again, neither had he.

Hearing Latin music suddenly playing from upstairs, Fiona looked up and curiously followed it. She noticed a few other people had gathered around the studio's door and were peaking inside. She quickly ran upstairs and joined them, shuffling closer to get a peak at what was happening.

The second she glanced inside, Fiona lost her breath and dropped her jaw. Adam and Kalo were there, Kalo in a red dress and Adam not in his usual gray sweats and black shirt, but a pair of black dress trousers and a white top. They were standing intimately, Kalo pressed up against Adam's chest and Adam looking down over her shoulder. The music played and they both moved.

Fiona watched. Kalo looked drop dead gorgeous, her body plump with curves accentuated by the tightly fitted dress with a loose skirt. She wore heels and had her hair pinned to one side. She danced like she had never done anything else in her life and moved perfectly in beat with Adam who now twirled her around.

They met, face to face, and Fiona watched as Adam lowered her body, bending her backwards with the help of his hand. Kalo tilted her head back, and as she did, Adam lowered his own towards her chest, his other hand running up her stomach to her cleavage slowly, then down again, sensually.

Fiona held her breath and felt something inside her stir from watching the two of them dance. She couldn't rip her eyes off of them; There was something different that happened today as Adam danced. Usually when he danced, he was happy and goofy, but this piece was... intense. And Adam played the part perfectly.

His face was set in stone, his brows furrowed in a way that made Fiona feel his passion and anger as he harshly twirled Kalo away, barely catching her on her wrist as she whipped away. He pulled her tightly towards him again and cupped her face, before jerking it to the side and leaning in. Kalo seemed distraught, yet emotionless. She kept her cool as

Adam released her and let her take a stride across the floor, circling back to him in a taunt.

His hand shot out, but she turned away from it. In synchronized movements, his hand then dropped and hers lifted instead, pressing her palm to his chest as he advanced and she backed away. Finally, he grabbed her arm and pulled her to his body again, twirling her around. They then ventured into a dueling tango that left Fiona speechless, had she wanted to talk. But she didn't.

Those steps said it all.

Fiona couldn't help but feel her stomach tighten slightly in anxiousness at Adam's serious face. His skin shone with sweat, but he dominated the dance, tossing Kalo around and lowering her like she was a doll, but then softening at the slightest movement from her side. He portrayed the battle of lust and love and it sent shivers through Fiona's body.

He really danced a little of everything. More than a little, she would say.

The dance finally came to a spiraling end as the music dropped and Kalo ended against his chest, caught in his arms, but her face turned away with a statuesque pose. Adam's was harsh and angry, and not a soul spoke as the music ended. Everyone was too stunned to speak, including Fiona.

Then, Adam cracked a slow smile.

The whole room broke into cheers and applauded them as he lifted Kalo up, who like him grinned and gave him a tight hug. He hugged her back and panted slightly, but then raised a questioning brow. "Like that?"

"Yes! We nailed it!" Kalo whopped and ran a hand over her hair. "Finally!"

"Guess Dimitri needs to up his game and practice those spins some more. You were perfect, Kalo, grade fucking A."

Kalo grinned back. "Thanks. Thank you for rehearsing it with me."

"Anytime, gumdrop."

It was then Adam turned with a smile and finally noticed Fiona. His smile broadened, and after quickly picking up his bag from the floor, he walked towards her. "There you are! Ready to get started?"

Fiona struggled to kickstart her body as he slung an arm around her shoulder and pulled her along. She awkwardly followed.

From what she had just witnessed, Adam could've fooled anyone into thinking he was a spurned lover of a woman who couldn't be tied down. His body had told a story through that dance, and it made Fiona think...

Had it all just been steps, or had he actually felt something in there?

"Why were you just dancing with her, just now?" Fiona asked, hoping she didn't sound jealous or anything like a bitch. In truth she wasn't, but the look on his face as he had danced had gotten her curious as to if... if there was something more between them. He did hang out with her after hours...

"Kalo needed my opinion on a piece she's choreographing. She's auditioning it Tuesday for a guy who's got her hooked up for a commercial gig," Adam replied. "Could be huge for her."

Fiona nodded. That wasn't the answer she was looking for, though...

They came to the studio, and Adam walked in, throwing down his bag and crouching down next to it. He searched through it, before finding his water bottle and taking a good gulp. Fiona herself laid her own bag down and realized then she was still in her church clothes. She hadn't had time to go home and change, but figured she could do it here. Except... her level of comfort with stripping down in public places was... very low.

"So, are you ready for more today?" Adam asked as he stood up. His body still shone with a light sheen of sweat, which didn't help how nice he looked, somewhat put together in real pants and a tight fitted top. His lean body peaked out with almost blatant transparency.

Fiona quickly averted her eyes. "Yeah. What are we doing today?"

"I was thinking we could do some contemporary and throw in some freestyle with what you've learned so far. Sort of like a little mash-up to see how much you remember."

Fiona bit her lip, hesitantly. Normally she didn't object to his lessons or his plans for their classes, but after today, the dancer in her had peaked with a strange and unusual curiosity.

Adam noticed her hesitance and rose a slow brow. "What? What's on your mind?"

Fiona hesitated a moment, feeling the slight prickle of nervousness tickle in her stomach. Should she ask? It was so outside her comfort zone, but she couldn't help but feel... drawn to it. "Could... could you teach me... what you did in there with Kalo?"

Adam lifted his brows in surprise. Then, with a broad smile, he crossed his arms and grinned. "Liked what you saw, huh?"

Fiona immediately regretted asking. She knew she should've just stuck to his regular teaching. "Forget it. Let's just get on with the program."

"It's not that I don't want to teach you, I don't mind at all," Adam voiced, walking closer to her as Fiona averted her eyes and pretended to busy herself with taking off her shoes. "I just don't think you're ready for that kind of dancing."

Fiona paused up. With slight confusion, she turned and gave him a little stare. "What do you mean?" Those steps hadn't looked too hard. They were certainly within her flexible limits, it was just the attitude that would take some practice getting down. But that was what Adam was there for.

"I mean," Adam came closer and suddenly Fiona felt his hands on her hips. "The tango is all about sexual confidence and tease. Passion," He whispered in her ear. Fiona felt the hairs on her neck rise and her cheeks burst into flames. "The bachata would be an alternative, but it all still comes from the hips. And you'd be dancing close to me. Very close."

Fiona held her breath. "H-how close?"

She felt as he grabbed her hips and tucked her backwards with a simple pull until her ass connected with his crotch with a small thud. "That close."

Fiona immediately jumped away. When she turned around, Adam was grinning smugly. She angrily pressed her lips together and folded her hands over her chest. "That's not dancing. That's something else."

"Not with Latin dancing it's not," Adam said and walked up to the stereo. He plugged in his phone and then muttered under his breath, "and if you think that was bad, I probably shouldn't even mention the reggaeton."

Fiona frowned, but wisely didn't comment when she noticed Adam's naughty grin. She reminded herself to google just what the hell that was later.

For now, Fiona took a deep breath and realized what she had to do. She could learn as many steps as she wanted, but they would be nothing until she could dance them like Kalo and Adam did. She needed to learn what they did, had to learn how to... dance close.

"Teach me," She determinedly said. She leveled her voice and hoped it sounded confident, because her chest was caving in and her stomach was in knots from merely speaking the words. Breathe. "Teach me to dance like that."

Adam stopped in his process of plugging his phone into the stereo and finding a song. With a slow raise of his head, he turned it and stared at her. "You want me to teach you that? Those steps?"

Fiona pressed her lips together. Inhale. Exhale. "Yes. Or whatever it is I have to do to dance like that." She wanted her own steps to look that good when she was dancing her ballet. More than just steps.

Adam kept staring at her, but then put his phone down. Without a word, he then walked up to her, keeping his eyes on her as he walked all the way right up to her and stopped in front of her. Then, he lifted a brow. "Who are you and what have you done to Fiona?"

When his lips split in a smirk Fiona rolled her eyes and turned away from him. If he wasn't going to take it seriously... "Forget it if you're going to be a dick about it. I was just trying to—"

"You have to feel every step," His hands were suddenly on her hips again, holding firmly onto them and pulling her close to his body. Fiona gasped. "Shit, you have to feel them to your bones, Fee. You gotta feel them, feel the beat, feel your partner, feel yourself. That's what this dancing is all about."

Fiona sucked in a breath when she felt how his hands smoothed up her hips to her sides. They paused there, sending a scorching heat through her already burning hot body. She had to feel.

"Give me you hands."

Fiona felt a zap of anxiety flee through her as Adam tapped her hip, wanting her to give him her hands. Her palms felt sweaty and her bones trembled, but she fought the sensation and shakily brought her hands to his.

Without wasting a moment, Adam grabbed her hands and plastered them to her own body. Fiona gasped again and looked down, seeing him place them over her hips. "Feel, Fiona. Feel the power inside your own body and channel it to your mind. Fucking feel this," He whispered and squeezed her hands tightly against her own hips. Fiona sucked a breath in. "This is your body, Fee. Identify with it. Own it."

Slowly, very slowly, Adam slid her hands up, keeping his own on top of them. Fiona could hardly breathe, felt his breath on her shoulder and right near her ear, felt his body heat behind her and the strength and callouses of his hands gripping hers. Slowly, he guided her hands up her own body, exploring.

"Feel that?" He murmured. Fiona closed her eyes and swallowed silently as he paused her hands on her stomach. He then slowly slid them up her sternum, up, up, up...

Fiona's eyes flew open when he brought her hands right on top of her chest. Anxiety pushed through when she felt how his hands practically rested on top of them – on top of her breasts. She was just about to jerk away and tell him she couldn't when Adam suddenly gripped her chin and turned her head sideways.

"Don't run," He told her. It was almost a whisper, but a prayer nonetheless. "Trust me, Fee. Please?"

Fiona's breath was hammering in and out of her lungs and her body felt on fire. Adam's voice pierced her ears and somehow made everything ten times hotter. She couldn't focus. "A-Adam..."

Suddenly, she was spun around and she stood face to face with Adam who held her face with a cupped hand on her cheek. They were inches apart, his breath striking her lips. Fiona froze up completely.

Then, she felt as Adam's other hand suddenly took hers. Lifting it and pressing it to his right pec, he copied the motion with his other hand and brought her other hand to his left pec. He kept his own hands on top of hers, letting her feel his calm heartbeat. They stood like that for what felt like centuries.

"Do you feel that?" Adam then said. Fiona who hadn't been able to tear her eyes away from his suddenly looked down when he did. They looked at their joined hands. "Physical contact is not something to fear, it's something to learn how to tackle. Everyone has a limit and that's okay. When dancing, you can't be afraid to touch your partner, Fiona."

Fiona released a shaky breath. Despite her angst in the situation, he was right. She knew it, he knew it, and it was something she had to admit. She was scared of contact, because the last man who held her closely... the last man who hugged her and loved her...

"We'll take it slowly, I promise you," Adam said. After another moment, he then released her hands, but didn't step back as she nervously drew them around herself. "You'll tell me when we meet your boundaries and I'll try and find ways for us to work through them. Then, once we get that down, that's when I'll teach you to dance like Kalo and I did. Deal?"

With a trembling breath, Fiona nodded. She felt her nerves slowly simmering down, settling as Adam finally stepped away and walked back to the stereo. She blew out a breath and closed her eyes for a moment. How the hell did he do it?

"I've had lots of practice, to be fair," Adam voiced, which made Fiona realize she had whispered her last thought out loud. "You kind of have to when you're a teenage boy and you have to dance with girls. Nothing is more awkward than a third leg amidst an emotional duet."

And just like that, the tension was broken as Fiona looked up flippantly and saw Adam grin to himself as he continued to scroll through his music. Did he just imply...?

"Relax," He said, after a moment, and looked up to see her uneasy grimace. "That won't happen with me. I'm a choir boy, baby. Jesus keeps me in line."

Him and Adam Jr, she hoped. If she thought physical intimacy was hard without a boner brushing against her leg...

"Oh, man, you really do look cute in red," Adam suddenly laughed and made Fiona jerk her head up to realize she was blushing profusely. What the hell! "Shit, your ears look like Christmas lights. Does it start around your neck? I think it does."

"Shut up," Fiona snapped. She embarrassedly tried to shake it off. "Just start the damn music, you dud."

"Dud? Man, I love it when you talk dirty to me," Adam suddenly tossed his head back with a grin and dramatically moaned. "More, baby! More!"

Fiona rolled her eyes and seriously contemplated walking out of there. He couldn't take anything seriously for more than a moment at a time before he reverted back to his immature self. She wouldn't get any work done like this. Maybe she should just dance alone today in an empty studio. "You know what, forget it. I'm out."

She grabbed her bag again and decided to go change and then go downstairs to see if there were any free studios left to dance in. She was just about to walk out when she halted in her steps.

"Fiona!"

Oh, hell.

The music blasted from the speakers, and for the first time she recognized the beat. Halting in the door, she clenched her teeth and then slowly turned around.

Adam was at the stereo, his hips already moving to the iconic number. He was smirking at her, then wagged his finger slowly as Fiona hesitated in the door. "Nobody walks out on the king, baby. Get yourself over here."

Fiona stayed put. She could leave now and have no regrets. She would disappoint Adam and he would most certainly make a dramatic scene about it, but she could leave and that would be that.

But, as Adam's smirk broadened and The Way You Make Me Feel by Michael Jackson played, Fiona turned her eyes to the sky and groaned. Oh, hell. She had lost her mind.

Dumping her bag down again, she closed the door and walked into the center of the dance floor as Adam whopped and then laughed, scraping the tips of his shoes over the floor as he danced towards her, going in a circle around her. "Fuck, yeah! That's what I'm talking about! Let's have some fucking fun, princess; Start walking."

With a small purse of her lips, Fiona couldn't help but feel her mouth turn upwards in a reluctant little smile. Shit, he was starting to rub off on her now, too. Maybe it was like a disease... if exposed to the bacteria for too long...

"Move, Fee."

With a deep breath, Fiona turned on her heel and shook her head as she started walking around the room – Adam following closely behind her, grooving along to the music.

Chapter 9

Monday morning, Fiona was in a rush to get to school. She had overslept again and had to hurry through her whole morning routine. Breakfast was out of the question.

"Oh, honey! Don't forget your lunch," Her mom called from the kitchen as Fiona rushed towards the door. She reluctantly halted and turned around.

"Oh, right..."

Her mom came up to her with her lunch bag. She smiled at her, and Fiona tightly returned it. "I feel like I hardly see you these days. You're always so busy running about."

"It's the audition, mom," Fiona reminded her and grabbed her lunch. "I'm rehearsing."

"I know you are, but it better not be affecting your school. I want to see your report card this week," She told and gave her a sharp look. "Anything below C's and I'm putting a curfew on you."

Fiona felt a hit to her stomach, like a cramp of angst catapulted from her throat to her abdomen. If she got a curfew, she couldn't dance... "Mom!"

"No discussions," She warned, then snapped her finger. "Off to school now, don't miss the bus."

Sighing and clenching her fists in frustration, Fiona left and rushed down the street.

With all the extra work she and Adam had been doing, she hadn't had much time to study. She wasn't a bad student, but she could maybe have done more for her grades lately. It all just didn't seem that important when the auditions were two weeks away.

Again, Fiona felt a sudden suck in her stomach. The pressure was building and it was making her want to vomit. If she failed both school and botched her audition... then it all would've been for nothing, and she would have nothing to fall back on.

Taking a shaky breath, she decided to get some homework done today during their breaks. Even if just a few minutes here and there, she would do her best to get it crammed in.

She wasn't sure she could survive disappointing both of her parents.

After school, Fiona arrived at the DanceDec to find a booming blast of music coming from one studio alone. Usually there were twelve different kinds of music playing from all the studios, but today it all seemed to be coming from just one. Fiona frowned and looked up to see everyone piling into the largest studio.

"There you are! Just in time!"

Fiona turned and found Adam rushing up to her with a grin on his face. He grabbed her arm and wordlessly started dragging her along with him.

"What's going on?" She asked when they rushed up the stairs, Adam and everyone else clearly worked up about something.

"It's dance circle time," He told and grinned as the people around him met him with hollers and quick clasps on his shoulder. It was like he knew everyone there.

"What's dance circle?" Fiona enquired.

Adam turned and broadened his lips into a full grin. "Remember when we first met? The shopping cart, the whole dance-thing?"

Fiona nodded. How could she forget? She thought that was him and his crew, but now after getting to know him, she realized they were just his friends here from the Dec.

"We do a dance circle every Monday," He told, now wedging them through the hoard of people who were also trying to get into the studio. The music was so loud, he almost had to shout to mask it. "We all gather around in a circle to dance our asses off! If you're invited into the circle, you gotta bust!"

Fiona widened her eyes as they finally made it into the studio and joined everyone else. Adam got them a good spot in the circle, which Fiona now saw was a literal circle that people had made where in the center there was a clean space of floor. It reminded her of fight club, except instead of fighting, they were going to be dancing.

"How does one get invited into the ring?" Fiona nervously shouted to catch Adam's attention over the boom of the music.

"You either get invited by the current dancer, get pulled in or you take the circle yourself!" He shouted back. His lips split in a grin when the music suddenly changed and some-one whistled loudly. Everyone cheered and Fiona guessed it meant the circle was open.

She wasn't surprised when she saw Kalo step into the circle as the first and made some gestures with her hands to get the crowd pumped up, even more than it already was. Everyone cheered her on and Adam even whistled loudly. Kalo then turned on her foot, and like that, she was in the zone.

Fiona had never seen anything like it; It was like a zoo, all of them acting like wild monkeys, roaring and shouting and acting like buffoons for the person in the center. Kalo owned the circle and showed off her multitude of dance skills with some freestyle and hiphop infused steps. She had the circle for almost a full minute before she walked up to someone in the crowd and smirked and pulled at his shirt, dragging him into the ring.

"That's Dimitri!" Adam shouted to Fiona who watched as the guy, Dimitri, took the circle with a smirk and let Kalo take his spot by the sideline. "He's her dance partner!"

Dimitri had a European look about him, but his footwork was otherworldly. His style was very much infused by street dance and Latin style. He had short black hair and a subtle goatee and seemed to love the attention just as much as Kalo. He worked the crowd up as well before taking the floor with his moves.

It went on like that for a while. Fiona watched as person after person was invited or dragged into the circle. Only one guy took the circle, and after seeing him dance, she didn't blame him. Fiona dropped her jaw when he laid down on the ground and started spinning and making these almost electric jolts with his body. He was the fastest dancer she had ever seen.

"That's Twitch!" Adam shouted. "His real name is Joe, but everyone calls him Twitch. I don't think I need to explain why!"

Fiona watched as Twitch got up from the floor again and took a stride around the circle. He made these twitches with his body that somehow looked cool in a way Fiona never could have imagined. She guessed he had found his trademark.

All of these people in the room seemed confident and happy. The ones who took the floor all danced like they owned it and everyone else as well in the room. They were masters of the dance floor, yet none of them had been professionally trained. They all came from the street like Adam, and just like him, they danced like it was the only thing that made the dark go away.

Fiona could relate to that, and yet when she danced, she still didn't look like this. And a cold feeling in her stomach was beginning to tell her she never would.

Fiona was just about to turn to Adam to ask if they could leave, when Twitch suddenly stopped in front of Adam. He clasped his shoulder and practically shoved him out there, making Adam stumble into the circle with a big fat grin. Everyone seemed to double their noise as he then straightened out his posture and brushed off his shoulder with a little goofy smirk.

And just like that, the Adam Fiona remembered from the first day was back; The wild, uninhibited 'zero-fucks-given' Adam who danced like his soul had no limits when he stepped on to the floor. He spun around and bust out more moves than Fiona could remember him teaching her. She watched him spin around on his head, his cap looking like a propeller against the floor before he jumped to his feet and swung around again.

The grin on his lips was the definition of happiness.

The music was upbeat, but Adam kept up with it and laughed when the girls and boys whistled at him. And then—just because he could—he made more of a fool of himself by dancing like any cliché teenage movie would have a pop girl dancing when the music switched.

Everyone laughed and whistled as Adam danced around like a flimsy gay parody, before shaking his head with a grin and waving his hands dismissively. He then walked up to a person in the crowd and yanked them in.

Fiona frowned. She seriously couldn't understand him sometimes. He both loved dancing so much he never looked happier than when he was out there on the floor, yet he still didn't take it seriously when he had the chance to show everyone what he could do. She wasn't opposed to a little fun, but nobody danced as great as he did and didn't have any aspirations in life to pursue it. He had to know he was talented, so how come he spent his time here goofing off?

These were the thoughts going through her head as Adam worked his way through the crowd, towards her. He was sweating, but he still wore the same grin he wore on the dance floor. When he came close enough, he swung a sweaty arm around her.

"Wanna get outta here?"

Fiona nodded, and then let Adam lead them out of the thick mob, his hand taking hers by pure instinct. She lowered her eyes to the action, watching how his palm fit comfortably in hers. Sweaty, but comfortably.

Breathe.

They made it out of the studio and down the hall to their booked studio. Everyone was still gathered for the dance circle, so nobody cared or noticed that the two of them slipped away. Adam opened the door and routinely walked up to the stereo.

"So, what are we in the mood for today?" He asked, humming thoughtfully as he scrolled through his phone. "If you're still interested, we can work on those boundaries of yours?"

Fiona swallowed and remembered the feel of his hand in hers. The feel of his hands on her body yesterday. Everywhere. Feeling her. If they were going to work on her boundaries, there was going to be a lot more of that today.

Breathe. Breathe. Focus.

Fiona felt slightly dizzy, her nerves spiking inside her, but shook it off and blamed it on the heat. Taking a deep breath, she looked up at Adam who awaited her response patiently. "Let's do it."

"Fuckin' A," He gave her a slow smile and then let his phone drop to the stereo as music started pouring through. It was slower, more sensual, with a bit of Latin feel to it. "Let's warm up and get to it then."

Warming up became nearly redundant seen as both of them were already dripping sweat from the heat. Adam who was wearing loose gray sweatpants and a red top was sweating through the fabric of both. Fiona herself who wore her usual leotard and cropped leggings was feeling the heat too. But in her case, the heat felt more internal than anything.

"Push against me," Adam held on to her hips as he guided her through a new choreographed slow dance, which included a lot of grinding and hands-on action. Fiona couldn't focus on her technique when his hands moved down to her thighs. "Stop turning out, this isn't ballet. Use your hips and push back against me."

Pushing through her discomfort, Fiona squeezed her eyes shut and tried to control her breathing. She couldn't do it. She couldn't... grind against him. It was too much.

"Alright, come here," His hands slid up to her waist again, clasping the most narrow part of her body. "Let's try something else. Just lean back against me. Relax your body against mine."

Fiona kept trying to breathe but found this no easier. If she closed her eyes, she could pretend he was a wall or her bed or something – anything other than what he really was; A dance partner who was touching her and leading her body into a pliant submission.

"It's alright," He whispered. As Fiona tried to lean back, she felt his chest and arms catch her. He was warm, and it almost felt like she could feel his heartbeat through her shoulder blades. "Now move when I move. Just follow my lead."

She kept her eyes closed and then felt as he slowly rocked his body from side to side. He started from the hips, his hands sliding down to hers again and making them follow his movements.

"That's it," His voice was right near her ear, breathing calmly against her rapid pulse. "Now put your upper body into it. Move, Fee. You got it."

She tried to move, but her body wouldn't obey her. Her hands started shaking, and it didn't help when she felt Adam's hands slide up her waist again, reaching just below her ribs.

– That was the final push.

Fiona snapped away from him and felt as her body shook. She was trembling all over, like ants crawling on her skin, and no matter how hard she tried, she couldn't push through it. Push through the fear. "I-I can't."

"You can, Fee," Adam voiced behind her. She heard the music stop while she wrapped her arms around herself and sought into her mental space of peace in her mind. Inhale, exhale. In and out. Breathe. "I know it's uncomfortable, but you just have to get used to it."

That was easy for him to say. Maybe he could prance down the hallway in revealing tights like it was nothing, but most normal people had problems with intimacy. Fiona felt vulnerable and outside her comfort zone, not to mention all this time, they had mostly danced side by side. Not together, like a couple. She was back to that day again, when he danced her through the pas de deux. Only this time, it was ten times worse and he wasn't annoyingly humming.

"Tell me what's going through your head when I touch you," Adam inquired, his voice coming closer. Fiona tried to block him out, but he kept coming closer. "Is it because it feels sexual? It's normal to feel uncomfortable dancing close at first, but you just have to get over the hump. No pun intended."

He was making jokes while she was trying to avoid having a mental breakdown. Fiona scoffed and shook her head. She was right. She would never be able to dance like the rest of them. "I can't do this."

"Why not?"

"Because..."

"Because what?"

"Because!" She shouted. She didn't want to answer his question, didn't want to tell him the last time she let anyone close, they died before her eyes while she was doing what she loved. How every step she took felt poisonous and like she didn't deserve to do them. How if she had never asked her dad to help her dance, maybe he wouldn't have...

"Is this where you run out on me?" Adam spoke right behind her. Fiona sucked in a breath when she hadn't realized how close he was standing. He couldn't be more than a foot away. "I won't block the door this time."

Angrily gritting her teeth, Fiona was just about to take him up on his generous preposition when she suddenly felt his hands grip her waist again. She jolted away like electrocuted. "Don't fucking touch me!"

"Then talk to me!" Adam yelled back. She spun around in shock when she had never heard him yell like that before. Or at all.

Shaking his head, Adam looked away and then walked away from her. He walked up to her bag and wordlessly dug through it until he found what he was looking for; her NYC ballet pamphlet.

"This is what you want, isn't it?" He asked and held the flyer up. His voice was angry, yet there was something else inside it as well. Frustration. "You want to be a professional dancer and I'm trying to help you, Fee, but to get to there from here you have to meet me halfway. I'm trying, but if you won't let me guide you through whatever's going on inside your head—"

"It's none of your business what happens in my head," Fiona snarled back, putting up all her defenses. "I asked for dance tutoring, not a damn therapist."

"Dancing is therapy!" He threw the flyer away and stalked up to her, the frustration clear as day. "Goddamn it, Fiona, dancing is supposed to feel like freedom of the body and the mind, but you lock up every time I tell you to move. What gives?"

"Leave me alone," She retreated and turned away to hide the tears welling up in her eyes.

"You won't let me touch you. You think I'm going to hurt you?"

"No."

"You think I'm trying to cop a feel?"

"No!"

"Then why are you afraid of me touching you?" He shouted. "Talk to me! Goddamn it, Fee!"

Fiona shut her eyes and felt the tears well over. She wanted to shove and scream at the sensation spreading inside her. It was like acid, ripping at her vital organs. Most of all she wanted to break down, once again seeing her father's face flash before her eyes right before he fell to the ground, dead.

"Shit," She then suddenly heard Adam whisper behind her. He sighed deeply and she then felt him move closer, carefully this time. "I'm sorry, Fee. I didn't mean to push. I just... I need you to give me something so I can figure out what I'm doing wrong with you. I can't read your mind, and you won't let me read your body. Help me help you, Fiona. Please."

Fiona dried her eyes and shook her head. She wanted to. She really did. He wanted to help her so much, but the problem was, she didn't even know how to help herself. She thought if she just kept pushing through and pushing the feelings down... "I can't, Adam. I just... can't."

"You keep saying that, yet you haven't run out on me yet," He pointed out. She slowly turned around and saw him lift a little smile onto his lips. "We just need to find a balance, yeah? Don't lose hope yet. There's still time. Have faith."

Fiona lowered her eyes and took a deep breath. Faith was not something she had a lot of these days, but with Adam... he really seemed like he did. There were 14 days left to practice before the audition. If nothing, then she could always bail and try next year...

"I'll never ask for too much, I promise," He said, his smile growing when Fiona sighed and then took another deep breath. "Just all that you are and everything that you do."

She lifted a brow when his grin broadened. "Everything that I do? What exactly is that?" Run out? Quit? Disappointed the people who loved her?

"Look, I don't really need to look very much further," He said, walking closer. "I just know I don't want to have to go where you don't follow me."

Fiona now seriously frowned. "What does that mean?" Where she didn't follow him?

"I won't hold this passion back again," He said and gestured between them. "But you can't run from yourself, princess. There's nowhere to hide."

"Wait... are you fucking—"

"So don't make me clooooooose one more doooooor!" He fell to his knees and theatrically lifted his hand in the air towards her. "Cause I don't wanna huuuuurt ya anymoreeee!"

Fiona rolled her eyes and spun on her foot, turning away from him. Of course he couldn't be serious for even one full minute... "You fucking asshole."

"Stay in my aaaaaarms, if you dare!" He shouted and got on his feet again, following her when she went up to her bag to grab it. She was so done here. "Or must I imagine you there?"

She was already on her way to the door when a pair arm warm arms suddenly wrapped around her waist and pulled her back. Fiona gasped, but then stopped breathing when Adam's voice lowered near her ear.

"Don't walk away from me, Fee. Please."

His voice sobered and Fiona turned her head slightly to feel his breath on her cheek. He held her softly against his body, but the strangest part was... she didn't feel nervous anymore.

Gulping, Fiona felt as his hands came to her hips, pulling her even closer back against him. She swallowed hard a second time, but this time the nerves she felt in her body were completely different. For one, they stemmed from another part of her anatomy.

"You're bravest when I annoy you," He then whispered in her ear, and she thought she heard the smile in his voice. "Because you forget all about being nervous when your attitude comes out. I think I know how to do this now, princess. Do you trust me?"

Fiona considered his words. She realized then he was right. Somehow, she always felt less anxious when she was annoyed with him, maybe because when he was being silly, it all felt less... serious. She got out of her own head and focused more on managing being around him without slapping him twice on each cheek.

She wondered if that's how Kalo had survived being his friend this long.

"Okay," She whispered, feeling Adam's smile broaden in her peripheral vision. "On one condition."

"No more singing?"

"No more damn singing."

He chuckled and then stepped back, swatting her ass. Fiona jumped and shot him a glare, one which he returned with a smirk. "I'll just have to compensate then."

And with that, he turned towards the stereo and put the music on.

Chapter 10

Fiona had thought a lot about Adam's words yesterday.

How he had told her she worked better when she was angry or annoyed with him and that it made her forget her fears for a moment. If that was true, were the next two weeks going to be insanely difficult with him driving her up the wall with his personality?

She couldn't decide whether or not she should feel happy or if she should be dreading this. After all, Adam hadn't showed her he had any boundaries of his own yet.

Coming into the DanceDec after school, Fiona sighed and prepared for a hectic day. If Adam was bringing his fullest, she was going to need to be on her top game as well.

The weather in New York continued to be scalding hot, and even inside the air conditioned studios, Fiona felt the warmth preen on her skin. She looked around and wasn't surprised when she found Adam in the foyer, standing upside down on his hands with his legs in the air.

A couple of guys were standing around him, familiar faces that Fiona recognized from the dance circle yesterday. There was Dimitri, Kalo's dance partner, Twitch, the guy with the sick body moves, and then a last guy she hadn't caught the name of. The were all laughing and messing around while eating a few snacks.

It was then Fiona saw something. Adam's loose blue top had slid down to his chest and revealed most of his toned stomach. And there, right on his left side was a large, purple bruise, staining his light skin.

Fiona barely had time to process what she had seen before Adam noticed her. He shot her a big upside-down grin, his face red from the blood streaming to his head. "Hey, princess! One second, just having a tête-à-tête with gravity!"

With a last grunt, he then flipped down to the ground again and got up, earning a few claps on the shoulder and handshakes from his buddies. He then grabbed his bag and turned towards Fiona, coming up with his usual smile.

"Alright, so are you ready for another day? Christ, this heat is burning me up from the inside out," He shook his head as they started ascending the stairs together, heading for their studio. "I can't imagine what it's like for you guys. Black attracts more heat, you reckon that counts for skin as well?"

Fiona couldn't concentrate on his usual amount of verbal diarrhea. She couldn't stop glancing down at his stomach, thinking about the size and color of that bruise.

She didn't get many bruises herself, but if she did, she never noticed on account of her skin tone. Adam's light skin had vividly displayed the bluish, half-purple bruise on his stomach, though. It had practically glowed. There had been no doubt as to what it was, but how it had gotten there was the far more interesting question.

"That's quite a bruise you got there," Fiona spoke up, just as they entered the studio and dropped their bags. Adam turned around with a raised brow and looked at her confused. She nodded down at his stomach.

"What? Oh, this?" He lifted his shirt and shot a grin towards his injury. He then shrugged nonchalantly. "I was trying out a new move and got a bit too enthusiastic. Don't worry about it," He chuckled and smoothed his shirt down again. "I get plenty of those daily. I play wild." He finished with a cheeky wink.

He turned towards the stereo while Fiona pursed her lips and started her usual warmup routine. She didn't know why, because Adam was the most open person she knew and she should have no reason to, but for some reason she wanted to doubt his words. She couldn't think of a single dance move that could give a bruise like that, but then again, he was a lot more vested in dance than she was. Maybe he had tried to do some weird belly flop onto the ground and bruised his stomach.

Or maybe he was lying and he was hiding something.

"So, are we ready?" He asked, after a moment of silence wherein Fiona had contemplated his honesty. If he said it was a dance injury, maybe that was what it was and she was overthinking like usual... in any case, it wasn't any of her concern. Yet a part of her couldn't help but still feel it was.

"I'm ready," She said, pushing it all out of her mind and taking a deep breath. She focused on what was about to happen right now, which was that Adam was coming closer, rubbing his hands together with a little grin.

"I'm going to annoy the living crap out of you," He snickered and made Fiona already roll her eyes, annoyed. "You have no idea what you're in for, tutu."

And yet, just like with his bruise, she had an inkling she did.

A scream pierced through the DanceDec and had Fiona and Adam both jolting around in the middle of a close dance. They barely got the chance to turn around before someone suddenly burst through the door to their studio.

"I got it!"

Adam nearly lost his balance, but caught it as Kalo came barreling towards him and jumped into his arms. His eyes widened and immediately so did his grin. "You got it?!"

Kalo screamed again and Adam then proceeded to spin her around in the air while laughing crazily with her.

"You got it, I knew you'd fucking get it, tu pinche—"

"I start tomorrow!" Kalo grinned as Adam finally put her down. "He loved my piece! He said I would be perfect for his project!"

"Does that mean what I think it means?"

"Celebration tonight, 8 o' clock," Kalo announced with a big grin. "Rani's coming as well."

"8 o' clock? That's in 20 minutes," Adam said, after a quick glance at the round clock on the wall. He then turned toward Fiona who had quietly been standing on the sideline of their little moment. He shot her a hesitant glance. "That means I have to cut teaching short tonight... if that's okay?" He looked imploringly at her.

Was he seriously asking for her permission like they were an old married couple? "Of course," Fiona replied and shot

Kalo a faint smile. "Congratulations on the gig." She assumed she had nailed the audition Adam had been helping her rehearse for.

"Thanks," She chirped and grinned back. "Do you wanna come? There's plenty of room for more."

Fiona immediately widened her eyes when Kalo looked expectantly at her. Go with them, as in... go out as a group? She wanted her to join? Or was she just being polite? "O-oh, no, that's okay. I, uh, I have dinner plans with my mom."

Kalo shrugged, but still shot her a friendly smile. "The offer stands if you change your mind. Anyway, see you later, chulo!"

Adam chuckled and then walked up to his bag and slung his towel over his shoulder, wiping off some sweat as Kalo walked out. Once alone again, he turned his eyes to Fiona who was packing up her things, now that their training was coming to an early end. "So now that Kalo's gone, what's the real reason you don't wanna come tonight?"

Fiona glanced at him and saw him giving her a no-nonsense glare. He had seen through her crap lie. He had his brow raised and was waiting for her actual excuse. "I just... I don't really know her that well and... it just doesn't seem like my thing."

"Fee, the way you make friends is by hanging out with strangers and getting to know them," Adam got up as Fiona stood up and pointedly took her time checking her bag that she had everything—avoiding his compelling gaze. "Come on! Kalo's nice, and it's literally right around the corner, this place we always come to. It's just food and bowling. You don't even have to participate, just come and watch me win. Get some fresh air."

Fiona paused and for some stupid reason actually considered it for a moment. She must've been dumb, or maybe the heat was finally getting to her. Going out with people like a normal teenager... having a night out...

With food.

"I'm sorry," She passed, quickly continuing her packing and then zipped up her bag. "I have to get home."

"If you go out with us tonight, I promise to never ever sing around you again, but if you don't..." Adam grinned as Fiona looked up slowly, already somehow knowing what he was going to do. "I will sing every word without even a tune or melodyyyy!"

Fiona rolled her eyes when he starting singing and vocalizing like a maniac, and even when she turned around to walk to the door she felt him following right behind her, singing annoyingly loud near her ear.

"Come on, Fee, you know you want too!" He sang, following her down the stairs, slinging his bag up on his shoulders. "I will keep singing every day unless you come out with us and just... enjoooooooy life! Lalalalaaaaa—"

"Oh my God, alright!" Fiona shouted and spun around, Adam abruptly halting up in his steps not to crash into her. He gave shit-eating grin when she irritatedly growled. "It is physically impossible to be as annoying as you are."

"And yet here I am," He chuckled. "Come on, it'll be great. Just one hour, then you can leave if you're not having fun. I'll even pay for your dinner."

Fiona kept her face as neutral as she could, but then sighed and bitterly turned and continued walking towards the bathroom to reluctantly change. She heard Adam snickering smugly behind her.

Tonight was going to be the longest hour of her life.

The bowling alley really was right around the corner and the place was exactly like Fiona had anticipated. Retro, loud, flashing neon lights on the wall and a pungent smell of foot spray and fried food. There weren't a lot of people on a Tuesday night, but a few bowlers had grabbed a couple of lanes and were laying pins with the heavy crashing of the bowling balls.

Fiona couldn't remember the last time she had been in a place like this.

"Alright, table!" Kalo said and eagerly led them towards the dining area where a couple of semi-dirty booths offered a seating area and plastic menus. "I am starving, so nobody better spend hours deciding what they want."

Fiona pressed her lips together. She had a good feeling that wouldn't be a problem.

Adam scored them a nice booth and they all got in. Fiona took the inner seat next to Adam who mushed himself next to her, while Rani and Kalo grabbed the opposite side. They all then grabbed the menu cards and started perusing the options.

Fiona looked into her own menu. Most of the food they offered was yunk food such as kebabs, pizzas, burgers, wraps or sandwiches. Almost all of them came with a side of potato fries and a selection of condiments. There was a small section for salads, but even they didn't offer any appetite for Fiona. They didn't look all that appealing on the plastic picture and there was no telling how old their produce was. She doubted a place like this prepared them fresh.

While Fiona contemplated her options, Kalo, Rani and Adam were all hungrily talking burgers and pizzas. Kalo wanted kebab on her pizza while Rani wanted two sides of fries to go with her wrap.

"I'm going with burgers," Adam announced and hummed to himself in what appeared to be starvation. "They better not be shy on cheese."

"Hey, Adam?" Kalo suddenly said. Adam lifted his head. She slowly smirked. "Are you horny?"

At that, Fiona blinked preposterously while Adam closed his eyes and laid a hand over his face. A grin then erupted from him and he shook his head. "Oh, man..."

Kalo started laughing as Adam groaned lowly, while Fiona sat on the sideline again, confused as hell. Why the hell did she just ask him that?

"Ahh, shit," Adam then suddenly said and looked up and around for some reason, his eyes landing on a waitress who was approaching their table. "Her? She looks so innocent."

"Do it," Kalo teased.

Still confused, Fiona could do nothing but wait and watch as whatever private thing between them played out. She looked at Adam, who with a last glance at the waitress then sighed and closed his eyes.

And the next thing she knew, he was moaning loudly.

Fiona's eyes widened into saucers as Adam tossed his head back and gripped the edges of the table with a loud moan. His body started jerking with small movements, his hips lifting off of the seat as his mouth opened with more moans. "Oh, fuck!"

·The waitress stopped as she came to their table and blinked just as confused and as mortified as Fiona. She watched as Adam gyrated in the booth while moaning loudly, his face screwing up in pleasure.

What the actual hell was he doing? Fiona thought and watched him in disbelief. Kalo sat completely cool opposite to him, acting like he wasn't doing shit, just as Rani did. They both innocently looked into their menu cards, while Fiona was the only staring stupidly, except for the waitress.

"Ahh..." Adam then finally stopped his moaning and slumped back in the booth, like he just had the orgasm of his life. Nobody said anything, but Fiona noticed the waitress looked absolutely beet red.

"Uhm... c-can I help you with something, Sir?" She hesitantly asked when Adam kept breathing heavily, catching his breath from his little performance. Fiona was sure if she had had the waitress's complexion, she would've been the same color of red as her.

Immediately after her question, Adam then shot up and sat straight in his seat like nothing had happened and looked into his menu. "Uh, yeah, I'd like two cheeseburgers with a sprite on the side and a side of fries. Make that two cups of sprite, actually. I'm feeling a little thirsty. Who's next?"

He looked on to Kalo who instantly continued to name her orders, passing it on to Rani who finally gave the lead to Fiona. She shook her head and politely declined. "I'm good."

"Nothing for you?" Adam lowly whispered. Fiona just shook her head. "Alright, then I guess that's it," He gathered all the menu cards and handed them over to the waitress with a megawatt grin. "Go medium on the paddy-fat, but lay that cheese on thick on one of them." He turned and gave Fiona a wise, pointed stare. "Balance."

With that, the waitress—who with a flabbergasted expression had written their orders down—then hesitantly took the menu cards and left. She glanced over her shoulder, sending a last odd glance at Adam.

"What the hell was that?" Fiona finally asked. It was the exact same second she spoke, Rani and Kalo finally burst into uncontrollable laughter.

"The 'Are you horny?' challenge," Adam elaborated with a chuckle and shook his head. "It's this thing we do sometimes."

"Whoever you ask has to break into a sudden orgasm like they're coming on the spot," Kalo bid in through her laughter. "Adam always does the best ones."

Adam grinned back, but then sighed dramatically. "That's the closest you'll get to hearing me actually come. Kalo's dreams revolve around it."

Kalo shot a long manicured middle-finger at him, to which Adam responded with a dirty hand gesture in front of his crotch and some small horny noises. At that, both Kalo and Rani shot some choice Spanish words at him, all of them curses and swears, Fiona was certain. All of them were still laughing and goofing off, though.

They were the craziest bunch.

The evening went on, and while they waited for their food, Kalo filled them in fully on how the audition had went and who the guy who had hired her was.

"Some big hotshot commercial agent who works for a large company that does advertising for fit wear," She told while slurping on her soda. Their drinks had arrived and they were all sipping on them, except for Fiona who hadn't ordered anything. "I don't care what he does honestly, as long as he lets me do it, too."

"Amen to that," Rani proclaimed.

"Oh, fuck, please let that be ours," Adam suddenly said and drew all of their attention towards a waitress who came over with a large tray filled with food. When she steered towards them, they all cheered. "Fuck, yeah!"

The waitress served them their food and no sooner had the plates hit the table before all of them dug in. Fiona sat quietly in her corner and watched, feeling like a fourth wheel.

But it's not like you're trying to change that, her inner voice pointed out.

All night she hadn't said a word. She had listened and nodded once or twice, but hadn't really spoken anything or bid in with anything since Adam's little performance. Any time she had felt the slightest urge to comment or ask something, her anxiety immediately talked her out of it. It was probably stupid anyway and who even cared...

"Hey," Adam gentle nudged her when Kalo went into a long talk about something or other Fiona didn't catch as Adam spoke to her. He looked down at her and cocked a little brow. "You okay?"

Fiona simply nodded back and gave a weak smile. At least attempt not to look miserable. These people were so friendly and had let her pathetically tag along on their celebration, and there she was, sulking.

"Here," He said, shoving his second burger towards her. "Eat it. You have to eat something. You haven't eaten since lunch."

Fiona looked down at the mess that was the burger. It was the one with less cheese, but it still looked like a hot, greasy mess.

"It's okay, it's yours," She said and smiled quickly. "You paid for it."

"I told you I'd pay for you," He said and pushed the burger towards her again when she tried to shove it away. "It's okay, I've got my fries."

Fiona looked down at the burger again and gulped. So many calories... but maybe if she excused herself to the bathroom afterwards...

She slowly picked the burger up and tried her best at giving a grateful smile to Adam who grinned back. He then turned back to his own burger, popping in a few fries before sipping one of his large drinks.

Fiona took a deep breath and then carefully took a bite of the burger, like she was expecting it to explode in her mouth. And in a way, it did. The greasy flavor imploded in her mouth and the combination of condiments, salads and meat swirled around in her mouth. She could taste the fat in the burger, and her throat struggled to force it down.

For ten minutes, she completely zoned out all conversation and focused on eating the burger, well aware that Adam was glancing at her once in a while. Around halfway through, he slowly pushed his second cup of Sprite towards her.

And that's when Fiona realized.

He had ordered double on purpose.

Pausing mid-bite, she looked up at Adam who was currently grinning at something funny Rani apparently had said. He was chewing on a fry, but once he registered her staring, he flipped his eyes down at raised a slow brow.

You haven't eaten since lunch, he said.

A cold sensation spread inside Fiona.

Did he... know?

Turning her eyes down and looking at the burger that suddenly became tasteless in her mouth, she forced herself to swallow the half-chewed bite in her mouth.

He knew. He knew and he was testing her.

Was that was tonight had been about?

Fiona's sight suddenly became blurry and when she realized she was tearing up, she quickly blinked it away. She swallowed fast when she felt like throwing up at the sensation spreading inside her. Her stomach started turning.

"Excuse me," She said and nudged Adam who once again lifted a brow. Fiona put down what was left of her burger and wiped her hands off. "Bathroom."

Adam chewed off his bite and then got up, letting her get up and pass through. After getting free, she didn't hesitate to walk as normally as she could towards the bathrooms.

The second she was inside the women's bathroom, Fiona ran towards the back booth and locked herself in. The tears were spilling down her cheeks, pain wrenching in her guts. She fell to her knees and shook as she lifted the toilet seat up.

She didn't even need to stuff her fingers down her throat this time. The urge came all on its own and came out in the bowl, accompanied with a sob.

After two more retches, she hit the flusher and sat back against the wall, clutching herself. The pain in her stomach had stopped, but not the one in her heart. Her tears wouldn't stop falling.

He had known and he made her come here tonight to eat, knowing full and well what it would do to her. Why? Why would he do that to her?

After minutes of crying quietly in the her stall, Fiona finally dried her eyes. She knew she couldn't keep hiding in there. She contemplated just leaving without a word, but even though she was mad at Adam, Kalo and Rani had done her no harm. Unless they were somehow in on it. Nevertheless, she decided she would make an excuse when she got out, saying her stomach was upset and that she had to go home.

To get away from Adam.

Unlocking the booth, Fiona sniveled quietly, but then halted up when a person was leaning against the sink, hands in his pockets.

"How long?"

Fiona stared at Adam, tears in her eyes. He looked as serious as he had ever been. "Does it matter?" She sniped back. No point in trying to hide it.

Adam's face grew hard. He unfurled his hands from his pockets as Fiona went up to the sinks and started washing her hands and rinsing her mouth. "You know damn well it matters, Fee. I'm not letting you leave this bathroom until you talk to me."

'Not letting her leave until...?' Who the hell did he think he was?!

Angrily, Fiona stood upright after rinsing her mouth and glared at him. She then swiped some paper towels from dispenser and gritted her teeth, trying contain her temper. "Is that why you wanted me to come along tonight? So you could get me alone to prove some stupid shit and make me feel like complete crap about myself?"

"I'm not the one shoving my fingers down my throat and making myself feel this way," He barked and walked up to her. Fiona widened her eyes. "You are doing that to yourself, Fiona. I brought you here tonight because I had an inkling and I wanted to see it for myself. I've been around enough dancers to know the signs," He said and looked down at her petite and skinny body.

Fiona wrapped her arms around herself and turned around to shield herself from his probing eyes. He had no goddamn right to judge her. "Every dancer does it, stop sounding so conceited. It's the fastest way to keep the weight off," She lied, knowing full and well it wouldn't hold up.

"How about you stop treating me like a fool and tell me how long you've been doing it and the real reason why," He lowly said, sounding as offended as she would've expected. She knew he wasn't a fool and he knew it wasn't because of her weight. But she was too angry to care.

"Back off of me," Fiona snapped, new tears welling up in her eyes. Breathe, breathe. Everything was culminating inside her. "I don't know why you think you have the goddamn right to ask me why—"

"Stop trying to make me your enemy, Fee, it's not working," He roughly spoke, cutting through her bullshit. He even saw through her plan to push him away. "Instead, start talking to me. How long have you been doing this? Are you still having your periods?"

Fiona spun around and glared up at him. He did not just ask her that. "That's non of your damn business, you wannabe shrink! Why don't you just back the hell off and leave me be!" She finally screamed, the tears now streaming down her face. She could no longer hold it back. "I don't want your fucking help! I-I don't want y-your stupid—"

Adam lunged out, and Fiona broke down as he wrapped his arms tightly around her and embraced her. He hugged her to his chest and let her cry as the tears fell without restraint.

Fiona sobbed and held on to his shirt as she felt his hand caress her back, softly. She couldn't keep it together any longer. She was still mad, but inside, she knew it was never at him the anger had been aimed towards. The resentment came from within.

Adam let her cry for minutes until she ran out of air and tears. She kept clinging to his chest and he never once stopped holding tightly on to her, like he knew she would break apart if he did.

And that hurt even more than what he had done tonight.

"I don't support this," He then finally spoke when Fiona had calmed herself enough down to listen. She sniveled quietly, but kept her eyes closed. "I don't support this, Fee. I can't. If you want to keep working with me, and I know you do, you have to stop doing this, do you hear me? Bulimia is not something to joke with. If I catch you purging again, I'm out."

"A-Adam—"

"I'm not kidding, Fiona," He pulled back to look down at her with a warning face. This was as sober as she had ever seen him. "From now on, I'm not leaving your side. If you go pee, I go pee. I don't care if it's the ladies room, I will start identifying as a lady if I have to, just so I can make sure you don't do anything stupid. Got it?"

And just because of the sober and sincere look in his eyes did she nod. She didn't know why, but for some reason... she let him pull her into his arms again and hold her close.

Laying a hand on the back of her head and the other one just on her back, Adam sighed and held her tightly as Fiona once again let a few small leftover tears trickle down her chin. "We'll talk about this tomorrow. It'll all be okay, okay? I'm going to help you get through this, one cheeseburger at a time."

Fiona swallowed, but didn't say anything. He was so sweet and so caring, and there she was, so broken and messed up.

He had wanted to help her right from the start and all she had wanted was to use him like a robot dance teacher.

And worst part was... she had a feeling he knew. And he just didn't care.

It made no sense.

"Thank you," She quietly whispered against his shoulder. With a deep breath, she then carefully locked her arms around his waist and let her hands rest on his lower back. "I don't get why you're so sweet all the time..." And why he still bothered with her.

"That's because I eat a shitload of candy," He told and smiled against the top of her head. Fiona let out a small, soundless chuckle. "Come on. Let's go out again. We've been away for 20 minutes. They must be thinking you're giving me a blow."

Fiona's eyes widened and she immediately pulled back, looking horrified up at him. "W-what?!"

Adam threw his head back and laughed loudly at her panicked expression. "Oh, Fee. I'm sorry, but your face, you have no idea. Come on, tutu. Let's go. Everything's going to be alright."

He grabbed her arm, but just then, Fiona felt something on the tip of her tongue.

"Hey, Adam?" She whispered as they walked up to the door, Adam keeping an arm wrapped around her.

"Yeah?" He looked down at her with a smile.

And that's when Fiona felt it; A tug in her heart and a tiny ball of nerves that filled her throat up.

Had she made a friend?

"I thought you said you needed longer than 20 minutes."

And with that, Adam broke into a loud laughter as they walked out together and joined the girls again.

Chapter 11

"S it."

The moment Fiona had walked into the DanceDec that following Wednesday, Adam had led her to the studio and proceeded to close the door. Fiona had dumped her bag down and taken off her shoes to start their usual warmup routine, but when she looked up, she saw Adam was nowhere near the stereo. Instead he had walked up to the wall, grabbed a chair and dragged it into the centre.

"I thought we were supposed to dance?" Fiona said, watching as he repeated the process and went to the wall and grabbed another chair, placing it so they were facing each other with a few feet's distance. The setup strangely reminded her of an AA meeting.

"We'll get to that," He replied and then slung himself into one of the chairs. He gestured towards the second and looked at her. "First, we talk."

Fiona felt the resistance in her body as she looked at the chair and watched Adam patiently wait for her to come sit in it. Suddenly the AA scenario turned into a shrink session. After last night, she knew they couldn't go on pretending. He had seen and she couldn't keep going on the way she was if she wanted to continue to dance with him.

'If you want to keep working with me, and I know you do, you have to stop doing this, do you hear me?'

Taking a deep breath, Fiona therefore reluctantly stepped forward and slowly took a seat in the chair. She felt herself close up like a shy clam when Adam eyed her with a long, probing stare, like he was trying to see through her. Fiona lowered her eyes to the floor and stayed silent, hoping to get this over with quick.

"When I was ten years old, I started to ask my grams where my parents were," He then suddenly started. Fiona blinked and looked up to see Adam pursing his lips. "I said to her; 'Grams, will I ever get to meet my family?' and she replied to me, 'that depends on who you see as you family.'"

Fiona watched him meet her with a small smile. It wasn't happy like his smiles usually were, though. There was a doleful glint to it.

"I didn't like that answer," He continued. "Not one bit. I knew my parents had left me at the orphanage for a reason, but I didn't know why. Around my 12th birthday, I started to lose hope that they'd ever come back for me. Kids at that age rarely get adopted. My only chance of having a family was either waiting for my mom and dad to come back, or go and make my own. You know which one I chose."

Fiona pressed her lips together. She remembered; "You joined a gang."

Adam slowly nodded and turned his eyes down again. "I was so ready to not be alone anymore. My friends were getting adopted, and the ones who weren't... they ran off and joined a gang," He exhaled and then ran a hand through his hair. "For someone who's never had a family, that was the closest we ever got to having one. They took care of us, they protected us, they fed us and said we were part of something bigger now. Something better." He slowly lifted his eyes and gazed at Fiona with a sad look. "I believed them."

Fiona's face softened. He was telling her how he had felt so desperate for a family, he had taken anything that resembled it remotely. And how his desperation to get what he wanted had led him down a dark road of mistakes.

"I hated doing what I did," He told, lowering his eyes and shaking his head. "I didn't know what I was carrying in those bags, but I know it wasn't spices. I hated that I was delivering them to people who passed it on to other people—people my own age. I was contributing to all the violence on the streets, but I didn't care because I finally had a home for the first time in my life."

Fiona watched as Adam sighed and then buried his head in his hands, rubbing it. He was silent for a few moments before starting with a new breath.

"When the police arrested me, I was almost relieved," He said and somehow managed to lift a little smile on to his lips. "Around this time, I was living half at the orphanage and half at the clubhouse. The police called the orphanage and told them of my situation, and that's when grams showed up. They told her I was facing at least two years in juvie because of the amount of product I had been carrying. Since I wasn't talking, they couldn't cut me any slack. You know what my grams did?" He looked up at Fiona.

She shook her head, but then saw as his smile evolved until he was almost grinning. But there was a teary glint in his eyes.

"She told them I danced," He smiled, shaking his head. "She told the officer who arrested me that I was a bright young kid who just desperately wanted to fit in somewhere. I just wanted to feel a part of something, and that I made some dumb choices along the way. That I was just a kid, but that I would never harm a soul. And what I had done, I had done so unknowingly and in the faith that God would lead me to my family. And you know what? He did."

Fiona lifted her eyes when Adam stood up and started walking the floor, taking a lap around the room. His smile softened to a warm glow.

"My sentence was reduced on the grounds that my grams would adopt me and provide me with a better home," He told, circling back to his chair. "The officer who arrested me was convinced that if I was released after my sentence was served, I would go straight back into old habits and I'd be right back in in a few months. Instead, he said that if my grams adopted me and kept me out of trouble, he would let me off with a reduced sentence, plus time served. I think my grams had the adoption papers filed within the hour after that talk." He chuckled.

Fiona smiled back faintly as he sat down again and then looked her in the eyes. She couldn't help but feel the same strange pull in her stomach like yesterday. Something was drawing her towards him in a way that made her feel... warm. And safe, somehow. Not exactly physically, though... it was more... emotionally.

"When my grams adopted me, she retired from the church at the same time and we moved to a different part of Harlem after I got out," He said. "She signed me up for dance classes here because she saw a spark in me whenever I used to dance at the orphanage. The moment I arrived here, I met Kalo who told me she had never seen a white boy with feet as fast as mine," He grinned. "She taught me how to get down the right way and introduced me to everyone here. And that's the moment I finally found my family. My real family."

Fiona didn't realize she was tearing up until she suddenly felt a salty tear on her lip. She quickly wiped her cheek and looked away. He had been truly blessed with a beautiful family.

"I'm not my grandma, Fee," Adam then said. "I didn't understand what she meant by 'spark' until about a week and two days ago when I happened to spot a certain ballet girl through the crack of a curtain."

Fiona felt her stomach tighten and a lump in her throat grew to the size of a baseball. She tried to swallow as she looked up through blurry eyes and saw Adam watching her with a little smile.

"She was spinning her foot off while crying her heart out, but she wasn't slowing down. Damn, no. She kept on going and going, even though it was clearly causing her pain to do so," He whispered. "She didn't stop, Fiona. She didn't care about herself, she cared about dancing. And here we are today, about to find out why."

Fiona swallowed the lump in her throat with difficulty. His words... his words were hitting her hard for some reason. The music from all the other studios weren't even noticeable anymore. It all faded away as they sat in their little bubble.

Breathe... breathe...

– And then for the first time in years, Fiona release a breath that contained everything she had been holding on to ever since she put her walls up.

"My... my d-dad," Her voice cracked, but she quickly sucked in another breath and wrapped her arms around herself so she didn't crumble. She shut her eyes and kept going, pushing the overdue words out. "My dad, h-he... when I was s-six, I really wanted to learn h-how to dance... my dad... my dad he helped me."

Fiona trembled inside when she realized that was the first time in years she had said that word aloud; Dad. The very thought of him always brought her pain and heartache, so she had blocked most of him away. Only when she danced did he come back to life.

"I w-was... I was learning to pirouette," She continued, trying to breathe and stop her hands from shaking. All of her was shaking, but she persevered. Adam was listening to her closely. "On my second try, h-he collapsed on the ground and had a heart attack. H-he didn't make it."

The tears fell down her cheeks now, and even though she wiped them away, they kept coming back. Adam sat there quietly and let her cry them out until she could breathe again. When she finally could, he slowly moved forward and somehow produced a handkerchief from his pocket.

"It makes sense now," He said while Fiona dried her eyes with his tissue and sniveled quietly. The ache in her chest hurt so much, but there was also a strange other feeling... or rather the lack thereof. She felt... strangely empty. "Why you cried during your spins."

"I haven't been able to do a proper fouetté since..." Her voice died out. "Much less a pirouette," She continued, hiccuping. "I-I can't... I just c-can't, every time I try I just—"

"You freeze up," Adam nodded when she looked up. "I saw."

Fiona lowered her eyes again and folded the handkerchief in her hand. There was a long, quiet moment, that finally got followed up by Adam's deep sigh.

"Tell me why you chose ballet," He then asked, making Fiona lift her eyes and her brow. "There are tons of dance styles out there. What made you choose ballet specifically?"

Fiona knew the answer to that one perfectly. "Because ballet... ballet is all about... control. You choose how good you want to be. How much you want to succeed." And it was all that had kept her together all these years. Constant discipline.

"That's present-day Fiona talking," Adam replied. "Why did six-year-old Fiona want to dance ballet?" He wanted to know, giving her another questioning stare.

The question took her back. Suddenly she was six years old again, sitting in her old living room, watching Swan Lake for the first time on the old grainy TV.

"Because... I wanted to look pretty like a princess," She awkwardly mumbled and felt her cheeks heat up. Adam's lips lifted in a little grin. "They were so graceful and elegant, and I guess... I guess I liked that..."

"That's more like it," He chuckled. "So, princess. Why aren't you dancing?"

Fiona looked up, but couldn't help but frown. "What do you mean?"

"I've only ever seen you dance once, Fiona," Adam stood up and walked into the studio. "You were right here and you were throwing it back so hard that when you were done, you started the happy waterworks."

Fiona remembered that day. It couldn't have been more than a few days ago, but it felt like ages. She remembered the feeling in her stomach after she had done that... the strange, bubbly sensation that had left her shaking afterwards...

"You were dancing, Fee," Adam slowly came up to her and knelt down in front of her chair. He smiled up at her when Fiona shyly looked away. "Shit, you nearly lowered my credentials. Ever since that day, I've tried to make you dance that freely again, but you keep locking up. Why is that?"

Fiona looked down into her lap, pressing her lips together. He would think it was stupid... "I..."

Adam's hand suddenly came on top of hers and took it. Both of his hands then enveloped hers and it made her look up as her heart jumped an extra beat. His jungly green eyes met hers.

"I know I'm not a shrink," He said, looking into her eyes and searching her face for a sign of retreat. She stayed put and didn't waver from his gaze. "But I want to help you work through whatever's holding you back. You have so much potential, Fee, but you're holding back on yourself. If I can help you unwind in any way, just know I'll do whatever."

Fiona couldn't help but tear up, smiling weakly. Adam smiled back and then lifted his thumb to wipe away a tear on her cheek. Her cheek suddenly felt hot where he had touched her.

"Why do you... care so much?" She whispered. She didn't mean to say the words aloud, but her thoughts slipped out. She had wondered so long why he cared for her so much when they never really knew each other that well until now. Why did he want to help her so badly?

"Because that's what friends do," He replied with a little grin.

"We're friends?" The words blurted from her mouth. She had felt it last night, but she hadn't been sure. Now...

"You're welcome," He winked and then stood up, patting her shoulder. Fiona blinked a couple of times, but then snapped out of it. Friends...

She heard him shuffle up to the stereo, and she then figured perhaps their talk was over. She stayed in her seat, though, looking into her lap.

"I owe you an apology," It then suddenly sounded from the stereo, instead of music pouring out. She turned her head and saw Adam lingering. He slowly turned towards her and shot her a little look. "For yesterday. What I did wasn't nice, but you have to understand that I've... I've been around enough people with these sort of problems to know how to approach them. It's hard, but it's the fastest way to get them to confess."

Fiona wasn't an expert on eating disorders, but she still knew a thing or two. She knew she would have never admitted to anyone who confronted her point blank that she had an eating disorder. It would've led to a lot of questions she didn't like and quite possibly more fuss than what needed to be made. Not to mention her mother would be so disappointed in her... she couldn't have survived seeing the pain on her face if she found out.

But yesterday Adam didn't give her a choice. He had payed attention to the signs and had been subtle about it until last night. He had provoked her with the burger he knew she wouldn't let stay down. When he followed her to the bathroom, he knew she couldn't have passed it off as food poisoning or anything like that. It would've taken longer to develop, and besides, her crying kind of gave away the act...

"I had to confront you to get the truth from you," He said, pressing his lips together. "We would've been doing a whole different dance if I hadn't. But I'm sorry I had to spring it on you like that..."

Fiona sighed and closed her eyes. She was mad, but still strangely not at him. She knew he had done it in good faith... but it didn't hurt any less that her secret was now out. She feared what changes it would make. "I just... please don't tell anyone. If my mom finds out, she won't let me come back here, and she definitely won't let me audition."

Adam pursed his lips and slowly placed his hands on his hips, before changing his mind and crossing them over his chest. "So your mom doesn't know. How long have you been—"

"Only a couple of months," Fiona truthfully replied. She swallowed and looked down when Adam clenched his jaw. "Only for preparation to the audition..."

He nodded, once. She knew he wasn't buying it, though.

"You and I both know you don't need to slim yourself down for the audition, Fiona," He said, slowly walking towards her. He held a pensive gaze on his face as he looked at the floor. "Tell me why you started doing it in the first place for real. And don't give me any crap about your physique and appearance. You're small as a bean."

Fiona lifted her legs up on the chair and hugged them. She realized then she probably looked even more like a bean right now. She didn't care as she folded her hands and leaned her forehead against her knees. "I... I just..." Her throat closed up and she gulped. She wasn't ready to tell him yet. Couldn't... she wasn't there yet. "I can't."

She heard him sigh, but then his footsteps came closer and halted in front of her. She suddenly felt his hand on her shoulder. "Alright. When you're ready, just promise me you'll tell me."

Fiona nodded silently, but didn't lift her head. She couldn't face him right now.

"Did you have breakfast this morning?"

Fiona pressed her lips together, but nodded.

"Did it stay down? Don't lie to me."

She thinned her mouth again, but then sighed and shook her head.

"Alright." She heard Adam sigh once more before taking a seat across from her again. "Here's what we're going to do, then. From now on, we eat together. Just you and me. I can't make sure you eat your breakfast or lunch on the week days, but on the weekends, you and I sit together in here and eat. You eat as much as you can without feeling sick, and in return, I won't hassle you about it. When you need to go to the bathroom, I go with you. That's my only condition."

Fiona finally looked up and carefully met his eyes. He sat perfectly calmly in his chair and looked at her, waiting for her reply. Fiona swallowed a lump, but then nodded. "Okay."

"And one more thing. Until your audition, I come home with you every night to eat dinner with you. That's not up for discussion either."

At that, Fiona's eyes widened and her head flew up. As Adam stood up and started walking towards the stereo again, she jumped up from her seat as well. "You can't. My mom will flip if I bring a boy home every day after hours. I'm already in trouble because of my grades," She confessed and watched Adam pull his phone out to plug it into the speakers.

"Two birds, one stone then," He said. "We study together and eat dinner together. Tell your mom I'm your new study partner. Trust me, she'll go apeshit once she sees my report card."

Fiona shook her head and tried not to flip out herself. Adam in her home, in her room, her mom around with the two of them sitting there, talking and Adam's mouth that had no filter... "it's not going to work out, I'm telling you."

"And I'm telling you, it'll work out just fine," He said, finally turning towards his phone to select a song. "Moms love me. I'm too lovable to not—"

The door suddenly burst open, and both of them spun towards it to see Rani looking around until she spotted Adam by the stereo. By the look on her face, something was wrong. "Es Kalo."

"¿Que pasó?" Adam abandoned his phone and quickly walked up to her when Rani shook her head.

"El pinché bastardo trato de to tocarla," She nearly spat the words out and Adam's face grew hard in one second. "Kalo llegó al lugar y él trató de tocarla."

"¿Donde está?" Adam shot out and ran at her when Rani gestured him along.

"En el baño," She replied, pressing her lips together.

Adam cursed under his breath and without a word ran out of the studio. Fiona quickly followed behind both of them, confused. What the hell had happened?

She followed Adam to the girls bathroom where a bunch of people seemed to have gathered around. Both girls and boys were forming a hoard in the doorway, making Adam yell at them all to get them to move and allow him passage through.

Once through, Fiona lost sight of him, but couldn't help but do like the rest of them, mushing around to get a peak inside at what the hell was going on. Finally, she managed to get to the front where she found Adam and Rani cuddled up on the floor next to a crying Kalo.

"It's okay," Adam said and held her tightly, slinging an arm around her when she buried her face in her lap. She was a whole mess, crying and shaking, but also shouting curse words and other things Fiona didn't understand. "It's over now, you're not going back there. Back the fuck off, guys!" He yelled at the watching crowd. "Give her some space, for fuck's sake."

Some of the people backed away, including Fiona, but once Adam spotted her, he gently waved her over. Fiona shook her head quickly. It wasn't her scene.

But Adam kept waving her over, nodding down at Kalo who was crying her eyes out. It was then Fiona remembered she still had Adam's handkerchief clutched in her hand.

Carefully walking in, she crouched down to Kalo who lifted her eyes for a second to see who had approached. She then lowered her eyes when Fiona held out the handkerchief to her. "I'm so sorry..."

She didn't know what the hell was going on, but if a girl like Kalo was crying, Hell had to have frozen over. She looked at Fiona for a moment before taking the tissue and nodding a thanks. Adam smiled beside her, mouthing the words.

"I want to kill him," She whispered, wiping her eyes and shaking her head again. "He fucking made me believe I actually had a chance when all he fucking wanted was to sleep with me—"

"Forget about him," Adam said, squeezing her shoulder.

"He's an asshole," Rani bid in, muttering something vehement in Spanish. "If he wants to sleep with something, I got a few choice things he can sleep with, starting with a motherfucking—"

"Rani, por favor," Adam warned. She shut up, but still whispered something in Spanish under her breath.

Suddenly there was more commotion behind them, and Fiona turned to find Dimitri, along with Twitch and a few other guys come to the doorway, all of them panting. Dimitri laid one eye on Kalo, then cursed. "What the fuck happened?!"

"Hotshot tried to touch her," Rani sniped before Adam could shut her up. "He tried to goddamn rape her and this asshole thinks just because he's got money, it's okay."

Dimitri gripped his head, and then before Fiona could process it, hit the door so hard, it banged against the wall. "I'm gonna fucking kill him. Let's roll out."

"Dimitri, no," Adam yelled, but he and the guys had already nodded to each other and were leaving. "Ay, dios mio." He shot to his feet and angrily growled. "I gotta stop them before they do something stupid. Stay with her," He turned to Fiona quickly and gave her a look. "Look after her, please."

And just like that, he ran out as well, yelling after the guys who were probably halfway down the stairs by now.

Everything was chaos. Fiona found herself in the midst of it, not knowing what the hell to do. She had heard what Rani said and now knew what was happening. She slowly turned towards Kalo who had cupped her face after the boys had left and was shaking her head slowly.

'Stay with her. Look after her, please.'

Fiona didn't know her from Eve, but she did know her from Adam. Even though they weren't close friends, there was one thing she could relate with her on. Being a minority.

"Fuck this shit," Kalo cried, but also angrily balled up her fist as Fiona sat down next to her. "I don't care what happens to that asshole, but if those guys go and get themselves locked up because of me—"

"Adam will stop them," Fiona found herself voicing, causing both Rani and Kalo to look at her. She swallowed, but somehow persisted. "He's good at talking to people..."

Kalo seemed to soften a bit. She sighed and then nodded, and before Fiona could move, she leaned her head against her shoulder and rested up against Fiona.

"He always looks after everybody," She mumbled, holding his handkerchief out and looking at it. "He's like everyone's big brother. Man, I probably would've done what those guys did. He always keeps us straight when we wanna do some shit. I don't know how he does it."

Fiona couldn't agree more. He had a natural talent for dancing, but his superpower was his heart. He only saw the best in people, and somehow in life, too. Even when it seemed like everyone around him was falling to pieces.

"He's a good guy," Fiona said, feeling Kalo settle down little by little. "He always makes you feel better."

Out of the corner of her eye, she saw Kalo smile a little. "When he's not annoying the crap out of you, anyway."

Fiona couldn't help but chuckle, but then quickly stopped when she realized it was inappropriate. She saw Kalo sit up and dry her eyes one last time before looking over at her.

"You know, I don't really know you or anything, but I like you," She said. Fiona slightly expanded her eyes. "You're quiet most of the time, but I think you're really nice. And I think you're good for Adam."

"W-What?" Fiona blinked. Somehow the topic had gone from her almost being assaulted to them talking about Adam. And her.

"Because you make him happy," Kalo smiled and leaned down on her shoulder again.

Fiona sat quietly as silence fell in the bathroom. Everyone but her and Rani had left, leaving the bathroom calm and peaceful. She had no idea how long they sat there, but it felt like hours. And through those hours, only one question rang in her head.

Did she really make Adam happy?

It was hours later when Adam finally showed up. It was almost 7pm and Fiona had long ago gone back to their studio, after Kalo announced that she was going home. Rani had offered to take her, which had left Fiona gravitating back towards the empty studio she and Adam had been supposed to be dancing in today.

Instead, Fiona's emotions had taken a dance of their own.

Something had happened today inside Fiona that made her realize something she probably should've realized sooner in her life, but it wasn't until Kalo had suddenly gotten off the bathroom floor and walked up to a sink and spoken, she realized it herself.

"Fuck this," Kalo had said and looked at herself. "I'm not going to let that bastard change me or hold me down. I'm not a fucking victim, I'm woman who's going to make his sorry ass regret what he did some day. Just watch me."

She had then walked out and Rani had followed her, leaving Fiona to think about a lot of things.

She had been holding herself back all of her life. She knew she had done it, but she hadn't stopped, because moving on like it hadn't happened... as if her father hadn't died... she couldn't forget it, and every step she had taken had showed it.

But now, after today, Fiona had realized she didn't have to forget it or even try and move past it. She just had to accept it, no matter how much it hurt. She didn't want to accept that her dad had died, she didn't want to accept that the hurt in her chest was probably there to stay. But she had to just keep on going anyway.

When Fiona finally saw the door open and an exhausted Adam stepped in, rubbing his face before looking up at her, she knew what she had to do. It had been a long day, but it wasn't over yet.

"It's because I don't deserve it," She spoke as Adam was about to say something, but instead halted up. He raised a confused brow, which made Fiona gulp and continue. "I don't deserve... food. I... I-I killed my dad when I made him help me dance, and I just have this constant guilt in my chest, and unless I somehow punish myself, I can't—"

"Stop," Adam said and lifted a hand. His tired face softened as Fiona shook and cradled herself in her arms. "You didn't kill your father, Fiona. That's simply not possible."

"But I did," She said, her voice cracking. He hadn't been there, so he didn't understand it. "One moment he was healthy as a horse, the next he was just dead. I pushed him too hard, if we had just stopped and called it a night—"

"He still would've collapsed, Fee," Adam walked up to her when she closed her eyes and let the tears fall. He cupped her face and leaned down. "Fiona. Whether or not you danced, it would've happened. These things just happen sometimes. We don't know why, but they just do. You couldn't possibly have provoked it. Do you understand?"

Fiona kept her eyes closed, but she felt his thumb rub her cheek, before his arm came around her and pulled her into his arms. He had probably spent all day fighting those guys, arguing and then comforting Kalo. And here he was, still selflessly giving out hugs, even though he was exhausted.

"That's why you hold back," He whispered against her hair. "That's why you do this to yourself. You dance for him, don't you?"

"He would've died for nothing if I didn't," Fiona quietly whispered back.

Adam pulled back and met her eyes again. He cupped her face with both hands. "Fiona, no. That's not why you're supposed to dance. You don't dance out of obligation; You dance in tribute," He leaned in and pressed his forehead against hers. "You dance, not just because that's what he would've wanted, but because you wanted it. Remember? You can still be a princess, Fiona." His lips curved up a little. "Princess Fiona."

"Stop," She muttered, closing her eyes and pulling a little away when he chuckled quietly. She was so tired, but his stupid joke still made her smile inside.

Adam leaned in, and then to Fiona's surprise, pressed a soft kiss to her forehead. "It's been a long day. I could use some dinner right around now."

When he pulled back, Fiona felt her cheeks slightly redden, but decided to ignore it. He was right, it had been a long, crazy day. A lot of emotions had been on the line.

"I'm not weak, you know," She whispered as Adam walked up to the stereo where he had left his phone. He paused and looked back at her. "I just chose my own way to be strong."

He sent her a little smile before nodding once. "I know."

She wanted him to know that just because she was wounded and just because she did what she did... she wasn't a weak girl. She knew what she wanted in life, she just... had to find ways to cope with her pain. Maybe it hadn't been the right way, but her choices hadn't weakened her. If anything, they had just taught her that one pain didn't mask another. It only made the internal pain that much worse.

"So what now?" Fiona said, looking around the studio, out into the hall, through the cracked curtains, to see the few people who were still there wandering around in a gloomy state. After today's event, everyone had been somewhat down and had retreated to their own corner. The family had taken a blow.

"There's only one thing to do at the end of a bad day," Adam replied. Fiona turned her eyes back and saw him lay down his phone. "Dance."

Music started playing through the speakers. Happy music. Fiona couldn't help but shake her head and smile as Adam walked into the center of the dance floor and stretched out his hand towards her. With a tired grin, he beckoned her.

Releasing the tension in her shoulders, Fiona stepped forward and let Adam swing her into his arms, twirling her against his chest. The song was much too upbeat, but it seemed neither of them cared. Adam chuckled as he pressed her back against his chest, wrapping his arms around her and rocking her slowly from side to side.

And for the first time since... forever, Fiona felt a burden drop off her shoulders when she rested against Adam and felt not even a quiver of fear or anxiety fill her body.

But something else entirely did.

Chapter 12

F iona had been anxious.

After everything, Adam still insisted to come home with her and eat dinner with her and her mother. He kept to his promise of helping her, even though the day had been beyond hectic. Fiona didn't know how he found the energy, but it was admirable.

– But that now also led to a very terrifying upcoming evening.

They had taken the bus and then walked to her home, and Fiona had been absolutely freaking out the whole way while Adam had chuckled at her. He had wrapped his arm around her and told her it would all be okay, just as they walked inside her house.

Her mom was in the kitchen with the dinner on the stove as Fiona walked in first. Her mom turned towards her and smiled, but then immediately froze up when she noticed Adam standing behind her. Her face went from loving to alarmed in a split second. Great start.

"Mom, this is Adam," Fiona quickly blurted and felt Adam give a wave behind her, probably followed by one of his megawatt grins. "Is it okay if he joins us for dinner?"

Her mom gave a deep and furrowed frown as Adam stepped forward to extend his hand. Politely, her mom shook it, but with a very guarded stare. "Adam? And how do you know my daughter?"

"We dance and study together," Adam prompted, and Fiona cringed at the flash of surprise that rolled over her mom's face. "I'm from the DanceDec. You have a really talented daughter, Mrs Torrence."

Now Fiona was the one who blinked up in surprise; Had he lurked their last name off the mailbox or something? He really was good.

"Thank you," Her mom replied, still giving him a slight skeptical glare. "You look a little old to still be in school. How old are you, Adam?"

"I'm 19, ma'am," He replied, giving a smile while her mom hummed quietly. "I'm in my senior year."

"Mm-hm," She looked him over thoroughly, doing the regular probing mom-stare. Fiona groaned internally.

"Please, mom?" She said, drawing the attention to herself. "We're just going to be studying and then he's going home himself. It's a school night."

Her mom gave one last long glare at Adam who smiled back. She then finally sighed. "Alright. But I want the door to stay open, that's not up for discussion. Now go wash your hands and help set the table."

"Thank you, ma'am," Adam grinned and then did as Fiona, following her lead. They both washed their hands and then set the table for the three of them, whereafter her mom came over with the food. Chicken breast with rice and curry sauce.

"Do you mind if I say grace?" Adam asked as they all sat down and placed their napkins in their laps. Fiona's mom raised a sharp brow, clearly not expecting that from him. "My grams would whip me if I didn't," He grinned.

Pursing her lips, Fiona saw her mom try and hide her smile, but she knew he had just earned a bucketful of points in her mom's book. With a nod, they therefore all joined hands and let Adam say grace.

Dinner went surprisingly smooth after that. Her mom eased off when Adam answered all of her grilling questions without pause and laughed when he told her about his grandmother. Fiona noticed that the more he told about himself, the more her mom started smiling. Adam had been right; he really was great with parents.

After cleaning up the dinner table, she and Adam then left for her room, keeping the door halfway open, as promised. Fiona knew her mom would be listening to every word they spoke, which made the whole thing that much more awkward. She hadn't brought a friend home since her dad died, and now she brought a boy home.

If that wasn't alarming in the Mom-handbook, nothing was.

The second they were alone in her room, Adam looked around curiously, like he had never seen a bedroom before. "Awesome room," He grinned and immediately walked up to her dresser where all of her hair styling products and makeup was. Not that she wore it much, but she had it, just in case...

"Thanks," Fiona muttered, taking an awkward seat on her bed. Why couldn't she think of a single damn thing to say?

"I told you, didn't I?" Adam chuckled when he looked back and noticed her face again. "I passed with flying collars. I'm every parents' dream."

Until he brought up the rapsheet, that was, Fiona thought, but decided to let him have his proud moment. He was grinning to himself and picking at her hairspray bottles, looking at- and reading the brands.

It was then Fiona happened to think back to dinner, at all that he had told her mom about him and his grandma. She already knew they lived alone together, but she didn't know that she knitted socks for the sick cancer children at the hospital. After retiring from the church, she had needed something else to occupy herself with. Adam had told she loved visiting the hospital and always joked about how she might as well get comfortable there soon. She had humor, and Fiona couldn't help but see where Adam had gotten it from.

"I like your grandmother," She voiced, folding her hands while Adam still animatedly looked through all of her things. "She seems really nice."

"Yeah, she's the best," He told with a grin. "She was actually the one who got me started with ballet when I wouldn't stop doing Tasmanian Devil spins around the orphanage. I guess she figured if I was going to keep doing it, I might as well learn how to do it properly."

"You started with ballet?" Fiona gaped. For some reason, that surprised her. "How come you stopped?"

Adam picked up one of her red lipsticks and pulled off the cap, twisted the colorful part up and watched it with curiosity while speaking. "I couldn't stay within the lines—literally. My teacher told me my lines weren't clean enough and also told me to start spinning on my feet instead of my head. I dunno, for some reason that was a deal-breaker for her."

Fiona rolled her eyes. "I can't imagine why. I mean it's—oh, my God, what the hell are you doing?"

He had put her red lipstick to his lips and suddenly begun smearing it all over and around them, pretending to do it classily by watching himself in the mirror and then smacking his lips. "Huh, well look at that, I guess red suits me, too."

"Adam!" Fiona couldn't help but burst into laughter when he put the lipstick down again and pretended to primp himself silly. "What the actual hell are you doing?"

He turned around and puckered his lips at her. "Kiss me, princess Fiona! Only a true love's kiss will break your spell!" And with that, he jumped across the floor towards her, arms spread wide.

"Adam, oh, my God!" She screamed as he bellyflopped onto the bed and then tackled her, wrapping his arms around her, whereafter he began smacking wet and red lipsticky kisses up and down her arm and what was exposed on her shoulder. "Adam!" Had he actually lost his whole mind?!

"You shall be hideous no more, Princess Fiona!" He chimed in a classic fairytale voice.

"Adam!" She shrieked when he wetly kissed the ball or her shoulder. "Adam, my mom can hear you!" Oh, God, if she walked in right now...

"She's also hearing you not saying stop," He pointed out with a smug grin. Fiona rolled her eyes as he then laughed and climbed off her. "Okay, okay. Let me just go wash this off, we'll get started on the homework. Bathroom?"

"Through that door," Fiona looked down at her arm and saw she was covered in red lipstick, too. Thank God for makeup remover. "You damn fool..." How the hell did Kalo survive him for years?

Adam laughed, but then shot her a wink before going to the bathroom. "I got you to laugh, tutu. That was all I wanted."

And as he closed the door and she heard the water start to run, Fiona leaned back on her bed and looked up at her ceiling with a small sigh.

She had a feeling he would be a fool any day if he just made people laugh.

The next morning Fiona felt kind of strange as she walked into the dance studio and met up with Adam. He was already setting up as usual and cast her a smile as she dumped her bag down. At that, she felt a strange flutter in her stomach she couldn't find end or beginning in. It only seemed to intensify when Adam finally laid his phone down and rolled his shoulder blades around.

"So, Kalo's back again," He voiced. Fiona lifted her eyes and looked him over.

"Yeah? Is she okay?"

"She's alright. Or at least she says so. I told her she could stop by if she wanted to. I hope that's okay?" He asked.

Fiona nodded, but in her stomach the fluttering changed. It suddenly twisted around, and it wasn't nerves.

"Alright," Adam slowly walked up to her, and with every step, Fiona noticed his expression changed. A slow frown formed on his face, and when he finally stopped about three feet away from her, something serious was definitely on his mind. "So about today's lesson..."

"Yeah...?" Fiona nervously replied. Had yesterday made things weird? By the look on his face, it felt like miles of shit had changed between them. He knew her so much better now, and even though that should have made her feel safer... it unsettled her when he finally looked up at her with a somewhat hard face.

"I noticed something yesterday when I was at your house," He suddenly said and threw her way off. Fiona blinked confused and raised a brow. "You don't have any pictures of your dad hanging around. Not in your living room, the hall, or in your bedroom. I even checked your bathroom. Nothing."

Fiona swallowed and looked down. Ah. So that was what was on his mind. After everything she told him yesterday... he probably expected her to have a shrine of her father somewhere at home. "I... my mom removed all the photos when I... when I couldn't look at him without crying. It reminded me what happened," She told, watching Adam nod slowly.

"Right."

That was it. He said nothing more and it only unsettled Fiona even more. She watched him turn and walk back towards his phone, hands on his hips and head lowered; Deep in thought.

Fiona tipped on her feet. She hated the silence, especially because it seemed to fill up with all of the unspoken. When it finally became too much for her, she opened her mouth to speak, but in that same second, Adam decided to speak as well. And what he said hit her hard.

"You're angry, Fiona."

He slowly turned around when she didn't move or reply. Fiona stared at him in astonishment as his words sunk inside. Why the hell would he say that? "No, I'm not?"

"You are," He said and started walking back to her. "It took me so long to figure out why you are the way you are, but after last night I realized what your problem was – why you can't dance; You're angry at your dad, Fee."

Fiona felt like he had stabbed her in the lungs. She couldn't breathe, but pushed out a breath anyway, a harsh one.

She loved her dad. How could he even have come to that conclusion?

"So just because I don't like to have his picture up, I'm angry? How the hell do you jump to that conclusion?" She argued, defensively. If he wanted to accuse her of being angry at her dad, he'd better back it up.

Adam came closer and met her head on. "You say every step you take reminds you of him. You starve yourself to punish yourself, but why would you need to punish yourself for something you know deep down you didn't do? It all leads back to that day, Fiona," He stopped in front of her and stared down into her eyes that had turned glossy. "You're angry that he caused you to hate dancing. Because he died. He turned something you loved into a bad memory, and now you have to keep dancing because otherwise you feel like he died in vain. You're angry, Fee."

Fiona's heart stuttered in her chest and her anxiety took a skyrocket blast into the ceiling. She stared up at Adam and he stared back at her, waiting for her to defy his words.

But the words on her tongue never came.

"Today we're going to do something different," He then said. He took a step back. "An exercise. I need you to break through your shield and let go of your anger. Today, you dance battle me."

"W-what?" Fiona stuttered shakily and felt her whole body tremble. Adam had turned towards his phone and was already picking a song while she tried to process his words. "B-battle you?"

"You have one and a half week's training to draw from. It doesn't have to be perfect or even decent, it just has to be." He laid his phone down again and then turned towards her and crossed his arms. "Let out all your anger in your steps. I don't care how you do it, just do it. Let me have it."

"I don't..." Fiona felt herself crimp as Adam walked up to her and stopped in front of her again. "Adam, I... can't. I'm not... I'm not a-angry."

"No?" He leaned down and stared at her.

Fiona swallowed and looked back up. "N-no."

"Time to get it then."

– And then he shoved her hard, just as the music started.

Fiona stumbled back and almost lost her footing, but managed to catch it in the last moment. She stared preposterously up at Adam and saw him glare at her as he stepped closer again. "What the hell are you—"

He shoved against her shoulders again and Fiona let out a sound as she stumbled again. When she caught her balance, she gritted her teeth and saw Adam was approaching again. He cocked a hard brow, almost arrogantly. It lit a fire in her stomach, but she pushed it down. He was just trying to provoke her.

"Stop it," She snapped when he circled around her. "It won't work. This is stupid—"

His chest pushed against her shoulder blades and Fiona stumbled forward. When she spun around to throw words at him, Adam stepped forward with a hard step. The floor slammed beneath his shoe and made Fiona take an involuntary step back. The music only grew louder.

"Your dad's dead," He then suddenly spoke up. Fiona blinked up at him, mortified. "Dead, Fiona. He died while you danced, but you didn't kill him. You think you honor him by dancing? You're mocking him," He sneered. "Starving yourself? You think he'd be proud of you for that? You think he'd like watching you cry while you pirouette? Is that what he would have wanted?"

"Shut up!" She shouted. Her whole body was trembling, but she could no longer keep it under control. She was shaking and glaring at Adam who kept provoking her with a hard stare. He started walking towards her. "You don't know shit about my dad, so don't you fucking talk about him!"

"Life's shitty, Fiona," He repaid with a harshly spoken tone. "You think you need to throw this kind of pity on yourself? Grow up. Face your fucking fears and move on."

He shoved her one last time, and that was it for Fiona. She let out a scream, and before she knew it, she was jumping towards him.

Adam stepped back fast when she spun towards him and let her anger out with the beat of her heart. It was drumming harshly and everything was rushing before her eyes. Adam stepped up to the floor again and suddenly his feet were moving, moving fast. He was dancing, but his hands kept shoving at her, provoking her.

Right until Fiona had enough and shoved him back.

She stomped her foot harshly into the floor like he had done and shoved him back with everything she had. Adam stumbled back, but Fiona didn't let her catch his balance. She shoved again and let him fall onto the floor. He landed on his back, and only then did she step back with gritted teeth. Adam glared up at her, but then, firming his gaze with a hard movement, he jumped up onto his feet again and vaulted his whole body up with one push.

He came at her like a bull, but Fiona didn't stand down this time or fall back. She was angry and she wanted to hurt him, even though her body felt like it was falling apart. Adam didn't seem to care, but only pushed her further.

"That's it?" He snarled at her and started circling around her again. He kept walking around her, making the circle he was creating around her smaller and smaller until his skin touched hers. His eyes stared her down from every angle, burning her.

Fiona snapped her eyes shut and then felt as his hands gripped her shoulders. The next moment, she felt his breath near her ear.

"Dance, Fiona," He growled. "Fucking dance or get the hell off the floor."

"You're an asshole," She whispered, feeling his snort against her neck.

"And you're a coward. You're only pretending to dance, but you're not even moving, Fee. It's pathetic."

"Pathetic?" The last straw was pulled, and with nothing else, Fiona spun around and let it all rip. He wanted angry? He got it. "I'm pretending? You're the one to talk! You walk around here and act like you're the happiest goddamn person alive, but I see through you!" She shouted and pushed his hands away from her when he tried to touch her. "You say I'm walking around with a guilt in my heart, but then how come you spend all day here helping people feel better? You used to deal drugs, Adam. You dealt drugs to kids, and that's still sitting with you."

Adam clenched his teeth, but didn't say word. And just as well, because she wasn't done yet.

"You pretend like you've moved past it—that you're okay and that you moved on to a better life, but it's all just a mirage," She breathed, angrily. "It's bullshit. You act okay to hide the fact that you still feel horrible that you did what you did because you were so desperate for the family you never had. You're trying to make up for all your past mistakes by dealing out happiness now, but it's all fake. So don't you dare come and tell me I'm the one carrying the guilt and anger."

The words from her mouth finally stopped, and so did the music. The whole room became quiet, and all that was left to hear was her harsh breathing. Fiona stared at Adam who stared back at her, showing nothing on his face. Almost a full minute went by where none of them moved.

Then, Adam moved.

Fiona broke down when he walked up and slung his arms around her. He pulled her against his chest and Fiona clutched on to his shirt with a trembling heart. Her cries ripped from her throat, from her lungs, from her soul. She cried and kept repeating the same words over and over again; "I'm sorry. I'm so sorry. I'm sorry."

Adam clutched her tightly and then exhaled near her ear. "Yeah... me, too."

Fiona shook her head rapidly and then looked up at him through her tears. "N-no. I'm so sorry, I-I didn't... what I said—"

"Wasn't a lie," He cupped her face, and it was only when she blinked away her own tears, she realized... his eyes looked wet as well. "I do try to make up for what I did, but I don't fake any of the love I give out. I turned my past into something good—you didn't. And I needed you to know that you should have," He whispered, leaning down and pressing his forehead against hers. "What happened to you wasn't your fault, Fiona. Stop blaming yourself for something you never had any control over. You were just a kid."

Fiona swallowed, but clutched tighter on to his shirt. She took a deep breath, but then met his jungly green eyes. "So were you."

Adam looked back down at her, and then with a softened look, he smiled. His hand brushed her cheek and then tucked a loose strand of hair out of her face. It was right then when their eyes met again that Fiona realized...

Their lips were just inches apart.

She felt his breath on her lip and looked up at him when she saw his gaze change. Something shifted inside his eyes, and with a firmer hand, he leaned even closer. Fiona stopped breathing all together, but realized her feet were pushing her body onto her toes...

The door opened abruptly, and Fiona pulled away so fast, she almost felt the whole earth come with her. She heard Adam clear his throat behind her, but then sensed him turn as a person stepped in.

"Hey," His voiced changed completely, and she instantly knew who had joined them.

As Kalo stepped further in, Adam stepped up to give her a hug. She smiled and patted his back.

"Hey, gringo. I thought I'd take you up on your offer and drop by. I'm not interrupting, am I?"

Adam chuckled hoarsely, but then looked towards Fiona who had cleaned up her tears and erased all evidence of her crying. She slowly turned and saw him look probingly at her.

"No," Fiona then spoke up. "We were just... taking a break."

Kalo looked between them, but then shrugged. "Alright, cool. I won't stay long, I just wanted to... say thank you for yesterday," She said and looked up at Adam again, then back at Fiona. "It was some messed up shit, but you guys were real sweet. I just wanted to say thanks for being there. It meant a lot."

"Hey," Adam grinned a little and then nudged her shoulder. "That almost sounded like a feeling. Are you growing goo-y on me? Soft coffee toffee?"

Kalo did exactly what Fiona would've done and rolled her eyes. She shoved him away and muttered something in Spanish under her breath. "Puto. Don't make me regret coming here." When Adam grinned again, she shook her head and turned towards Fiona. "You're officially a part of the family, girl. Ever need anything, you know who to call."

Fiona looked perplexed for a moment, but then realized she was talking to her. "Uh... t-thank you."

"Alright, I'm out again," She rolled her eyes when Adam threw his arms around her for a hug. "Urgh, I don't know how you stand him for a whole day."

"No, stay," Adam insisted. "I have to use the ladies' room anyway. Keep her company?" He said, then eyed out Fiona.

Fiona blinked in startle when Kalo shrugged, but then pushed Adam away who ran to the door with a grin. "Don't forget to wash your hands after you wiped your vagina!"

"Why does he use the ladies' toilet?" Fiona spoke before she could stop herself. Kalo snorted and shook her head.

"Because it's the only place the locks work."

"Why is—"

"The guys have sex and smoke weed in the boy's room."

"Ohh." Fiona finally understood. Now it made sense that he preferred to use the girls' bathroom; It was hard taking a dump with people groaning and moaning in the next stall over.

Kalo slowly walked into the studio and looked at herself in the big mirrors, checking on her clothes and hair. She had a gorgeous body; curvy hips, a nice bosom for a dancer, thick thighs and a juicy bottom. And she knew how to work it all.

"You know, I meant what I said yesterday," She then suddenly spoke. Fiona tore her eyes away from her body and quickly tried to hide her obvious ogling.

"Huh?"

"He really likes you—Adam." Kalo turned around and smiled at her, the most genuine and down to earth smile she had ever seen on this girl's lips. She was always up to something mischief or teasing, and her smiles always portrayed it. But right now, she was coming up to her with a friendly smile.

"I, uh... I..." Fiona didn't know how to respond. First of, she was certain she was wrong. After all... how could you notice someone like her with someone like Kalo around? "I think maybe you're wrong... I mean, I just don't think I'm his type." She was much too un-happy and introverted for someone like him.

"Listen," Kalo came up to her and laid a hand on her shoulder. "You wanna know how I know he likes you? Because in all the time I've known and danced with that boy, he ain't never ever had a girlfriend. He's never even expressed a crush, he's just been doing himself and dancing around like a hyped up kid on Adderall."

Fiona slightly frowned and tried to see what she was saying. "And...? What's... your point?"

Kalo slowly smirked. "It means I know when he's acting different around a girl. He's into you! I don't know what y'all are doing up here every day, but whatever it is, it's working, girl. Keep it up."

Fiona blinked, absolutely shocked. When Kalo patted her shoulder and grinned, then took a step back to walk up to the mirror again, Fiona tried to process the facts she had just gotten. He had never had a girlfriend here? Why was that so hard to believe? He was Adam—someone had to have scooped him up, or at least tried to. Or he had to have tried someone else.

But now Kalo was saying he wasn't that kind of guy.

Swallowing a lump, Fiona slowly walked up beside Kalo and tried to keep her nerves in check. She was about to ask a question she had been dying to ask since she first got here. "I kind of thought you and him were..."

"Me and Adam?" Kalo snorted preposterously, then broke into a laughter. She waved her hand dismissively, but then caught her breath. "Hell no, girl. There's nothing wrong with Adam, but he is just waaaaay too... Adam. You know what I mean? He's not my taste. Nah, he's too good for me."

"Too good?" Fiona slowly questioned.

Kalo sighed and then turned to look at her. "He's a real good guy. Been through some shit, but he made it through, you know? He's not into being a daredevil anymore, doesn't break the law, doesn't even smoke. He's not a ride or die, he's a choir boy. Maybe there's something wrong with me then, but he's just not what I want."

Fiona nodded slowly and thought about her words. The Adam she knew loved messing around, but when she thought about it, he was pretty good. For some reason, in her head, his bad boy looks had somehow put him in a box, even when she knew he was the opposite. Maybe that's what she liked about him; he had the bad boy vibe, but chose to be good.

And unlike Kalo, it sounded like something she could like.

But why would he ever like someone like her? What did she have that anyone else couldn't give him?

Fiona shook her head. Why was she even entertaining this thought? Nothing was going to happen between them. They were just friends.

The door opened behind them and Adam came in, drumming on the door jamb. "I'm back. Don't tell her you taught her anything I can't do. It'll make me look bad here."

Kalo scoffed and turned, walking back as Adam came forward. Meeting him halfway, she flicked his forehead. "You always look bad standing next to me, gringo. Laws of nature, women are the fairer sex."

"No arguments there," Adam teased and looked her up and down, then whistled lowly to annoy her. It worked; Kalo muttered something, but then brushed past him after saying something about boys will be fucktoys.

"Have fun," She tossed over her shoulder and turned to look at Fiona in the door. "He's all yours," She smirked, then tapped the door and walked out.

Fiona felt her cheeks redden when Adam raised a slow brow and looked at her. "All yours? Did she make you sign the custody papers while I was gone?"

Fiona laughed nervously when he grinned, but it sounded strained to her own ears. She needed to forget the conversation with Kalo ever happened, especially if she was going to get through the rest of the day. Things were weird enough as they were.

"Hey..." Adam slowly came up to her when he noticed her awkward face. "We're alright, right? About before..."

"We're good," Fiona promised. When Adam lifted a questioning brow, she released a shaky breath. "Water under the bridge. I... I know why you said it." Because it had to be said.

"Alright..." He slowly nodded. "So... friends?"

When he stuck out his hand and looked at her with an unreadable face, right then, she knew there was nothing between them. He was making it clear to her, whatever moment might have passed, had passed. Moving forward.

So reaching out, she squeezed his sweaty palm. "Friends."

Chapter 13

"So, by factoring the basic trinomials of the form x2+bx+c into 2 binomials—"

"Stop. I think I need a break," Adam sighed and rubbed his hands through his hair as Fiona and he laid stretched out on her bed after dinner at her house, doing their school homework. They had been at it for nearly two hours, and it was almost 10pm. As Adam laid down his pencil, Fiona couldn't help but yawn as well, and then nod in agreement; She was exhausted, too.

"Okay, but we have to finish these before I go to bed. What time do you need to be home?"

"2am," He replied. When Fiona blinked in slight shock, he shook his head with a little grin. "I'm going to work after this."

"Wait, wait," She held up a hand and stared at Adam preposterously while he picked up and sipped his second energy drink of the night. "Are you saying you work on top of everything else you do?"

"Do you think expenses pays themselves, tutu?" He mused with a tired smile. "Clothes, bus fare, school, books—"

"No," She broke in. She just couldn't believe it. How the hell did he find the time? "Where do you work, then?"

"The Junk Joint downtown. Three nights a week, from 11pm to 2am," He told and then reached for the bowl of chips Fiona's mom had put out for them. While he crunched on the crispy treat, Fiona summed it all up in her head.

"So you go to a public high school, work three night shifts a week down at the Junk Joint, and you still have time to come and dance with me every day, on top of keeping up with homework and taking care of your grandmother?"

Adam shrugged and gave a little grin before twirling his pen around on his worksheet. "Yeah. I'm healthy, I'm young and I'm blessed to have so many good things in my life. It's not really about having the time, it's about making the most of every moment. You know?"

"I... I guess," Fiona mumbled and looked down at her own homework. She still had a hard time believing she never knew he worked. He did so much... "But... don't you ever just get... exhausted?"

"Oh, trust me, I sleep well at night," He laughed and then grabbed another chip from the bowl before rising up from her bed and stretching his back. "But I count myself lucky to even be able to maintain a job with my history. Imagine if I was black, too," he teased.

Fiona glared.

"Not funny?" He grinned lopsidedly.

Fiona sighed, but then sat up as well and stretched her stiff body. Adam sat down beside her again, and then for a moment a silence stretched. There was a question in her mind she wanted to ask, but she wasn't certain it was her place to ask about...

And yet still, she did.

"It's what happened to Kalo, isn't it?" She slowly said. She knew he knew what she was referring to.

When Adam didn't move, but merely pressed his lips tightly together, it almost answered the question before he did.

"Yeah," He then said, quietly.

Fiona felt a familiar stab in her chest.

It wasn't often it happened to her, but sometimes she had run into people on the street who had looked at her funnily or failed to hide their opinion of her because of her... appearance.

Once, when she walked into a clothes store to pick up a birthday present for her mom after school, a security guard had told her to leave her backpack up at the counter. At first she didn't think anything of it, until a smaller kid with his mom walked in—the kid wearing a Spider-Man backpack whom the guard conveniently didn't ask him to leave at the counter. Both mom and the kid had been white. As had the guard.

Discrimination and sometimes being a minority still affected Fiona here and there, but it had never been as bad as it could've been—nothing like what happened to Kalo. To think someone would ever try to exploit someone because they thought they were easier to set up because of their skin color... like they were more stupid because they looked different—it was disgusting. And who decided what different was, anyway?

"He told her she was a nobody," Adam silently voiced, as if he had been reading her thoughts and thinking along the same lines as her. "He told her she was just another kid from the ghetto, and that in their business, you had to do things to get ahead. And then he said something crude about which head she could choose to use," He scoffed, angrily.

Fiona didn't realize her fists had curled up until she felt her fingernails poke into her palm. She quickly unfolded them and then exhaled what was meant to be a calming breath. It wasn't.

Adam, on the other hand, stood up and started walking the floor, as if to burn off some angry energy. By the look on his face, the issue clearly still bothered him.

"I hate this shit," He told and shook his head as paced back and forth on her floor in front of her bed. "I hate that it happens and that some people actually get away with it. She was one of the lucky few that managed to get out of it. I honestly don't know what I would've done if she... if she hadn't..."

Fiona looked up when he paused and saw him close his eyes tightly. The pain on his face was obvious, and out of pure empathy, she carefully reached out and took his hand. "Hey... she's okay. Nothing happened, and she told me she's moving on from it."

Adam slowly looked down and then grabbed her hand, giving it at clench. Then blew out a breath. "Yeah... I know. She's just... she's my best friend," He confessed.

Fiona stayed silent as Adam sat down beside her again and rubbed his face. Another question now burned on her tongue, but this one was much more nerve wracking than the last one. Did she dare ask?

"Do you... like her?" She whispered, barely audible.

Adam lifted his face from his hands and rose a crooked brow. "Like her? As in... like like her?" When Fiona gave a hesitant nod, his lips split in a quick laugh. "Fuuuck, no. She's waaaay too much trouble. Greatest human alive, but she's too much for me. No, we're just friends. I consider her my sister."

Fiona didn't want to exhale loudly, but it was as if her lungs cleared out and her stomach eased. Small stirrings started rolling around in there instead, tickling her lower abdomen and her heart, but she ignored it steadfastly. Adam and Kalo were friends, and so were they; Just friends.

"Kalo told me that you don't date," She suddenly blurted. When she realized she had spoken aloud, it was too late to take it back.

While Fiona felt the sweat run down her back, Adam's lips turned upwards in a modest little grin. "Yeah... that's true."

"Really? Never?" Fiona asked, surprised. With his looks and personality...

"I did some stupid shit back when I was younger that I wish I could undo, so I'm making up for it by... being more selective," He slowly chuckled and then laid down on her bed with a groan. "I just... I guess I haven't found the right girl to break my celibacy yet," He told, but then swallowed and cleared his throat as Fiona pursed her lips in thought. He really was a choir boy, wasn't he. "What about you?"

Snapping out of it, Fiona looked back at him and saw him raise a brow. "What about me?"

"Come on," He grinned. "Are you still a virgin? I want to say the answer is obvious, but I've learned not to judge a tiger by its stripes – or a ballerina by her tutu."

Fiona felt her cheeks slightly redden. She looked away, but honestly had no idea why she felt embarrassed. There was nothing wrong with being a virgin. She was only 18 years old, and she wasn't in a rush.

"I'm a virgin." She mumbled.

Adam's smile widened. "I figured. You have a very innocent glow about you. Except for when I bring out your attitude," He reminded her, which made Fiona roll her eyes. "That's why I felt I needed to ask." He sat up and suddenly leaned in towards her ear. "Maybe you have a secret alter ego I know nothing about." He teasingly whispered.

Fiona snorted as he laid back down again with a grin. Alter ego? Her? Hardly. "I haven't even seen a condom before, that's how virgin I am," She replied—and then instantly regretted.

"Hold up—you've never seen a condom before?" Adam echoed in disbelief. He blinked in shock for two seconds, then shook his head and abruptly dug his hand into his back pocket. "Okay, hold the phone."

Widening her eyes, Fiona then watched as Adam nonchalantly fished out what turned out to be his wallet. After opening it, he pulled out a small square packet from one of the slips; A foil packet.

Fiona gaped. Then, before she could think, she jumped up and hurriedly closed her door so her mom couldn't see the giant red flag Adam had just brought into her house. He brought a condom with him to her room; The 'celibate' boy. "Adam!"

He chuckled when she came back on the bed again and looked alarmed at the deceiving, innocent-looking little packet. "You look like a deer in headlights. You should see your face." He laughed, pleased with her reaction.

Gritting her teeth, Fiona decided to toughen up, even though she was freaking out inside. He brought a freaking-fracking-fucking condom with him to her home. "You know they say that keeping condoms in your wallet isn't good. It dries them out."

"That's only if you keep them there for too long," Adam chuckled, stuffing his wallet back into his back pocket while holding up the foil packet between two fingers.

"And don't you?" She pointed out, almost hoping to catch him mid-lie in his good boy behavior.

He laughed shortly, but then shook his head. "Always better safe than sorry, tutu. Anyways; Behold," He then said, waving the condom in front of her nose with a grin. "Your very first Trojan."

Fiona felt her cheeks heat up again as Adam kept it held up in front of her, as if it was some holy treat she'd never seen before. Which it kind of was.

"So? Are you gonna open it?" He asked when Fiona didn't take it, but simply just stared at it. "Or do you want me to do it?"

"What?" Fiona exclaimed. He didn't mean that, did he? He wasn't really going to open it... was he? "Uh, no. I-I think we should just keep it wrapped up, there's no need to—"

Adam placed the corner of the foil wrapper between his teeth, and then with a gruff, doggish sound, tore the packet open. Fiona's mouth fell open as he spit out the little foil piece and then held up the now opened condom. "Too late," He grinned.

Oh God, Fiona thought as she watched him now pull the little rolled up condom out, the latex looking... sticky. She swore she also smelled a scent coming off it. "Is that..."

"Apple?" He finished for her with a teasing grin. "Yup."

God help them if her mom was to walk in right now. Fiona was an absolute nervous mess. Her hands were sweaty and she was certain it couldn't get any worse, but then, what Adam did next, had Fiona going completely red. And that was saying something with her skin tone.

He started shaking the condom, thus making it unfold until it was completely out. In his hand, it now dangled like the sloppiest, thinnest excuse of a balloon in the world, looking so very... flaccid. Fiona couldn't help but just stare. That was slightly unimpressive.

"Well?" Adam questioned curiously, raising his brow. He waited for her reaction. "Everything you wanted it to be?"

Yes, this was exactly how she imagined looking at her first condom would be like; in her room with a way too smug-looking guy, with her mom right outside, probably finding her sandals as they spoke.

"It looks... kinda gross," Fiona stated and wrinkled her nose when he with a laugh jiggled it in the air like a worm and moved it closer to her face until she had to move back and push him away with a screech. "Ew, stop! Get it away from me!"

"Might look gross like this, but not on a dick," He laughed and then suddenly climbed in over her, still lolling it in her face. Fiona screeched again and then tried to avoid it by pushing it away, yet still not touching it. "Come on, Fee! Don't be scared—one day these'll be your best friends!"

"Not anytime soon!" She shouted back, squeaking when it graced her cheek. She felt a slimy sensation. "Ew, get it away, Adam! Throw it out!"

"Throw it out? So your mom finds it in the trash and gets a heart attack? What are you going to tell her then?" He wheezed and shook his head while Fiona hid her face in her hands. "'Oh. It was just some private thing between me and Adam. Don't worry about it.' I'll tell you right now, I won't be welcomed back then."

"Oh, my God, just get rid of it!" Fiona flipped. She swore if her mom actually walked in right now...

"Oh, so you wanna go naked?" Adam teased smugly, but then finally conceded and leaned back to toss the condom into her paper waste basket. She heard the limp splat of it hitting the bottom. "Well, get ready for lots of babies then. That's what happens if you don't wrap it before you tap it; baby batter makes the belly grow fatter. Quote me on that."

"You are so impossible," Fiona shook her head and now sat up, just as Adam slung himself back into her bed with a grin.

"Am I lying, though?"

"Shut up," She demanded. Adam continued laughing while Fiona palmed her face, trying to calm down. Her heart was racing, but it wasn't from fear. The excitement in her stomach told her... she was happy.

"Hey," Adam then suddenly said. The grin in his voice was gone, but a little smile remained on his face. "I'm sorry if I crossed a line. Sometimes I get overexcited."

Sometimes? When was he not excited?

"It's fine," Fiona sighed and then laid back down again, folding her hands on her stomach. She looked up at her ceiling, but sensed Adam watching her from the corner of her eye. The small flutter in her stomach returned.

"Can I ask a last question?"

Fiona slowly turned her head and then met his eyes and saw they had softened quite a bit. Her own expression melted, and with a last sigh, she nodded. "Fine."

He watched her closely, looking between her eyes and then finally down at her lips. "Have you ever kissed someone... or been kissed?"

All of the air in the room seemed to go on an instant vacation. Fiona's breath froze up, and with a shaky heartbeat, she looked back at Adam and swore that for a moment... she saw something in his eyes...

"No," She replied.

His lips twitched ever so slightly, but there was nothing teasing about it anymore. "Good. You should wait until you find the right person, and then wait for the perfect moment, too. Nothing will feel better, I promise you. Not even dancing."

Fiona let out a quiet snort. Nothing felt better than dancing.

"Wait and see," Adam turned his head up at the ceiling and grinned a little at it. "It'll be worth the wait."

"Yeah, well..." Fiona also turned her eyes away and forced herself to swallow the ball in her throat. "I'm not planning on having my first kiss anytime soon. It's one more week of this and then the audition. And then after that..."

Her words trailed off when she realized she hadn't planned after that. If she got in by some miracle, she would be training with a ballet company. If she didn't... well, then what?

Luckily in that moment, just as she was about to reply, the door burst open and Fiona's mom came in. Both of them jolted upright when she stared at Adam, harshly. "It's 10am, time to go."

Fiona blushed, but Adam just grinned and nodded. While he started packing up his books and her mom retreated to the living room, Fiona spent a few seconds gathering her thoughts. What was her plan if she didn't get in?

Would she stay at the DanceDec?

"Fee?"

"Hm?" Fiona looked up and saw Adam packed and ready. His school bag was slung over his shoulder, and he was lingering in the door.

He gave her a slow smile. "Bring your pointe shoes tomorrow."

The next Friday afternoon, Fiona should've been used to walking into the DanceDec nervous. She had done it almost every day for the past two weeks, but after Adam's last words yesterday, today felt... different. She didn't know what to expect when she would walk through that door, but she had done as he had asked and brought her pointe shoes.

Did it mean what she thought it meant?

She exhaled one last time before then turning the doorknob and walking inside their studio. She immediately halted.

Adam was standing by the stereo as usual, but unlike his usual sweatpants and t-shirt attire, he had dressed differently today.

Wearing a simple white T-shirt and a pair of black tights, he turned and looked up from the stereo as she walked in. Their eyes met, and with a little smile, he lifted his hand and gestured into the studio where two warmup barres were pulled up to the centre.

Ballet.

Fiona's breath hitched and her eyes dropped to his feet as he slowly approached her. He was wearing ballet flats, and from the lack of lines on his tights, he was also wearing his dancer's belt.

She had been right; Today would be different.

"Did you bring your pointe shoes?" He asked. Fiona's eyes snapped back to his and laid eyes on his face. He looked calm, but why did it feel like a warning?

"I... yes," She whispered.

They were dancing ballet today. Not contemporary, not jazz, nor hip hop or salsa. Ballet. He was finally dancing what she wanted to dance...

So how come she wasn't excited?

"Go warm up," He told her, gesturing to the barre before turning to walk back to the stereo. "I'll be with you in a moment."

Fiona stayed rooted for another couple of seconds before her brain would cooperate. She slowly started walking forward, her knees feeling shaky. If they were dancing ballet today...

Slow piano music started flowing through the sound system, and with a last adjustment on the stereo, Adam walked up and joined her by the barre. He gave her a little smile, then let his hand fall to the wooden barre. "Show me your warmup routine."

He was following her. Already the whole routine of their daily flow had been altered. She had never been the teacher, but now he was telling her to take the lead.

Fiona slowly swallowed, but then turned and looked at her reflection in the mirror. Her black tights and her purple top didn't resemble her old appearance, always in a leotard and pointe shoes. The girl who stared back at her was someone else... or a newer version of herself.

And maybe that's why taking the first step felt hard as she folded her feet against each on the floor.

Breathing out, her right hand fell to the barre while the other floated in front of her stomach. In the mirror, she saw Adam copy her moves and wait for her next one. He looked all wrong too, dressed up in ballet clothes.

What had happened to her?

Slowly moving her hand, she pushed up on her feet, seeing Adam doing the same. Then, lifting her arm and slowly bending down, she let the tip of her fingers graze the floor as her forehead met her knees. When she slowly arose again, she saw Adam do the same.

Throughout her whole routine, he followed her, making every one of her moves seem so elegant, yet handsome when performed by him. She kept checking to see if he was keeping his posture and his lines straight, and surprisingly he was. His arabesque was a little lower than hers, but his pliés went as far down as her own. By the time they had done the routine for 15 minutes, all of her muscles ached, both inside and out.

Two weeks without ballet felt like an eternity to the muscles.

Finishing with a last plié, they came back to first position. Fiona let go of the barre and saw Adam smile at her. He didn't say anything, simply just lifted the warmup barre and carried it back to the wall.

Fiona exhaled, but the ease didn't come to her. The hardest part didn't feel over yet. Even as she without a word went up to her bag and started tying on her pointe shoes without his command. They slipped on, shaping after her foot like an old friend.

"Sugar Plum Fairy. Do you know it?"

Fiona froze. Staring through the mirror, she slowly looked up and saw him look at her from the wall, slowly coming towards her. "Adam."

"I'll assist you. We'll make it a pas de deux, and I'll be right there with you, Fiona."

Fiona shook her head and immediately stood up. She wasn't ready for that. "The sugar plum fairy has—"

"Tchaikovsky's sugar plum fairy has 17 fouettés and 23 pirouettes. And I'll be there through every single one of them."

"It's too difficult," Fiona protested, already backing away when he came up to her. "I can't—"

"You and I both know you can do it. Not only physically, but mentally. You can do it, Fee," He said, stopping in front of her.

She kept shaking her head. She wasn't ready for it. The pirouettes—him, the whole dance. It was too much, and she liked him too much to watch him—

"Hey," Adam suddenly cupped her cheeks in his palms when she was spinning out. Maybe he could see it in her eyes, or maybe it was evident in the way her knees buckled. "Breathe, Fiona. Look at me. I said, look at me."

When she refused to look at him, he hooked her chin with his knuckle and forced her to meet his gaze. Her breath froze in her throat, as did the sob about to spill from her lips.

"I'm right here," He whispered, brushing his thumb over her cheek. "I'm here, and I'm not leaving your side. You've come this fucking far, Fiona. Two weeks ago, you wouldn't even trust me with your foot. Look at us now."

Her eyes dropped and saw how close they were standing. He was less than five inches from touching her body.

"You're dancing for him today, Fee," He whispered, smiling a little. "But you're doing this for yourself. You know you can, and I'll just be holding your hand through it. Do you trust me?"

Fiona held back the tears in her eyes. She knew it was irrational, but the fear was rooted so deeply inside her. But Adam...

He made her feel so safe.

Seeing the slow change inside her eyes, Adam slowly nodded and then pulled back. He wiped a single fallen tear from her eye, then exhaled and squeeze her hand. "From the intro. I'll follow your lead."

As he walked back towards the stereo to start the music, Fiona took a couple of deep breaths and tried to shake the fear from her body. Squeezing her eyes shut, an image of her dad popped up.

He was smiling. He was watching her dance, just like in their old garage, but he was alive in her head.

In her heart.

'Today you're dancing for him.'

As the intro started playing, Fiona exhaled a last time and then laid eyes on herself in the mirror.

Dance for him.

Closing her eyes, Fiona didn't even register as the music transitioned into the dance portion, but her body did. Without even having to tell herself to move, her feet lifted her up until only the tips of her toes were carrying her whole weight. All of the weight she had cut down so dancing wouldn't feel so painful.

But the pain came from within.

Warm hands came to her waist, and with a small gasp, Fiona opened her eyes, but moved as the music continued.

She didn't focus on the body that followed behind her and stabilized her when her legs shook.

"Feel it inside," He whispered in her ear, moving close enough as she extended her leg and let him support it. The first pirouette was coming up, and as if her body's movements gave it away, Adam gave her a little clench. "Let go of the thoughts that doesn't make you stronger, Fiona. You can do it."

She couldn't do it. She couldn't do it. She couldn't do it...

"You can do it."

With a sob, Fiona's body trusted Adam's words as he steadied her for the first pirouette. Her leg bent up and then she was turning.

It was over so quickly before she could process it had happened. Something inside her hurt, but the music waited for no one. It kept on playing, and right after the pirouette came three fouettés. Adam was still there, holding on to her.

She couldn't do it. She couldn't do it. She couldn't...

Her leg kick out and her spot blurred on the wall, but feeling Adam's hand clasp her waist when she started to spin out of control, she sucked in a shaky breath and found her spot again.

Keep going. You can do this. You're doing this. He's watching you. You're doing this for yourself. You have to get through this.

Fiona kept spinning and lost sight of Adam in the process. She knew he was around, but she couldn't tell if the words in her head came from the outside or from herself. The music kept playing and she kept dancing. The whole room was spinning.

She couldn't do it... but she was doing it.

The tears on her face dried and turned into silent, trembling breaths as she spun around in a large circle in the dance studio. The sugar plum fairy was technically difficult, but that wasn't what today was about. Adam didn't want her to look perfect. She had chased that for so long, but no more.

He just wanted her to dance and feel happy and free.

Just like her dad.

Fiona spun and spun and spun around, but the ache in her chest disappeared with every spin. Every time she kicked her leg out, she felt like screaming as she pushed away all of the old shit stuck inside her.

Loving dancing. Hating dancing. Loving her father. Hating him for leaving her. Hating Adam. Hating him for making her dance like this. Hating him for bursting through to her. Loving him for...

For helping her come back to herself.

"Fiona."

Her body was caught as she lost footing and crashed against a hard body. She was sobbing full on and she didn't even realize. Adam was holding her so tightly, cupping her face in his hands and brushing the strands of hair that had escaped her bun away from her face. She was shaking all over, her body feeling so completely bared and so vulnerable. So empty.

It felt like every hard breath in her body had left her, and suddenly she was breathing fresh air for the first time in years.

She had danced for him. She had showed him she could do it without him.

She was strong enough by herself after all.

"Fiona," Adam's voice sounded gravelly, and as she opened her eyes, she first thought she was seeing things, until she blinked a couple of times and cleared the water in her eyes. He was... was he really crying with her?

There was water in Adam's eyes, but the most beautiful smile on his lips as he brushed her cheeks with his thumbs and looked at her. "You did it, Fiona. You fucking did it. You danced so goddamn beautifully, I couldn't even—you let go of my hand and you just fucking spun on your own. Fiona, you did it."

Fiona let go of a sob and cupped her mouth, shaking her head as it all came out of her. The strength had been inside her all along. She had always known, but it had always hurt. She had starved herself, punished herself, tortured herself for years—of course it had hurt. Adam taught her how to stop and then taught how to let go – literally.

'You let go of my hand and you just fucking spun on your own.'

"Adam," She cried.

"Fuck, yeah," He whispered back, then clutched her into his body so tightly it almost hurt. She felt his lips press a hard kiss to her head, lingering for several seconds before he pulled away and brushed her back with his hand. "Fuck yeah, Fiona."

It felt like she had reached her goal. All this time they had trained to ready her for her audition, but it felt like none of it mattered in that moment. Right in that moment, this had been what it had all been about; Letting go; Dancing for herself; Showing to herself she could do it; Proving that her dad's death wasn't going to control her steps for the rest of her life.

"How are you feeling?" Adam pulled back and cupped her face again, looking into her tear-filled eyes. His own were still wet, but the smile on his lips shone through them. "Did it feel good?"

Fiona was lost for words. She didn't know why it had taken her so long to fight through it. Had the circumstances done it, or was it the boy standing in front of her who had helped her? Or was a hand really all she had needed to do it herself?

Mutely, Fiona simply just nodded frantically, more tears falling from her eyes with a little sob. Adam's smile broadened and he chuckled a little, almost laughing and crying with her. "Yeah? Do you want to keep dancing?"

Did she want to keep...

She swallowed hard and looked up at him through her tears. Did she want to keep dancing? "Yes... with you."

Adam's lips, if possible, turned up even more. Then, with a laugh, he leaned in and pressed a kiss to her sweaty forehead. "You fucking got it, baby."

And then he crouched down and lifted her up by her thighs, whooping loudly. Fiona screeched and quickly grabbed on to his shoulders, but couldn't stop laughing as he spun her around and howled joyously. He grinned up at her, shaking his head while splitting his cheeks with his smile. She couldn't help but automatically smile back and look into his brightly shining eyes.

She really did it.

And she owed all of it to him.

By the end of the day, both of them had danced so much that they could no longer keep going. As the clock turned 8pm, both of them were laying down flat on the floor with each their water bottle, panting. Adam was chewing on a candy bar. The day had been absolutely amazing, and Fiona still felt high from all of it. It was as if she had jumped out of her own skin and done what she never thought she could do.

She had proved to herself she was much braver than she originally thought.

"Come dancing with me tonight," Adam then suddenly voiced. Fiona turned her head towards him and gave him a turned up brow.

"Excuse me?" He had just spent all day dancing with her until every limb in her body hurt. More dancing didn't seem like an option at this point.

"There's this club not too far from where I live," He said, sitting up and leaning his elbows on his knees. He curled up his candy wrapper and looked at her. "They don't check ID and I know the doorman. He can get us in."

"You... you mean, like... go out with you?" Fiona carefully whispered. It sounded like a date. Didn't it sound like a date? Was it a date? It couldn't be a date...

"To dance, yeah," Adam smiled softly. "It's a Latin club, so it's mostly salsa. You already know some, and I'll guide you through the rest. What do you say?"

A club. A night out with him. Him, alone.

Fiona bit her lip. Everything inside her old self wanted to scream and run away, but after today, a part of her felt like... like... like this was something she had to try as well. Going out like a normal teenager, having fun with friends... being a part of the youth...

But the anxiety bubbled in her stomach.

"I... I'm not sure," She said, sitting up and wrapping her hands around her legs. "I'm... I don't think my mom would let me go."

"Call her and ask her. Tell her you can stay at my place so you won't have to travel home at night."

Fiona nearly choked. "Your... place?" Breathe. Breathe. Where was all the fucking air at?

Adam's lips twitched into a little grin. "My grams will be there. Call her and ask, I'm serious. If she says no, I'll get it, but if she says yes..."

Fiona knew she wouldn't say yes. Not even a little. Going to a club in an unknown part of Harlem with a boy she already had a stern eye on, only to spend the night at his place, too? Yeah, there was no way in hell she would approve.

"I'll give her a call," Fiona said, seeing Adam grin and get up. He grabbed his bag, then went to the door.

"I'll go change in the meanwhile. I love your gift, tutu, but another part of my anatomy is really having a stringent fight here."

Grimacing, Fiona watched as Adam then chuckled and left. He went to the girl's bathroom to change, and with a sigh, Fiona therefore reached for her phone in her bag.

Should she really call her?

Chewing on her lip again, she thought for a couple of minutes about all of it.

She wanted to go... but she also feared going. If she called her mom, the answer would be a definite no and she would tell her to come home immediately. The choice would no longer be hers, but if she didn't call...

With a pinch in her stomach, Fiona put her phone away and zipped up her bag, just as Adam came back in, changed to his usual black top and denim pants. How he could even wear that in this heat was beyond her.

"So? What did she say?"

Fiona looked up at him as he came in, raising a questioning brow. The words almost got stuck in her throat. She was about to lie, but wasn't it okay if it was for the greater good?

Then how come it still felt wrong?

"She, uhm... I had to convince her, but she eventually said yes," She boldly lied, seeing Adam's eyebrow lift even more. "On the condition that... I text her to let her know I'm okay."

Adam watched her for a moment, but then slowly nodded. "I thought for sure she'd say no. She seems like the type, no offense. Not that I know much about parents," He chuckled.

Fiona nervously chuckled back. "She is. She just, uh.... she's been wanting me to get out more and see some friends. I think that's the only reason she said yes."

"Well, let not take that for granted," Adam grinned. "Let's go."

Fiona stood up, but then immediately looked down at herself when she realized... she didn't have any other clothes with her to go clubbing. She would have to go home to get some, and if she did... "I... I have no clothes to wear..." This was already becoming a worse and worse idea. Should she just back out while she still could?

But Adam merely shook his head and smiled. "You can borrow something from Kalo, I'm sure. She always has clothes lying around. Let's go find her."

"I—" Fiona didn't get a chance to argue with his proposal before he grabbed her hand and led her out of the studio with him. They hurried down the hall to another studio where Adam poked his head inside and looked around. She spotted Rani and some of the other boys hanging out in a corner.

"Hey. Any of you seen Kalo?" Adam asked.

All of them shook their heads. "Check with Dimitri, maybe he knows," Twitch, the dancer from the dance circle, suggested. "He just went to the bathroom."

"Thanks," Adam grinned.

Without further ado, he dragged Fiona along to the girls bathroom. Fiona awkwardly followed along, feeling weird. He seemed so set on getting her to come with him...

Bursting the door open to the girls bathroom, Adam stuck his head inside and hollered. "Dimitri!"

They waited, but didn't hear a reply. All the stalls were closed, so maybe it was occupied.

"I'll check the boy's room," He sighed and shut the door, walking two paces to the left. "In worst case of emergencies when all the toilets are occupied, we—oh, shit!"

Opening the door to the boy's room, there came a screech and a shocked outburst.

Right there, against the sink, stood Dimitri.

– With Kalo bent over it, right in front of him.

"Holy shit," Adam burst into laughter and hurried out as both of them yelled at them to get out. Fiona had caught their faces though. They had been red as hell, and it hadn't been because of...

"Were they just—"

"And that-" Adam, who couldn't stop laughing as he leaned up against the wall outside, said, "-is why we use the girl's bathroom."

Chapter 14

After the initial shock and laughing on Adam's side, Kalo eventually came out of the bathroom with Dimitri following behind. Some perverted and inappropriate remarks from Adam later, Kalo finally agreed to lend some of her clothes for clubbing.

Fiona had been standing by in the corner, hopelessly watching the whole thing while trying to convince herself this wasn't completely crazy. She was already regretting saying yes to this, but by the time Adam had gotten the clothes from Kalo, it felt too late to change her mind.

Therefore, with Adam waiting outside the bathroom stall, Fiona quickly changed into a red salsa dress from Kalo's pile. As for shoes, she was lucky that Kalo used the same size and borrowed her a couple of modest heels. She hoped she wouldn't break them trying to dance like they did.

"Have fun tonight, alright?" Kalo said as she loosened Fiona's bun from her head and let her curls fall free in a haphazard mess around her face. She sprayed something on them that made them shine, then grinned at her through the mirror. "Good luck with him. Man, you'll need it."

Then, without further explanation, she and Fiona came out of the bathroom to a waiting Adam who stood leaned up against the railings to the staircase. He looked up from his tapping foot on the floor and laid eyes on Fiona.

"Oh, shit," He said, smiling slowly. "Shit, shit, shit. I'm not sure I'm authorized to take you out like that. I'm only one guy."

Kalo rolled her eyes dramatically, but then urged Fiona towards him. "Seriously. Good luck."

Adam chuckled and slung an arm around Fiona. Then, leading her down the stairs, he gave her a glance. "Do you trust me that I'll make sure that tonight will be fun? Say no and I won't hold it agains you."

Fiona took a deep breath and looked down at her getup. She had come this far, so what was the point of going back now? She might as well get it over with. "I somewhat trust you."

Adam's grin broadened. "Good enough. I'll take it. Let's go, tutu. Shit, you're going to knock them dead in that dress."

The second they walked into the Latin club, the booming music hit them. Fiona dropped her jaw and gawked as Adam pulled her inside with an amused grin.

The vibe in the club was so lit and so alive, everyone was moving and dancing to the music almost without stopping. The crowd was thick, the people were nearly impossible to get through, and the air was so humid you felt like you were walking into a sauna. Everyone's skin glistened and made everyone in the room seem like they were glowing. Fiona felt completely overwhelmed, but Adam seemed to know what to do.

He very quickly led them along the side of the room, around the dance floor where couples were dancing all different kinds of dances. Fiona could recognize a few basic steps here and there, some batchata, a little salsa... and a few dancing reggaeton; It was impossible to miss those couples. They were practically grinding publicly on the dance floor.

And they looked good while doing it.

"This way," Adam chuckled at her shocked expression. Her mouth was probably hanging half open. She quickly closed it and let him lead her on.

There was no such thing as an empty space in the club, but Adam managed to find a less crowded area of the dance floor and immediately pulled her to his chest. Fiona gasped, but Adam just smiled and caught her hips.

"Are you ready?" He whispered in her ear, sliding his hands up her sides. His hands caught hers and braided them with his own. Fiona suddenly couldn't breathe.

"No," She whispered back, her heart pounding almost as loudly as the music. She couldn't believe she was here in a club with him... surrounded by people dancing who could see them...

But Adam was standing so close to her and he was holding on to her. He wouldn't let her make a fool of herself.

His left hand hooked under her chin and lifted her face when she looked down shyly. Fiona nervously looked up at him and saw him smile slowly before poking her nose.

"You're ready, princess. Now move."

Fiona's breath froze in her throat when he then let his hand curl around her back and let the other clench her hand. Grinning, he nodded, and before she could argue, he pushed them into motion.

Panicked, Fiona looked down at their feet, deadly scared to step on him or someone else with her high heels. Her feet moved on their own accord though, and Adam lifted her chin once more and made her meet his eyes.

"Don't think," He reminded her and leaned in to her ear. "Feel, Fee. Feel the music. Feel the room. Feel this."

He grabbed her hand and placed it over his chest, tapping his finger against hers to the same drum as his heart and the music. Fiona exhaled shakily, the anxiety still tickling in her body.

Let go. Just let go this once, she kept telling herself. Stop thinking and just... let go.

Almost as if sending her ease up, Adam tugged her closer to his chest and pressed a hand on her lower back. She didn't even realize the music had switched, but suddenly it was faster, moving on eight beats rather than four. Salsa.

"You got this," He pecked her cheek with a little smile. "Show me what you got, tutu."

And then he pushed her away and swung her around.

Fiona expelled a little shocked squeal, but then quickly fell into the beat as Adam pulled her back and caught her. He grinned like a sonofabitch when her hands automatically fell to his shoulder and caught his as well. She pressed her lips together and decided to keep going.

Let go. Just let go.

The people around them were dancing salsa as well, spinning and twirling around, but Fiona found herself forgetting the surroundings when she caught Adam's smile on his face. There was something in it... pride? Or was it just plain happiness?

And that's when she realized.

He was mirroring her own face.

Her lips were split and her cheeks were hurting from grinning too hard. When he spun around, she spun around afterwards, and then he spun her around some more. Then she was against his chest, then she wasn't, and then she was facing him again.

She was doing it. She was dancing in front of others, spinning and twirling for the first time in... forever. She was really doing it.

She was dancing.

"Fuck, yeah," Adam grinned when she twirled around and spun against him. He caught her and kept on dancing, shaking his head and laughing. "Fuck yeah, Fiona!"

She let out a small scream and couldn't help but laugh with him, quickly pressing one hand in front of her mouth before he caught it again and spun her around once more. He dipped her down, then pulled her up again and to his chest. He kept her there and swept a hand over her hair, pushing it away from her face.

"There you are," He whispered, his lips still split in a proud smile. "There you so fucking are. You're dancing, Fee. How does it feel?"

Fiona was panting. She didn't realize how much air you needed when you were happy, dancing and grinning all at the same time. Adam was breathing hard against her as well, both of them out of breath. How did it feel? It felt... "I..."

The music suddenly changed again. The beat dropped way down, and the people on the dance floor seemed to grind into a slower motion. Fiona looked around to see the women moving closer to their partners and their partners taking a better hold of them. And then that first beat hit.

Reggaeton.

Adam pulled her closer and made Fiona snap her eyes back to him. He smiled mischievously and then patted her thigh. "It's reggaeton mixed with a little kizumba. It's not that hard, just follow my lead."

"But I don't know how to—"

He shut her up by placing a single finger over her lips. Then, meeting her eyes, he slowly slid his hand down her side... down to her hip... to her rear...

And then he moved.

Fiona's breath vanished and her skin felt hot as he moved her hips slowly, grinding them against his as he stepped forward, then backwards. He tapped her thigh again, and Fiona instinctively moved her hips, letting him guide them. Her eyes shut when he then lowered his head and slowly continued their sensual dance. He was right there, lost in the music with her.

Fiona felt the air thicken in the club, getting harder to breathe, but easier to move. With her eyes closed, she felt him spin her around and press her back against his chest. She exhaled slowly and let the music lead her body.

Just let go.

Her head fell backwards against his shoulder and he slowly lifted her arms and hooked them around his neck. Then, breathing against her skin, she felt as Adam slowly let his hand slide up her legs, landing on her hips. Fiona felt absolutely scorched when he exhaled hard and then arched his hips towards her, the same time he made her own grind backwards.

The sweat dribbled off her skin.

It was like everything had faded away except the two of them. Adam's body pressed tightly against hers, every hot, hard inch grinding against her own. He was murmuring the words to the Spanish song right against her ear, and suddenly it wasn't so annoying. The Spanish words did something else to her, and the breathy, deep rasp of his voice mouthing the words sent nothing but heat through her body. It felt like everything inside her was melting.

His hands then suddenly moved again, pressing over her lower belly in a sort of triangle before they slowly slid up again, following the length of her body and up her arms. While swaying side to side, still grinding, their fingers intertwined behind his neck.

He exhaled against her neck again, and the hot air sent another feverish shiver through Fiona. Something stirred inside her, something that had been stirring for weeks; Now, it felt more awake than ever, right in this moment as she and Adam were the only people left in the world.

"Adam..."

He spun her around and pressed a leg between hers, keeping them moving as he hummed. She opened her eyes an inch and saw his were completely closed as well, lost in the rhythm.

Her gaze then fell to his lips.

"Kiss me," She whispered.

As if awoken from a spell, his eyes slowly opened and met hers. But instead of the shock she thought would meet her, all she saw streaming from his eyes was...

Need.

"Kiss you?" He whispered, swiping her hair away from her sweaty neck. He cupped it and met her eyes. "Are you sure?"

He didn't even question it. Didn't even object. Fiona felt her breath leave her, and with a pull inside her, she tugged at his shirt, wanting him closer. "Yes."

Wait for the perfect moment, he said.

He was her perfect moment. He had been for weeks.

His lips twitched ever so slightly, but then he moved down, smiling harder. "Thank God."

And then he pressed his lips against hers.

Fiona felt everything inside her light on fire. His lips were so soft, but so persistent. He kissed her hard, but with gentle movements, his hands sweeping across her face softly and cupping the nape of her neck. Without even thinking, she pulled him even closer and curled her fingers into his hair. She felt his lips tug upwards.

It seemed so completely crazy. Fiona couldn't help but smile back as he begun chuckling lowly and pecked her mouth as they slowly swayed to the music, still.

There they were, in the middle of the club full of dancing people... and they were kissing.

And not a single fuck was given.

Slowly pulling apart, both of them stared at each other for a moment before they both started grinning. Adam smiled the hardest. Without wasting a moment, he pulled her into his chest and hugged her tightly while chuckling. "Thank God," He said again.

"Why do you keep saying that?" Fiona asked when he pulled back. He shook his head and just cupped her face again, leaning down to her forehead. With a soft peck, he kissed it.

And then the music filled the room again, just as Adam pulled them into motion. For once, Fiona let it all go and didn't think as she let him take the lead. She was so perfectly happy, nothing was going to ruin this night. Not her stupid thoughts or her anxious concerns.

Tonight, it was just the two of them.

—And a hundred other people who suddenly seemed to scamper around them.

The music was almost overruled as someone suddenly shouted something loudly in Spanish into the whole club. Everyone seemed to snap out of it, including Adam who lifted his head and looked around. People immediately started rushing towards the exit.

"What's happening?" Fiona asked, panicked. Was the police raiding the place? Were they going to get arrested? Oh, God. What if it was some sort of mob war—

"Come on," Adam quickly tucked her along and pulled her towards the entrance as well. With some effort, he managed to mash them through the crowd and get to the outside. And what met them... had everyone hollering.

"¡Lluvia!"

Thick, loud and countless drops of water droplets had started to fall from the sky in what felt like a blessing from above—literally. For the first time I over three weeks, it finally, finally rained; The drought was over.

Everyone started cheering, and all of a sudden the party seemed to move outside. Everyone started dancing in the rain, the music still booming from inside now pouring out onto the street. The roads quickly became a wet mess, puddles forming faster than fast and splashing everywhere. And right there in the centre stood Fiona and Adam, caught in the middle of all the madness.

Adam laughed loudly and turned his head to the sky, lifting his hands up. With a loud whoop, he bellowed out with the rest of them; "Fuck, yeah! Finally!"

Fiona couldn't help but laugh as well. When Adam shook his head like a dog, the water sprayed everywhere. They were both already soaked, the rain coming down hard. Thunder echoed ominously in the background of the music.

"Come on," Adam then chuckled, taking her hand and pressing a quick kiss to it. "Let's go!"

And then, with nothing but the clothes on their backs, they ran down the street in the pouring rain, laughing and screaming like maniacs.

By the time Adam had led them to their destination, the thrill of the rain had passed. It was now pouring down buckets and the thunder was rolling in over the whole city. One moment it was warm and humid, the next it was shivering and cold.

Adam quickly led them up the stairs to the most modest little apartment Fiona had ever seen, in the most dodgy neighborhood she had ever been in—and she had been to her fair share of dodgy neighborhoods, but this was one she wouldn't even walk a hypothetical dog in. Even the bushes looked sketchy.

Unlocking the front door in two places, Adam let her walk in first before following behind her. He closed the door and locked it up tightly, and whilst doing so, Fiona looked around.

The world's smallest kitchen and dining area was crammed into one corner of the tiny apartment while the living room seemed to connect through it. Just on the other side she could see a black figure sleeping on a futon couch, a small flickering of a TV illuminating the person's body.

"My grandma," Adam whispered. "Come on." He then wordlessly took her hand and pulled her along to a closed door.

Stepping inside what had to be his bedroom, Fiona looked around and hugged herself from the cold and the jitters nipping at her skin. His room was even smaller than the kitchen, barely able to fit a bed and single small dresser. The rest of his stuff laid spread around on the floor in an unorganized mess; shoes, food boxes, dirty clothes, deodorant bottles and energy drinks. There even laid a small teddy bear in one corner.

A loud sound from a TV suddenly came from the other side of the wall of his room, opposite the living room where his grandma slept. Adam seemed to routinely walk up to the wall and banged hard at it, before shouting something in Spanish. After a moment, the TV sounds lowered a bit.

"Here," He then said, quickly walking back to his dresser and grabbing something from it. He handed her a large T-shirt. "You can dry yourself with that."

Fiona hesitantly took it and gave a nod as a thank you. She didn't trust her voice right now, not when he grabbed another shirt himself and started drying off as well.

Both of them silently dried off, and while they did, Fiona felt how hard her heart was beating in her chest. She couldn't stop looking around at his room, taking in all of the impressions. The walls seemed moldy, and the carpeted floors were dirty. Even his bed seemed more like a bad spring pallet rather than a mattress. Worn out and misshaped.

He really lived like this, she thought. This boy who deserved the world lived like this... and still smiled every day.

Fiona slowly turned around when she sensed Adam looking at her. It was completely dark, and the only window in his room was a thin basement-like window at the very top of his wall. The rain beat against it and the lightening flashes occasionally lid it up and gave them a few seconds of light.

And it was in those seconds of light she saw how his entire face had changed as he looked upon her.

Slowly stepping closer, he carefully cupped her cheek and looked at her. Fiona felt her breath shallowly come out between her lips as their eyes connected in that moment.

All the joking was gone. He was looking at her like... like he had been waiting for her—waiting for this moment where he could finally kiss her and she wouldn't run away. Maybe he had even prayed for it...

'Thank God.'

Without overthinking, Fiona stepped closer and wrapped her hands around his neck. She dropped the shirt in her grip, just as Adam pulled her closer and breathed slowly against her lips.

Leaning down, just as she pushed up on her toes, they met halfway. Fiona felt the rush inside her when his mouth came down on hers and kissed her, slowly, deeply, but also couldn't deny the need in her own. His hand knotted in her tangled hair, desperately pulling her closer. Fiona responded by tugging him closer by pulling at his wet shirt.

This was crazy. Fiona couldn't breathe as both of them seemed to surrender to whatever heat seemed to have left the city and all but flown into this room. Her hands were gripping on to him, and surprisingly, they weren't shaking. She felt so safe and so comfortable, and it was all because of him.

Kissing him harder, Fiona let out a small, involuntary sound when his tongue tryingly swept along her lower lip. Then, with a hard breath, he dipped into her mouth and let his tongue slide against hers, Fiona following his movements as if they were dancing. He took the lead, but she somehow knew what to do.

But more importantly, she knew what she wanted to do.

Fear was not going to control her for one more second of her life.

Ripping at his wet shirt, she started tugging it upwards the same time he pulled away a single inch. He met her eyes, molten and so ready for her, and without further ado, he lifted his shirt and pulled it off. Throwing it away carelessly on the floor, he cupped her face once again and brushed her cheek before dipping down once more.

Fiona felt so lost. She clung to his shoulders and didn't stop to think when his hands picked her up off the floor. Suddenly she was seated on his lap, arms around his neck, his lips still pressed hotly against hers. The thunder loudly rolled over them again.

Adam's hands rested right around her hips, tucking up her dress so she could straddle him better. They found solace at the top of her ass, squeezing her closer as their lips fused together harder. Fiona braced herself on the wall behind his bed as he breathed erratically and pulled her closer.

God, she didn't want this night to stop.

Tucking at the straps of her drenched dress, Fiona managed to pull her arms free, the same time she felt Adam reach for the zipper on the back. Zipping it down, he helped her tug it up off her body, pulling back to let her hoist it up and off. They both tossed it away to join his shirt on the floor.

Sitting in only her underwear, Fiona knew she should've felt conscious somewhere, but she didn't. Adam's hands came to her skin the same second the dress was gone, and the way he touched her made her feel appreciated and beautiful with a single hot breath. A groan grated at the back of his throat as his lips traveled down her neck to her cleavage. Fiona tilted her head back and buried her hands in his hair.

"Fiona," He gutturally whispered against her skin—almost cursed her name in a sacrilegious way. When his mouth kissed her chest, she felt it rise and fall with erratic pants, sweat beginning to form on her skin. His hands slid up her sides again, before going down and landing on her ass. He squeezed hard and dragged an involuntary moan from her lips. The sound even surprised Fiona.

All that could be heard in the darkness of the room was the silent sound of their lips meeting accompanied by the heavy rain and thunder that raged outside. Fiona ignored all of it as she gripped on to Adam's head and met his lips kiss for kiss. Both of them were breathless, panting against each other's mouthes, but couldn't seem to stop.

"Fiona," Adam whispered again, breaking her name in in between kisses. He groaned in his throat when she moved her lips down and kissed it, sending shivers down her own spine at the vibrations of his voice. "Fiona."

She pulled back and met his eyes, seeing his own heavy lids lift to look at her. His jungly green eyes were almost black with desire, but he stilled anyway as they both caught their breath. Fiona felt him cup her face and peck her lips one last time, before pulling back with resolution.

"I don't want to rush this," He whispered, brushing his thumb against her cheek. "I waited too long to ruin it in one night. Tell me you understand."

Fiona tried to find her voice, but her breath was still missing. She therefore had to settle for a nod, her fingers curling in his hair.

She hadn't stopped to think about any of it. Once you let go, it was really hard to stop. She would've gone all the way simply because of the way he made her feel.

But now that someone seemed to have turned on their brain, she realized he was right; tonight wasn't supposed to be about that. In her own way, she had been waiting for this, too. But not tonight.

Tonight had been the best night of her life, and this was more than enough to complete it. She had finally broken through her lifelong fears and had found something truly special on the other side.

– And she wasn't going to ruin it by rushing through it.

With a smile, Adam therefore kissed her one final time before he pulled them down on his bed. Unbuttoning his still damp pants, he quickly kicked them off before tucking his sheets over them.

Fiona snuggled back against him as he laid an arm around her and pulled her to his chest. With a sigh, both of them then fell into a peaceful lull from the rain.

"Hey, Fee?" Adam then suddenly whispered near her ear.

She hummed silently, almost asleep already. There was something so comforting about being in his arms all the time...

"Isn't this the life?"

There was a smile in his voice, and even without looking, Fiona smiled back silently.

With him in it... yes, it was.

And it would never be the same without him again.

Chapter 15

The next morning when Fiona woke up, she couldn't remember the last time she had slept this great. But she knew exactly why she had slept well.

Adam still slept soundly next to her, his arm wrapped around her middle section as it had been almost all night. She remembered waking up once and finding him pulling her closer to him when she had somehow managed to scoot away on the already cramped bed. He had gently kissed her shoulder, but then drifted off to sleep again.

It was such a strange feeling. She felt giddy and infinitely calm all at once, like she wanted to jump his bones but at the same time she wanted to lay there for another whole decade. She was exhausted from yesterday, but it had been the greatest night of her life.

Smiling to herself, she snuggled closer to Adam and laid a hand on his chest, feeling his steady heartbeat thump all that potent love he kept in there. He was such an amazing person... how did she ever get lucky enough to be here? Why did he even like her? Would she ever be enough for him? How could she ever match his energy and emotions? Whatever this was, would it even... last?

She had just started overthinking things when Adam suddenly stirred and mumbled something incoherent. Slowly shifting, he then opened his eyes and looked around until he found her. And then, just like yesterday, a tired grin evolved on his whole face.

"Holy shit, it's a good morning," He said and rolled on to his side, capturing her face with his hand. Fiona grinned back, but for some reason blushed. It was so weird... being here with him, like this. But it felt so nice.

"Uhm... good morning to you, too," She whispered back and covered her mouth to hide her morning breath. Adam chuckled and grabbed that same hand and dragged it away.

"You've gotta be kidding yourself if you think I'm not gonna grab a stinky morning kiss from you. It's part of the experience. Get used to it."

"Ew, Adam, nooo..." She protested, but couldn't help but laugh when he did. He moved closer and kissed first her cheek and then the other, but then moved down and covered her lips with his own.

Fiona's eyes fluttered shut by themselves, and she couldn't help but give in. She was still so new to kissing, but Adam made it all so... easy. He kissed her gently and swept her tangled hair away from her face, rolling her onto her back to kiss her properly. Fiona shivered and wrapped her hand around his neck, pulling him closer as the kiss deepened. She almost didn't care that they both probably had terrible breath. He was right. It was what it was, but it was needed.

An involuntary wince then went through her when his body started pressing down on hers. Her bra, which she had slept in, was digging right into her ribcage and the clasp was gnawing between her shoulder blades. Adam noticed her discomfort.

"I'm sorry, am I hurting you?" He quickly pulled back, removing his weight from her body. "I didn't mean to squash—"

"It's my bra," She told, shaking her head. "Not you."

"Oh," He looked relieved for a moment, but then glanced down. "Do you want to change? I have a shirt you can borrow."

Fiona shook her head. She was so nervous, but... she didn't want to borrow a shirt from him.

But she did want her bra off.

"Will you help me with this?" She nervously whispered. It was strange. She wasn't shy as such... or maybe she was? Or maybe, it was because of the reaction she was scared of getting. Being rejected, or being told he didn't want to...

"You want me to...?" He looked down at her bra strap, then slowly wrapped a finger around it.

She nodded. She was so nervous, but she knew what she wanted, even if it felt so... sudden. She just knew she wanted to be closer to him, close in a way that... that made her feel even safer with him. Even if that seemed impossible at this point.

Adam brushed her cheek tenderly, but then leaned down to her lips. His eyes were so deep, so... God, the way he looked at her made her feel so special. It made her shy, but somehow made her want him even more.

He slowly brushed his lips against hers, pulling her neck up to arch her lips. She breathed shakily, but then felt as the anxiety vanished into thin air as her arms wrapped around him and held him close. He kissed her deeper and let a strangled sound escape his lips as she lifted her chest up to him.

His hand sought under the gap beneath her back, and with a bit of fumbling, he managed to unclasp her bra. She felt the instant relief as the tight device was unstrapped from around her chest and let her ribcage exhale freely. It really had ached.

With some awkward maneuvering, she then carefully pulled her bra off of her shoulders and slipped it onto the floor, and as Adam pulled back to look into her eyes, she felt a nervous flutter in her stomach. But the really good kind.

"I won't look if you don't want me to," He said, keeping his lips inches away from hers.

Fiona gulped. She wanted him to look. Wanted him to... God, she was crazy.

Arching her chest up slowly, she ran a hand through his soft hair, but then pulled his lips against hers. His eyes shut, but his lips parted with a low sound and kissed her back. Fiona shifted beneath him, and with some more awkward maneuvering, she managed to fit his body between her legs and wrap them around him.

Adam moved closer and rested his weight on his forearms, just as his lips slowly moved down her neck and took a tentative path down her neckline. Fiona curved her neck up and let herself just focus on the feeling of his lips against her skin. Hot, slow kisses, moving down her chest... her cleavage...

She bit her lip to hide a small moan when she felt his lips touch her breast for the first time. He circled the areola, tracing it with light kisses, before finally... he closed his mouth around it and made her toes curl.

Her throat released a moan she hadn't authorized, but at the sensation of Adam's mouth gently sucking on her nipple, she couldn't help but mewl quietly and cup her mouth to stop more embarrassing sounds from escaping them. Her body burgeoned at his touches, and before she could prepare herself, she felt his hand grasp around her thigh when she was practically clinging to him, arms and legs.

"I don't know what the fuck you're doing, but I'm losing my mind over you," He suddenly breathed hotly between kisses. Fiona bit her lip when he moved up and feathered his lips against hers again. "You're so going to make me break my celibacy streak."

Blushing, Fiona felt him smirk slowly against her lips before kissing them. She hadn't exactly planned on making him break any promises to himself... but she was glad that he did.

Nestled beneath him, Fiona let herself get completely absorbed in Adam's kisses that he couldn't stop giving to her lips. She hardly sensed anything else but him, and she had a feeling he was a goner, too, purely from the depths of his kisses.

And she suspected that was the reason why neither of them heard any footsteps before the door to his bedroom was suddenly opened.

Fiona screeched and quickly pulled the covers up to her chin, while Adam cursed under his breath and awkwardly cleared his throat. Then, turning his head, he gave a sheepish grin to who Fiona had to assume was... "Hiiiii, grams."

An elderly black woman with white hair weaved up into a bun stood in the doorway in a vintage kanga with a floral print. She wore a set of thin glasses and simply shook her head as she looked upon Adam and her. She had a stern face, but the way her eyes sparkled told Fiona she wasn't one you wanted to be a fool around. She would whop your ass.

"Adam, give that poor child a chance to have some breakfast," She then said, and Fiona now realized she also walked with a cane. She pointed it shortly at his messy floor, then shook her head. "And don't think I can't see this mess you still haven't cleaned up. I told you to get that done last week."

"Sorry," Adam mumbled, dipping his head down into Fiona's chest. "I'll do it today."

"Mm-hm. Now you two kids get dressed, and then you come introduce this lovely girl to me," She told, giving Adam a last reprimanding stare. "And then I believe some church time is in order."

She walked off, muttering under her breath, but then shut the door and left them be.

Fiona was embarrassed... to her very soul. "Oh... my God." She couldn't walk out there. She just couldn't. The woman used to be a nun for crying out loud! And she had just walked in on her trying to corrupt her Christian foster child.

"We better get up," Adam chuckled and pecked her lips one last quick time. Fiona remained frozen. "I promise you she's not that bad. She's actually really excited to meet you. Might've mentioned you a few times."

Fiona could still feel her cheeks burning when Adam slowly untangled himself from her and left her with the covers. He grabbed his pants from the floor and dragged them on before standing up.

"Do you wanna borrow the bathroom first? Get dressed?"

"Uhm... yes," Fiona carefully said, still very reluctant to move. If the earth could just swallow her, that would be real nice. "Please."

Offering her a clean t-shirt, Adam then turned around like a gentleman while she slipped it on, even though he had already... seen everything. Fiona then slipped out of bed and tip-toed over to the door that led to the bathroom.

Once locked inside, Fiona caught herself against the sink and cupped her cheeks. Dear lord, how was she going to face going out there and talking to his grams? What had she even been thinking, asking him to take off her bra when it was morning time?!

Shaking her head, mortified at herself, Fiona then lifted her eyes and then had to hold back a shriek.

Her hair... looked hideous.

Thanks to the rain, it was an absolute mess, and with no help from Adam's touchy hands, it was a complete tangle. Her curls stuck out everywhere, and she didn't even have anything to detangle it with. Dear God, why did God hate her? Not only did she get caught in bed with a boy, but she now also looked like a complete mess. And had nothing to fix it with.

Deciding that water was her best option for now, Fiona tried her best to slick her hair back and used the hair tie around her wrist to pull it back into a somewhat decent bun. Then, quickly using the toilet and cleaning her face with another quick splash of water, she came back out into his bedroom, ready to face the horror of meeting his grams.

But instead of finding Adam getting ready, she saw him sitting on his bed, elbows on his knees. He wore a dark expression.

"Adam?" Fiona approached him with a terrible gut feeling. His face was all wrong. "What's wrong?"

Adam slowly lifted his head and looked at her, and it was right then he lifted his hand as well and revealed... her phone.

– The phone she had kept in the pocket of her dress all night, the same phone she had kept on silence ever since... ever since she lied to him about getting her mother's permission.

"It was ringing on the floor," Adam said with a detached voice. "So I answered it. You had 32 missed calls."

Fiona felt all of it slip and slide inside her. "Adam—"

"Your mom wants you to come home straight away," He said and stood up, handing over her phone. "She's not happy, and neither am I, Fiona."

"Adam, I'm sorry," Fiona tried, feeling her gut tear when just shook his head and turned away. She saw his chin jut out as he clenched his jaw. "I wanted to tell you, but I just—"

"You lied," He said. He turned and looked at her with a confused, but hurt face. "Why lie, Fee? What were you actually thinking?"

"I was thinking she wouldn't have let me go, and I really wanted to go with you," Fiona explained with a shaky voice and walked up to him when he turned away again with a disappointed look. That look almost hurt more than the face she knew her mother would greet her with. "Adam..."

"We could've gone out any other day, Fiona," He said, shaking his head. "I wouldn't have minded waiting if she said no. I never wanted to let her think I was stealing you away. Did you ever think how that would make me look?"

"Adam—"

"I think you should go home and solve it with your mom," He said, shaking his head. "And I should come too so I can apologize. Christ, Fee, you didn't even let her know where you were. You had her sick with worry, she was fucking crying on the phone!"

Fiona felt the tears burn in her eyes as well. She had never meant to cause this much trouble. She knew what she had done was wrong, but she had never thought... never expected it to go this far. She knew her mom would've been worried... and she hadn't cared anyway. Just for one night, she hadn't cared.

"Get dressed," He said, giving her a last look before going up to his door with a tired face. "I'll go explain to grams why breakfast will have to wait."

"Adam, I'm so sorry," Fiona whispered. She felt sorry with all of her heart.

Adam looked at her for a long moment before sighing and walking out. "So am I."

Fiona had barely reached the perimeter of her house before she saw her mother bursting out of the front door. She had probably been waiting by the window, waiting to see her coming down the road.

"Fiona Eluka Torrence, who the hell do you think you are?!" She shouted. Fiona cringed already and felt the tears well up in her eyes. "You get inside this house right now, young lady! You are grounded!"

"Mom, please," She feebly tried, but she didn't even get a chance to break through.

Turning her attention to the person walking behind her, her mother glared at Adam who silently looked back. She pointed a hefty finger at him.

"I don't ever want to see you come around here again," She snapped, and despite all that Fiona knew had been waiting for her when she came home, she never expected that.

"No! Mom! Please, it's not his fault," Fiona said and pleaded her mother. "He didn't know—"

"Fiona, it's okay," Adam said, making her stare up at him in horror when he just accepted that he wasn't allowed to see her anymore. What? "Ma'am, I want you to know how sorry I am. I take full responsibility, I shouldn't have—"

"Adam, stop, you didn't know I—"

"—taken her out before asking you personally," He said, looking at her mom remorsefully. "I apologize, and I don't expect you to forgive me. I just wanted you to know that."

"Duly noted," Her mom replied, shortly. Then grabbed Fiona's arm and pulled her towards the front door. "You get inside right now, missy."

"Mom!" Fiona cried and twisted to look back at Adam who stood with a sullen expression and watched her get dragged away. "Mom, please! He didn't do anything!"

"We'll talk about him later," She snapped and dragged her inside the building. Shutting the front door, she then let go of Fiona the second they were inside the kitchen, safe from the outside. But unsafe from all that followed.

Tears caught in her eyes, Fiona sat down on one of the dining chairs and watched her mom pace back and forth in the kitchen, gearing up to what she was about to say. She could see the fumes practically coming off of her, steaming out through her flaring nostrils.

"I can't even find words to begin," She then slowly started, turning towards Fiona who kept her head down. "to explain how much you hurt and scared me last night. When you didn't come home, I assumed the worst. You don't even leave as much as a text message?! Do you have any idea how damn scared I was, Fiona? Do you?!"

"I'm sorry," She cried, hiding her face away in her hands.

"You don't get to be sorry!" Her mom yelled. "The child I raised did not act so irresponsibly and careless! She didn't worry her mother who already lost one person she loved! You don't ever do that to me again, Fiona!"

Fiona was sobbing now. At the mention of her father, it all just ripped inside her. Like a suture rupturing, she felt all the pain inside her run loose inside her veins.

"I lost him, too," She whispered, still crying uncontrollably. "I miss him, too."

Her mom cupped her forehead, but then shook her head. "I know you do, but that doesn't excuse your behavior last night. From this day on, you're grounded until further notice.

That means no more dancing, no more friends, no more ballet audition."

Fiona's head flew up at the sound of that. "What?"

"I want you to go to your room and clean yourself up," She said and gave her a stern glare. "And then I want you to take a damn pill so I know you didn't do something so foolish last night, I—"

"Stop!" Fiona screamed. It all just burst inside her, ringing through her ears. She clenched her eyes shut and felt the tears stream down. "Just stop! You don't even care! If you did, then you would've seen how good Adam has been to me!"

"That's how it starts," Her mom scoffed back. "But all boys his age are the same. I don't care what you say, I don't trust your judgement after last night—"

"He's been helping me!" She shouted, refusing to let her insult him. She had done everything wrong, but by God, she wouldn't let Adam take any of the blame. "He's been so sweet and understanding, and he's helped me in ways you won't ever understand!"

"Well, that's mighty kind of him, but you're my child, and I'm the only one who needs to help you," She stated. "Now get into your room and start—"

"God, will you just listen?!" Fiona screamed and broke down into tears. She let her face fall into her hands as she sobbed helplessly. "He's... been... there... for... me... when yo u... weren't."

A brief silence fell, but it was broken shortly after. "What the hell are you talking about?" Her mom said, harshness tainting her voice.

Fiona sniveled and tried to collect her words. She dried her eyes and then slowly looked up at her mom. "I couldn't... I couldn't... I couldn't dance before Adam helped me," She whispered, feeling more tears well over the rim of her eyes as she remembered that first day where he stepped up behind her and supported her leg. "He helped me... move on." And just move.

"What are you saying?" Her mom knelt down when Fiona kept hiding her face. "Sweetheart, what are you talking about?"

Fiona took a deep breath. She had to get all of it out now. It was due time.

"I haven't eaten... in months," She quietly whispered. She saw her mom's eyes widen and her lips part. "I would throw up... because I didn't deserve it..."

"Fiona..." Her mom's voice broke in half. "Baby...?"

"I couldn't pirouette," The tears rolled down her cheeks, and she closed her eyes. Her breath stuttered in her chest. "I was scared to dance every day, but if I didn't, then dad would've died in vain, and that's why I had to get the into the company, because if I didn't—"

"Fiona," her mom said and immediately cupped her face. She swept her cheeks with her thumbs and looked into her wet eyes. Fiona looked back and saw her mom look completely lost at her. "My sweet baby, why haven't you told me any of this before? Why have you been hiding this from me?"

"Because then you would've been disappointed in me, too," She squeaked, barely audible. Her mom let out a broken sound, but then abruptly pulled her into a bone-crushing hug.

"Baby," She whispered and stroked her over her hair. "Oh, honey. How could you ever think that? Your father and I love you very much. We could never be disappointed in you."

"...Not even after last night?" She reasoned.

She heard her mom sigh deeply. "No, baby. Not even then. I was so angry and concerned about you, but I could never be disappointed in you. You make me proud every day you live and breathe. You're my beautiful baby."

She heard her mother's voice crack, and as if she wasn't crying enough herself, she now heard her mother hiccup, which made her cry even more. "Mommy..."

"I love you so much, Fiona," She gave her a hard kiss on the side of her head, and then pulled her tighter to her body. Fiona shakily brought her own hands around her as well. They hugged each other for what felt like minutes.

"I love you, too," She whispered back, brokenly. "And I miss dad... so much," She cried and buried her head in her neck.

Her mom cupped the back of her head and softly stroked her back. "Me, too, baby. Me, too."

They sat like that for what felt like a whole hour, an hour wherein Fiona didn't let go of her mom and her mom didn't let go of her. She couldn't remember the last time she had gotten a hug that lasted that long... and had felt so strong and full of love.

Not even Adam could top this one. Her mom's hugs were the best thing in the world.

"I'm sorry I yelled at you," Her mom then said, after a long moment. "You just scared me so much last night."

"I'm sorry I didn't say anything," She replied, sniffling a little. "I never meant to scare you."

"Promise me you'll never do something like that again."

"I won't," She promised, but then glared out of the kitchen window, down the street where she and Adam had come from. He was long gone. "But mom... Adam really didn't know. He's only ever been good to me, you have to believe that."

Her mom gave a deep sigh and finally pulled back. Her eyes were a little shiny as well, but she mustered up her stern face. "I'll choose to believe that for now. He did seem like a good kid, but I just don't trust boys his age, sweetheart. They're all up to one thing."

"Adam's not like that," Fiona said, honestly. She smiled faintly at the floor as she remembered how he had pulled away last night right when it seemed like things were going to move too fast... "he doesn't want to do any of that. He just..." She almost said something she realized she wasn't sure about.

They had kissed... but what exactly did that mean for them? They hadn't even had a chance to talk. Things had been so crazy and hectic, they never got a chance to sit down and figure out what this new step in their friendship meant... if friendship was even what you could call it anymore.

"Please don't tell me I can't see him anymore," She begged and saw her mom press her lips tightly together. "Please. He's helping me eat, he's eating with me every day, and he's helping me dance better, and I've gotten friends thanks to him, and—"

"Alright," her mom held up a finger and took a deep breath. "I need to have a serious talk with him, and I think you and I need to talk about all this eating business too, but... until I figure out how to punish you for what you did... you can continue seeing him," She said, making Fiona's heart race. She nearly jumped out of her seat right then, but her mom raised her hand again, "on the condition that we drive over and see him right now, and talk this whole thing out. If he's helped you as much as you say, I believe I owe him the benefit of the doubt."

"Thank you," Fiona surged forward and nearly tipped her mom backwards when she jumped her with a hug. She clung to her and almost shook to her bones in happiness when despite it all, she would still get to see Adam. If he still wanted to see her, that was...

They had driven to his house where his grandma had told them he had taken off to be at the DanceDec. They had briefly exchanged a few words with his grams too, where Fiona's mom got a few words of peace as well, regarding Adam. It was just like Adam had said; his grams wasn't all too bad. She was mostly just talk and sass.

They had then driven to the DanceDec, after saying good-bye to his grams, and pulled up at the front. Fiona had then asked her mom if she could get just a few minutes alone with him first before she came in with her. She just needed to talk to him alone before they even started anything else.

Allowing her a few moments, Fiona therefore found herself ascending the stairs alone and walking towards their usual studio. She could feel her heart pounding in her chest, already emotionally spent enough. She wasn't sure she could handle two trips down the emotional lane...

Twisting the doorknob quietly, she silently peaked in and found him all alone.

He was practicing a few new steps, but from the looks of it, his concentration was somewhere else. When the door opened, he looked up and spotted her through the mirror. He sighed deeply, but his face then softened, probably from looking at her swollen eyes. When he smiled faintly, it gave her just the inch of hope she needed.

Walking inside slowly, she closed the door and watched him abandon the dance floor. He slowly came towards her as well, his body seeming as exhausted as she felt herself. The last 24 hours had been a crazy mess.

Stepping forward, Fiona then looked up in surprise when Adam suddenly wrapped his arms around her and pulled her to his chest. Fiona nearly broke down crying again and clung to his shirt. He didn't hate her. "Hey."

"Hi," She shakily whispered back. They stood like that for a few moments before Adam pulled back.

"Did you talk things out with her?"

Fiona nodded. "Yeah." And then some.

"Did you tell her everything?"

She nodded again and looked up at his eyes. "Everything."

A relieved look slid over his face, and he then pulled her into his body again. Pressing a faint kiss to her forehead, he sighed. "Good."

"Adam, I'm so sorry," She whispered, hoping he understood how much she truly meant it. She never meant to lie to him, but last night had meant so much to her, she couldn't even tell if she would've done the same again. "I'm so sorry I lied to you."

"Don't do it again," He whispered quietly and softly pecked her head again.

"I promise," She whispered back. She was done with lying.

"I like you more than you know, Fiona," He said and suddenly pulled back a little to look into her eyes. His jungly green ones were an array of emotions. "I don't want there to be any lies or secrets between us, not if we're going to do this."

"Do... what?" Fiona felt her heartbeat slowly speed up. Was he talking about...?

His lips twitched a little, and with his thumb, he brushed her cheek. "I hope you don't mind dating a white guy. I still twerk better than you."

Her lips split in a wide grin. Did he just...? "You're so stupid."

"That's girl for shut up and kiss me," He grinned, just before leaning down and capturing her lips. Fiona rolled her eyes, but couldn't help but grin back and wind her arm around his neck when he pulled her real close into his arms.

Feeling his lips kiss her tenderly, but passionately, Fiona threaded her fingers through his hair and felt his body tense up against her. He slowly pulled his lips back, a little out of breath.

"Any chance you think your mom will let me take you out again tonight on a proper date?" He then said against her lips.

When he gave her a cheesy grin, Fiona chuckled dryly. "I think that might be pushing it. But speaking of my mom..."

And as if on cue, that was when the door opened behind them and her mom cleared her throat loudly.

"Shit," Adam cursed under his breath.

That made them two for two.

Chapter 16

They had talked everything through.

After talking with Adam and eventually thanking him for all that he had done for her, Fiona's and her mom had driven home to talk more privately. It was an emotional Saturday to say the least, but Fiona felt they got to say what needed to be said. Now that everything was out in the open, it felt like a burden had fallen off of her shoulders.

That next Sunday morning, against all odds, Fiona's mom had let her go to the DanceDec after church, but now with a new 6 o'clock curfew. At least until her mom found a better way to ground her, she was allowed to see Adam and dance with him, after having explained what dancing meant to her now. Whether or not she would be allowed to go to her audition was still to be determined, though.

But as Fiona walked into the DanceDec that morning and greeted Rani and Kalo and Dimitri and some of the others with a smile and a wave, she realized... she almost didn't care if she couldn't go. The audition had been her goal for so long because she thought that's what she needed to do to honor her father. Now, after working with Adam for some time... she just wanted to dance every day, regardless of the end result in a week.

Walking inside their usual studio, Fiona's lips and mood automatically lifted as she saw Adam warming up on the floor. He was stretching out his hamstrings with a foam roller, but shot a look her way when she came in. His lips turned up in a smile as well and he got up to greet her. "Hey."

"Hi," Fiona let her bag dump down to the floor and tugged a loose curl behind her ear. She had kept her hair down today, but clipped back the front pieces for dancing.

Adam came up to her and looked her over. He couldn't stop smiling as he cupped her face a little and then moved a little closer. Fiona felt her heart flutter, and then felt her cheeks warm up too when he slowly moved down and kissed her gently.

"So, are you ready for another day?" He asked, carefully. After yesterday, she understood why he was being considerate.

"I am," She replied. All she wanted to do was dance with him, especially now when it seemed so much more important.

Adam grinned slowly, then nodded. "Let's get you warmed up then."

They very quickly got warmed up with a quick dynamic stretch and then moved on to what was planned. Adam wanted to go over a few of the steps that they had danced back at the club. They hadn't been all bad, but there was room for improvement.

"So when you move your upper body to the steps of a regular reggaeton, you want it to be an extension of what happens below the waist," He told and stood behind her. He laid his hands on her hips and slowly swayed them from side to side, then around in a circle. "So back, forward, and around in a circle."

"Okay," Fiona concentrated and tried to follow the movements his hands were trying to make her do, seeing him do the same moves right behind her so they followed along. It still sometimes felt weird doing moves she weren't used to doing, but she no longer felt embarrassed. Adam made her feel comfortable enough to do them without fear of feeling stupid.

"So you want to feel it, like this," He said and connected her rear with his right side. "It's a slow grind, but if it sits right, it's going to be great. Let's try it."

He turned on the music and then they both waited as the beat counted down. Fiona concentrated and then kicked into motion when Adam did.

Hand on her hips, he guided her along to the same movements he did, doing them slowly for the sake of practicing. Fiona watched herself closely in the mirror, hoping she was doing it right. Adam nodded slowly and then lowered his gaze to her hips again. He kicked up the tempo just a little, patting her hip whenever she fell out of rhythm. After a few minutes, she finally caught the move and flowed with him as they danced.

"Good," He proudly said and gave her a little grin. Fiona grinned back and watched as Adam then nodded again. "Real good. Are you up for a routine? I'll keep it simple."

"Give me your worst."

He raised a brow. "Damn, what've you done with shy Fiona?" He chuckled and poked her side. "Last week you were wheeling out over twerking. Now you're grinding up against me like it's a piece of cake."

Fiona couldn't help but grin again and shrugged. She really couldn't explain it, other than he brought out a side of her that she didn't think she had. "That better not be a complaint or I'm walking out that door."

"Wouldn't be the first time," He winked at her through the mirror before grabbing her hips again. "Get ready then. I'll amp up the difficulty and see what you'll do about it."

For some reason, she felt so ready for that. Fiona grinned in the mirror, but then got serious as the music started. The beat counted down and Adam took the lead. Fiona felt him guide her hips, felt his hands slide over her body and his chest brush against hers. Spinning her around, he then pulled her into his chest and led her along to the beat as it dropped.

Grinding up against his right hip and leg, Fiona concentrated on keeping the beat and not messing up. Adam was working alongside her, and so far he hadn't corrected her. His hands were on her lower back and her thigh, keeping the rhythm as they took a small step back, then a small step forward. Fiona tilted her upper body back a bit and felt as his hand swept up and caught her between her shoulder blades. But when she moved up again and swung her arms around his neck, Adam abruptly pulled away.

"I'm sorry, did I do something wrong?" Fiona instantly panicked when he walked away with a curse. He strode across the room and stopped in front of a wall and pressed his hand against it with a deep sigh, glaring down at the floor with a bent head. "A-Adam?"

"No, you did good," He said in a slightly disturbed voice. He took a deep breath, then blew it out and turned to walk back. "Sorry. Let's go again."

Confused, Fiona didn't get a chance to ask anything more when he started the music again and picked up where they left off like nothing had happened. She hesitantly brought her arms back around his neck, but he then surprised her by spinning her around. Facing the mirror, Fiona frowned a little, but decided to forget about it for now and focus on dancing. Adam was gripping her hips again and trying to get her to fall in with the rhythm.

"Don't forget your left leg," He said and tapped her a little. "You tend to favor your right side a little more. Get both working."

Fiona nodded and quickly tried to do as told. She payed attention to her movements and moved when he did. She slowly ground her hips around and leaned her body a bit back against his, brushing up against his chest.

"Fuck," Adam muttered under his breath and abruptly pulled away again. This time Fiona spun around in confusion when he once again walked up to the same wall as before and leaned against it with one hand.

"Adam, what the hell is going on?" She exclaimed. Why did he keep walking away? If she was doing something wrong, why wasn't he just telling her? Had she stepped on his feet without noticing or something? "Adam."

"Sorry," He said, but cursed again under his breath before taking a new deep and very slow breath. "It's not you. I just... need a moment. For fuck's sake."

Need a moment...?

And that's when it clicked.

Fiona slowly cupped her mouth, but almost couldn't hold back her grin when she put two and two together. No fucking way.

"Tell me Jesus did not leave you?" She laughed when he kept cursing at the floor and taking controlled breaths. "Need me to step outside and go find him for you?"

He lifted his head and shot a glare at her over his shoulder, but she saw the corner of his mouth being tugged up in a little grin. "Real funny."

Unable to hold her laughter back anymore, Fiona laughed loudly and shook her head as he finally took a last breath and came back towards her. "I'm so sorry, but I thought you were immune to that sort of thing. I mean, we've been dancing for weeks."

"Yeah," He said, stepping real close to her, which immediately cut off her laughter. "But then you slept in my bed and stripped down in front of me. Not so much immune to that."

Fiona shook her head, but couldn't help but smirk up at him. So that was the reason why? He couldn't stop picturing her half naked?

"You know, my mom warned me that boys your age are only about one thing," She teasingly said and slung her arms around his neck when he rolled his eyes. "I promised her you weren't like that."

"Yeah?" He said and then slowly cupped her face with a slight tease to his lip. He chuckled lowly and leaned down to her mouth. "Oh, you really shouldn't have done that, baby."

And then his mouth crashed against hers.

Fiona nearly lost her balance, but that same second, Adam's arms curled around her back and below her ass, and without further ado, picked her up and made her automatically cinch her legs around him. His lips were on hers, and without any incentive needed, Fiona parted her own lips and kissed him back, heat and excitement running through her whole body. Oh God, it was happening again.

Clinging onto Adam, pressed to his hips, she could feel the slight bulge pushing against her inner thigh, growing more and more as their kiss grew more heated. Fiona couldn't help but let a moan slip past her lips when he clenched her ass just right and pressed her up against his crotch.

Shit, she couldn't breathe.

Panting, Fiona felt hot all over and heard Adam breathing just as heavily beneath her lips. Still, neither of them broke the kiss, too lost in the moment. Oh Lord, if none of them took control of this soon...

Fiona felt a wet heat spread in her lower abdomen. She gulped when Adam's bulge pressed against her inner thigh again, moving a bit closer to where her legs met...

Pulling apart abruptly from his lips, Fiona sucked in a loud breath of air. Adam panted against her lips, but still didn't set her down. She didn't dare open her eyes, didn't dare to look and see how deep his eyes were...

"I-I think we need to c-catch our breaths," She stuttered out, completely winded.

"Yeah..." Adam breathed back, "let me catch yours."

And then before she could object, his lips captured hers again and sucked out whatever remaining air she had managed to find with another scorching kiss.

Letting go of an embarrassing sound, Fiona clenched her legs around him when he suddenly moved. The next moment her back crashed against one of the walls, the cold surface making her gasp.

"You make me lose my fucking mind," Adam cursed against her lips, still breathing hard. He pulled away a little, but not enough for her to find more air. "You don't even understand how crazy I am about you, Fee. God."

Oh, but she think she knew. If it was just half of what she was currently feeling, she had a pretty good idea of exactly what he felt.

"I'm crazy about you, too," She whispered back, dragging her palm down his cheek. She never noticed the faint trace of shaved stubble on his skin before.

"I mean it when I say I want to take things slow with you," He breathed back, calming down a bit. Fiona slowly dared to open her eyes and found him already looking at her with a little smile.

"Yeah," She agreed. Slow was good... temptation was hard. And speaking of which... "so what are we going to do about your new... problem?"

Adam's lips slowly widened in a little grin. Then, kissing her lips gently, he slowly set her down on the floor. "I'll figure something out, don't worry."

"I don't mind... helping you," She whispered, looking up to gauge his reaction. Adam chuckled and shook his head, then leaned down and cupped her cheek.

"Dancing is all about confidence, Fee, and damn yours has grown," He said, keeping his grin. "But you don't get it from a dick, you get it by teasing one, not riding one."

"How about... blowing?" She leaned in and whispered in his ear. She had no idea where this sudden confidence was coming, but... she think Adam was slightly wrong. She was pretty sure a lot of her new confidence had something to do with the fact that she made him lose his mind. Him – the choirboy.

Adam let out a slow, controlled breath, but grinned down at her. Shaking his head again, he then smacked her hip lightly. "Don't test me like that, princess."

She grinned back and then curled her arms around his neck when he leaned down and gently kissed her lips. She couldn't believe this boy was her boyfriend—she had a boyfriend. Her. The shy girl.

Adam was right; Who was this Fiona, and what had she done with the old one? Did she even exist anymore?

The door was smacked open, and a loud howl erupted from the hall.

Pulling apart as fast as possible, Adam cursed under his breath and rolled his eyes as Kalo stood in the doorway, bent over in laughter. Fiona awkwardly hid her face in her hand and Adam stepped behind her to hide... well, his problem.

"I fucking knew it!" Kalo screamed and kept on laughing, pointing at Adam. "It was only a matter of time! My little boy is all grown up, puta madre—"

"Go to hell," Adam replied back, flatly. "Get out."

Kalo chuckled and shot a look at Fiona. "Fucking knew it. Good luck with him, girl, he doesn't eat any bread without cheese—"

Adam stalked up and almost shoved her out of the door before slamming it shut. They could still hear Kalo howling out in the hall, and Adam shook his head.

Well... this made them three for three.

"So I guess we're telling people," Fiona said, still feeling her cheeks flaming. So the other her did still exist.

"She won't tell anyone," Adam promised, slowly walking back to her. "She's fun and games, but Kalo ain't one to spread gossip. Do you want me to go after her?"

Fiona instantly shook her head. "No, no. It's okay." She wasn't really scared that anyone would find out, but at the same time, it was all so... new. She wasn't ready if anyone started asking questions.

Adam pulled her in for a hug and laid his head on top of her head. "We really need some damn locks in this place..."

Fiona couldn't help but grin, but silently disagreed. No locks.

Because without the lack of them, Adam never would've found her.

After a long day of dancing, it came to a reluctant end as the clock struck 6pm. Even though she understood why, Fiona hated that she didn't get to have the last few hours dancing with Adam like they used to. But, to every problem there was a solution.

Walking home hand in hand with Adam, Fiona couldn't help but constantly grin at the pavement. She heard Adam chuckling as well when he saw her face, reading her mind. "I think we're breaking the rules, aren't we?"

"She never said you couldn't walk me home," Fiona pointed out. The trick to getting away with things was in the loopholes of the agreement. Her mom said she had to be home at 6pm on the dot, but she never said that Adam couldn't be the one to make sure she made it there in time.

"She's gonna beat me as if she sees me, won't she?" Adam laughed and bent his head. He then looked down at their joined hands and swung their arms back and forth. "Worth it, though."

Fiona shook her head and felt her whole body warm up. All of the constant questions bubbled up in her head. It just didn't make any sense. Why did he like her? Why was he even attracted to her? She just wasn't this lucky. A guy like him didn't fall for someone like her. Her mind needed a rational explanation, and yet every time Adam looked at her and nearly split his cheeks from smiling at her, all of her worries just seemed so stupid.

He liked her, and that was that. Period.

...But why was that?

Sighing, Fiona moved closer to Adam and laid her head on his shoulder as they walked. Adam clenched her hand in return and laid his cheek against her hair.

"I really want to take you on a date," He then said. Fiona lifted her head and blinked in slight shock.

"What?"

He stopped walking for a moment and turned to look at her. "I know you're grounded and I know you have a curfew, but I'm gonna talk to your mom real soon and ask her if I can't take you out. I want to do right by you before... if anything else happens," He said, taking a curl of her hair and tucking it into place. "Do you mind if I do that?"

Fiona's heart was soaring. She really just didn't understand what she had done to deserve him... she must've killed Hitler in a previous life or something. "No. I... I-I would like that."

Adam's smile broadened, and with that, he then leaned down and pecked her lips lightly. Fiona enjoyed the few seconds of intimacy, but then reluctantly had to pull away when her curfew was getting too close.

They continued walking to her house where, not surprisingly, her mom was waiting in the kitchen, looking out of the window as the came down the road. Adam clenched her hand, and with a last hug, Fiona embraced him tightly before feeling Adam hug her back and then let her go. He watched her walk inside her house safely before turning and walking back the way he came from.

"Was that Adam walking you home?" Her mom asked the second she stepped into the kitchen, taking off her shoes and jacket. She saw her give her a firm look, but then sighed and dumped her bag down.

"Yes."

Her mom didn't reply to that. Fiona sat down in one of the kitchen chairs, watching her mom continue to chop some veggies for the casserole on the stove.

"How serious are you with him?" Her mom then surprised her by asking. Fiona looked up, seeing her mom looking at her with a stern, yet genuine face.

"I... I want it to be serious," She whispered, afraid to call it anything more. These were the questions she was talking about earlier. "And I think Adam wants the same."

Her mom watched her for a moment, narrowing her eyes a little, but then turned back to her cooking. Fiona waited for a few minutes, expecting her to follow her question up with something, but when nothing came, she finally picked up her bag and went for her room. "I'm gonna take a shower."

She had just gotten up from the chair when her mom then finally spoke up.

"Have you had sex yet?"

Fiona stopped dead in her track and felt as every blood cell in her body relocated to her cheeks. "Mom!"

"Have you?" She insisted. Fiona damn well nearly died from embarrassment. "Or anything like that? Has he tried to touch you?"

"Mom!" Fiona hysterically said again, feeling her cheeks burn. This just wasn't happening. "No, we haven't! Adam isn't like that—I'm not like that." But weren't she a little bit, though? "I... we've only just started dating."

"So you plan on going there?"

Lord, if the universe could erase her existence right now, that would be just might great. "I-I don't know! Mom, can we please not talk about this?"

"Oh, we are gonna talk about this," Her mom stated. "You hardly even know this boy. I don't want you doing something stupid just because some guy smiles your way."

Like that wasn't how her and her dad met, she thought to herself. Fiona remembered her mom telling her when she was little how she fell in love with her dad in church after he smiled at her. Their parents disapproved of their love, and it looked like it was about to become a family-thing now. "You don't know him that well, but I do. And he's a good guy, mom. He's never not treated me nicely, and you'd know that if you bothered to get to know him better."

Fiona turned on her foot, ready to march off into her room and escape this conversation when her mom then spoke up again.

"Alright. Let's invite them over for dinner then. Him and his grandma," She said, making Fiona freeze up in her steps again and drop her jaw. She slowly turned around and looked at her mom as if she had grown an extra head. Or maybe just a new one, because the old one would never have allowed this.

"R-really?" Fiona said, almost tripping over the one word. "You... you mean..."

"If you're thinking about getting serious with this boy, I need to know him and his family better. You're about to start therapy next week, and if he's going to be a bad distraction for you, I need to know beforehand."

Fiona shook her head, but couldn't help but grin. "He won't be! Thank you, mom!"

"This doesn't mean I approve yet," She sharply said. "Ask them if they want to come over for dinner tomorrow night, then afterwards we can talk."

Fiona ran up and hugged her mom from behind, squealing into her ear. Her mom coughed a little, but patted her hands. "Thank you, thank you, thank you!"

"Go take that shower now," Her mom demanded, and with a kiss on her cheek from Fiona, she then did just that and ran off to her room.

For the third time that day, Fiona had to ask herself the same question again; how the hell did she get so lucky?

Everything was just coming together perfectly.

Chapter 17

When Fiona left school that afternoon and headed for the DanceDec, she was a bit of a nervous wreck, but that was nothing new at this point.

After the talk with her mom yesterday, she had promised to send the invite onwards to Adam and his grams about the dinner offer. She had never asked anyone over for dinner before, much less with family included, but if this was what it took for her mom to trust her with him, then dinner it was.

… But wasn't it truly just a polite opportunity for her mom to grill Adam some more and ask him the same questions she had asked Fiona yesterday?

So with slightly sweaty palms, Fiona jumped off the bus and walked towards the DanceDec, only to come to a slow halt outside of it when she spotted something unusual.

Adam was standing on the curb in front of the building, still in his school uniform, backpack slung over his shoulder, and was talking to… some guy?

Fiona frowned a little and watched as Adam appeared to be caught in a deep conversation with the man standing in front of him, a guy who appeared to be somewhat mid- to late twenties. He was reasonably tall and had black hair and olive skin. He looked friendly from the looks of his calm demeanor, but there was just something about him that made Fiona feel slightly anxious. He looked... official.

Who was this man, and how did Adam know him?

Carefully walking up to the two of them, Fiona hesitantly cleared her throat when she paused up right behind Adam. He turned around at the sound and then immediately grinned when he saw her standing there.

"And when speaking of the sun!" He laughed and wrapped his arm around her. He tenderly pecked her head. "This is her. Fiona, this is Matteo Jackson, my parole officer."

"Oh," Fiona's eyes widened when Matteo Jackson smiled her way. "It's nice to meet you."

"It's nice to meet you too," Mr Jackson extended his hand, and Fiona politely shook it. "Adam's talked a lot about you."

Fiona looked surprised up at Adam who smiled sheepishly. "He has?"

"I told him you're the one keeping me out of trouble," Adam replied and tugged her closer to him. "And also promised not to get you into any either."

"If only all parolees were as well-behaved as you," Mr Jackson shook his head, but grinned. Fiona couldn't help but notice he spoke with a slight accent, but she couldn't quite pin it down. "Anyway. I just dropped by to say my goodbye. You'll get a call from your new parole officer sometime later this week."

"He's transferring to the west," Adam filled in when Fiona frowned confused. "He's leaving tomorrow, but I was his first assigned case, so I'm actually surprised he hasn't brought me a goodbye gift. Like a bag of coke to reminisce the good ole' days."

"Watch it," Mr Jackson pointed a reprimanding finger at him, but did so with a crooked smile. "Alright, I gotta get going. You two take care."

"Whoa, whoa," Adam held up his hands and stepped in Mr Jackson's way when he tried to leave. "It's dance circle Monday. Don't tell me you're trying to leave without a proper goodbye."

"Well, actually, I—"

"Unless you didn't bring it, of course," Adam challenged and looked him up and down with a teasing grin. "I bet old age took it from you and that's why you never show up anymore."

"Oh, so that's how it is?" Mr Jackson replied, chuckling with a shake of his head. "Old man, huh?"

"You know where the circle is," Adam gestured towards the doors and wagged his eyebrows. "Prove me wrong, grandpa. You know, my gram's still single. I could give you her number—"

"Alright, you little asshole," Mr Jackson laughed and then snatched the cap off of Adam's head. He propped it on his own and flipped it around for good measure. "Lead the way."

Adam howled with triumph, then grabbed Fiona's hand and ran inside, dragging her on tow.

"This is going to be amazing, wait and see," He told, grinning to her.

They ran upstairs, where everyone was gathering in the big studio, already starting to form a circle and gearing up for the big event. Rani, Kalo and the gang were there too, and as soon as they saw Adam and Fiona, they all grinned and waved them over.

"What's up?" Kalo wanted to know when Adam headed straight for the stereo. He shook his head and pulled her phone cord out, only to plug his own in.

"MC's outside, he's here for a last dance, so I'm throwing the beat down for him," He rapidly told with a sly grin. "Fuck, he's gonna hate me."

"What are you picking?" Kalo leaned in over his shoulder to follow along, and so did Fiona, only to hear Kalo let out a low laugh when he finally selected a track. "Oooooooh, man. You're dead."

The track started playing, and just in the same moment, Matteo Jackson came into the room, everyone making way for him. Some shook his hand, others fist-bumped him, while a few simply just whistled – mainly the girls.

"Who is this guy?" Fiona whispered to Adam who chuckled and crossed his arms.

"Watch this," He laughed as Jackson stepped into the circle, glaring at Adam with a teasing grin. "He's pure legend. He busts like nobody else, I swear."

Fiona turned her head and now watched curiously as the man everyone apparently seemed geared up to see dance again smirked slowly at Adam.

And then, with a chuckle, Matteo Jackson truly did break it down.

Fiona dropped her jaw and heard as Adam howled and whistled while his parole officer tore up the floor. His feet and his rhythm was something so incredible, even Fiona couldn't believe it. It was like he was on beat with every movement and every loop in the music. He moved his body in ways that looked so effortless, yet so impossible, Fiona could only stare.

But she also couldn't help but notice something else: A lot of the steps he did were steps she had seen Adam do.

Had he been his mentor?

Fiona cheered along with the rest of the crowd as Mr Jackson danced the floor raw and finally ended it with walking up to Adam and pulling him out to join. Adam laughed and stepped right up next to him, and then did a routine that seemed so rehearsed, it had to be a private thing they had together. Fiona couldn't help but smile, seeing how happy Adam was. How come she never knew about this guy before now?

The song eventually came to a finish and transitioned into the next one, and just like that, Adam and Mr Jackson ended their number with a glorious cheer from the crowd. Adam then turned towards Jackson and stuck out his hand, to which Mr Jackson grabbed it and pulled him in for a short hug.

"Give it up one last time for the real MC!" Adam then shouted over all the cheers, which only made the crowd that much wilder. Everyone walked up to say their goodbyes to him, and while they did, Adam sneaked his way back to Fiona, who still stood hidden by the speakers.

"Ready to go?" He asked, panting lightly while picking up his bag, but still smiling like a mad man.

"Are you?" She asked him. "You don't want to say a proper goodbye...?"

Adam shook his head and slung his arm around her. "I don't believe in goodbyes. Especially with feet like that. Believe me, I'll be seeing him again."

He started dragging them out of the studio, but Fiona couldn't help but look back and get one last look at the tall, black-haired man who was still shaking hands with everyone. "Yeah... he really was great out there."

"Yeah," Adam agreed, just as they made it into the hall. "Guess that's why they call him Jagger."

They made it to their studio where Adam walked in first and dumped his bag down, whereafter Fiona did the same. They both sat down on the floor where Fiona watched as Adam started tugging his school tie loose and peeling off his uniform shirt. He wore a white tank top beneath.

"So, one week left," He finally said and stuffed away his things into his bag. Fiona, who had been staring at his muscular arms, snapped her head up and looked confused at him.

"Huh?"

"Your audition?" He reminded her with a raised brow.

Oh, right. The life important audition that her whole life had revolved around... that one. "Right."

"Are you nervous?"

It was strange, but suddenly the audition seemed like the last thing she was worried about. She had a million other things that seemed so much more important... and right now she couldn't even remember why she was auditioning. "Uh... I guess? A little?"

"I think we should start preparing your piece," He stated, then walked up to the one of the walls where a foam roller laid tucked into corner. "You have two weeks of copped attitude and different dance styles to express yourself with. I want to see what we can do with it."

"Okay..." Fiona slowly said, watching him smirk and then toss the foam roller at her. She narrowly caught it.

"Time to stretch you out then," He cheekily winked, but then joined her on the floor for warmups when she rolled her eyes.

But why did that slightly also make her blush?

The day then went on with them first warming up, using the foam rollers and a bit of resistant band training to warm up all their joints. Adam then watched her closely while she warmed up by the barre and helped stretch out her legs and press down on her hips so she got the last inch eliminated in her deep pliés. All of her limbs ached and felt wobbly afterwards, but she hadn't felt this stretched in weeks. Her feet were working overtime and they hadn't even switched to pointe yet.

"Separate those shoulder blades," Adam corrected while she did her routine by the barre. "Elongate your neck. Don't worry so much about looking perfect, focus more on your technique. They're gonna scrutinize you in there if you don't extend your leg straight behind you."

She had always wondered how he knew so much about all these different kinds of dancing, but ballet in particular. She remember he told her he started with ballet, but did he really learn that much from just that?

"Alright, I wanna see you en pointe again," Adam then said, after another fifteen minutes of watching her do her routine. Fiona immediately turned and headed for her bag. "I wanna see if you still remember what I taught you when we first met."

Oh, she didn't think she would ever forget that.

Tying up her shoes and fastening them securely around her feet so they were comfortable, she stepped up to the centre of the floor. Adam stepped up right behind her and lightly gripped her hips as she slowly went on pointe. Then, lifting her leg backwards and slightly letting herself lean forward, she watched and felt as Adam adjusted her posture.

"Keeping that foot tugged in," He noticed with a satisfied chuckle. "Good. How far is your extension?"

"Pretty far," Fiona lifted her leg a bit more and continued to lower her upper body. Adam stabilized her and raised a brow as she kept going down and down... and then down some more.

Standing in an almost perfect vertical split, Adam whistled lowly and then helped her up again to both feet. "That's more than pretty far, show-off. Alright then, let's work some more on your feet. To the barre."

Fiona grinned but then went back to the barre. Together, they then worked on a few different moves that he deemed she was a little rusty in. Since she had never received professional training, all she had had to go from in the past were videos, books and learning by herself. That meant a lot of her techniques weren't up to scratch, according to how the companies wanted you to dance. Every company wanted a different style, but the New York Ballet was looking for the classic and contemporary artists.

After about two hours of dancing, working on her feet and perfecting a few dance moves, Fiona was feeling sore, but good. Adam was sweating behind her as well as he lifted and supported her around on the floor. Around mid-afternoon, they finally both decided on a snack break.

"What've you got?" Adam grinned and looked into her lunchbox where her mom had packed her some healthier alternatives. A sandwich with lots of tomatoes, avocado and chicken slices and an added apple on the side. "Looks so damn good."

"What about you?" Fiona watched as he pulled a lunch sack out of his bag. He had granola bars, a few orange slices and a peanut butter jelly sandwich.

"Want a bite?" Adam offered when he pulled up his sandwich. Fiona eyed the sandwich out and mentally counted the calories. Peanut butter... dense fats... the jam... pure sugar... and the bread... complex carbs...

"Can I... can I have a piece of one of your granola bars instead?" She carefully asked, not feeling quite ready for the sandwich yet. She was getting better at eating bigger and more calorie-dense meals, but... she still had problems when it came to carb bombs.

"Sure," Adam pulled up one of his granola bars which were oats, protein and chocolate-chipped. A bite of that was less damaging than a whole bar.

Fiona nervously watched as he opened the granola bar and broke off a little piece. When he handled it to her, she smiled back and then weighed the piece in her hand. It was just one piece.

"So about your solo," He said, biting into his sandwich. Her attention shifted and she quickly snapped out of her inner turmoil.

"What about it?"

"I'm not sure the song you picked is enough to show off your full range of abilities. Especially now when you've learned so much more and have a whole lot more to add. Would you be interested in changing it up?"

"You mean... learning a whole new solo a week before my audition?" Fiona questioned and suddenly realized she was chewing. She blinked in almost shock when she tasted oats and chocolate. She hadn't even registered she had put the granola piece in her mouth.

Adam nodded and grinned, taking another bite of his sandwich. "Yeah. It's gonna be a challenge, but if you trust me, I'll help you. I think I already have something in mind."

Fiona swallowed the granola piece in her mouth and realized she had liked the taste. She smiled a little to herself, but then picked up her apple. "Can I make up my mind after you show it to me?"

"Sure. I can show you after we're doing here," He waved his sandwich and quickly licked the side when the jam was dripping out. She chuckled a little, but then suddenly remembered something. She had gotten completely sidetracked this morning and had almost forgotten she had something important to ask.

"Speaking of... eating," She said and instantly felt her stom-ach squeeze together tightly and do a flip. "My mom wants to invite you and your grams over for dinner tonight. Would that, uhm... be something you'd want?"

Adam raised a brow, but smiled slowly. "Your mom asked? Well fuck, then I'm not saying no. I'll ask my grams, but any food we don't have to cook ourselves, we'll usually take. We're in."

"You do realize it's my mom's way of feeling you out... right?" Fiona questioned and raised a brow as well when Adam grinned, but then sighed.

"Damn. Sounds kinky," He chuckled, before leaning in to-wards her and pressing a quick kiss to her lips, before smirk-ing slowly. "Good thing you bought me a thong then."

Oh, lord.

Fiona had been so nervous about tonight. After confirming with his grandma, the dinner was officially on and her mom had cooked up a whole meal. Everything had been set up nicely, but in truth it was all just a pretty disguise her mom put out so she could question Adam without them feeling uncomfortable. And that was exactly why Fiona had been pacing the floor in her room for half an hour before they were set to arrive.

What if his parole came up? His prison time? What if her mom found out somehow, and what if that was what made her change her whole mind about him? She was already on the edge with him, even though he had won some points after she found out how he had helped Fiona. Even still... her mom was even more protective of her now that she knew what problems she had been dealing with. If just one thing went wrong tonight...

Fiona had been a mess when they finally showed up, and as if noticing that straight away, Adam had pulled her into a hug and discreetly kissed her neck while her mom and his grams were saying hi. He had squeezed her hand and then whispered quietly in her ear; "I told her not to bring up my past."

Fiona exhaled visibly after that. It wasn't that she was ashamed of his past, it was just that their whole future together was hanging on the thread that was her mother's approval of him. She would tell her about his past when the time was right, but tonight wasn't it. Tonight was all about kissing up and making sure they could still dance together every day.

"Thank you so much for this lovely invitation," Adam's grandma voice as they stepped into the kitchen, after removing their jackets. "I can't remember the last time I had a good home cooked meal that actually tasted good."

"Hey?" Adam said, looking at his grams with a mock-offended look. "I can cook, alright? You just always need fifty pounds of hot sauce before you can taste anything."

"Hush now," His grams patted his shoulder and instead grabbed his elbow. "Help me to the chair, please."

"Of course, sit down," Fiona's mom smiled and gestured towards kitchen dining table. "Dinner's gonna be ready in a second. You want water or some wine? We got both."

Adam helped his grams wobble into a chair and take a seat. You could tell she wasn't walking very well any more, and getting into the chair took Adam lowering her in carefully. Once she was seated, Adam took a seat next to Fiona, who had sat down at the end of the table.

"Water, please," His grams replied. "Everything smells just delicious. Let me know if you need any help, Adam will get it for you."

"Yes, ma'am," Adam prompted and smiled up at Fiona's mom.

"You can help lift that heavy pot there over to the table, if you please," Her mom responded curtly while tossing the salad around, after mixing in the dressing. "Just right over there on the wooden block. Grab the oven mitts on the wall over there, the pot's probably still hot."

Adam immediately got up and effortlessly lifted the heavy pot to the table, after taking the oven mitts. Fiona watched nervously as everything seemed to be going well so far. But for how long? Tonight was going to be a long night.

Pretty soon they all got seated around the table and got ready to eat. Adam's grams led the prayer and they all waited till she had blessed the food. After that, Adam helped plate the food for his grams and offered the same for Fiona and her mom. Fiona was too nervous to even focus on the food, she merely looked between her mom and Adam, waiting for something to happen. Whenever she caught Adam's eyes though, he smiled calmly at her and somehow eased her worry. If only for a few moments at a time.

They made it through the whole dinner and onto dessert, which was coffee cake and coffee, without a single incident. Her mom had asked a few personal questions, but Adam had responded as openly as he usually did. The topic of his past didn't come up, but around dessert, another topic did.

"He was such a sweet boy, right from the start," His grams said and looked at him as he and Fiona sat at the end of the table with a couple of her pointe shoes. After today's dance lesson, she had to repair the seams and change the laces. Adam had offered to help her. "He was delivered to our doorstep sometime in the early morning, we think. It was something right outta an old western movie. A little basket with the sweetest little boy sleeping with his stuffed animal. We don't believe his mother meant him any harm or abandoned him out of hatred. We merely believed she knew his future would be better with us than with her. God bless her soul."

"So you never knew your parents?" Fiona's mom asked Adam.

Looking at the shoe he was sewing, he peaked up with a little smile and shook his head. "No, ma'am. But I've never needed to, either. The orphanage took better care of me than any other place could have. I can't imagine my mother having been able to match their love."

"He's being too kind," His grams reached forward and pinched his cheek like he was still a little boy. Adam actually blushed and looked down. "We did the best we could with him, and he repaid us in all the love he could give us. Adam's always been such a happy soul. I don't know where he gets it from. God sure did give him a heart worth more than gold."

Fiona was actually feeling her heart ache, but also had to press her lips together not to smile. Adam was blushing something furiously and was trying to hide it by keeping his head down and pretending to be focused on repairing her shoe. Even the tips of his ears were red.

"Well... sounds like he found his joy in life," Fiona's mom replied. "He dances well, according to my daughter. She says he's a real pro at teaching."

"Well, he teaches all of the residents over at my friend's nursing home," His grams prompted after sipping her coffee with a smack of her lips. "He visits once a week and helps all of us keep our hides from getting glued to the couches and chairs, pardon my language. He does a real good job of it."

"Actually, speaking of that," Adam now broke in and looked up at Fiona's mom. "Tomorrow's the next time I visit, and I would love to bring Fiona if I could. I know the guys there will love the chance to dance with a pretty, talented girl. Brings them so much joy to just dance."

Fiona widened her eyes. Shit. He just looked her mom in the eyes and asked to take her daughter out without breaking a sweat. How could he even dance with balls that big?

"Dancing at the nursing home, you say?" Her mom pursed her lips ever so slightly. "What time does this... event start?"

"It starts at 6 and ends around 8," Adam replied. "It wouldn't be late at all, and my grams would be there, too. I would have her home within half an hour after 8."

Fiona turned towards her mom in shock and watched her narrow her eyes. Oh, she knew what he was playing at. Using sweet talk and dirty tricks to get her to say yes. The only question was... was she falling for it?

"Please, mom?" Fiona pleaded, carefully. She really wanted to go. Any time she could spend with Adam, even if in the company of a bunch of seniors, she wanted it. "It would just be a little longer than usual. I promise I'll be up and early for school in the morning—"

Her mom lifted a hand. Fiona shut up immediately and held her breath as she watched her mom think. After another moment, she then finally unclenched.

"I suppose I could make this one exception," She then slowly said, watching Fiona's smile almost burst in happiness. "Even though she is grounded. But I suppose a little dispersion couldn't hurt, and especially for such a good cause."

"Thank you, thank you, thank you," Fiona squealed quietly and leaned over to hug her mom with a grin. Her mom hugged her back briefly before pulling back and looking Adam in the eye.

"I want her home no later than 8.45pm. I understand you're very fond of my daughter, but you must also understand that she's currently going through a lot. I have her best interest in mind, and I'm not sure a boy is what she needs right now."

"I understand," Adam replied. "I do really care for your daughter, Ms Torrence, and I want the best for her, too. She lights up like nothing else when she dances, so if she wants to continue to dancing with me, I'll consider it my privilege to be her dance partner. Anything else is just a bonus."

Her mom hummed in response to that and pursed her lips a little. Fiona could tell she really wanted an excuse not to like Adam, but she was finding it very hard. And maybe that was because Adam really only was a sweet boy.

"Well, then," His grams then said, wiping her mouth down with her napkin. "I think we're gonna head home then. Thank you for an absolutely lovely and delicious night, Mrs Torrence. You sure do know your way around a kitchen."

"Thank you," Her mom smiled back and stood up as Adam started helping his grams get up as well. "Would you me like to call you a cab home? Busses can be so unsafe at this time."

"I think we'll manage," Her grams smiled back. "I like to stretch my legs when I can. Lord knows they need it."

They all got up and moved towards the tiny hall where Adam helped his grams put on her jacket. Fiona felt like she could breathe for the first time that whole night as they all started to say farewell, and when it became her turn to say her goodbyes, she got a firm hug from Adam's grams and and even firmer hug from Adam himself.

"I'll see you tomorrow," He whispered in her ear before giving her cheek a chaste peck. Fiona knew her mom was watching them, but she almost didn't care. Adam pulled back after a moment and gave them both a smile. "Thank you so much for tonight."

"Bye," Fiona waved goodbye as they walked out, feeling the urge to run after him. Her mom waved goodbye as well, but left to go clean the kitchen as soon as they were on their merry way. Fiona, on the other hand, stayed and watched them walk down the street, seeing Adam supporting his grams, but glancing back over his shoulder instinctively, as if feeling her still looking.

He shot her a big grin, to which Fiona couldn't help but reciprocate. Then, with a last look, Fiona finally closed the door and sighed happily.

She couldn't wait until tomorrow.

Chapter 18

It was late in the afternoon, almost evening time, and Fiona was walking side by side with Adam, feeling nervous butterflies in her stomach as they neared the building up front.

With her mom's permission, Fiona had come with Adam after a full day of dancing, now heading towards his gram's friend's nursing home to help teach dancing. Some of the other nuns who had retired from the nunnery where Adam had grown up lived there and that's why they so often visited. They were as much a part of Adam's family as the DanceDec was.

Fiona found it almost ironic. For a boy who was an orphan, he had more family than she had. She guessed he had found the family he had always wanted.

"Come on," Adam smiled down at her when she took a deep breath as they walked in through the doors. They were meeting up with his grams who had already gotten there earlier while they were still dancing at the DanceDec. She spent most of her days here with her friends, playing cards and having fun while Adam was out handling the grind.

Fiona smiled back up at him and let Adam take the lead as they walked up to the sign-in counter. The receptionist of course smiled brightly when she saw Adam, and Adam happily introduced Fiona. Fiona felt herself blush, but only because he introduced her as his girlfriend.

Girlfriend.

"It's right down here," He then said, after they had signed in and greeted a few more nurses in the hallway. He led her down another hallway, towards what seemed to lead to a larger, open space. A make-due living room.

"So how does it normally work?" Fiona hesitantly asked. She had never done something like this, and she wasn't quite so sure what they were supposed to do. What she was supposed to do.

Adam grinned a little. "Just follow my lead, tutu."

Grabbing her hand, he then burst into the large living room that was full of seniors sitting around, watching television, talking to each other, knitting, or half-sleeping in their various couches and chairs.

"Alright, everybody get up!" Adam shouted with a wide grin, and Fiona watched as all of the seniors faces instantly looked up and brightened at his arrival. Adam walked into the centre of the room and started pulling all of the crafting tables out to the side of the room and stuffing them away in corners like it was all pure routine – which of course it had to be. "Goddamn, it's like a funeral in here! I see a lot of handsome, sexy people sitting around on their asses and I wanna see you up on this dance floor, guys! Come on!"

Several of the elderly people laughed and started getting up from their chairs, Adam walking around and helping a few of them. There were a few nurses as well, Fiona realized, when she saw a few men and women in scrubs help the ones lying in the couches get up as well or rolling the ones in wheelchairs more to the centre.

"I hope you don't mind, I brought a little assistant to help me today," Adam then announced as he made it back to the centre where Fiona was still shyly standing. "This is Fiona, everyone!"

He gestured towards her with a big smile, and she blushed and nervously waved into the room as all the eyes turned to her. Almost all of them smiled back with a kind look.

"She's gonna help us out with a few steps tonight, but fair warning, gentlemen," He chuckled and walked up to Fiona, wrapping his arm around her. He gently kissed her cheek. "She's taken."

Fiona blushed even more when a few of the seniors aww'ed and even whistled in admiration. Age really didn't define the universal reaction of seeing young love.

"Alright, guys!" Adam then stepped out and clapped his hands, just as most of the seniors had made it to their feet. "Find a partner, don't you dare be shy or I'm gonna grab you first! We're gonna start up with a little salsa for a warmup, and then I want to see those feet of yours show me what we went over the last time – and no Alzheimer's excuses, I know y'all remember it, I thrive on my unforgettableness."

Everyone let out a laugh, including Fiona. Adam's energy was amazing and adaptable as ever. He truly had a charismatic gift for making people feel good and happy instantly the moment he walked in. She really couldn't understand how he had fallen for her, the complete opposite.

It didn't take long before everyone had found a partner while Adam walked up to what turned out to be a closet with a stereo. He plugged in his phone and turned the music up, setting it to something very modern and hyper. Just like he had done with Fiona, back in the start.

"Alright, everyone! Ready to begin! And one, two, three, four!"

Fiona was surprised to see everyone start dancing, suddenly seeming ten years younger as their old bodies shuffled around and their smiles went wide. Adam was right in the centre, having teamed up with an older woman who looked to be happy dancing in his arms. Fiona chuckled and shook her head, cupping her mouth a little when it all just made her feel so... happy.

But it was Adam's face as he salsa'ed around the room with the seniors that made her heart soar.

Her heart was pounding hard in her chest when she suddenly felt a finger tap on her shoulder. She snapped out of her daze and looked to her side to see Adam's grams standing beside her. "Oh! Hi!"

"He sure is great, isn't he?" His grams smiled proudly as Adam shouted instructions to get those arthritic hips shaking and made the room laugh again. "I don't know where he gets that energy from. Lord knows it's as bad as it was when he was a kid."

Fiona smiled a little. She suddenly remembered him telling her that he used to dance around the orphanage so much, his grams signed him up. "Adam told me he's been dancing since he was little...?"

"Mhm. And he hasn't stopped since," She grunted and nodded towards Adam who now spun one of the seniors around who gushed and blushed.

Fiona smiled and couldn't help but shake her head again when the woman patted his cheek lovingly. He chuckled back, but then turned his eyes towards Fiona, as if sensing her looking. He sent her a grin and waved her over a quick hand gesture.

"I guess that's my cue," Fiona nervously said and excused herself. His grams merely smiled and nudged her along.

"Go have fun, child."

Fiona made her way through the dancing crowd, towards Adam until she managed to make it to his side. He smiled brightly at her, but then bowed to his dance partner. "Alright, guys! Time for some new lessons! Let's have a circle so me and Fiona can demonstrate a few new steps for you to practice. Robert, I'm gonna walk you through them in a moment."

Fiona followed Adam's glare, which happened to land on what appeared to be a blind man. He was standing with his dance partner and smiled back towards him with an off-kilter wave. "I'd rather have your girlfriend help me," He rasped with a cheeky grin.

Adam laughed while Fiona blushed. "Watch it, Casanova. Alright; everyone take a step back and watch what me and Fiona do! We'll show it fast first, then break it down to you."

Adam quickly leaned in towards Fiona who felt a nervous spike in her stomach. She didn't want to make a fool out of herself in front of all these people, but as usual, Adam had already read her mind.

"It's bachata, just like we did in the club," He whispered in her ear, before taking a hold of her hand and hips. Fiona quickly gulped, but then nodded, hoping she wouldn't accidentally trip. She knew bachata.

The music started, and Adam led them through the simple steps they danced in the middle of the circle, the seniors around them watching along. Adam then slowed it down for them and instructed them, both from the male and female point. He used Fiona as a model, and she merely let him work, silently admiring his passion as he spoke.

"So it's left foot front, left foot back, then right foot front, then right foot back," He instructed loudly, showing the steps with Fiona slowly. "Put your hips into it and keep the count of one-two-three-and-four! Are we ready to try it? Come back on the floor and show me!"

Everyone shuffled and found their partners again, and on Adam's count, everyone followed his lead and did as he and Fiona. They danced along with them, Adam pulling Fiona to the front of the room so everyone could keep their eyes on them. He kept showing them for about five minutes, before he took a round through the room and helped guide the few that required assistance. Fiona stayed up front and watched them all dance; Watched Adam work, but also saw how his eyes kept fleeting up to hers with a quick grin.

He was always looking out for her.

Fiona's heart was soaring throughout the whole dance lesson, and about 20 minutes later, Adam slowed it down for the elders who were already running out of energy. Some had already retired to the chairs, but as he put on a slow song and announced this was the time to relive their high school prom, he advised everyone to grab the last dance with that special someone they secretly liked. This was the perfect excuse, he had vowed.

With that, a few more had gotten up from their chairs, and Fiona had watched as a man bid his grams up to dance, who with a humble smile took his hand and went to the dance floor. Fiona cupped her mouth to hide her smile when the gentleman seemed to puff out his chest in pride. Oh, yeah. He knew he just landed himself a prize.

It was about five minutes later, Adam appeared from the crowd and went towards Fiona. He was still smiling, but came up to her with a deep sigh, pulling his arms around her and kissing her cheek chastely. "Hey. Are you having a good time?"

Fiona smiled back and leaned into his touch as he grabbed her hand. "The best."

"Come on," He said, now suddenly pulling her along. "Come with me for a moment."

Fiona lifted her brows in confusion, but let him pull her out of the living room, just across the hall to another room. "Where are we going?"

Opening the door, Adam pulled her inside what turned out to be another living room, but much smaller than the other and completely deserted. It was shut off in darkness, only the light from the door filling up the room with a notion of light.

"What are we doing here?" Fiona asked as Adam turned towards her. He smiled a little, but then suddenly pulled her close.

Fiona gasped silently, but then realized when his hand kept holding hers and his other hand fell to her back, that they were dancing. He rocked her back and forth slowly, listening to the music coming from the other room.

"Oh," She whispered, smiling a little as she leaned her head against his chest. He chuckled a little and placed a kiss on her head.

"I just wanted you for myself for a moment," He murmured, breathing in her hair.

Fiona felt her cheeks hurting from smiling too much tonight. Even so, her heart somehow ached more.

How was he this perfect?

"You're a really good teacher, you know," She said, letting him rock them back and forth while the music faintly played in the background. "Have you considered... becoming one?"

"I have," He murmured back.

"Good," Fiona agreed. He really would be a good one. It seemed like his calling.

"Did you really have fun tonight?" He then whispered in her ear, after a few silent moments of dancing to the music.

"Mmm..." Fiona hummed back, closing her eyes. She felt so peaceful, leaning against Adam's chest and feeling his thumb rub her back, gently. "It was perfect. Thank you."

"Good," Adam echoed.

Minutes seemed to pass in absolute silence where all they did was dance to the fading music. Fiona couldn't stop her heart from aching. It hurt so much, she was beginning to realize what it truly meant...

The music faded out in the other room and came to a stop, but to Fiona's surprise, Adam kept rocking them back and forth. He kept going long after the music had stopped, so long she suspected he might not even have noticed.

"The song ended," She whispered against his chest. He hummed quietly and then pulled her even closer, sighing deeply against her neck.

"You make me want to keep dancing, even when the music stops."

Fiona felt her heart stutter in her chest.

Lifting her head, she peered up through her lashes and found Adam meeting her gaze. He slowly cupped her face and brushed her cheek with his thumb. Her heart ached even more. "Adam..."

He pressed his lips against hers before she could say anything else. A small gasp fell from her lips, but she didn't hesitate to kiss him back as he leaned down and deepened the kiss.

Moaning softly, Fiona stepped onto her toes and wrapped her arms around his neck as he pulled her closer, so close that all space between them got eliminated. Fiona felt her chest rise and fall rapidly as he pressed her against his hard body. The body she always seemed to miss feeling under her fingers.

When she suddenly felt another hardness pressing against her lower abdomen, a garbled sound fell from her lips when he at the same let his tongue sweep across her lips. She moaned softly into his mouth. "Adam..."

"Fuck, don't make that sound," He whispered. When she felt him stiffen slightly, she definitely felt his bulge growing against her abdomen now.

"What sound?" She breathed back, nibbling against his ear. He groaned lowly and squeezed her ass in response.

"That sound," He cursed under his breath again when she breathed against his neck, almost out of air. "And don't breathe like that either... God, you're driving me insane."

He gripped her ass roughly with one hand and then steered her mouth towards his before roving his own against hers. Fiona trembled and moved even closer, gripping onto his shirt and clawing her fingertips down his chest until she couldn't take it anymore. His bulge was rubbing against her pelvis and she couldn't hold out any longer. She had to.

Moving her hand down, Adam let out a low groan when she carefully cupped him and felt him for the first time. Holy shit.

"Christ, Fee," Adam jolted with a hot sound when she hesitantly ran her palm against him to feel his full size. She has never felt one before, but he felt... equipped. "You fucking blow me away sometimes."

She felt his lips twitch upwards a little when she moaned silently. She was too busy exploring this erotic and thrilling moment to worry. She could feel his bulge pulsing in her palm and the feeling of it made her unconsciously rub her legs together. Why did he feel so good?

"Someone could walk in," He reminded her against her lips, breathing shallowly when she continued to rub him. "Maybe we should... oh, fuck," He cursed when she clenched him again and she felt him shudder in pleasure against her. "Fiona."

He gripped her chin and slammed his mouth against hers before she could protest. The next moment he had her spun against a wall, capturing her face and body in his hands.

Lips woven together, Fiona mewled as Adam pressed her up against the wall and kissed her. He couldn't keep his hand off of her, and she could say the same about her own hers as well. She was gripping tightly onto his him through his pants and couldn't stop rubbing him while his mouth worked against hers. Adam groaned into her mouth with every hot breath they took and shuddered when she touched him just right. Things were heating up fast, and pretty soon they wouldn't be able to turn back.

"Adam," She whimpered into his ear when he pulled her hips towards his own. His bulge pressed perfectly against her and she was losing her mind. "Please..."

She didn't know what she was begging for, but she just knew she needed it and it was Adam who had it.

"Come here," He breathed against her lips. Kissing them, he then pulled her with him, fumbling in the dark as they made it across the room to a separate door.

Shoving it open, Adam clicked on the lights and then locked them inside what turned out to be a bathroom. It had the handlebars around the toilet and everything, but more importantly right now, it was completely closed off for anyone who might walk in.

Not wasting a moment, Fiona tugged on Adam's shirt and watched as he moved closer without hesitation. Pushing her up against one of the walls, he instantly cupped her face and lowered his lips against hers again with a deep groan.

Finally alone, Fiona wrapped her arms around him and pushed her hips towards his when he started grinding against her. She mewled softly again, but then let go of a gasp when he suddenly dug his fingers into her ass and squeezed tightly.

"I need to hear you moan, Fee," He gutturally spoke against her neck, moving closer and cursing against her skin. "It's all I can think about. I need to hear you moan right now."

"Adam..." God, she already couldn't breathe. Now his voice had lowered into that deep, husky voice that made her inner thighs tickle and her knees shake. And then he said that.

"Fiona," He responded with a breathy whisper. Pulling back, he then cupped her face and looked deeply into her eyes. "Can I?"

When his hand slowly tickled up her thigh and under her dress, Fiona nearly melted. Suddenly she knew what she needed. "Yes. Yes, yes, please."

Adam groaned softly at her pleas, but then moved down and kissed her lips gently. Fiona almost couldn't even think anymore when she then felt his hand move up under her skirt and softly trail up her inner thigh.

Trembling with pleasure and heat, she waited anxiously and impatiently as his hand finally made it to the place where she felt like she was melting. She could actually feel how damp her panties were and wondered how wet she would be without them. Those thought quickly vanished when she finally, at last, felt Adam's finger seek out her warm folds.

Gasping, Fiona closed her eyes and nearly felt like fainting. Adam's lips were pressed against her neck, but his fingers were softly pressed against her folds, rubbing her just like she hand rubbed him. The sensation was out of this world and she couldn't keep a pleasurable whimper from escaping her lips. "Adam..."

"God, that sound," He groaned and scraped his teeth against her neck before kissing it hard.

His fingers started moving a little faster and more persistently, and Fiona felt as he slowly started working up her... her orgasm.

Whimpering and moaning, Fiona couldn't help herself from grinding against his hand like he had done with her, and felt as his fingers pressed down on the spot that made her knees turn to jelly. She was shaking everywhere and she couldn't stand still, and out of pure instinct, she reached for his throbbing bulge and started palming it once more.

Groaning and moaning into each other's ears, none of them were made to last long tonight. Fiona was squirming to stop herself from crying out loud in pleasure, and Adam was panting hard against her neck. She could feel his fingers pressing into her panty and touch her swollen folds, seeking out her little bud that would send her right over the edge.

"Adam," She gripped tightly onto her shoulders as her breath grew faster. Adam's hand was moving with determination, and her she could no longer think any coherent thoughts. "Adam...!"

She clung to him as the feeling inside her lower abdomen exploded and extended to the rest of her body. She cried out, but couldn't stop herself when the sensation took a full hold of her body and controlled every movement and sound she made. She was shaking and twitching, spasming as she felt Adam's fingers continue to rub her until she hardly could stand.

"Adam," She cried against his neck and tried to capture her breath when he decided to melt his lips against hers. She clung to him desperately, brushing her fingers through his hair as the feeling inside her slowly subsided and gave her the control back of her body.

After a final few moments of panting, she finally seemed to calm down. She was still a mess, but at least now she could control her breathing. Adam's lips continued to kiss hers slowly, sinking the pace down until they came to a halt together.

Pulling back less than an inch, Adam was panting just as hard as her. He slowly cupped her face and looked her over with a little smile, admiring her probably flushed cheeks and big pupils. Fiona gulped slowly, but then softly brushed his hair back, seeing his eyes as well being about the color of ink.

"You're so beautiful," He whispered heartfelt against her lips. Fiona felt her chest cave in, but at the same time explode with a feeling that almost ached at the intensity. She smiled back up at him, seeing him watch her back so closely and with so much adoration, she almost felt shy.

It was when he carefully leaned down to peck her lips, she felt a hardness against her hip. That's when she realized he was still...

"You didn't..." She said, almost awkwardly. He chuckled a little and shook her head.

"I think I did a little, but I can't come in my pants," He grinned silently and rested his forehead against hers. "It's gonna leave a stain I don't feel like explaining to anyone."

Fiona blushed a little, but then hesitantly bit her lip. He had a point. But what if... "What if you didn't do it in your pants?"

He swiped a lock of her hair away from her face, but then pecked her cheek. "You're not ready for that, princess. And it's not gonna happen here in a handicap bathroom. Another time."

"But... then how are you going to—"

"I'm gonna need a moment alone," He grinned lopsidedly, and she swore that she saw him blush ever so slightly. It was unfair, though; He could watch her come, but she couldn't do the same?

"What if I was ready?" She tried, seeing him pull back and shake his head nonetheless.

"I don't know how to put this delicately," He chuckled and grinned lopsidedly again, lifting her hand and kissing it. "But if you do that for me, I'm gonna make a mess that you won't want to explain to anyone. I promise you, some other time, Fiona."

She sighed with resignation. He had a bit of a point, even if she disliked the truth of it. She really wanted to do this for him, but it was the wrong time and place. Another time... preferably when they were alone and in one of their beds.

"Okay," She therefore said, pouting ever so slightly when he brushed her cheek with his thumb. "I'll... step outside and give a moment then."

He nodded and then leaned down and kissed her lips one last time before pulling back finally. "Thanks."

She stepped out after a last glance and then quickly fixed up her dress and her hair. Then, hearing the door lock up after she was out, she patiently waited—a little awkwardly—while Adam finished what they had started.

It was so crazy to think how fast their relationship had moved forward. Fiona bit her lip to conceal a smile, when against all odds... moving forward fast had felt right. Maybe it seemed fast because... well, because it was, but somehow it didn't feel fast to her. It felt like she had been waiting for this moment her whole life... had been waiting for him... and now that he was here, she didn't want to spend another second waiting.

It was right then a thought struck her. It nearly floored her as it passed through her head and took all of the air from her lungs.

She realized how much she liked Adam. Like, a lot, a lot. Maybe even too much... maybe even...

"Oh, there you are! Have you seen Adam?"

Fiona yelped and spun around to come face to face with Adam's grandma. She quickly smiled to her and then cleared her throat.

"Uhm, he's just using the bathroom," She said. Technically she wasn't lying. "We'll be back in in a moment."

"Actually, I was gonna say I think we're ready to pack up for the evening," His grams replied. "Let Adam know to come help put everything back where it belongs when he's done. I think we're gonna head home after, if you don't mind."

"Of course," Fiona smiled, hopefully not visibly strained. "I'll let him know."

His grams left, and Fiona quickly let go of a whooshing exhale the second she was gone. She then cupped her mouth with both hands to stop her laughter. Holy shit... if she had come in five minutes earlier...

A few minutes later, she heard the toilet flush and then the water tap run. A moment later, Adam walked out with an awkward grin. He pushed his hands into his pants and cleared his throat, but then pursed his lips and looked into the hall, trying to act nonchalant. "So... was that my grams I heard?"

"Yup," Fiona affirmed, biting her lip not to laugh again. "She, uhm, said they're packing up and you should come help. We're heading home afterwards."

"Cool beans," He started laughing at her face and then shook his head and palmed his own face when they finally both cracked. "Sweet Christ, Fee. You're gonna put me back in jail some day soon. I swear."

"I'm so sorry," She laughed back and then pulled him in for a hug. He wrapped his arms around her and then kissed the side of her head with a deep sigh. "I promise I'll try and behave in the future."

"Don't you dare," He whispered lowly in her ear, before swiftly smacking her butt. "We should probably go help my grams. Or she's gonna start to assume things."

"Your grams ain't dumb at all," Fiona chuckled when Adam guffawed out a snort.

"Holy shit, no," He shook his head and rubbed his chest with a laugh. "She's smart as a whip, but she's also deaf without her hearing aids."

Fiona raised a brow. She had never noticed his grams wearing hearing aids. Then again, her hair and scarfs usually hid most of her ears. "Really? So she won't hear whenever you..."

Adam tilted his head back and expelled a loud, exaggerated moan to that as reply.

Fiona cupped her mouth in horror, but then quickly slapped his back when he started walking towards the hall. "Oh my God, shut up!"

"What, baby?" He moaned out and grinned hysterically at her. "Whhhhyyyyyy—ah-ah-ah!"

Fiona slapped his shoulder to shut him up, and it finally worked. But not in the way she had expected, though.

Adam made a loud wince, but quickly tried to mask it by straightening out his face. But it was too late; She had seen.

"Are you sore there?" She questioned, but knew instantly he would just smile at her question and brush it off. And that's exactly what he did.

"Another dance injury," He smiled and held out his hand. "Don't worry about it. Come on."

She looked at his hand, but felt a sudden hesitance in her chest. She would bet almost all of her pointe shoes and money on him having another large and purple bruise on his shoulder.

But why was he brushing it off, was the real question?

She knew that bruise hadn't been there a few days ago, and he knew she knew as well.

"Fee?"

And that's why, despite her inner desire to, she didn't take his hand.

Chapter 19

Flashback ~

"Fee? What's wrong?"

She looked at his face and couldn't help but search for any sign of his lie. He was looking at her with a worried, but slightly furrowed expression. She had to confront him. It was now or never.

"Take off your shirt."

His brows immediately rose. "Damn. Not even a drink first?"

"I'm not kidding," She said sternly and crossed her arms with a serious look. "Take it off and show me your shoulder."

His little grin fell and he slowly looked down. "Fee..."

"Why are you lying to me?" She stepped forward right in that moment as his defeated face gave it all away; he wasn't trying to hide it no more. "Adam."

"Because it's not worth worrying about," He sighed and met her eyes. "It's nothing, I promise you. I've got a handle on it."

How funny was it? He sounded exactly like she did when he confronted her with her problems. "We said no lies—YOU said no lies. You said that you couldn't be in a relationship with—"

"I know what I said!" He shouted and palmed his face. "But you wouldn't understand this, Fiona. There's nothing to be done about it, it is how it is."

"You are getting hurt by someone!" She shouted back. She was not gonna stand there and listen to him say there was nothing that could be done about that. "Are you honestly telling me right now that if I was in your shoes, you wouldn't be yelling at me right now, too?!"

"But you're not!" He said and met her with a hard glare. "You're not in my shoes, and if you were, you would be able to see that I'm telling the truth here, Fee. This is how it is. I can't change it, it's just something that I can't control."

"What do you mean by that? Who's hurting you?" She stepped even closer when he closed his eyes and turned away. "Don't fucking turn away from me! Tell me who's hurting you!!!"

"It's THEM, alright!?" He yelled back and whipped around. "It's the old kids I used to hang with in the streets. Satisfied?"

Fiona was speechless for a moment. Then, with tears pressing in her eyes, she took a step back. "I thought you had quit all your connections to your past."

"I have. It's not like that," He sighed and dragged a hand down his face. "They go at my school. They roughhouse me a little to show some pussy-ass form of dominance and practice their thug skills. Sometimes it leaves bruises, but it's really not that bad. They're just bored and pick on me because I don't fight back."

Fiona gaped. Did he just say... he didn't fight back? "Why the hell would you do that? You just... just stand there and take it?" She couldn't believe she was hearing this. Was this part of his whole 'I sold drugs to kids, so I deserve this' punishment he was giving himself?

"Because if I fight back, it makes it worse," Adam walked up closely to her and tried to cup her face, but she pushed his hands away. She didn't know how to feel, but she couldn't handle his touch right now. Even if she craved to hold him tightly. Or slap him. Or something. She was mad at him, but also... hurt. Why was this happening to him?

Fiona stepped back and wiped her cheeks down when it felt like they were wet. She took a moment to think and felt as Adam watched her.

"This is why I didn't tell you," He silently said. She could hear him coming closer, standing behind her and looking down at her with a soft look. "I knew you'd worry for me, but I promise you, Fee. They're only hassling me because they're bored. It'll all be over when I graduate. They won't be graduating, believe me, but I will, and then I'll be out of there. Do you trust me to handle this my way? ... Fiona?"

Fiona opened her eyes and held back the tears that threatened to spill over as she currently sat in the bus after school. She quickly blinked them away and sat straighter up, looking out of the window.

Right at that point, his grams had shown up to get them to help with the cleanup, so she hadn't been able to reply. They had worked silently while cleaning up, none of them speaking to each other, and the bus ride back to her place had been even more silent.

Adam had carefully reached for her hand and she had let him take it, only because she really needed it. She didn't want to be mad at him. It just... it hurt being angry with him, because she... liked him so much. Thinking of someone hurting him... even if he said it wasn't that bad... she almost couldn't breathe at just thinking about it.

– He was the best thing that had ever happened to her, and maybe even to the whole world. She just couldn't lose him.

And that's why, with a hike in her bag she stepped off the bus and found herself standing in front of the one building that almost everyone drove past on purpose without stopping.

– McCuvie's High School for all of the misfits.

Adam's school.

Taking a deep breath, Fiona held a tight grip on her school bag as she on shaky legs found herself moving forward, heading for the school's entrance. She didn't know what her plan was yet... only that she had to see these bullies for herself and see if Adam was telling the truth or not about not having to worry. But from the size of those bruises...

Fiona had managed to get there just in time for class to end, only by cutting the last class of her own school. She had never cut school before in her life, but for this, she could see no better reason. She had jumped on the bus and rushed over to McCuvie's to see... well, she didn't know what she expected to see yet, but a part of her almost hoped all of this had been in vain.

That it wasn't as bad as she was imagining it.

Walking into the school, Fiona was shocked to see the giant metal detectors and the security their school had, simply upon entering. There were guards with vests like at the airport, and the ones working the metal detectors glared at her sternly as she hesitantly approached. She didn't wear a uniform, so it was obvious that she didn't belong here.

After explaining that she was here to visit a friend, the security people let her through the metal detectors after a pat-down and a search of her school bag. Then, letting her through, Fiona made it into the large hall, just as the bell rung.

A myriad of students rushed out from the respective class-rooms, heading for their lockers and jostling around each other to get ahead first. A few boys were plowing through the hall, playing with someone's backpack, while others simply scurried on as fast as possible, heading to the metal detec-tors where Fiona was standing in an effort to get out.

Looking over the crowd, Fiona stared in slight shock. If she thought her own high school was bad, this was absolutely mayhem. The teachers walking down the hall completely ig-nored the group of teens who were teasing another teenager by taking his hat. They also looked the other way as the future baby mamas of tomorrow were making out with their future baby daddies right in the middle of the hall. Some of the girls even looked to already be pregnant. Of course there were pregnant girls at Fiona's school as well, but just front looking, Fiona could count at least... four in the crowd. Yes, four.

She had never seen such an out of control school before, so full of all the deviant kids you could possibly imagine. But what she didn't see was the face of the one person who didn't belong here.

Squirming nervously, Fiona kept scanning the crowd of identical uniforms, hoping to spot a familiar tuft of hair amidst it all. So far, all she could see were people hassling about and shoving each other aside to get through. It was right when she was considering finally giving up and waiting outside, her head whipped to a boy coming out of a class-room as the last one.

Her mouth fell open when she saw him. It was that same moment she also realized why she hadn't been able to find him.

At the DanceDec, Adam was always the centre of attention; the loudest person in the room and the joy that started the party. Always smiling.

But the boy walking down the hall? He had his head down and was dodging the arms and sharp shoulders and looks of other people. He looked nothing like Adam, and yet... it was him.

Fiona gaped. She almost didn't recognize Adam as he quietly trudged to his locker and narrowly avoided getting smashed by a flying basketball slamming against one of the lockers. He jerked to the side and let it bounce off and disap-pear into the crowd again. Then, like nothing had happened, he unlocked his locker and started collecting his books.

Fiona was speechless. She could faintly see the way his face was concealed in a mask of indifference, but also discomfort as people around him started to clear out and head for the metal detectors.

He looked nothing like the happy Adam she knew. If anything, this was the closest she had ever seen him looking
like... herself.

Watching him gather all of his books and finish up, Fiona
felt a stake go through her heart as he with a tired sigh leaned
down to pick up something that fell out of his locker – a sock,
it looked like. He stuffed it into his bag and stood up again,
but just as he did – it happened.

Four large guys walked up behind him and made Fiona's
throat close up in a gasp. She hadn't seen them coming and
neither had Adam, because the second he stood up and spun
around, they were on him.

Shoving him against the locker, Adam let out what appeared to be a grunt and pulled a face as one of the leaned
down and spoke something to him Fiona couldn't hear. Her
mouth fell open when the guy in the front, a black guy with
a tattoo on his neck, jabbed a finger at his forehead, poking
him with a taunting grin. The boys around him laughed and
stood by as Adam did nothing but press his lips together and
lower his eyes.

Fiona gaped. He had been telling the truth. He really did
just stand there and let them bully him.

Looking around the hall, Fiona was furious to see the
teachers merely walking by or standing idly in the hall, talking to some of the other teachers, smiling and laughing like
nothing was wrong. Fiona felt the wrath inside her boil up,
because couldn't they see what was happening? Why was no
one doing anything?!

The hallway started to clear out, and pretty soon there were only Adam and the four other kids left, aside from a few more students standing by their lockers. Nobody was looking at them, as if merely looking was going to earn them a target on their back as well.

The emptying of the students allowed Fiona to actually catch bits and pieces as the four guys continued to talk to Adam when he tried to push past them and placate them. It was obvious he was trying to just leave, but they kept shoving him back up against the locker.

"Going over to dance, twinkle toes?" The one in the front voiced with a condescending smile. "In a rush to see your boyfriend?"

Fiona could tell Adam was fighting an eye roll. For the sake of the situation, though, he only sighed and gritted his teeth. "Come on, Grip."

Fiona gritted her teeth as well. Oh yeah, because being gay was such a bad thing. Dancing, too. Adam was right; these guys weren't graduating school, or life.

"Tell me, does he give you special privileges too?" The guy in the front, Grip, as Adam had called him, now spoke and leaned in towards Adam. "You flash your little white ass at him and he lets you fuck his?"

Fiona had heard enough. With anger boiling inside her, she hiked up in her bag and marched forward. Enough was enough.

All of the guys were laughing at Adam as he turned his head away at their taunts, hiding his growl. It was right then he looked up and noticed Fiona marching down the hall with goddamn daggers in her eyes. His mouth dropped.

"Adam!" She called out, causing all four heads to snap towards her as she came running down the hall, screwing a smile on her face. She would show these assholes. "Baby!"

All of the guys stepped back when she jumped Adam and embraced him tightly, hearing him let out an oomph and stumble a step back. He caught his balance and carefully wrapped his arms around her when she pulled back to look at his shocked face. "Wha—"

She leaned in and pressed her lips firmly against his, knowing full and well the guys were watching with slightly open mouthes. Adam let out a surprise sound, but hesitantly kissed her back, although she sensed his unease stay as he held her.

Finally, after a good moment, Fiona pulled back and looked at him. He stared back at her, still seemingly in shock, but swallowed as she pulled back some more and allowed some space between them. "Fiona... what the hell are you doing here?"

"I wanted to surprise you," She said, still keeping her smile on for theatrics. The guys were still watching them, clearly trying to find a new angle on the situation. "I just couldn't wait any longer."

"Who the hell is this?" Grip, the front guy, then finally snapped when Adam still seemed to struggle for words.

At that, Adam seemed to wake up. "She's—"

"His girlfriend," Fiona voiced, cutting Adam short. She said it harsher than she meant to, and she never knew she could sound so territorial. These assholes needed to know they couldn't just mess with him without messing with her, too. She felt quite proud of herself for that.

Adam, on the other hand, closed his eyes and looked like she had just stepped in something she shouldn't.

"Your girlfriend?" Grip remarked. He sounded unimpressed and took a good long look at Fiona, to the point where she felt like he should've stopped five years ago. The other guys merely exchanged a look between each other, something passing through them.

"And you are?" She quipped, sounding more brave than she felt. She didn't like the way they looked at her, and she was starting to understand why Adam hadn't looked pleased with her coming here and announcing herself.

Did she just get a target on her back?

So what, she angrily thought. She would rather be right here with Adam than watching helplessly from the side.

"We're Adam's friends," Grip then said, looking over at Adam with a little smirk. He only glared back, darkly. "Hasn't he told you about us? Yeah, we're best friends, right, Adam? We go way back."

Adam clenched his jaw and Fiona felt as his grip suddenly tightened around her hip. "Come on," He then said, nudging Fiona. "Let's just go."

Adam almost pulled her along when the guys finally seemed to step back, but followed a few steps behind them. Fiona felt the hairs on her back rise as she heard them grin under their breath. She swore she heard one of them whisper someone about her.

About her ass.

"Walk faster," Adam muttered the second they made it through the detectors. The guys behind them were still caught in the process of going through the detectors, so while they were held up, they made a break for it.

Going outside the school, Fiona felt herself breathe out as the fresh, unencumbered air hit her face and cooled her off. She didn't realize she had been sweating until she felt her neck being clammy.

She had barely gathered her composure when she suddenly felt a hand yank her to the side. She let out a startled yelp, but then felt as Adam pulled her to the side of the building where nobody could see them.

"What the hell are you doing here, Fiona?" He barked out. He was mad, just as Fiona had expected.

"I came here to see the truth for myself!" She yelled back, shoving his hands off of her. He palmed his face and gritted his teeth when she defiantly crossed her arms. "I can't believe what just happened in there."

"I told you," He snapped and pulled his face out of his hands to give her a hard glare. "I had this under control, Fee. I don't need you to interfere for me. It's better this way."

Better? Better for him to get beat up? "They were fucking harassing you!" She shouted when he closed his eyes and tilted his head back. "They were calling you whack names and accusing you of being some white privileged kid and—"

"And who says I'm not?!" He suddenly shouted back and spun towards her. Fiona dropped her jaw. He did not just say that. Him of all people. It was almost ridiculous.

"You're an orphan," She said, seeing him roll his eyes. Oh, no, he was not going to dismiss the truth like it wasn't real and didn't matter. "You grew up on the street, you live in a tiny apartment in the worst part of your neighborhood, and you fight for every penny you own! You work harder than any person I've ever known, so don't you dare stand there and tell me some stupid shit about white privilege. You served you time like they did, you got out on parole—"

"Yeah, and five months earlier than any of them," He cut her off with a harsh voice. Once again, Fiona felt her mouth fall open, speechlessly. Adam gave a sigh and then rubbed his face. "Shit..."

Fiona closed her mouth again and swallowed after a moment. "What are you saying?"

"I'm saying, you said it all," He said and looked down at the concrete with a hard clench of his teeth. "I come from the exact same shit that they've gone through, yet I was let out of juvie with a slap on my wrist while they served almost a full year sentence."

"You got out because your grams spoke for you," Fiona reminded him. "You weren't bad, you were just on the wrong path."

"Yeah, and so were they, but they didn't get any mercy like me. Nobody spoke for them," Adam pointed towards the building, then let out a furious sound and locked his hands behind his neck. Fiona watched him pace back and forth for a moment, breathing deeply to try and contain his temper.

She had never seen him this agitated before.

"Look. I don't blame them for accusing me of white privilege," He then said, pushing out a breath. "I got out of juvie and was given a second chance. They weren't. So if they're angry at me and want to bully me, then—"

"Stop," Fiona said. She saw Adam angrily bite his teeth shut, but she couldn't focus on that right now. "Tell me something. Were they arrested for the same shit as you did?"

"No. They were in the gang a few months before I was. They were dealing, I was only in training, but—"

"So they did worse than you," She stated, walking up to him when he closed his eyes. "This was never about color, Adam. It's about punishment fitting the crime, and I don't give a shit if those assholes in there say you got white privilege, because I know for a fact that you don't," She snapped angrily. Adam slowly looked up at her, his face crumbling. "You chose to do better once you got out—you chose to spread positivity and never to harm another person again in any way. Those assholes in there didn't. That right there is the proof that you were let out on the truth, not skin color."

Fiona was the first to say she had seen white privilege happen almost every day of her life. But she would be damned if she was going to stand here and listen to the one person who couldn't be fitted into that category. Adam had done everything he could to make it on his own since he made his mistakes. If someone had done something more for him because of his skin color, then he wasn't to blame, and he had certainly not taken advantage of his advantage if it had been offered to him.

But she understood why it was easy to feel guilty anyway when you walked the halls with people who were never even offered the same.

"Hey," She quietly whispered, slowly stepping closer towards him when he had closed his eyes and pressed his lips together. She cupped his cheek and carefully stroked his hair out of his face. "I'm sorry if I crossed a line today. I just couldn't... I couldn't stand anyone hurting you. Tell me you wouldn't have done the same if it was me."

"Shit," Adam shook his head and then suddenly wrapped his arms around her and pulled her to his chest. "Don't even say that. I can't even think of someone hurting you."

When he pressed his lips to the side of her head and hugged her tightly, Fiona felt her heart blossom again and allowed herself to melt into his touch. "No one will. And I don't want anyone hurting you either. I just can't, I can't—"

"Hey," When her voice broke, Adam pulled back and cupped her face with a sad little smile. "Look at me, princess. I promise, I'm fine. In less than two months, this is all going to be over. I'm gonna graduate and then I'll never have to seen them again. Okay?"

Fiona pressed her lips together. She still didn't like it. It was still almost two whole months of this, and she just couldn't stand it, dancing with him and knowing now where all his bruises came from. And all the new ones that would follow...

"Can't you tell anyone? The teachers? The principal? The police?"

Adam shook his head and softly cupped her head. "You don't snitch in these situations, Fee. I know it sounds bad, but you have to believe me on this. It'll only become worse if I go to the teachers."

She believed him... but she hated it. She really hated it, and she wanted it to go away. It wasn't fair. It wasn't fair it was him.

"Come on," Adam finally said, when all she did was struggle to find words. She wanted to hug him and never let him go, as if that could protect him. "Let's head to the Dec. Everyone goes sane if I'm not there to annoy them."

Despite her aching heart, he managed to pull a little smile onto her lips, but it faded very quickly as he gently took her hand and started leading her towards the bus. Her insides still hurt and her heart twisted in pain, and she had a feeling it wouldn't go away until they did.

God... two months of this... She wasn't sure she was going to survive having all these feelings...

All these feelings of love.

Chapter 20

The next day, Adam and Fiona walked into the DanceDec together, hand in hand. She had just gotten off the bus as Adam came running up behind her. He had missed his bus again, but at least now she knew why. Even though she couldn't see them, she was sure he was sporting some new bruises underneath his shirt today.

"Don't think about it," Adam had murmured against her ear, after seeing her worried expression. He softly kissed her cheek, as if to help remove any pain. It didn't work; Her heart was burning and her eyes stung. Was there really nothing that could be done?

The next moment, her thoughts were pushed from her head as they walked into the foyer and were met by a cheer from the usual group of friends. Rani, Kalo and Dimitri were all sitting with some of the other guys, some already doing homework, while others were stretching out. As if nothing was wrong, Adam's lips perked up and turned into an instant grin at the sight of of them. "Hey, guys!"

All of them greeted them back with a shout and a wave, but then Rani all of a sudden cleared her throat and held up her hand, as if in class.

"Sooo... are we like, supposed to keep ignoring this or what?" She grinned and pointed between the two of them and their joined hands. Fiona immediately widened her eyes, not even having realized they were still intimately holding hands, fingers braided. Oh, God.

"Ah, shit," Adam cursed under his breath, his eyes turning to Kalo.

"I didn't tell them anything!" Kalo swore, to which Adam snorted. "You haven't exactly been subtle, guys."

Okay, she had a point, Fiona silently thought. But was she ready to go public with it? Were they?

"So, are you together or what?" Rani pressed on, still grinning ear to ear. Fiona felt her face turn red as Adam let out a little groan, but accompanied it with a little smile. "We're gonna find out either way soon enough, so just tell us!"

"Curious fuckers," Adam whispered, but then carefully looked down at Fiona, raising a little brow. Asking for permission.

She guessed there was no hiding it any longer...

– And that's why she gave a timid nod back. There went all or nothing.

"You caught us," Adam confessed with a sly grin when everyone jumped up with a howl and loud cheering. "Christ. Here we go."

"Congrats, gringo!" Kalo cheered and slung her arms around him, rubbing his hair. "They grow up so fast!"

"– I'm older than you."

"But not hotter," She patted his cheek, to which he rolled his eyes and chuckled. Then, turning towards Fiona, he took her hand again.

"Alright, we're gonna change and go dance now, if you all are done with the interrogation," He voiced, a disappointed, but theatrical 'aww' coming from all of them.

"You know we're gonna have to steal Fiona later for some girl talk," Kalo called after them as he begun tucking her away from all the attention. "Just to prepare her for all your STDs and what to do in case she chokes on that tiny—"

"Puta!" He yelled over his shoulder, but then broke into laughter when he got a very long, very heated Spanish reply back. It probably wasn't compliments.

Fiona couldn't help but grin ever so slightly, but her stomach was still bothering her. She was starting to think it would never go away. Maybe she was getting an ulcer simply from worrying.

"I don't have any STDs, by the way, just to be clear," He voiced, just as they came to the girl's bathroom. He opened the door for her and let her step in first.

Fiona rolled her eyes, but then shook her head. "I figured as much."

"And it's not tiny either," He whispered in her ear, leaning down behind her to peck her cheek. "In case you didn't know that either."

Well... technically she didn't, but then again, he had brushed up against her enough times for her to be moderately sure it wasn't. "I figured that as well."

"Good," He grinned, then smacked her ass. "I'm gonna go change then. I'll grab the corner booth."

"I'm just gonna..." She pointed to the first stall, the one furthest away from the one he had claimed. "Use..."

"See you in a sec, baby."

Normally she would be self conscious about peeing in public bathrooms, especially with the boy she liked just a few very short and sound feet away, but the music was booming so loud from the other rooms, she almost couldn't hear him humming to himself in the other end.

And since she had forgotten to use the bathroom before she went on the bus, it was either now or five hours from now.

So, stepping into the first booth, she listened to Adam hum along to the music playing through the wall while doing her business. It was when she came to the... end part, a gasp flew from her lips. "Oh, my God."

"What's up?" She heard Adam finish up and come out of the last booth. Meanwhile, Fiona felt her face redden. "Fiona?"

She looked down into the toilet bowl and felt her heart begin to race. The last time was... three months ago... and now it decided to show up? "Uhm... It's nothing. I just..."

She heard Adam shift on his feet, then step a little closer. "What's wrong, Fee?"

"Nothing!" She fussed, trying to think of a solution. No tampons and no complementary pads... and paper was not an option here.

She heard Adam go silent for a moment, but then heard the door open and close to the bathroom. She thought for a brief second someone had come in, but it was after a second more she realized... he had left?

Blowing out a breath, she palmed her face and tried to think now that she could focus.

She hadn't packed any tampons because it hadn't shown up the last two times. She thought... she thought that maybe... because of her eating habits...

The door abruptly opened again, and this time she heard a distinctively lighter pair of feet come in. "What's up, girl?"

It was Kalo. Fiona almost let go of a cry.

"It's... it's nothing," She whispered, but she wasn't so embarrassed any longer. Only a little. "I just... I got my... period."

"Oh! Damn, you had us worried there for a moment. Do you need a pad or a tampon?"

Just like that; No questions asked. Kalo was increasingly becoming her favorite person at the Dec.

"Tampon, please," She mumbled, and a short second later, Fiona heard the sound of a small pouch opening. Some rustling later and then a hand suddenly appeared below the rim of the stall.

"Here you go. Man, I hate when that happens and you're unprepared. Mother fucking nature sneaking up on you like the bitch she is."

Fiona awkwardly took the tampon, but felt how much she suddenly felt like crying. Oh. Maybe that explained the stomach pains, too. "Yeah. Thank you."

"Don't mention it! I'll wait outside. Adam seriously thought you crapped yourself or some shit," She laughed, before the door then opened. "Seriously, good luck with him."

Fiona laughed nervously, but then palmed her face.

Lord.

Walking out of the bathroom a few minutes later, she walked towards their studio where Kalo told she had sent Adam off to when he wouldn't stop asking questions. Fiona timidly walked in, now suddenly aware of the ache in her lower abdomen and the heavy sensation that followed. Today was going to be great, wasn't it?

The second she came inside, Adam spun around, standing by the stereo, and hurriedly came towards her. "Fiona. Is everything okay? You didn't..."

Didn't what? "What?" She frowned, confused.

He clenched his jaw a little, but then sighed. "Throw up."

Oh. Oh! That's why he had panicked?

"No," She replied, seeing him give her a thorough stare, perhaps checking if she was lying. "I promise. It wasn't that..."

"Then what's wrong? You got me worried," He said, cupping her cheek. "Please, Fee."

Fiona blushed a little. He was really forcing her to say it, wasn't he? He wasn't going to let it go. "Nothing is wrong. I just... got my.... per...iod," She mumbled, looking away and at the floor.

Adam froze for a moment, but then gripped her chin and turned her eyes back to his. When she looked up, she was surprised to see a grin rising on his lips.

"You got your period?" He said, looking almost... excited? What? "Fee, are you telling me..."

"I know, so gross, but you wouldn't let up!" She huffed out, rolling her eyes when he started chuckling. "Asshole."

"You got your period," He repeated, and before she could react, he leaned down and planted a hard kiss on her lips. One that left her momentarily breathless. Whoa. What again?

When he pulled back, Fiona looked at him as he cupped her face happily and couldn't stop grinning. "Okay, you're acting really weird. Stop that. You do know what period means, right?"

"It means you're so fucking healthy, Fee," He said and suddenly hugged her to his body. "Fuck yeah, I know what it means."

Fiona let his words settle, and that's when she felt a soft blush and another kind of ache happen in her body. A little higher, just around her chest. He had been worried about her...

"Yeah, I got it," She whispered, laughing nervously. "But it's been a while. That's why..."

"And that explains the 'oh, my god'," He chuckled, brushing her cheek with his thumb.

Fiona blushed a little again. "I just wasn't prepared..."

"But you're all good now?"

She nodded, reassuringly. "Yeah."

"Do you have any cramps...?"

"A little, but nothing I can't dance through."

"Are you sure?" He asked, looking sincerely at her. "Because we can take a day off and just relax."

"No, I'm good," She promised, smiling up at him when he assessed her words. "Come on. Just teach me something."

He looked at her for a long moment, but then sighed and nodded. "Alright. Just one thing first, though."

"What?"

He jerked her chin up, and without another word, pressed his lips against hers. Fiona stumbled a step back and let out a small squeak, but quickly caught onto his shoulders as he leaned down and kissed her thoroughly.

Looping her arms around his neck, she couldn't help but laugh against his lips when he hummed and pushed her up against the wall, pecking her lips with happy little kisses. He chuckled back, but then brushed her cheek and dipped down low.

His tongue grazed hers, and just like that, Fiona felt her mood change. She felt his hands slide down and grasp her ass, giving it a good clench, before he lifted her off the floor. She quickly cinched her legs around his hips and then felt as he kissed her deeply while keeping her in his arms.

Despite the fact that her mind was all in a scramble and her body ached, Fiona could feel a different kind of feeling suddenly taking a hold of her body. It was hot, sweaty and almost made her heart pound harder than the spot between her legs. Rubbing herself against Adam was only a mild cure that did little to satisfy her. She wanted... needed more.

But it was right about then, Adam kissed her a last time and then slowly lowered her to the floor. Both of them were panting and feeling hot, but Adam, as always, had come to his stupid senses.

"We should... get started on your routine," He breathed against her lips while quickly licking his own. "Needa practice."

Just like that? He expected her to just go along with it after he kissed her like that? Nuh-uh. He wasn't playing fair. "Can't we dance something else today?"

Adam lifted a little brow. "What do you wanna dance?"

Fiona hummed to herself, but the choice was obvious. "I wanna dance reggaeton."

Adam chuckled lowly and leaned down to peck a lips to her cheeks when she pressed her body closer against his. "I don't think you wanna dance reggaeton, baby."

"No?"

"No," He grinned, letting his eyes drop low to where she had slowly started to grind against him. "I think you're trying to push up on me."

"You have a dirty mind," Fiona declared, but of course he was right. She didn't want to dance reggaeton. She didn't even want to dance. God, out of all days, today was the day her period decided to show up.

"And you've got filthy ways, baby," Adam chuckled when her hand bravely crept down to his crotch. "Fiona..."

"You promised I could do it some other time," She argued with almost a whine to her voice. It just wasn't fair, though; she was so horny and she really honestly felt like she wanted to, and here he was, being the perfect gentleman. She didn't want to come off as a horny bitch all the time, but had he met himself? Because he was a hard guy to resist, especially when his lips were quirked sexily like they were now.

"And you think now is a good time?" He teased when she couldn't keep her hands off of him.

"Yes." Period or not, she wanted to do something for him today. Not just because he always supported her and cared about her, but because she really wanted to.

"Baby, you know I'd let you," He whispered in her ear, brushing her hair away to peck her cheek. "But these doors don't lock, remember?"

Right now, the locks were her last concern. "Adam..."

"Jesus Christ. What did I say about breathing my name like that?" He grunted when her hand once again cupped his bulge. "Fuck, Fiona—"

"Please," She whispered, feeling her cheeks flush with color. She really couldn't stop it, because the next words that slipped from her lips were the crudest she had even dared to speak; "I wanna suck you off."

She felt Adam stiffen against her, but definitely not out of shock, but more out of pure lust. The bulge in her hand did a hard jerk, and she most certainly felt him grow. "Jesus Christ, Fiona."

She pushed up on her toes and claimed his lips, and to her delight, he didn't fight her. If anything, she felt him give in and heard him groan as her hand started rubbing his now very prominent bulge in his slacks.

Placing his palm over her hand, Adam kissed her back and followed her movements with his hand over hers, doing slow, upwards tugs until he was groaning in her ear. He bit into her earlobe, before cursing lowly under his breath.

"You're gonna bring me straight to hell," He groaned into her ear, hissing quietly when she boldly clenched him through his sweatpants. "Christ, Fee..."

He had said that before, but for some reason she couldn't find it in her to feel guilty. Instead, a little vixen grin spread on her lips when he kept whispering quietly into her ear all the things she made him feel.

Well... since they were both already going to hell...

"Jesus Christ," Adam cursed loudly when Fiona dropped to her knees and took a hold on his the band of his sweatpants. "Are you sure about this?"

She had never felt more sure about anything.

"Yes," She whispered, peaking up at him, searching his face for his permission. When he sexily bit his lower lip and gave a low grunt, she took that as his green light.

Tugging carefully at his sweatpants, she lowered them just enough to expose his boxers where his bulge was outlining the shape of what lay beneath them. Fiona's eyes slightly widened, not prepared for the full size that hit her. It looked so much bigger up close. Not that it had ever looked small, of course...

"Fee, you don't have to if you've changed your mind," Adam voiced, perhaps mistaking her shocked face for intimidation or fear. Sure, she was a little intimidated, but no matter what, she knew in her heart that this was what she wanted; Him. Adam.

...And making him moan his heart out as she made him feel as good as he had made her feel these past many weeks.

And that's why, waiting no longer, she tugged his boxers below his hips and slid him into her mouth without hesitation.

"Shit!" Adam cursed out loudly and snapped his head back with a throaty groan, gripping onto the wall behind them with a hefty move. "Jesus Christ, Fee..."

Taking him to the back of her throat, Fiona had no idea what she was doing, but going by Adam's reaction, she was doing something right.

She was a virgin through and through, but it wasn't like she was an idiot; she knew the basic principles of what a blowjob consisted of, but all of that seemed so meaningless right now as she had a cock in her mouth for the first time. It was surreal—felt surreal, but most of all, it felt... so good.

Moving her lips up and down his shaft, Fiona looked up to watch Adam as his lips parted in pleasure and groaned out the most sexiest of sounds. He was completely transformed from a moment ago; she had never seen his face be so fragile, yet so beautiful as she sucked on his dick, giving him all that she had to work with.

"Oh, fuck, Fiona," He moaned quietly when she pulled back and placed a few kisses up and down his shaft. "You're so goddamn crazy..."

"Is this... okay?" She whispered, wrapping her hand carefully around his length and testing his firmness. He let out a low grunt, but then saw as his face melted.

"It's more than okay. God, Fiona..."

She took his appraisal with a new dose of confidence and then wrapped her lips around him once more. He immediately groaned again when she starting bobbing back and forth, letting him slide inside her like he would one day soon, somewhere else.

"Your mouth," He groaned, his hand suddenly coming to her hair when she started moving a little faster, testing to see what he liked best. "Fuck. Why are you so... f-fuck..."

His incomplete sentences got lost in translation when he suddenly stiffened and let out a low curse. Fiona then suddenly felt a salty nip on her tongue as she sucked him, and when she glanced up, she saw the perspiration on his chest gleaming.

"Fiona," He ground out, shaking his head. "I can't hold back much longer..."

He was close. Fiona took that as her cue to continue, letting go of a moan herself when his groans grew deeper and started to break in half. It was right when she took him as far back as she could, his hand clumped in her hair and kept her put.

"Fuck!" Adam let go with a hard exhale and panted harshly as he with little jerks unloaded in her mouth. Fiona felt shivers of something go down her back, just as the first load of his juices hit her tongue.

And that's when she realized... she was dripping wet herself.

A couple of seconds later, it was all over. Adam released her hair and Fiona pulled back, swallowing what he had given her. The taste wasn't bad at all, just a little overwhelming at first because she hadn't expected it. From the looks of it, neither had Adam.

"Jesus Christ, I'm so sorry," He panted, helping her up from the floor as he himself struggled to stay upright. He seemed

a little weak in the knees. "Are you okay? I didn't mean to...
it's been too long, I didn't—"

"I liked it," Fiona whispered, her cheeks blushing furiously
as she gave a nervous smile. She had just sucked him off and
swallowed his product. Was that excitement or pride? Or
both?

Adam watched her for a second, but then broke into a
breathless chuckle and turned his head up. He laughed quietly, but then pulled her into his arms and hugged her. "Christ,
Fee. You amaze me."

She grinned against his chest, feeling that happy flutter in
her own chest spread to her stomach and even her hands.
She sighed contently, closing her eyes when Adam softly
kissed the top of her head.

"I think I fucked up your hair," He then murmured with
what sounded like a crooked smile. She couldn't help but
smile back.

"It was worth it."

"I should've taken you on a date first," He then voiced.
Pulling slightly back, Fiona frowned a little when he cupped
her face and looked down at her with a tender look. "We're
doing this all backwards, princess. Shit, I'm supposed to feed
you before I try and get with you."

"We had that date at your grandma's friend's nursing
home," Fiona pointed out. Then let a cheeky smile spread on
her lips. "And I think you did just feed me."

Adam smirked slowly, but then rolled his eyes and shook
his head when Fiona couldn't keep a laugh back. "You little..."

Looking back at her, he then leaned down to her lips and smirked against them. "When did these lips get so naughty?"

"Hmm," Fiona pretended to think. "Maybe it's the company I've been keeping lately."

Adam's grin widened, and with a slow kiss on her lips, he then sighed deeply and rested his forehead against hers. "Fucking corrupting you, baby."

Maybe he was corrupting her. And maybe she was turning a little more naughtier and bolder.

But she loved every last part of it.

"I'm taking you on a date," He then whispered, cupping her face and rubbing his thumb over her cheek, just as her chest started constricting again with emotions. "Tomorrow night. And this time, I'm asking your mom. In person."

Fiona immediately froze up when a vivid fantasy then suddenly played before her eyes.

Adam asking her mom if she could take her daughter out on a date; Her innocent, sweet and virgin daughter, who not minutes ago had sucked his cock in the middle of an unlocked dance studio.

What could go wrong?

Chapter 21

When Moses parted the Red Sea, it wasn't even half as shocking as when Fiona's mom had given in to Adam's request of letting him take Fiona out on a date.

Fiona had watched, gobsmacked, as Adam had followed her home the night before and then talked to her mom for a solid ten minutes alone in the living room while Fiona waited with her ear pressed to the door. It was then both her mom and Adam had come back out to the kitchen, Adam looking rather pale, but nonetheless victorious. Her mom had then proceeded to tell Fiona that the agreement would be that the date would be no longer than two hours long and there would be no alcohol, no partying or any kind of behavior that wouldn't pass in church. Both of them had nodded and agreed, and that's how Fiona found herself going on a date with Adam tonight.

Standing in the DanceDec, in the girl's bathroom with Kalo working on her makeup, Fiona felt nervous ants crawl through her stomach for some reason. She didn't know why she was so nervous all of a sudden—or maybe she did, because this was her first actual real date with a boy, if you looked past the night where they went dancing together.

Tonight would be completely different, wouldn't it?

"You look so fucking nervous and cute," Kalo grinned at her as Fiona tried to breathe without accidentally choking on the ball in her throat. "Relax, girl. Adam's got you covered. I'm sure it's just gonna be a nice, quiet evening."

To that, Fiona couldn't help but send a flat stare back up at Kalo who bit her lip not to crack. Nice and quiet didn't go in a sentence with Adam.

"Okay, you're right. He's probably got something big planned and you're gonna need all the help you can get."

"Oh, God," Fiona let out a shaky breath and started picking at her bottom lip. Kalo quickly flicked her forehead to make her stop.

"Hey, don't ruin the gloss. You look perfect right now and so help me God, I'm not doing your whole makeup again. Girl up."

She was right. Fiona tried to take a calming breath, but the nervous butterflies stayed in her stomach.

After a long day of dancing and rehearsing the new routine Adam had come up with for her audition, the clock had struck 5.30pm. Kalo had burst in and announced it was time to get ready for the big date night, whereafter she had stolen Fiona away and locked them inside the girl's bathroom. The following thirty minutes had been filled with Kalo stuffing her into different outfits (all sponsored by Kalo herself) and doing her hair and makeup, which then finally brought them to now.

"Alright, you're done," Kalo announced, pulling back after coating one last coat of mascara on her lashes. "Jeeeesus, you're gonna knock him over. This I gotta see."

She grinned smugly while Fiona only managed a strained smile. Her hands were clammy and her knees felt oddly wobbly. Was the air in the bathroom becoming thicker?

"Come on," Kalo pulled her up from the floor and then dragged her to the door, where, on the other side, Adam had been waiting impatiently for them to finish up. His frequent knocks on the door and irritated outbursts of "what's taking so damn long?!" had only made Kalo work purposely slower. She had said it was good for him to learn some patience.

But now, as Kalo opened the door, Fiona suddenly felt another kind of nervous as they stepped out and found Adam leaning against the rails, checking his watch. It was the moment he lifted his gaze and laid eyes on Fiona, his whole face went slack.

"Here you go," Kalo grinned and pushed Fiona towards him. "Have your girlfriend back. Don't mess up her hair."

Adam shook his head and slowly cupped his mouth, just as Fiona nervously stepped closer. He didn't tear his eyes off her, but drank up her low-cut, ripped jeans and the tube top that Kalo had borrowed her. Her hair was styled freely with her curls loose and bouncy. Her makeup was kept simple, just some dark liner and mascara with a bit of concealer here and there. A transparent gloss had finished the look, along with a pair of gold hoop earrings.

"Christ," Adam kept shaking his head, his eyes gliding over Fiona until she felt her cheeks redden. "No, no, no, holy shit. You gotta give me a moment here. I gotta call God real quick."

And then he proceeded to fall to his knees and pick his actual phone out of his pocket, pressing it to his ear with a dramatic glance towards the sky. Both Kalo and Fiona rolled their eyes when he then let out a deep holler.

"Yo, God, my man," He spoke into the phone, clutching his chest. "It's Adam. Why the fuck is my girlfriend so hot, man? Seriously? What are you doing to me?" He whined dramatically into the phone. Kalo let out an exaggerated groan, but Fiona couldn't help but burst into laughter and blush. "I'm only one man here, God. How am I supposed to handle all of this? How? Oh shit, I gotta talk to you later," He then finally said, shaking his head and climbing back up to his feet. "I've gotta go kiss her now before she realizes she's way too good for me."

"You're too much." Kalo flatly grunted as Adam stuffed his phone away and ended his little performance with a grin. When he stuck his tongue out at her, she grunted again and then mumbled something in Spanish before turning and walking off. "Too much!"

Adam chuckled after her, but then turned towards Fiona with a little smile, before leaning down and pressing a soft kiss to her cheek. "As long as I'm not too little," He then added in her ear, smirking.

Fiona couldn't help but grin when he pulled back. "You definitely are not," She assured him. Knowingly.

Adam gave a last naughty grin, but then sighed and let his face form into a soft expression. "You look so beautiful, baby."

Fiona's cheeks and insides instantly warmed. She smiled a little, but then looked down, shyly. "Thank you."

"Ready to go?" He asked, to which Fiona instantly nodded. He took her hand and kissed her knuckles, then started leading her down the stairs. "Let's go, princess. I've got a big night planned for you."

The "big night" turned out to be dinner at the best pizza place in the area. When they showed up, Adam had reserved them the best corner booth, where a vase with a single red rose stood. They had since then sat down and ordered a pizza to share with a few cokes.

Fiona knew that with Adam's salary and the fact that he had even been able to do this at all meant he had to have put aside a lot of his savings, if not all of it. He paid for their whole meal, and along with the red rose he had clearly bought for her as well, she knew this was the best he was able to offer her.

And that's why Fiona ate every last bite of the calorically dense pizza and finished every drop of her soda, simply because she knew how much this really truly meant. Her heart ached when he had asked if she wanted dessert as well. She had politely declined.

After finishing their meal, they had then taken a walk through a park to burn off some calories and enjoy the warm night air. Someone was playing music somewhere and Adam had purposely steered them in that direction. They talked the whole way through, getting to know each other on topics they had never talked about before.

"So that's when grams brought me to the DanceDec," Adam told, telling the tale of how he first met the whole gang. "Kalo was already there with Rani, and the second I walked in, they looked at me like they knew I was gonna be trouble," He grinned. Fiona couldn't help but grin too. "Anyway. So my grams drops me off, and that's when Kalo walks straight up to me and pokes me in the chest."

"She poked you in the chest?"

"Poked me in the chest," Adam laughed and shook his head. "And told me if I didn't come here to bust moves, then I should just keep on walking that skinny white ass along to somewhere else."

"So did you? Bust out, I mean?" Fiona asked.

"I did what anyone would've done in that situation," Adam told with a grave expression. "– I laughed my skinny white ass off."

Fiona let out a laugh herself, picturing Adam doing exactly that and a stunted Kalo staring at him like he was crazy. Fiona had been around Kalo enough now to understand what Adam meant when he had said that she was "too much" for him. She acted all high and mighty on the outside, but when you got close to her, it all turned out just to be an act she played to always stay on top of bullshit. No one was gonna pull shit over on her, and the only way she stayed immune was to control the room. The fact that Adam had laughed at her words back then must've done something else to her.

"So what happened then?" Fiona curiously wanted to know, just as they came to a water fountain in the park where a few people had gathered to sit and eat or talk with their friends.

"Well, she got over herself and let me in on her and Rani's dance routine," He told. "Remember the twerk routine?"

Fiona would never forget that; The first day where he had started to teach her and tried to get her to throw it back. When she hadn't, he had proceeded to bring in Rani and Kalo who then showed her, with Adam's unforgettable help, how to throw it back, African style.

"I remember," She affirmed, biting the inside of her cheek.

"Well, they taught me that only to test how far I would go—they even taught me how to whine. When they realized I wasn't half bad and had a few moves of my own, they started to dance more and more with me for real. Then Dimitri came along and wanted to push up on Kalo," Adam grinned, smugly. "So I stepped aside and let him get his ass burned. Or so I thought until... well."

– Until they had walked in on them together in the bathroom less than a week ago.

Fiona bit her lip and felt herself blush, remembering how they found them... she had seen much more than she needed to.

"Anyway, that's how we became friends," Adam told, giving a grin.

Fiona grinned back, but then let a comfortable silence fall as Adam took her hand and braided his fingers with hers. They continued to walk through the park, simply enjoying the night air.

There was a question that had been burning in the back of Fiona's mind for days. Ever since they had had that talk together, that evening in her bedroom, about... his past. About... his "celibacy". She wanted to know what he meant about 'having done some stupid shit in the past he wanted to make up for'.

"Adam?" She carefully asked. He hummed back. "Can I ask you something personal?"

He looked down at her with a little smile. "Of course. What's up?"

Fiona bit her lip a little. How did she start? "I... I just wanted to know... when you told me back in my bedroom... that you had done some stupid shit... what did you mean by that?"

Adam slowly stopped walking. Fiona instantly looked up, afraid she had pushed a bad button, but to her surprise, she only heard him give a little sigh.

"I meant I... did some unchristian things I'm not proud of," He replied, tilting his head down a little. He cut a grimace, but then shook his head. "You need to understand something before I explain. You see, on the street, the only thing that keeps you safe is your rep."

Fiona frowned a little, but listened. "Your rep?"

"People respect you if they know certain things about you. How much cash you've got, which friends you keep... how many girls you've been with," He eyed her out slowly just as Fiona's face fell. "I was just trying to fit in, Fiona. I was so young and dumb and desperate, I did some stupid, stupid shit I regret so much."

"What... did you do?" Fiona gulped, not sure she wanted to know the answer.

Adam sighed again and brought a hand to the back of his neck. Taking a deep breath, he then shook his head. "I slept with this girl. The guys told me you couldn't be a virgin in this whole shit or you'd be a fucking joke, so they... set me up with this chick who was a few years older than me."

Fiona processed his words. The message hurt a little, but the thing that hit her the hardest was how much she could hear the regret in his voice. He had been peer-pressured into sleeping with someone he didn't want to sleep with, all so he could earn the respect of a fake family.

"I'm so sorry," She whispered, lifting her hand to his cheek.

Adam shook his head a last time, then sighed and took her hand. He kissed the top of it. "I made my own choices and they weren't good. I never went back to her and I never went in with someone else. I was ashamed of myself... I still am, but... I'm working on it."

Fiona pressed her lips together. She could see the real repentance on his face as he glanced down at her, trying to give her a smile. It seemed half-broken, but she knew there was something good in there as well.

"I think you're amazing," Fiona whispered, stepping closer to him and wrapping her arms around his neck. "You came back from something bad and you came out a better man. Just look at how well you've done."

He smiled faintly, but then leaned down and softly kissed her lips. "I am. I'm holding the proof in my arms."

Circling his arms around her, Adam then dipped down and kissed her lips deeply, causing Fiona to tremble. His lips were tender, but so passionate, she stopped breathing and simply dwelled in the sensation. It took what felt like several minutes before they finally pulled apart.

"For what it's worth, though," He then said, taking in a deep, shaky breath. "If I had known I was going to meet you, I would've waited. I would've liked to have been with you... as my first."

Fiona felt her heart melt. It pounded so hard in her chest, it almost hurt. She looked up at Adam and saw his gentle face smile so softly down at her, and right then she knew. There was no doubt in her heart any longer.

She lo—

"Shit," Adam then suddenly cursed, taking a step back. "I broke your mom's rule. I'm not supposed to be kissing you."

The bubble burst, and Fiona couldn't help but let out a breathless laugh when Adam, of all people, was suddenly following the rules. What in God's name had her mother said to him in the living room? "Since when do you care so much about the rules?"

"Since your mom will castrate me if I try and get in your pants," He laughed back, taking a step back. He carefully took her hand and started walking again. "And believe me, she meant it. I might not fall asleep tonight."

Fiona laughed again. She couldn't believe he was actually sticking to his promise. That just wasn't going to work. "Hey Adam? Can I ask you one more question?"

"Sure," Adam said, giving her another smile. Fiona took a deep breath, feeling her heart pound. Do it.

"Are you horny?"

Adam immediately stopped walking again and stared down at her in disbelief. Then, after several seconds of shock, he finally let his head tilt back and burst into laughter. "Oh, God."

And then, just as Fiona broke into laughter as well, Adam slapped his hands over his chest and started rubbing himself with a loud, high-pitched moan.

"Oh, God yes!" He hollered, causing the other people in the park to abruptly turn around and glare after Adam who was gyrating on the spot. "God, yeah, I'm so horny, baby, I'm gonna bust so hard! Give it to me, awhhh!"

Fiona was a flaming red color, but couldn't stop laughing as Adam continued his high-pitched moaning. Several people were now glaring after them as Adam finally came down from his fake orgasm.

Turning towards her, he then laughed with her and shook his head, before leaning down and capturing her lips with a surprising hunger. Fiona squealed, but let him tuck her into his body and kiss her passionately. When his tongue swept across her lips, she had to fight not to moan herself.

"I'm such a bad influence on you," He then chuckled lowly against her lips. "Minx."

Fiona grinned and pecked his lips back, but then shrugging innocently. Her little plan had worked though, hadn't it?

"I am horny, though," He then added, cocking a slow, challenging brow at her. "The question is... are you?"

Fiona's eyes slowly widened. He wasn't asking her to... was he? "Adam. I can't."

"Yes you can," He encouraged, grinning wildly at her. "Come on, tiger."

"No, really, I can't," Fiona protested, feeling her heart pound nervously. She respected Adam for not giving a damn, but there was just so many people around, it was too embarrassing. She didn't have his confidence. "I can't."

"Just one big moan," He dared, smirking against her lips. "One big, horny moan and then we'll run. On three, alright? One..."

"No, Adam!" Fiona panicked.

"Two..." He smirked wider.

"Adam!" Oh, God, she couldn't—

"Three!" He shouted.

Fiona felt her cheeks burst into flames. Then, without letting herself have time to think, she expelled her best impression of a loud moan.

– Adam howled, but Fiona didn't get a chance to see his face, because she was already bolting. She was gone like the wind, hearing Adam speeding after her behind her, but still laughing like a mad man. She couldn't believe she had just done that.

She didn't stop running until she was several blocks away, absolutely certain that anyone who could've heard or seen her was at least far enough away to not be able to see her red face now. She hadn't even stopped to check if anyone had turned to look at her, but she also didn't take the chance; She was positive she was burning up, heat practically coming off of her cheeks.

"That—" Adam finally caught up with her as she leaned up against the wall of a building in a fairly deserted area. "Was... the best thing ever! Jesus Christ, I can't believe you actually did it!"

"Shut up!" She flushed, cupping her mouth. Her heart was still racing, still caught on adrenaline. "Oh my God, oh my God..."

"Come here," He said, still out of breath from running. She shook her head wildly, still too embarrassed to function. "I said come here right now and let me kiss those lips."

Adam didn't give her a choice as he pulled her to his chest with a grin and then dipped down to her lips. Fiona squeaked embarrassedly, but felt as the angst melted away from her body as Adam kissed it away with a deep kiss. She slowly loosened up and let herself melt into his touch, moaning quietly as his tongue teased the seams of her lips. That brought on a whole new sensation inside her body.

Standing in the deserted street, Fiona felt herself shiver with warm when Adam then suddenly turned the kiss softer. He cupped her cheek and gentle stroked her cheekbone with his thumb, before pulling back and resting his forehead against hers.

Fiona didn't think this night could've been any better. Everything was as perfect as she could possibly have imagined it. Right until...

"I love you," Adam breathed shakily against her lips. Her eyes flew open and saw him looking down at her, nervously.

Fiona's mouth fell open. Not out of shock, but out of pure... happiness. She replayed the words in her mind, making sure she had heard them just right. He really loved her?

"I love you, too," She whispered back, squeezing her hand into his shirt, right over his heart. His eyes widened just like hers, but she saw the fireworks burst alive inside them.

"Really?" He asked, breathlessly. He sounded as amazed as she felt. How was this even possible?

"Really," She assured him.

It was when his face suddenly became blurry, she realized she was welling up with emotional tears. Adam instantly leaned down and pressed his lips over hers, pulling her tightly into his arms. Fiona didn't hesitate to wrap her own arms around him, clinging to his body.

This was the first time since her father died that any man had told her he loved her. To have Adam's warm arms wrapped around her, to feel his heart beat so rapidly against her own...

Fiona felt as if a part of her that had been missing finally got found. Not in a creepy way, but as in... she finally found what she had been needing all this time. She had loved ballet desperately for years, but ballet was a cruel love, so unforgiving.

But Adam... he loved her unconditionally.

Her father would've loved to meet him.

Smiling happily, Fiona managed to stop crying and pulled away from Adam long enough to give him a bright, if not a stupid smile. Adam smiled back down at her, then slowly chuckled, just as Fiona shook her head. They were being so silly.

"You've no idea how long I've been waiting to say that," Adam then finally said, sighing contently. "Shit, I was so scared it would be too much for you. I was scared that you would..."

"Run away?" Fiona offered. She couldn't believe there had ever been a time she tried to run from this guy. "I'm not going anywhere."

Adam smiled slowly, but then leaned down to place a final kiss on her lips. His mouth lingered a second, simply just dwelling in the closeness...

"Hey!"

Both of them broke apart, but Adam was the one to jolt his head and turn abruptly. Fiona looked confused and followed his gaze, when, suddenly, she realized what had had him startled.

Down the street, a group of four guys came walking down the road, heading their way. The guy in the middle looked familiar and seemed to be pointing at Adam. And that's when Fiona realized why Adam's face suddenly paled.

– It was Grip.

"Yo! It's the ballet boy!" He hollered at Adam, to which his friends snickered loudly like that was the joke of the year. "Damn, I almost didn't recognize you without your tights on! What's doing, twinkletoes?"

Adam clenched his teeth and instantly looked away from them, grasping Fiona's hand. "Come on. Just ignore them."

He started walking her down the street and Fiona followed with a sudden knot in her chest and a lump in her throat. He was walking faster than normal. "They're not gonna try anything, a-are they?"

When she nervously glanced over her shoulder, she noticed they were still following them – also seeming to have sped up their pace.

"Adam," She stressed.

"Just keep walking," He warned. But he couldn't hide the panic in his voice as well.

"Yo, twinkletoes, where are you going so fast?" Grip shouted after him. Fiona whimpered when she heard their voices get louder and closer. "Yo, wait up! Looks like you've got some company."

Fiona felt the terror in her stomach roll over her when Adam clenched her hand tightly. He let out a breath, but then lowly spoke her way.

"Don't speak to them," He whispered. Anxiety bubbled inside her when she saw his face twist in a way she had never seen it twist before. "And whatever happens, don't provoke them."

Fiona quickly nodded, only seconds before they both felt the four guys finally catch up to them. Adam breathed slowly, but kept his hand firmly clenched around Fiona's.

"Hey, twinkles," Grip mused with a big grin, clasping his hand on Adam's shoulder and stepped up beside him. "Out for an evening walk?"

"Come on, Grip," Adam slowly spoke his way. Fiona kept her head down when she noticed a muscle in his jaw work.

"And you've got your girlfriend with you," Grip commented, now stepping in front of Adam. Adam halted in his steps and now Fiona felt as he clenched her hand so tightly, she almost felt her bones crack. "I never caught her name. Why don't you introduce us, Adam."

Adam glared up at Grip while Fiona became acutely aware of the fact that the three other guys had circled them. Her eyes scanned the area for any other people around to help, but the street was still deserted.

"Her name's Fiona," Adam reluctantly pushed out, before pulling her closer to his body. "Now let us through."

"Whoa, whoa, what's the rush?" Grip mused, pushing Adam back when he tried to walk around him. Fiona swallowed a gasp. "We're just talking here. Where'd you find her? Fiona," He spoke out her name slowly, then let his eyes slide up and down her body. "I think we should definitely be friends."

"Come on, Grip," Adam lowly spoke again. He stared up at him, giving him a serious look. "Please. Not tonight."

"We just wanna know where you found her," Grip insisted, once again pushing Adam back when he tried again to walk around him. This time, Adam ground his teeth tightly. "Or should I say, how much are you paying her to stay with you?"

His friends all snickered lowly, passing around low high fives and shoulder bumps. Fiona suppressed the urge to roll her eyes, only because she knew it would only piss them off more.

"We just want to be alone," Adam harshly replied, meeting Grip's eyes. "Just leave us be tonight, Grip. We can do this after school."

"You wanna be alone?" Grip voiced, raising his voice a little. He then glanced over at Fiona who squirmed in her spot. He then let out a dry snort. "You wanna be alone? Shit, poor girl. Maybe we stay and keep you company. Make sure she's properly looked after."

"That's enough," Adam snapped, stepping up to Grip. "I'm not biting tonight, so whatever you wanna say, just leave it. Or better yet, we're leaving. Come on, Fee."

Adam had barely pulled on her arm before Grip shoved him back violently. Adam stumbled a few steps and accidentally backed up into one the guys behind him, who shoved him forward again. He managed to catch his footing, whereas Fiona felt like her knees were gonna give out. God, no, this wasn't happening.

"Please just leave us alone," She feebly said, despite having promised not to say anything. Grip turned his eyes towards her and cocked a sharp brow. "Please?"

"You really wanna be with this pussy?" He lowly spoke, stepping closer to Fiona. "This sorry ass, rat-mouthed little snitch who can't even keep his woman safe?"

"I didn't rat," Adam snapped, but that was apparently it.

The guy behind him reached out and grabbed Adam before he had a chance to see it coming. Yanking his head back by his hair, he then shoved a knee into his back, causing Adam to grunt painfully and fall to the ground. Fiona let out a scream and instantly jumped towards him to help him, but she never got that far.

One of the other guys, a guy with red-dyed hair, gripped her arm and yanked her back, just as Adam jerked his head to the sound of her screaming. He instantly got to his feet again and glared at Grip who was smirking at Fiona.

"Don't touch her. Please, this is between you and me, Grip. Don't bring her into this," He tried to reason with him. Grip slowly turned his eyes back to Adam and watched him press his lips together. "Don't do this while she's here."

"I wasn't talking to you," Grip sneered back, pushing closer to his face. "I was talking to your girlfriend." He turned his head back to Fiona and shot her a smirk. "What do you say, baby? You want some good company?"

"Back off of her," Adam barked when Grip stepped real close to Fiona, who noticeably shrunk down.

In one fluid motion, Grip swung around and rammed his fist into Adam's face. Fiona screamed out loud and watched in horror as Adam collapsed to the ground with a terrible crunching sound. When he looked up, she saw that his eyebrow was severely bleeding and his eye was swelling up. "A-Adam!"

"I said she can speak for herself!" Grip roared down at Adam. "Unless you think she needs your little white ass to speak for her? Is that what you think?"

"Please!" Fiona shouted when the two other guys suddenly grabbed Adam and pushed him down when he tried to get up. Panic rose in her voice, just as her entire body starting shaking with fear. "Please just leave us alone!"

"Fiona, run," Adam groaned out, just as one of the other guys kicked him.

"No, she fucking stays!" Grip yelled, just as Fiona cried out, watching Adam let out a holler of pain. The guy's shoe hit him directly in the stomach and made Adam curl up. "She gonna stay and watch what kind of white scum she's dating. The kind of shitpiece that stabs his family in the back because he's a little fucking spineless coward."

"I didn't rat!" Adam shouted back from the ground, just as another boot landed in his stomach. He coughed hard and finally twisted with a painful grimace.

"But you got out," Grip snarled into his face, leaning down to him. "You fucking got out and continued life like you ain't fucking owe us all a debt. They just put you in a fucking school, give you a nice little job and let you walk around without a leash like you're some harmless fucking poodle. And then you take our women, too?"

Fiona's eyes widened. She couldn't believe the words that had just come out of his mouth. He did not just say...

Grip's fist smashed into Adam's face again, and Fiona screamed at the sight and tried to lunge out. It only resulted in the red-headed guy pulling her back and keeping her pinned to his chest. "Stop! Stop hurting him, please!"

But they didn't. Adam curled up in a ball as all three of the guys pounded Adam while the fourth guy made her watch. When Fiona started screaming for help, he clasped a hand over her mouth and shut her up, only to keep her head turned towards Adam who was moving less and less with every punch, kick and blow. He stopped grunting after a few minutes, and that's when Fiona feared the worst.

"PLEASE STOP!" She cried hysterically, pure panic, fear and hopeless anxiety coursing through her body like a never-ending rollercoaster. She was shaking everywhere and couldn't control her sobs, not even when Grip finally landed the last blow in Adam's face and stood up. She noticed his knuckles were bloodied.

Adam didn't move on the ground, but rather laid lifeless, looking beaten and bruised. He was bleeding from his mouth, ear, brow and nose, not to mention the swollen eye that had swelled so much, his eyelid was stuck shut. Fiona cried hysterically at the sight and twisted and turned to get free.

"Please," She cried, when the redheaded guy finally let go of her mouth to let her speak. She was so busy never ripping her eyes away from Adam's unconscious form, she didn't notice Grip walking up to her.

"He deserved all of it," Grip spat at her, gripping her chin and turning her face his way. "He had it fucking coming. You should be ashamed to be fucking seen with him."

Ashamed? Because of what he had done? Because of his white privilege or the fact that he had chosen to do better than come back to these assholes that claimed to be his family?

"What the fuck's the matter with you?!" Fiona cried, wrestling the red-headed guy who still wouldn't let her go. "He wasn't hurting anyone! You're fucking animals!"

Grip instantly dug his fingernails into her chin and glared harshly down at her. "You said something to me, bitch? You wanna join your boyfriend on the fucking ground?"

"Don't... touch... her..." A weak voice suddenly rasped from the ground. Fiona jolted towards the sound and saw Adam stirring softly on the ground, his face twisting in pain as he did.

"Keep your mouth shut, ballet boy," Grip barked at him, turning to kick him one last time in the stomach. Adam wheezed out a breath, wincing once again. Fiona let out a sob, but didn't get more time to cry as Grip once again turned towards her. "When you're ready to be with a real man who's gonna protect you, you know where to find us. The street's got your back."

Fiona only pressed her lips together to stop herself from saying anything else. She wanted to say a million more things, but knew they would do no good out in the open. She therefore lowered her eyes in defeat, whereafter Grip finally let go of her, same as the red-headed guy. Fiona instantly lurched towards Adam, who once again had stopped moving.

"Let's roll out," She heard Grip announce.

Fiona didn't even bother turning around to watch them run off, but kept her eyes on Adam who looked to be bare-ly breathing. She still couldn't stop crying, but desperately shook all over as she carefully touched his hair.

"A-Adam? Adam, please," She cried, just as she heard him hiss out a pained breath. She immediately went for the phone in her pocket, not hesitating to dial 911. "Just hang on."

He begun coughing up blood and tilted his head to the side, blood dripping from his mouth. Fiona cried out and tried not to panic, but rolled him onto his side so he could breathe.

"F-Fee..."

Deja-vu. Fiona was sucked into her past and suddenly knelt besides her father. "Adam..."

"Am...bu... lance..." He wheezed out, closing his eyes and wincing again when he tried to move. Fiona nodded frantically, already getting passed through to the emergency responder who wanted to know what had happened. He was too far gone to register what was happening.

"I-I need an ambulance immediately," She cried into the phone as the operator asked what had happened. "I-I think he's dying, my b-boyfriend was attacked by s-some guys and I—"

"Not dying..." Adam rasped, quietly. Fiona felt her heart get knocked out of her chest when he then sighed out, closing his eyes. "Not going... anywhere, Fiona..."

Chapter 22

Fiona had ridden the ambulance with Adam, watching while the paramedics worked on him, checking his vitals and hooking him up to all sorts of equipment. It took a little while, but eventually Adam came to, just as they arrived at the hospital. Fiona followed as he was driven into the ER, her heart still stuck in her throat while her mind was caught in the past.

Much like her father, Adam had looked as pale as he had done as they arrived at the hospital. Of course her father had already long ago passed by the time the ambulance picked them up, whereas Adam kept his good eye open, if not looking a little distant. He had lost a lot of blood, not to mention the harsh bruising that contrasted his pale skin in a grisly manner.

Fiona held back her tears as the doctors and nurses hooked him up to a station in the ER. They started by asking him his name and social security number. Thankfully Adam was lucid enough to give them the answers they needed, but he still looked faded. Exhausted. When a nurse then came to palpate his chest and abdominal regions, he winced out loudly in pain.

Fiona then listened to the doctors exchange words. Fractured ribs, possibly broken. A broken nose and a busted ear drum. Possible concussion. A few minor cuts and bruises. Possible blood in the lungs and stomach from choking on the blood from his broken nose. His one good eye that could still open responded well to the flashlight, but the other one was swollen shut.

Fiona felt herself hyperventilate as everyone around her started working on Adam, cleaning up his blood and applying ointment to his bruised eye. When a nurse then finally came up to him with a vial and a bag filled with some liquid, Adam groaned out hoarsely.

"Is there something fun in there?" He rasped, causing Fiona to flip her eyes up and look at his face. He winced shortly as the nurse pricked his arm with the needle and laid a drip. "—Ahh, it better be fun, because that really wasn't."

The nurse smiled softly and wrapped a bandage around the drip to keep it put. "It'll work in a few minutes. It'll help with the pain before we take you up to X-rays."

"Great. If I start singing before, please record it. I've never been high before," He weakly spoke to the nurse who smiled again and took off her gloves. "Promise me?" His lips turned up in the faintest smile. Fiona couldn't believe what she was seeing.

"Alright," The nurse spoke. "You just relax, and don't bother the nurses while they work, alright?"

"Yes, ma'am."

"Alright. Now things might sting a little, too," She warned, turning to Adam's bruised and scraped stomach as she picked out an antiseptic wipe.

"Wait wait, is there alcohol in that?" He slurred tiredly at the nurse, just as she hovered the wipe over his stomach with a raised brow. "Because I can't have that. My grams told me... not to mix alcohol with drugs," He said, cracking a little smile. The nurse let out a chuckle. "She'll kill me if she finds out."

"I'm sure she'll forgive you just this once," The nurse admonished and then started to clean his wounds where the shoes of those assholes had scraped his skin clean off.

Adam winced a little, but didn't let out another peep. It was right then he turned his eyes towards Fiona who was caught in a stiff trance of surreal shock. His smile instantly faded. "Fee? Fee, come here, please."

Standing just outside of his reach, mostly so the nurses could work, Fiona's eyes met Adam's between the blur of her tears. He beckoned her closer with his good eye, and with wobbly legs, Fiona shuffled closer.

Adam extended one hand and didn't hesitate to grabs hers the second she was within his reach. He lifted it to his lip and then kissed her knuckles deeply with his cut lip, closing his eyes and lingering there before finally opening them again. Fiona couldn't help but let out a sob when he looked up at her, so deep with remorse. "Fiona..."

"Adam," She cried. She didn't want to cry in front of him, didn't want to be weak now when he needed her to be strong. She tried to keep them at bay, but it seemed her shock was still in effect; she couldn't control them as they rushed down her cheeks. "Adam..."

Adam pulled her a bit closer and looked up at her with anguish, squeezing her hand a little. "Fee, please don't cry. I'm okay. It's over now. It's alright."

It was over now? How could he even say that? Shit, she was scared shitless and she wasn't even the one who had been jumped. She was afraid to step out onto the street, but much more so, she was scared of him ever doing the same as long as those sick assholes were around.

"No, it's not," She fought, sobbing frustratedly when Adam's brows furrowed with concern. "Nothing is okay and I don't understand how you can sit here and smile and act like all you got was a lovetap!"

"Well... I wouldn't call it a mild lovetap..."

"Adam, I'm serious!" She looked him in the eyes to sober him up. "How can you even want to be near me? They beat you up because you were out with me, because—"

"Hey," He said, and now his eyes hardened. "It had nothing to do with you, Fiona. They already hate me. They just needed one more reason."

And a reason they had gotten. They had been waiting for another reason to beat him up, and as Adam said, they'd found it. Her.

And that's why Adam had looked so regretful when she had told them she was his girlfriend back at his school.

Because she was half-black.

"I don't give a fuck about them," Adam rasped, squeezing her hand when Fiona tried to think straight. Her mind was in shambles and she had no idea what to think or what to do. "Please, let's just forget about them. I'm gonna be fine, okay?"

But she couldn't and wouldn't forget about them. They wouldn't stop coming after him, would they? And now that they had another reason to pick on him, what more did they need?

Would her being with him make him even more of a target?

Fiona pressed her lips together and looked down, feeling her chin wobble. When tears began to well up in her eyes again, she felt Adam take her hand and squeeze it aglain, braiding his fingers through hers.

"Please stop crying, Fee. You're so fucking beautiful and special to me," He whispered, Fiona pressing her lips together to stop her whimpering. "Now get those lips down here so I can kiss them, please."

When he softly pulled on her arm, Fiona didn't hesitate to lean down and press her lips carefully against his bruised ones. The cut on his lip was bad, but Adam still kissed her back gently and groaned softly when she brushed his hair. The nurses around them looked away, but smiled at their little encounter. Fiona then felt Adam softly peck her lips one last time, before drawing back and suddenly began chuckling.

"What?" She asked, confused when he didn't stop.

"Sorry," He continued to snicker and leaned back, cupping his own head now. "I'm so sorry, that's the drugs. I feel them," He laughed and then blinked twice, looking around in amazement. "Shit, that's good stuff. Hey, can I start singing now? Ask the other patients if they have any requests, because

I've got a lot of songs in my head. I'm kinda leaning towards John Legend though," He told and then looked up at Fee with a considerably more wobbly expression than before. "Cuz' aaaaaaaall of me – loves, aaaaaaaall of you..."

Fiona closed her eyes and stepped back as Adam began belting out in the middle of the ER, soaring higher and higher on his drugs as they took a hold of him. He kept singing while nurses worked and tried to shush him down when he was getting too loud. At last, the drugs started to make him sleepy and finally shut him up, making him mumble he was gonna nap now and he'd like a volunteer to cuddle with.

"We're going to take him up to X-ray now," The nurse then announced to Fiona who had stood by and watched Adam finally slump off to sleep, getting some much needed rest. "You should go home or call someone to come get you. It's getting late, and he won't be discharged until the morning. Do you have someone you can call?"

Fiona had already thought that far. While the nurses had called Adam's emergency contact person, which was his grams, Fiona herself knew she eventually had to head home – to her mom, who there would be no escaping from, once she came to pick her up from the emergency room and asked what had happened.

In one night, everything had fallen apart.

Her mom had screamed her off, the second she had showed up at the hospital to pick her up. Fiona had been forced to tell her the truth about what happened... and why it happened.

"A criminal!" Her mom still yelled as they stepped through the front door to their house. "You neglected to tell me your new friend was an ex-gang member and now you expect me to act calm after what just happened?! God, Fiona!"

Fiona who had stayed quiet the whole ride home, took off her shoes and jacket. Her mom kept ranting hopelessly on about how she could've kept this from her. Deep down, she knew she was just shocked and scared about the fact of what had happened tonight. How close it had been... to her being on that gurney.

"Now you see what I mean?!" Fiona's mom kept yelling as Fiona continued to walk through the house until she made it to the bathroom. "You can never trust boys that age, they're always up to no good! And clearly he's had a bad influence on you since you've started lying—"

Fiona had barely fallen to her knees before she felt the bile in her throat. She hurled into the toilet and then felt as all of the adrenaline that had kept her going until now finally wore off. All of tonight's events came rushing over her, and she vomited into the toilet once more.

"Fiona!" Her mom gasped and immediately fell to her side and helped her hold her hair as broken, uncontrolled sobs started falling from Fiona's throat. Everything kept coming back to her, the crunching sound of Adam's face, the horrible cries he had expelled as they had beaten him to near death... his face as he had collapsed on the ground, spitting up blood...

Fiona retched over and over, until her stomach refused to expel any more. She didn't even need to stick her fingers down her throat – the shock did all the work for her, her body shaking uncontrollably and tears welling down over her cheeks.

A guy she loved nearly died tonight and for the second time in her life, it was all her fault.

She stayed by the toilet for hours while her mom brushed her hair and tried to calm her down. It took a long time before she finally managed to coax her into the bed to lie down. She wasn't yelling anymore, but rather seemed to have grown mute as Fiona closed her eyes, hiding her pain.

How could everything have fallen apart so fast? One second everything perfect... and then everything just... collided.

"I love him, mom," Fiona whispered brokenly, sobbing quietly into her hands. Her mom brushed her hair, and for the first time in a long time, she heard a crack in her mom's voice.

"I know, baby," She whispered back. She leaned down and gave her a long kiss on her cheek before pulling back and stroking her hair. "Oh, baby... I'm so sorry..."

"Mommy," She whispered when she started to pull away. More tears welled down her cheeks and she pulled her mom closer again. "Don't leave me, p-please."

"Okay," She whispered soothingly, while keeping her hand gliding over her matted hair. "Alright, sweetheart. I'm right here. I won't leave."

And that's how Fiona managed to catch some sleep. It took hours and she kept waking up and remembering everything all over again, which caused her to start crying and having to start over with her sleep. Her mom stayed with her in her room, sleeping beside her and holding her whenever she woke up.

The last time they had done this was when her father died.

The next morning, Fiona woke up feeling like she had been the one to get beat up. Her body felt sore all over, her eyes felt swollen and there was a hollow feeling right where her heart used to be. The first thought that struck her as she awakened was that Adam was being discharged today.

After a long candid talk with her mom about everything, Fiona managed to convince her that Adam wasn't some common criminal. Deep down, Fiona knew that she had known yesterday as well – she had just been too upset and frightened about the fact that she had called from the hospital. She had feared for her daughter's safety.

Now, though, after having calmed down and seen what it had done to Fiona, her mom knew there was no escaping the fact that Fiona had to see him again. She wouldn't rest until she saw that he was doing better – that he wasn't on the brink of death any longer and had been stitched up.

And that's why, as Fiona left the house that afternoon, after having promised to call her mom if anything at all happened, Fiona now stepped onto the bus that would take her to Adam's place. He had texted her about an hour ago that he was home again, discharged and ready to be nursed.

Half an hour later, she reached Adam's place. Jumping off the bus, she walked the last mile while her heart caught in her throat, unsure of what would meet her. He would still be severely bruised, but maybe at least the pain wouldn't be so bad. He had put on a brave face last night, but the second that nurse had examined him, it had been obvious; they had gotten him good.

Now, though, no longer being in a hospital had to mean he was well enough to be home. So perhaps it wouldn't be that bad...?

Fiona kept lying to herself as she stepped up and hesitantly knocked on the door. She knew deep down he would be every bit as messed up as last night, but every time she thought about it, she wanted to throw up all over again.

All her fault...

The door finally got opened. It was Adam's grandma who gave her a warm smile as she came inside. She thanked Fiona immensely for having been there for him last night and for calling that ambulance, and Fiona had done nothing but smile silently back. If only she knew it was because of her they had attacked him...

"He's in his room," His grandma then finally said, whereafter Fiona nodded shakily and then began walking towards it. Breathe, breathe...

Knocking quietly on his door, Fiona stepped in, not prepared for what would meet her.

Laying on his bed, head plopped against a few pillows and a pack of ice over his chest, Adam turned his eyes the second she stopped up in the door. His face looked every bit as grim as yesterday – if anything, the colors had deepened and his swollen eye was still glued shut. His broken nose had a metal plate on it, but his torn lip was patched up though, and with a little crooked smile, he met her with a tired gaze.

"Hey," He hoarsely spoke, just as Fiona's chest caved in. "There's my nurse."

She couldn't stop it. The tears welled up the second he spoke, and shutting the door, Fiona came towards him and saw his smile fall and turn into a pained frown as she dropped down beside him. He didn't hesitate to reach for her hand, clutching it tightly. "A-Adam..."

"Hey," He whispered, lifting her hand like he had done yesterday and pressing it to his lips. "Shit, Fee. No more tears. I'm in enough pain as is and watching you cry is making it worse. Please..."

But she couldn't stop. Fiona shook her head and hiccuped through her tears, feeling Adam lift his hand to swipe them away. He gently smoothed his thumb over her cheek, but then cupped her face.

"Fiona," He spoke softly, watching her try and control her sobs.

"I'm so sorry," She finally managed to get out. "Adam, I-I..."

"There's nothing to be sorry about," He replied, tugging at the corner of his lip again. "It happened and now we're moving past it. Alright?"

"I can't," Fiona cried, refusing to just let it go. It would never stop haunting her. "Adam... they beat you up. They beat you up b-because... because you were with me."

"What?" Adam slowly asked. She saw his good brow crease into a little line. "No, Fiona. Last night had nothing to do about you, I told you. I promise you that."

"But you heard what they said!" She exclaimed. He couldn't do this. This was not one of those times where he would try and remove the guilt from her shoulders by denying the obvious facts. "They said that stupid shit about you being with me and—"

"Stop," Adam harshly spoke before she could finish her sentence. He removed the ice pack from his chest and winced as he tried to sit up. Fiona immediately tried to make him lay down again, but he pushed her hand away. "No. You need to hear me clearly when I say this now, Fiona; it had nothing to do with you."

"But—"

"It had nothing to do with you," He repeated, looking sternly at her. Fiona pressed her lips together, not believing him; She had heard every word they had spoken.

"Then why did they beat you up?" She whispered back crossly, even though she knew she shouldn't be arguing with him right now. He was in no state to be getting riled up.

"Because they hate me," Adam replied. "And when you hate someone, everything you do becomes another reason for them to hate you."

Fiona's bottom lip wobbled. She fought with his words internally, because... "So what if I hadn't been black?"

"If you hadn't been black, then they would've found some other reason to jump me. They just needed one more reason, Fee. But it had nothing to do with you."

She wanted to believe him. She really did. But even if he was right, then... she would still be the reason they jumped him.

And that was exactly it; She didn't want to be another reason for them to bully him – for him to become a punching bag for their stupid agenda. She wanted to believe what Adam said, but she also knew that if she had been white, they wouldn't have gone off on him like that. It was a backwards mindset and it was a fact she hated, but a fact nonetheless.

– Cultural preference. It existed, and even though she couldn't deny it, it still happened all around them, in all races and cultures. It had even happened in her own damn family. It was that very same reason that she had never known her grandparents.

– Her dad fell in love with her mom, who was white. Her mom had told her many times that his parents didn't like her – that they didn't want him dating a white girl and bringing her back to home to meet them. They didn't trust her and didn't want anything to do with her. Her dad hadn't cared, and the moment her mom fell pregnant with her, she had told Fiona, it hadn't even been a choice for him; he had wanted to stay and raise his daughter, even if it meant he would get disowned.

He loved them that much.

It was many years ago, but even to this day, though, Fiona knew there were still parents who didn't want their kids to date anyone outside their culture or religion—who would also get disowned for bringing home an 'outside' kid. She just never thought that she would be on the receiving end of it, getting discriminated for wanting to be with a white guy. It was insane. For God's sake, it was the 21st century. She was half-black, but she was also half-white, so what was the big fucking deal? Just because her skin was a bit more on the melanin-side, it made it not-okay for her to date someone pasty like Adam? Where was the line?

And as her eyes fell to Adam's, that's when she got her answer.

"Come on," Adam whispered, brushing her cheekbone with his thumb. "I don't want to talk about this anymore. I just want to hold the girl I love in my arms. Fiona?"

Fiona had stilled, but swallowed heavily. She didn't want this to end... but as long as they were out there, he wouldn't be safe if she stayed with him.

"Did you... did you talk to the police?" She finally spoke after a full minute. She heard Adam sigh heavily before giving a curt nod.

"Yes."

"So you told them it was them who assaulted you?"

His jaw clenched, and lowering his hand, he closed his eyes and turned his head away. "No."

Fiona blinked twice and replayed his answer in her mind to make sure she didn't mishear him. He did what? "You didn't tell them?"

"No," He repeated, a little firmer this time. "I told you; you don't rat in these situations."

Fiona sprung up from the bed. She saw Adam turn his head and stare after her as she started backing away. She couldn't believe this. "No..."

"Fiona—"

"No!" She shouted. Angry tears welled up in her eyes and she furiously shook her head. "Are you fucking stupid?! Adam, they b-beat you up! They fucking beat you to near d-death and you won't even press charges!" She shouted, not caring that his grandma could probably hear her. "Are you fucking kidding me?!"

"Fiona, please," Adam pleaded, pressing his lips together, but she was beyond listening to him now. Enough was enough.

"No," She said, hearing her voice break. Everything inside her broke, only because she knew what this meant. "No... I just can't..."

"Fiona, please, come back," Adam begged her and tried to sit up when she backed up against the door, fumbling for the doorknob. He winced loudly and had to lie back down. "Fuck, Fiona, please just stay and let me explain—"

"No," She exclaimed, holding up her hand as the tears rushed down her cheeks. Her whole body was shaking. "I've already lost one person I love. I won't lose another one because you're too fucking stupid not to put these assholes behind bars."

Adam's face dropped. "Fiona..."

But she was already gone.

Ripping the door open, she heard Adam call her name, but she didn't come back. With tears streaming down her face, she ran out of the house and out onto the street, shaking everywhere.

It was one thing to try and be strong for someone you loved who had just survived a brutal beating... but it was another thing to stay by that person, while knowing every wakening moment, it could happen again... all because he refused to give them up.

– And that right there, was the line Fiona couldn't cross.

Chapter 23

The next morning, Fiona woke up before her mom did and got showered and ready. Grabbing her bag and her ballet shoes, she left a note on the dining table before then walking out the door.

It was Sunday, and although she usually went to church with her mom on Sundays, she couldn't today. There were too many thoughts on her mind and today, she needed to be alone with them.

Well... almost alone.

A short bus ride later, Fiona stood in front of the church before it had even opened. It was still too early, the sunrise barely coloring the sky a beautiful rich golden color, and yet as Fiona breathed in the lukewarm morning air and stepped into the cemetery, she already felt as if a warmth had swept over her.

"Hi, dad," She whispered, standing in front of his headstone. The beautiful white marble with the black, slanted name carved on was all she had to talk to, but it was enough as she knelt down and smiled with a trembling lip to her dad.

When she was little, she had missed his presence. She had missed dancing with him, had missed him picking her up from school... had missed having him around the dinner table and had missed him tucking her into bed. All the little things most kids that age took for granted, she had missed more than anything.

But as she grew up, Fiona stopped missing his presence as much as she missed his words and his voice. She wasn't quite sure she remembered exactly how his voice sounded anymore, but that wasn't even the worst part.

– The thing she missed the most was his advice.

Looking down at his headstone, Fiona found herself over-whelmed with all of the questions she wanted to ask him. Why did he love her mom enough to choose her over his own family? How had he made the choice? Did he ever regret it?

Did he ever regret having her?

Fiona felt a tear slip down her cheek as all these questions filled her mind, knowing she would never get any answers. She knew in her heart that he had loved her and her mom, but... had it been worth it, getting thrown out by his own mom?

"I love you so much, dad," Fiona whispered through her tears, cupping her face to stop the sobs from coming.

All of this business with Adam had her more confused than ever. And not just what had happened recently, but all of it; Tomorrow was the day of her audition, the thing she had been training for all these weeks, but now... now she wasn't even sure she wanted to go.

Her dad had been her age when he had made the toughest decision of his life; choosing her mom and her over his family. Now as Fiona found herself faced with two tough choices, she wished more than ever she could've talked to her dad about it.

"I don't know what to do, dad," She cried, wrapping her arms around herself.

She loved Adam, but could she stand being by his side, knowing that at any moment, he could be taken from her side? Death was always inevitable, but if you could do anything at all to prevent it...

Her dad had died out of the blue. If there had been anything she could've done to prevent it back then, Fiona would've done it, no question or hesitation.

– Adam was refusing to report Grip and the other guys who assaulted him, which meant he was inviting every possibility of it happening again into his life. How was she supposed to stay beside him, knowing that?

She just couldn't support it.

But after all that Adam had done for her to support her... even when she had been making stupid choices...

Squeezing her eyes shut, Fiona felt so torn. A few more sobs broke from her throat, unwilling to stop them.

She would have to choose sooner or later, just like her father had done. Was she going to put everything on the line for him... or was she going to stay where everything was safer? If her being with him put him at risk...

Opening her eyes, Fiona looked at her father's headstone. He had been brave enough to go for what he wanted, but she wasn't sure she was as strong as he was.

He had chosen love: Could she do the same?

About an hour later, Fiona was at the DanceDec. She had been the first one there, everyone still being in church or asleep at home. She had gone up to their usual dance studio, but as she walked in alone, it suddenly felt... empty. Like something was missing.

Or someone.

Strapping on her ballet slippers, Fiona had warmed up and continued doing her old routine until she finally heard life begin to come in downstairs. She heard music begin to boom from the other studios, heard the usual chatter and laughter from around the place, people having fun and enjoying themselves, dancing.

But as Fiona finally stepped out onto the floor to begin her new dance routine that Adam had made for her, she found her legs trembling, just like they used to before she met him.

It felt like the room was coming at her from all angles. Her bones felt insecure, just as the mirror seemed to skirt around on the wall, unable to provide her with a spot to hold. It felt as if everything hurt when she took those first steps, and it didn't take long before she had to stop.

Guilt was weighing in her stomach again. Too many thoughts, too many concerns, too much... everything.

Was this what she wanted? Was ballet still all she wanted in life, or had something changed within her? Did she even want to dance at some ballet company, and was it even worth all of the grueling work that she knew would come in the future?

Just as Fiona felt like she was having an existential crisis, there was a sudden knock on the door. Her heart flew up into her throat, for some reason expecting him to walk through the door, but... as the door opened, it was Kalo's face that met her.

"Heya," She softly spoke, sending Fiona a careful smile. She obviously knew what had happened, which meant the whole DanceDec also knew. "I saw the shades were down, so I figured you were in here."

Fiona swallowed a ball. As Kalo came in and closed the door, she realized she wasn't just here to check up on her. Was she about to get reamed out by Adam's best friend for storming out on him in his condition? "Uhm... y-yeah. My audition is tomorrow, s-so I have to practice."

Kalo nodded, sticking her bottom lip out. "Cool, cool."

Fiona watched as Kalo slowly walked around the studio a little, looking around at seemingly nothing. She continued doing that for another minute before Fiona decided she should say something.

"I'm... I'm really sorry about what happened," She whispered, hearing her voice crack. Kalo shot her a look, but then raised her eyebrow when Fiona started shrinking under her gaze.

Kalo watched her for a long moment, so long that Fiona finally had to lower her eyes to avoid the tension. She didn't know what else to say, even though the words 'I'm sorry' kept playing over and over in her mind. She felt so guilty for what had happened.

"Do you know why dogs love everyone?" Kalo then suddenly spoke.

Fiona blinked twice in astonishment. Then, shaking her head no, she let Kalo continue.

"It's because they don't see color," Kalo grinned. "Yeah. I always found it kind of funny how for example, that LGBTQ flag keeps getting more and more colors and shit, more letters and more definitions? It's strange isn't it, that they say we shouldn't focus on color, yet that flag is all about accepting the whole gay rainbow. I say fuck that. Let's all go colorblind like dogs."

Fiona opened her mouth, but nothing came out. She slowly closed it again and tipped her on feet when Kalo then sighed and crossed her arms.

"Alright, I know what happened," She then finally said. When Fiona's face paled, Kalo shrugged indifferently and looked around the studio again. "And I've got some things to say even if it's not my place to, but I've never been one to shut up, so here goes," She announced in a rapid speech.

Fiona held her breath, expecting worst. She was expecting Kalo to give her a hard lecture on hurting her friends, on hurting Adam and running out on him like that, leaving him helplessly behind in his bed. But none of that came.

"Adam doesn't like to talk about color," Kalo instead started. She shrugged again and held up her hands. "And shit, neither do I, but some things just fucking are and needs to be said; We're all different here and that's okay, except for when we start judging each other on the bases of it. Right?"

Fiona listened, surprised. This wasn't where she thought things would go today, but it seemed, just like Kalo said, that some things just needed to be said. And spoken about.

"We chose to be black no more than Adam chose to be white, right? So, he didn't actually choose his white privilege card, no more than we got robbed of one. The system gave him that card," She said, meeting Fiona's eyes. Fiona didn't quite know what to respond, so she gave a half-hearted shrug with one shoulder.

"So he has a white card," Kalo pointed out. "but, does he use it like some of these other white mo-fo kids out there do? Never."

The honest truth was, Fiona hadn't known Adam long enough to be the judge of that, but purely from what she did know about him, she knew that he never would. Not knowingly, at least. He was young and he was scared, but he was also smart; he had been to juvie and maybe that had scared him enough to do whatever it took to make parole—maybe even if it meant using his white card. And maybe that was why he hadn't reported them.

Maybe he thought he deserved it.

"Adam got white-carded once," Kalo now continued. "Once. And even if that's still not great and doesn't excuse anything, does that make it okay for these punkass bitches to go after him for it like that? Nah. That's not how we achieve justice here," She scoffed, angrily. "My point is, Adam did a stupid fucking thing, but he's spent every day since to try and make up for it, and that's all you can do, except these assholes don't see that. Some people will always hold grudges and hate on people for something that's happened, and usually they have a reason for it, and sadly, that's a truth, too."

Fiona let her words sink in, standing quietly and swallowing heavily as the emotions built up inside her. She agreed that that wasn't how justice was served. On some twisted level, she even understood their anger and reason for beating him up—but it still would never be okay in a million years. Hatred would never be the solution. Their act of crime had now only resulted in more crime, and unless Adam decided to do the right thing, then justice would never be found.

An eye for an eye made the whole world blind.

"Now, I know this shit doesn't work for everyone," Kalo now said, firmly. "Don't get me twisted, I know in most cases, that white card is flexed hard, that it is overused and abused, and that's why these grudges stick, and that's why some invent their own justice system. But that's also not how it is for every white person out there," She spoke, twisting her lip a little. "Most, but not all. Now I can't speak for all of those other cases, I can and will only speak about what happened to Adam because I'm not about to get my grill on, so that's what I'm gonna do; Adam is one of the sweetest guys on this earth who would never intentionally harm a fly, but some just don't see that. Like those assholes."

Kalo took a deep breath, and Fiona automatically followed her lead after she had spoken. They were making it towards her point, and Fiona felt it creeping up like precipitation.

"Adam made a bad mistake and they're going to keep punishing him for it even while he's trying to repent, but that's because they're shitheads," Kalo stated, pursing her lips, but then provided her with a sharp glare. "But you're not, though. So I'll be damned if you go and quit on his ass because you think it'll save him from himself if you stay away, because it won't. He'll always have his little white annoying ass as sure as mine will be juiced with melanin, and there's nothing we can do about that. He will always get into some kind of trouble, just as sure as his past will always haunt him one way or another. So the only question you need to ask yourself is whether or not you love him enough to stay with him throughout all his bullshit."

Fiona let everything sink in. Along with all the other thoughts that had been floating around in her head, this was a lot to take in. Adam had done a bad thing, but what they had done wasn't right either. Him not reporting them felt worse, but her leaving him for it... was the final nail in the coffin. So many wrongs couldn't make a right, so where did that leave them?

"I've said my peace," Kalo finally said, holding up her hands, before placing them back on her hips. "If you want to be with Adam, then fuck those guys; Be with him. But if you want to go, then put him out of his misery and end it before it goes too far. That's all I ask, as his friend."

Fiona understood. He was already in enough pain as it was, and leaving him thinking he was about to lose her as well wasn't right either. She knew she had to talk to him. It was just...

"I'm just scared," Fiona whispered, brokenly. She looked towards Kalo who softened up and dropped her arms to her side. With a sigh, she then walked up to Fiona and placed her hands on her shoulders.

"I know. But you'll only truly lose him if you leave him. Nobody knows what the future holds. If you love him enough, why not just get the best out of it?"

Fiona lowered her eyes, feeling tears creeping up. Kalo instantly pulled her in for a hug she didn't expect at all, but a hug she realized that she needed. She wrapped her hands around her and hugged her back.

"Thank you," She whispered, sniveling quietly.

"Anytime," Kalo replied, a smile to her voice. Adam was right; she was big and bad on the outside, but just a big softie on the inside. "Now, keep practicing for that audition, but don't keep Adam waiting for too long. Or I'll kick the color off of your ass."

Fiona let out a weak laugh, but then pulled back and dried her eyes. "I promise. And thanks again. I... I really needed someone to talk to."

"You can come to me any time," Kalo started walking back towards the door, but shot her a grin over her shoulder. "You're part of the family now. That means you're stuck with me."

Fiona smiled back, but then watched as Kalo stepped out, leaving her to her practice. With a deep sigh, Fiona then turned towards the mirror and looked herself over for a long time.

She had a lot of work to do.

It was around noon and Fiona was still at the DanceDec, rehearsing her routine while also going over everything she wanted to say to Adam. She had decided that after lunch, she was taking the bus to his and his grandma's place to talk things over with him and get everything out in the open.

But as it turned out, she wouldn't have to.

A loud cheer, followed by a startling applause suddenly came from downstairs, and it drew Fiona towards the door, opening it to see what was causing all of the commotion.

There, limping in through the front door, surrounded by almost everyone they knew in the DanceDec, Adam with all his bruises and bashed up face came walking in slowly, a smile stretching on his face as everyone welcomed him back.

Fiona's heart immediately went into her throat as she watched people come up to him and ask him how he was, telling him stuff she couldn't hear, but no doubt were words of praise and courage. Everyone knew what had happened, and they had all been worried, but seeing Adam still alive and well enough to show up, was enough to have everyone gathering around in a relieved circled.

"Seriously, what does it take to kill you?" Kalo hollered loudly, to which Adam chuckled hoarsely. He grimaced and then pressed a hand over his fractured ribs.

"Yeah, come on, we were counting on some quiet around here for at least some days," Rani bid in, coming through the crowd to carefully hug him as well and welcome him back.

Adam kept smiling and meeting everyone who wanted to greet him, but Fiona noticed the way his eyes darted around the crowd, as if looking for someone in particular. It was when his eyes finally lifted and gazed upstairs, his eyes locked as he found her.

Fiona's breath caught, but she saw his eyes didn't waver as he started making his way through the crowd, people giving him space and helping him as he started climbing the stairs. Everyone finally left him alone and went back to their own stuff as he made it to the top, but Fiona was certain it was because they knew as well as anyone where he was headed.

Fiona slowly swallowed as he limped towards her, grunting ever so slightly while supporting his ribs with his good arm. The other one was in a sling, resting his shoulder that had been severely bruised as well. Other than a few sprained limbs and cracked ribs, it was a miracle he hadn't broken anything other than his nose.

"Hey," He spoke gravelly as Fiona clutched herself not to start crying again.

"Hey," She whispered back, seeing him halt a few feet away from her.

"Can we talk?" He asked, looking briefly towards the dance studio, before pinning his eyes back on her. Fiona nodded and instantly went to open the door for him.

They walked in together, and Fiona made sure to close the door after him as he walked further into the studio, looking around.

"Kalo said you were here," He then started quietly, breaking the silence only disturbed by the music from the other studios. "You weren't responding to my texts, so I called her."

"I needed some time to think," Fiona elaborated. She swallowed hard, but then lowered her head. "Adam..."

"I'm scared, Fiona."

Her heart stopped in her chest, and as she looked up to meet his eyes, she saw that they were filled with tears. Her heart broke down the middle. "Adam..."

She rushed towards him when a tear fell from his eye, a tear he quickly wiped down before taking a deep breath.

"I'm scared shitless, Fee," He told, shaking his head when she carefully placed her hands on his shoulders. "I've got my grams, and I've got Kalo and Rani and even Dimitri, and now I've got you too. I'm scared to lose any of you."

"Adam..."

"And I'm scared that if I do go to the cops, someone will catch wind of it and they'll come after me and everyone I love, and I just can't fucking bear that, Fee. I don't want anyone getting hurt because of me."

"Adam—"

"And I love you so damn much, Fiona," His voice broke as he leaned down and cupped her face. Tears were still welled up in his eyes, but he didn't let any more fall for now. "And I was so scared that they were gonna hurt you, I would've broken my own back to get up and protect you if they tried to even lay a finger on you. They can beat me up twice over, but if they ever came close to even touching you, I—"

"Adam," She broke through his frantic talking that became more and more desperate with every word. Another tear finally fell from his eye, but this time it was Fiona who wiped it away. "I love you. I love you so much, and I don't want to lose you either."

"But you're scared to be with me," He whispered, shutting his eyes and breathing shakily. "I know you lost your father, and I know you're scared of losing me too, but I—"

"I'm more scared of not being with you," Fiona broke in, pulling him even closer and meeting his eyes as he slowly opened them again. "I thought it would be better i-if I stayed away, but then I realized I didn't want to and I just... I'm so sorry for leaving you, Adam, I was just so scared and—"

His mouth was on hers before she could finish, and she desperately clung to his neck, kissing him back carefully as his cut lip moved against hers.

For what felt like minutes, they just stood there and kissed and let that kiss heal whatever had happened between them. There was still a lot they needed to talk about, but for now, this was good enough.

After a long moment, they both finally pulled away for air. Fiona stayed pressed up against him, careful not to put pressure on any part of his bruised body, but she also couldn't get herself to move further away. If she could, she would've clenched him to her very soul.

"I never understood why you wanted to be with me in the first place," She then carefully whispered. She looked up to see Adam's face soften and melt. "And then when they said what they did, I thought for sure you wouldn't want to be with me then either. You're the best thing that's ever happened to me, and I just don't understand... what I've done to deserve you."

Adam looked at her for a long time, simply cupping her face and brushing her cheek. Then, pecking the corner of her mouth softly, he sighed. "You need to hear this, Fiona. And I need you to believe me when I say it's true; I was in love with you before I even met you. Shit, before I even knew myself that I was in love with you... I loved you."

Confused, Fiona frowned up at Adam and allowed him to pull back. She watched as he walked to the very centre of the studio and looked down at the floor, as if looking for an exact spot.

"You were standing right here when I saw you for the first time," He then told, a little smile tugging at his lip at the memory. "You were dancing around, all caught up in your little routine, and I was just passing by when I saw you."

When he turned around and laid eyes on her, he shook his head and gave a hopeless sigh.

"I always thought that love-at-first-sight shit was a fairy-tale they made for kids to keep hope or something. I never once believed it was true, not until I saw you. I swear to God himself, Fee, I felt something when I saw you dance. I don't know whether if it was the fact that you were dancing so fiercely and with so much passion, it made my heart skip a beat, or if it was because you were crying throughout it. I just know the moment I saw you there, I wanted to know you, know your story and wanted to dance with you at least once. But I also realized you were so closed off, you'd probably never go for a guy like me."

He looked her over, and his lips then stretched as he walked his way back over to her to cup her face once more, leaning down and sighing against her lips with a smile.

"Little did I know you were gonna fall straight into my arms," He chuckled.

Everything inside Fiona melted into pieces. She didn't realize tears were steaming down her face until Adam wiped them away.

"I am a hundred percent certain that I found my passion in this life because God knew it would lead me to you," He solemnly spoke, smiling when Fiona couldn't stop crying. "I've loved dancing my whole life, but I've never loved it as much as I do as when I dance with you. You're just it, Fiona."

Fiona shook her head, unable to speak. She was at a loss for words, completely. To think he had loved her that long... and then fallen in love with her, too, despite everything...

"I love you," She whispered as the only thing she could think of. "I love you so much."

"I love you more." He leaned down and pressed his lips over hers again for a long moment, both of them simply dwelling in each other. Then, Adam pulled back, exhaling slowly. "... and I'll report them if you really want me to."

Fiona squeezed her eyes shut, but then buried her face in his neck. She didn't know what was right do this very moment, she just knew that she didn't want to do anything that could make her lose him.

"We'll figure it out later," She whispered, feeling him lean down to take a deep sniff of her hair. He then let go of another deep exhale.

"You're right. Right now, we have more important matters; you need to practice."

When he pulled back, Fiona looked up with a confused look when he started limping towards the stereo. Without a word, he pulled his phone out of his pocket and plugged it up to the stereo.

"While I was in the hospital, I found the perfect song for your new routine," He told, scrolling through his phone with a little smile, before pressing his lips together. "I left my phone on shuffle, and it just came on."

"Adam..." Fiona took a shaky breath, not sure if she should tell him. "I'm... not sure I want to go to the audition tomorrow."

As if he wasn't surprised at all, Adam merely smiled and turned to shoot her a look. "Whether or not you want to get in, I still think you should go. You've been working on this for three weeks; Go to the audition, dance for them, if not for yourself, then for your father. Listen."

And as he pressed play on his phone and the music started pouring through the speakers, Fiona cupped her mouth and felt new tears welling up.

He was right; this was the song.

Chapter 24

Adam had stayed with Fiona and helped her rehearse her routine for another hour before they decided to head back to his place. Since he was still healing from his injuries, he tired quickly and needed to lie down.

But they also needed to talk.

"I never got an anklet," Adam had told. Fiona knew the shortened version of how he got behind bars, but to make the decision about whether or not to go to the cops, she needed the full one – with all of the details.

"What...?" She whispered, watching him close his eyes tiredly and press his lips together.

"After I got cleared for probation. I got a five-year sentence and only served about 3-4 months in the actual slammer. I got out on 'good behavior' and with my grams' support and promise to look after me. My deal was to have weekly meetings with my P.O, land good grades in school and stay away from all of my old gang friends. That's why the DanceDec happened.

"But when I got released into my grams' custody, they didn't put an anklet on me. Not even for the first year," Adam opened his eyes and stared into his room. Fiona saw the pain in his eyes as he then shook his head and sighed. "I got caught with drugs, muling them around town, and they gave me a weak-ass sentence, Fiona. And I took it."

Fiona was silent for a moment, trying to reason with his words. Even if... even if a part of her tore apart.

"You were just a kid," She finally said and swallowed hard, reaching for his good hand when it started shaking. "You were scared."

"We all were," Adam objected. "We were all fucking scared in there, Fee, it doesn't excuse that I let myself be coddled. I should've served my sentence and not... let them give me all those chances. They beat me up because I rightfully deserved it, Fee. They hate me because they should. Shit... I'm so sorry."

Fiona furrowed her brows and pressed her lips together when he cupped his face and started shaking with tears. The pain in his voice was hurting her heart so much... but what hurt even more was that he thought he deserved to get beaten up for his poor choices.

"Adam," She carefully spoke, clenching his hand. "No matter what happened in the past, you didn't deserve this. They shouldn't have beat you up, that's not justice. That's not how we fight white privilege. You might've done something bad, but it was the system that failed in the end."

Everything in this situation spoke to what was wrong in the world; Adam had done something wrong, and yet the system had barely punished him compared to what his old friends had done. All on the basis of their skin. The system was faulty, and that's why Fiona hated the situation; she hated that she knew why they were angry at him, but also hated that if they reported what they had done, they wouldn't just receive a slap on the wrist like Adam had gotten. They would get much worse.

"I just don't want to stir up anymore problems," Adam finally said, taking in a deep, trembling breath. He shut his eyes and let his head rest back against his pillows. "They beat me up, they evened out the scales. If I call on them now, it'll only provoke them again."

Fiona bit her lip, resenting how complicated the situation was. There was no justice in any of this, but perhaps he was right... perhaps it was best just to leave it for now and let the fire die out. But...

"If they ever hurt you again, though," She whispered fiercely, shutting her eyes. She couldn't believe this was what it had to be, but she sure as hell wouldn't let them get away with it twice. "If they ever come at you again or anyone we know, then we go to the cops, okay? I'm not gonna let them control your life over one stupid mistake you made."

Adam looked up at her. Then, taking her hand, he braided his fingers with hers and brought her knuckles to his lips. He kissed them softly. "Okay."

"Promise me."

"I promise you."

Fiona released a breath. Then, nodding, she laid down beside him in his bed and snuggled up to his good side – the side that wasn't wrapped up in a sling and battered too badly.

"So... this is it?" Adam whispered.

Fiona drew in a fresh breath, but then nodded against his shoulder. This was it; she was letting go of the past and focusing on the future. Their future together. In the end, that was all one could do; Work for a better future.

She felt Adam turn his head and place a kiss on top of her head before he like her released a deep breath. Moving forward.

"Are you ready for tomorrow then?"

Fiona slowly opened her eyes. Tomorrow. It was so far away, yet so close. The very thing she had been working for all these weeks and months, just a few hours away now. Months of preparation, but was she actually ready?

"I guess we'll find out."

"Number 46."

It was the strangest thing. As Fiona stood ready, hair pinned in a bun, legs clad in pantyhose and her body fitted into a tight leotard, she looked towards the lady who called her number... and felt not a shred of nerves.

Standing besides her, her mother and Adam had come with her to her audition which had been scheduled in a ballet studio on the upper east side. They both looked at her with a nervous, but proud look as she took a deep breath.

"Good luck, sweetheart," Her mom whispered, leaning down to quickly peck her cheek. Fiona nodded and smiled back, but then looked towards Adam.

"Go get em', tiger," He winked, getting a small laugh out of her. She then took a last deep breath before turning around and walking towards the lady.

The New York Ballet didn't usually hold open auditions. Usually you had to be professionally trained by some other company or ballet school, by whom you could get in through.

But this year, in honor of their 75th anniversary, the New York Ballet was celebrating the school by opening up auditions country-wide for all who enjoyed dancing ballet. They had set up auditions in 20 states and granted a total of a 100 people to be auditioned over 3 days. Today was the first day, which meant testing of basic barre skills and simple routines. And finally, it was on to the solos.

– And they had already gone through the barres and routines of today.

Now, after several hours of waiting, it was finally Fiona's turn to showcase her solo. Each dancer was allowed a total of 3 minutes to perform a solo that would then be graded on creativeness, technique and execution. The judging process took another 5 minutes, depending on the solo, and then it was either win or lose. If you made it through the first day, you got a callback to the next and so on.

But if you didn't...

Fiona walked up towards the slim lady with the glasses who had called her name. She held a chart in her hand and looked towards Fiona as she came towards her.

"Fiona Torrence?" She confirmed, looking down at the number pasted on her stomach.

"Yes," She replied.

"Follow me."

Stepping through a door, she came to a private dance studio where, through a window, the people outside could look in and watch the audition. One of the requirements were being able to perform in pressure and in front of a crowd.

– Fiona's very worst nightmare.

But as she stepped into the centre of the studio and looked towards the table of judges who sat idly in their chairs, ready to do the very thing she had feared all of her life, Fiona felt nothing but ready. There was no tingling in her body, no nausea welling up her throat or any panic crawling up her spine.

She was ready.

"Ms Torrence," A man in the middle spoke, looking into his papers. "You may begin when you're ready."

Her heart started beating fast, but not out of angst. As she nodded in confirmation and took her position on the floor, she closed her eyes as the moment finally arrived.

The moment she would make her dad proud.

The music that Adam had chosen started playing from the speakers, and without a glimmer of hesitation, Fiona went en pointe. She remembered all of Adam's notes from yesterday – keep your chin high, make sure your arms stay fluent – but they all melted away as she started dancing. Suddenly, it wasn't Adam who was dancing with her anymore. It wasn't the judges sitting in those chairs, looking at her. The crowd beyond the window disappeared, and the only person that was watching her... was her dad.

Smiling, Fiona felt her eyes well up as his happy face watched her twirl around perfectly, never slowing down, never hesitating. She spun around in pirouettes as the music soared, she jumped into the air as the beat swelled, and as everything culminated together, she came to a beautiful halt on the floor, moving her arms around herself.

She had danced for him, but danced for herself. The joy she had felt when she was little had come back to her right in this moment as she felt all of her emotions translate into her dancing.

She was dancing because she loved it. Not because she had to, but because she needed to. This feeling in her heart right now...

That was her reason for dancing.

'I'm so proud of you. I've always been proud of you. I will always be proud of you, princess.'

Smiling as she remembered her dad's voice, the music finally came to a stop. The world came back to her and the judges reappeared in front of her. The room slowly became bright again and the crowd outside the window returned.

Looking over at the judges, their faces remained impassive, but she saw them scribble a lot down on their paper. After a moment of waiting, the guy from before lifted his head and nodded to her.

"Thank you, Ms Torrence. If you'll please wait outside, we'll have your result in a moment."

Doing a polite curtsey as was mannered in ballet, Fiona then tiptoed quickly towards the exit and back out to the crowd.

Right towards Adam.

He had seen the whole thing through the window, just like her mom, and as she came towards them both, it was Adam's face that caught her attention. He was rubbing his cheeks down, while her mother was dabbing her own with a tissue.

"How did I do?" She asked, looking between them. Her mom broke into a new fit of tears and blew her nose into the tissue.

But Adam smiled lovingly at her and stepped towards her. "You did so great, Fee. You looked so beautiful... you were dancing, tutu."

A small laugh bubbled from her throat, and cupping her mouth, Fiona felt involuntary tears well up inside her eyes as well. Adam pulled her in for a hug, squeezing her to his bruised chest as well as he could, before pressing a small kiss to the side of her head.

"It doesn't matter what they say in there," He then whispered. "You danced perfectly, Fiona."

Fiona closed her eyes and smiled silently, squeezing him back gently. After a moment, she then pulled back to receive a hug from her mom as well who immediately broke into a rant about how beautiful it had been. It wasn't until her name was suddenly called again, they all went quiet.

"Fiona Torrence?"

This was it. The moment of truth. Had she made it on to the next round or was this the end of the road?

Looking at Adam and her mom one last time, she saw them both nod before she with a deep breath turned around and walked back to the lady.

And as she walked inside to get her result, she realized... she didn't care at all what happened.

– She had gotten what she came for here today and it wasn't this result.

The cork of the sparkling cider popped and was immediately accompanied by a loud cheer from Kalo, Rani, Dimitri and the rest of the gang as Adam and Fiona entered the DanceDec and told them the news.

"To overcoming shit!" Kalo announced, pouring the cider into all the plastic cups that were being passed around. Fiona grinned quietly. "And to those shitheads for being blind, stupid fuckers with no sense of what's good moves! If it means we get to keep you around here for longer and get you to absorb Adam's annoying ass shit, then it's a fucking win! To Fiona!"

"To Fiona!" Everyone cheered in agreement.

Beside her Adam chuckled, shaking his head as Fiona blushed. Trust Kalo to be the one to turn a rejection into a party of celebration.

"They said her moves were great, she just wasn't what they were looking for," Adam reiterated the same words Fiona had told after she had gone inside the studio to receive her judgement. Her mom had been furious, Adam had been saddened, but Fiona... truthfully, she had almost felt relieved.

If she had gotten through, that meant intense day-long training at some fancy studios uptown. She wouldn't have had time to come here, to see Adam and all the others, wouldn't have been able to make it in and enjoy just a few hours at the DanceDec with the people she liked the most. The company would've kept her busy, and after meeting Adam and coming to terms with what dancing truly was to her, she had realized the NYC Ballet was no longer her dream.

"Well, lucky for us then, she's exactly what we're looking for!" Kalo announced. Adam chuckled, shaking his head again. "We're doing this dance piece and we could use a third dancer. Interested?" Kalo turned towards Fiona and asked.

Fiona felt a nervous pull in her stomach. She had only ever danced with Adam before. Was she ready to dance with other people? "I... I, uh, I don't know yet..."

"Well, let me know within the next few days," She grinned, but then raised her cup of cider of gulped down her entire cup in one large sip and followed it up with an equally large burp.

Everyone broke into laughter and talking, and soon everyone had gathered around, drinking the cider and passing around food. Chips, fries and candy made its way around the group while Fiona stayed close to Adam who was getting his word in on the new routine Kalo and Rani were making. Eventually everyone was talking about their own thing, and that's when Adam had turned towards Fiona and gently pulled her away from the crowd to a quieter spot.

"So are you really okay?" He asked, leaning down and giving her cheek and quick brush with his thumb. "About the decision?"

Fiona nodded slowly and hummed. She gave a little smile. "I am." And she truly meant it.

"You're not even a little disappointed?" He asked, furrowing his brows a little and studying her face closely. "It was your dream for so long."

Fiona shook her head and felt her smile grow. "My dreams changed."

When she cupped his face slowly, she saw his lips turn up as well. He grinned a little, but then bent down to her lips.

"I'm looking at mine right now."

Pressing his mouth over hers, he kissed her softly, but deeply, and Fiona couldn't help but return the feeling. She carefully ran her hand up his chest to the nape of his neck and kissed him back with everything she had. It finally felt like everything was as it was supposed to be.

After a moment, Adam pulled back ever so gently and then exhaled against her lips. "And about... the other decision...?"

Fiona felt her cheeks heat a little.

After their heavy talk yesterday, they had gone on to discuss another few important issues that they had glossed over during the couple of weeks that they had known each other; the direction of their relationship.

It seemed like everything had gone so fast, so quickly, that they had barely had time to stop to think about... what they were doing. And if they should be doing it. They had done some stuff, and there was no doubt in their minds they both wanted to do more, but yesterday when they had talked, they had both agreed on one thing.

"We're waiting," Fiona hummed, smiling happily up at him. Adam grinned back.

They had barely known each other three weeks, and in those three weeks, it was safe to say they had fallen pretty hard for each other. With everything else that was going on though, Fiona's therapy and now Adam's rehab, not to mention both of them were graduating in only a few weeks, it seemed like slowing things down was the right thing to do. There was no need for anymore big steps right now.

More specifically, one big one.

"We're waiting," Adam echoed, leaning down to press a quick kiss to her lips.

It would give them a chance to get to know each other better, and to Fiona, it meant feeling sure about giving up her first time to someone whom she really loved – even if she was certain on that point already. But if that love could stand the test of time and patience, then nothing could break them apart.

Kissing Adam back gently, Fiona let go of a deep breath. Waiting. "You better not cheat on me with anyone else." She warned him.

"With who?"

When a megawatt grin spread on Adam's lips, Fiona rolled her eyes, just as he leaned down and pressed a thick kiss to her cheek. "You're so annoying."

"Yeah? Well, you're stuck with me now," He promised with a chuckle. "Sorry, tutu."

Smiling against her will, Fiona shook her head and sighed again. "Hmm... I think I'll survive."

"Good," He hummed, leaning down to press his face into the crook of her neck. He pressed a series of small kisses up and down her throat, causing Fiona to shiver lightly and curl her toes. "But you know... since we're waiting, you better hope I survive, too."

Fiona frowned a little confused and watched as he pulled back. "What do you mean?"

Adam chuckled lowly. Then, leaning into her ear, he whispered hotly; "Because I'm probably going to get sooo horny."

And with that, he snapped his head back and expelled the loudest moan yet, making Fiona blush and everyone around them to turn and stare.

Maybe she wouldn't survive after all.

Chapter 25

3 MONTHS LATER

– The second the music started booming from the dance studio down the hall, Fiona knew exactly who was dancing.

Rolling her eyes, she walked up to the studio and stopped up in the door, leaning up against it with a grin on her lips. Peering into the dance studio, she instantly bit her lip and felt her stomach clench.

Kneeling on the floor, wearing his loose sweatpants and his black tank top, his upper body was sweating from the heat outside, but also from the routine he was doing. The music was slow and sensual, and as it kicked off, so did he.

Catching himself on his palms on the floor, Adam slowly started grinding his pelvis into the ground, a concentrated look on his face. Then, rolling his shoulders, he twisted around and up on his feet, popping his chest and then swerving around to face the mirror. His head snapped to the side as the beat hit, and before Fiona could react, he had launched himself across the floor, sliding on his knees until he came to a halt. His hips undulated erotically, and Fiona was forced to catch her breath when her eyes fell to his ass that looked way too good in those slacks.

His upper body was glistening with sweat and his unruly brown hair was falling onto his forehead. His cap was snapped on backwards and did little to hide his face as he once again rose to his feet. The way he moved to the sensual beat made Fiona sweat herself, watching her man work out his routine.

Her man.

Dancing around on the floor, Fiona watched for minutes as Adam practiced the routine he had been working on for a few weeks. It was supposed to be a contemporary hip hop piece, but somewhere along the line, it had become an erotic magic mike performance. Fiona couldn't help but bite down a grin when she figured how it had happened.

Three months of no action... they had both stayed true to their promise, and Adam had been more than a champion about it.

But it now seemed he had found another way to channel his... frustrations.

Just then, Adam stopped dancing and instead caught his breath. A slow smirk then spread on his lips, before his head turned towards the door and busted her. "Enjoying the show, tutu?"

Rolling her eyes, Fiona heard him grin as he extended a hand towards her, before wiggling a finger at her. She shook her head, biting her lip, and that only made him chuckle lowly and start creeping towards her.

Like a predator stalking his pray, Fiona felt her breathing become bothered as he finally grabbed her hips and pulled her out onto the floor. The music still boomed in the lyrics were making her sweat.

'I'm a freaky-deeky lover, wanna hit you from the back and other ways that you have never experimented under the covers—'

Just as the beat hit Adam twisted her around and pressed her back against him, brushing her hair away from her ear. She could feel his dirty smirk as he slowly started swaying with her to the beat, while whispering along to music.

"Imma' make you scream my name—imma' make you glad you came," He chuckled when Fiona squirmed against him, barely controlling herself. He teasingly bit her ear, before kissing her down her neck.

"Adam," She breathed out. Shit, she was about to throw every their promise so far away—

"Alright bunnies, that's enough public dry-humping!" A voice cut through the music and officially made Fiona jump in shock.

Kalo stood in the door with a knowing and pleased grin on her face as Adam turned his head to shoot her a flat glare.

"Vete a la mierda," He rolled off his tongue before flicking her a long finger.

"Cállate la boca," Kalo scoffed back. "Now give me my dance partner back, I need her."

"She'll be with you in a minute," Adam snapped, to which Kalo rolled her eyes and stepped out to give them a moment.

Which was good, because Fiona was about the color of a cherry.

"So are we still on for tonight?" Adam finally said, chuckling as he turned around and made her meet his eyes. Fiona gulped and quickly nodded.

"Yup, yup."

"Good. Now bring those lips up here, tutu."

Fiona didn't hesitate to step onto her toes as Adam wrapped his hand around her head and pulled her to him. Their lips met in a hot mess, Adam running his tongue over her seams before dipping into her mouth. A feeble moan escaped Fiona as heat started licking itself against her skin, just as Adam reached down and cupped her ass.

Whimpering when he gave it a good squeeze, Fiona gripped onto his shirt and couldn't go amiss of the hard bulge that was pressing against her stomach. When she returned the favor and cupped him, Adam cursed against her mouth.

"You better run after Kalo right now or you're not leaving this room anytime soon," He told her as a matter-of-factly. Fiona almost contemplated staying. "Go, baby."

With a reluctant huff, Fiona pulled away from Adam who smirked down at her. She gave him a grumpy look, but then turned and started heading for the door. "I'll see you tonight."

Every week for the past three months, Adam and Fiona had had a date night. It had taken some time to figure out a schedule, but after graduating and Adam recovering from his injuries, they had agreed upon one night a week, Saturday to be precise. Which happened to be tonight.

"By the way," Adam called out, just as Fiona stopped up in the door. She glanced over her shoulder and found him grabbing his water bottle with a smirk. "My grams won't be home tonight."

Fiona paled and felt her eyes widen. His grams wouldn't be there...? "Oh...?"

"Nope," Adam kept the smirk as he suckled on his water bottle and took a sip. "We'll have the place to ourselves."

Fiona's stomach exploded with butterflies. She had to remind herself to breathe—a thing her body suddenly refused to do as Adam kept smirking suggestively at her, teasing her by wagging his eyebrows.

"Okay," She merely said, before swallowing dryly, trying to seem indifferent. They were waiting after all. "I'll see you later then."

With a last grin from Adam, she then hurried out of the dance studio, out into the hall where Kalo was tapping her foot impatiently and sending her an accusing stare. She finally snorted at her red face.

"I don't know how you haven't jumped him yet," She declared, shaking her head disapprovingly as they started walking down the hall. "With Dimitri, I hardly lasted a week."

And as they entered their dance studio down the hall from Adam, Fiona silently chewed her lip and thought to herself.

Maybe it was time to jump.

"... and then Dimitri accused me of not having enough fucking rotation on my turns, so I showed him that thing I did last week, you know that spin I do on my cap, and he told me even a newbie could do better."

Adam came out of the bathroom, throwing away a towel and scoffing with a shake of his head as Fiona grinned at him from the bed. Freshly showered and shaved, he clicked off the lights and then crawled in over her, laying down behind in bed with a sigh, pulling the covers over them both.

"Calling me a fucking newbie. I taught him to dupstep. I'm insulted."

"Your poor ego," Fiona sarcastically sympathized as he settled in. When she sent him a grin, he chuckled and shook his head again.

"Shut up. What movie did you pick?"

Fiona pressed, play and as soon as Netflix had loaded the screen, Adam let out a groan.

"Burlesque, really?" He grinned, pinching her side.

"Shut up, it's a great movie!" Fiona argued with a pout. Adam hummed behind her, but then reached for the bowl of fruit on the floor. He picked a piece of mango and plopped it in his mouth.

"I watched Ninja Turtles with you last week, so you better shut up and watch the movie," Fiona ordered, to which Adam snickered.

"Fine," He conceded, pressing a kiss to her shoulder.

Wrapping his arm around her, they then started to watch the movie, Fiona unable to fully concentrate as the butterflies in her stomach from earlier continued to flutter around inside her.

Adam had spoken the truth; his grams was staying at the senior care center for the night, celebrating one of her friend's birthday. They were completely and utterly alone.

Chewing on her lip, Fiona dared a glance up at Adam who was staring at the screen, watching the dancers dance around on stage in the movie.

Fiona's mom allowed her to spend one night a week at Adam's place, sleeping over. Despite all the progress they had made, her mom still didn't trust Adam a hundred percent, but she also couldn't deny any longer that Fiona was grown and deserved to live her own life; Meaning, spending nights with her boyfriend was going to happen.

Still, despite telling her mom that they had decided to wait on the whole sex thing, Fiona's mom had taken no chances and taken her to the doctor to get her started on the pill. She also told her that as long as she lived under her roof, she was going to also dedicate time to her family and not neglect her studies.

Yes, studies.

As it turned out, a lot could happen in three months.

After having gone to therapy and having begun working on her complicated issues with food, Fiona's therapist had encouraged her to look into the actual foods she ate to understand the nutritional values they had, as a way to combat the fear of them. It was because of that and after having actual done as her therapist recommended, Fiona had realized what she wanted to do with her life.

– Nutritional specialist.

Learning about food, health and how it all worked together had given Fiona the confidence to eat without fearing gaining weight, at least the wrong way. Through muscles, protein and healthy fats, she had begun eating carefully and seen the results her body was able to make with just the littlest adjustment to her eating habits. Three months of eating regularly, and now she was at a normal weight, but with no less muscles than she had before.

That success had inspired her to want to help others who struggled with food the way she had. Whether it be obesity or anorexia, she knew she wanted to help others find the courage to change their lifestyle as well. Food was such an important part of living, and for a long time, she hadn't felt alive. Adam gave her the courage to try, but food gave her the energy to continue.

And today, she had never felt more alive.

But Fiona wasn't the only one who had gone through a lot of changes.

After what had happened—after Adam had been through recovery—they had stuck to their decision about not reporting to the cops. It had been months since they had last heard anything from them, anyway. What Adam had said about getting even had perhaps been true; maybe now that he had gotten his 'punishment', they would finally let him be. Fiona truly hoped that in any case. The good news was, he would no longer have to see them on a daily basis anymore.

Graduation had rolled around fast, and the moment Adam had received his cap, gown and diploma, he had been out of that school for good. Fiona had attended his graduation and had never been so happy as when he had walked off stage and saw the way his chest had deflated; he was finally free.

Shortly after that, Adam had received a call from his new parole officer, who had delivered the surprising news that his parole was coming to an end. After years of sticking to his word and being a model student in school, his P.O had told him his sentence was nearly served. He had a court date in a few days where he would appear in front of a judge to make it official. If everything went through, his criminal slate would also finally be clean as well.

It felt like everything had fallen into place over the past three months. Fiona had gotten over her fear of dancing with others—hence her reason for dancing with Kalo earlier. She, Kalo and Rani were working on a dance routine together to showcase on dance circle Monday. So far, Fiona hadn't dared to step into it yet. But maybe that was about change soon as well.

Three months was all they had needed to make everything come together. Now, lying here in bed with Adam, Fiona had never felt happier in her life. She couldn't help but smile as she felt Adam hum along to the music playing in the movie, telling her that he had most definitely seen this movie more than once or twice.

"What?" He asked when she wouldn't stop giggling. "What's funny?"

"You know the songs," Fiona pointed out, to which Adam pursed his lips.

"Shut up," He muttered, to which Fiona only burst with more laughter. He clamped a hand over her mouth, and it only resulted in Fiona biting into his hand, licking his palm until he cursed and removed it again. "Christ, Fee."

"What?" She teased, squirming when he caught his arms around her.

"Keep moving and licking me like that, I fucking dare you," He chuckled, but she saw the serious glint in his eyes.

"What would you do?" Fiona breathed back, swallowing when she caught his eyes. He saw the look inside hers. With a slow hand, he therefore brought his thumb to her lip.

"I'd show you what my tongue can do to you," He whispered, rubbing her bottom lip. "I'd spread your legs and crawl between them and not leave until you're dripping all over my mouth."

Fiona felt the air get knocked out of her chest. She opened her mouth to respond something, but nothing came out. Her body felt uncomfortably hot, and the spot between her legs was pulsing.

"Do you want me to?" Adam whispered against her lips, moving lower until there was no escaping him. He'd caught her against the mattress and pinned her down. "One word, Fee. Tell me if you want me."

Three months. They had been waiting for three months, and all of a suddenly Fiona couldn't remember why. She wanted him more than anything. It was time.

"Yes," Fiona therefore breathed back, seeing Adam's eyes flash with surprise. Maybe he didn't think she'd go through with it. "Only if you want to, too, though."

"Is that even a question?" Adam groaned and pressed his hips against hers, giving her the proof of how much he wanted her. "Christ, Fee, I wanna taste you so fucking bad. I wanna feel you come against my mouth."

A feeble sound left Fiona—something completely hot and bothered and embarrassing. His words had made her pussy clench and there was nothing she could think of that could stop her from wanting this. She was done waiting.

"Please," She begged when he kept hovering over her lips, grinding his hips against her. "I want you, Adam."

"Fuck," Something inside him seemed to snap, and with no further incentive, he pulled the covers off of them and reached into her pajama shorts. Fiona gasped, but only spread her thighs further apart when his fingers found her soaking panties. "You're already so wet, Fee. What the fuck."

Rubbing his palm against her mound, Fiona finally succumbed and dragged his lips down on hers. Adam didn't hold back and kissed her back passionately, sliding his tongue along hers with a strained groan.

Bucking against his hand, Fiona moaned and whimpered as Adam slid his finger along her slit and rubbed her clit until she was soaking through her panty. Adam groaned into her mouth, and with a final peck to her lips, he then pulled back.

"Come here," He whispered, moving back to steer her legs up, only so he could hook his fingers around the waistband of her pajama shorts and panties. Fiona complied and lifted her hips to help him pull them off.

Throwing both items away on the floor, Fiona felt herself flush instantly as she found herself lying bottomless in front of Adam. When he slowly parted her knees and gazed upon her dripping sex, he shook his head and whispered a sacrilegious curse under his breath.

"Why the fuck..." He breathed, slowly dipping down to kiss her mound. "... are you so fucking beautiful?"

"Adam," Fiona cried out softly as his lips kissed around her sex, trailing up her inner thigh and kissing right above her mound.

"Are you still sure you want this?" He asked between her legs, his voice sounding as messed up as she felt. Even if she hadn't wanted this, she felt like there was no way she could've ever pulled away from this.

"Yes!" She whimpered, just as his lips finally sealed over her pussy. "Fuck!"

With a slow, measured lick, she felt as Adam's tongue slid between her folds and sought out her clit, gulping loudly with a groan before grasping tightly onto her thighs. And then, it happened.

Fiona screamed and had to slap a hand over her mouth, just as Adam sucked her clit into his mouth and began thrusting and grinding his tongue against it. Her body arched off the bed and her legs snapped shut in reflex as the pleasure tickled up inside her and made her insides clench. Wetness started dripping from her core and she felt with deft moves as Adam lapped it up with his tongue.

"Oh, fuck!" She cried out, twisting and turning in his bed. When he started flattening his tongue and letting her hips grind against his face, she cursed out and nearly jolted up, gripping onto the roots of his hair. "F-fuck! Adam!"

He made a sound at the back of his throat, before she heard the heavy gulp again, her juices flowing down his throat. She was coming apart fast and there was no way she could hold back.

It was the moment she felt him insert two fingers inside her, it was game over. Fiona cried out and felt herself come apart against his lips as he had wanted it, hearing him drink up all her creamy juices with satisfied groans. She was panting by the time she released her hold on his hair and slumped back into the bed. Through wet lashes, she saw Adam sit up and wipe his mouth down, before moving in over her.

"Are you okay?" He whispered when all she could do was pant and whimper, still feeling the aftershocks pulsing through her. Her pussy was throbbing, but God she was feeling great.

"I want more," She pleaded, wrapping her hands around his neck and dragging him down to her lips.

"More?" He spoke, almost in disbelief. He chuckled breathlessly before pecking her lips. "Are you sure you can handle that?"

Fiona shook her head. He had misunderstood her. She didn't mean more of him licking her up; She meant more of him.

"I don't want to wait any longer," She whispered, seeing as truth slowly dawned on him. His face sobered up and he looked down at her with a serious expression.

"You wanna...?" He left the sentence hanging for her to finish, but all she could do was nod. He shook his head at that. "I need to hear you say it, Fee. I need you to speak the words."

"I want you to fuck me," She told him, wrapping her legs around him and boldly reaching down between them to cup his very hard erection. "I want you, Adam. All of you."

With a groan, Adam succumbed to her plea and leaned down to her lips. "Baby. Are you sure?"

"Yes," She whimpered, reaching into his sweats to cup his length. He was commando. With a quick tug, she started rubbing her hand up and down his shaft. "I want you, Adam."

"Fuck," He groaned out throatily, straining his neck back when she kept rubbing him. And that seemed to be game over for him.

Leaning down, he mashed his lips against her with a fervid groan, before reaching down to her pussy again, not wasting a moment to thrust two fingers inside her still dripping core. Fiona jolted, but instantly felt how her pussy stretched and accepted the intrusion, feeling as he started to jerk them slowly in and out of her in a rhythmic pace. Her core started clenching around him, her hips undulating to the motion.

In less than a minute, they had both removed what little clothes they both had left on. Fiona pulled off her shirt while Adam stood up to slide off his sweats and discard his t-shirt. Then, they were both on each other again, Adam groaning as Fiona wrapped her hand around his pulsating cock.

"Condom," He panted against her lips when they were both spinning out of control. "Hold on, tutu."

Tilting his hand out over the edge of the bed, Adam pawed around under his mattress while Fiona tried to catch her breath. Finally, after what felt like eternities, he procured a little foil package from under his bed, sitting back on his haunches to quickly tear it and roll it on.

Watching as he safely sheathed his length, Fiona then spread her legs and wrapped them around him as Adam came back on top of her, cupping her face. He slowly rubbed his now covered length up and down her folds, letting anticipation build up inside her stomach.

"Are you still absolutely sure about this?" He whispered, catching her eyes to see the truth in them. Fiona hummed and cupped his cheek, and with a little smile, she nodded.

"Yes."

With a last look, Adam then leaned down and kissed her deeply, Fiona moaning against his lips as his hips now again started sliding up and down her folds. His thick, steely warmth made her pussy squeeze in need, begging to feel it slide inside her.

But then, reaching down, Adam slowly guided himself inside her, granting her her wish.

Fiona's mouth opened and shaped an 'O' as the pressure of his cock invaded her virgin opening. It was so much different from his fingers, the pressure and aching so much more... intense. She felt as his tip entered her completely, before he slowly slid inside her, inch by inch.

"Tell me if I'm hurting you," Adam murmured near her ear, concentrated on carefully entering her and letting her adjust. It was right about then Fiona realized she had dug her fingertips into his back.

Letting go of a small whimper, Fiona bit her lip, but was surprised to discovered she hardly felt any pain. She felt the large intrusion inside her that her body was trying to get accustomed to, but other than that, there was only an uncomfortable pinching. But no pain.

"It doesn't hurt," She breathed, flattening her palms and stroking his back. "Keep going."

Adam gave a grunt to let her know he heard her. Then, sliding further in, he slowly sunk all the way inside her.

Fiona gasped as Adam settled within her with a groan, fully sheathed inside her. The pressure felt so much, but Fiona loved it. All of him was inside her, nestled in her pussy.

"How are you feeling?" Adam spoke into her ear. He brushed her cheek with a little smile, to which Fiona returned it.

"Good."

"Good?" When she nodded, he smiled broader and hovered over her lips. "I'm gonna make you feel great, baby. Just wait."

And then he slowly retracted his hips, before pushing inside her again.

Fiona gasped and felt something pleasurable run up her spin. Oh. When Adam repeated the motion and struck even deeper inside her, her pussy clenched around him and made her release a sound. Pleasure released inside her and started wrapping around his cock as he slowly found a rhythm. With each thrust, he went a little faster, giving her just a tiny taste of the pleasure that was currently coursing through her lower belly. It felt like all of her nerve endings were getting zapped and electrified as he continued to strike a spot within her.

"Shit," She breathed out quietly, just as Adam kissed her neck with what she could feel was a smile.

"Feel good, baby? You like that?"

Fiona nodded rapidly when he suddenly gripped her thigh and hoisted it over his shoulder.

"Good, because I'm so far from done with you," He whispered hotly in her ear.

And then, he stopped holding back.

Fiona let out a cry and had to quickly grab onto the headboard as Adam slammed his hips against hers, the new angle making him slide so much deeper. Fiona screamed out and then heard his harsh groan as his hips started jerking fast. The entire bed started moving with them, banging against the wall behind them.

"Fuck! Adam!" Fiona cried out as she felt her pussy begin to bathe in juices, the wet slap of his balls striking her making her blush. Adam gripped her chin right then and steered her lips to his, taking them harshly, just as Fiona felt herself come apart.

If an orgasm by his tongue had felt great, she had no words for what this felt like. Feeling Adam's cock slide within her, rubbing against her most sensitive parts, whilst hearing him moan into her ear at the feel of her tightening around him... there were no words as Fiona felt herself slip into another world of pleasure.

Her whole pussy clenched and retracted uncontrollably as Adam continued to plow through her orgasm, leaving her crying until she had no air left to spare. Only then did he slow down and allow her to catch her breath, which turned out to be a difficult task when his lips veered down and found her peaked nipples.

"You are so sexy," He breathed against her chest, kissing her up her neck and releasing a groan as he slowly circled his hips and made Fiona tremble at the sensation. Oh God, she felt like she could come again any second. "I love you so much, Fiona. God, I love you."

He pulled back to meet her eyes, and with tears in her own, Fiona smiled and laughed in agreement. "I love you, too."

Adam smiled brightly down at her, then swept a lock of sweaty hair away from her forehead and brushed her cheek. "Hey."

"Hi," Fiona giggled, suddenly very aware of everything. They were having sex. "Is, uhm... does it feel good for you, too?"

Adam barked out a laugh, dipping his head down into her neck. Then, lifting it up again, he shook his head. "You fucking kill me, Fee."

"Is that a yes?" She tried, laughing nervously.

"It's a dead yes."

"Are you sure? Because I can move more. I-I mean, I could maybe—"

Adam silenced her with a kiss. Pecking her lips softly, he then hummed against her lips, shifting the weight on his elbows. "First time's on me, tutu. I want you to feel good. We can do me later."

"But I still want you to come," She stated, gripping onto his hair tightly. "I want you to... come inside me."

His cock did a jerk inside her, and with a surprised yelp, Fiona blinked up at Adam who's jaw had locked tightly.

"Death," He then shook his head, before slowly starting to move his hips again. "You're gonna be the death of me, tutu."

And with that, he pinned her to the mattress and gave her her wish.

But not before making sure she knew exactly how to pirouette in bed as well.

Epilogue

7 YEARS LATER

"We are so gonna win today."

"Most definitely."

"The boys don't stand a chance."

As Fiona, Rani and Kalo walked into the studio with their bags, they found Adam, Dimitri and Twitch already inside, standing by the stereo. When they entered, they all turned and shot them a look.

Fiona instantly caught Adam's eyes and saw him grin.

Resisting a smile herself, Fiona reminded herself what they were here for today and soldiered up.

Last week, the boys had told them that out of the six of them, they were the best dancers. That they created better routines than the girls, and outraged, Kalo had challenged them to a dance-off; one week to prepare, losing team had to clean the DanceDec's studios for a whole month.

The boys had accepted, and today was finally the day where the dance-off was happening. So when Adam waved to Fiona, she had to remind herself that today, the boys were the enemies.

"Ladies," Kalo spoke to the boys and walked in, dumping her bag down. "Are you ready for this or nah?"

"Bring it," Dimitri countered, sending her a smirk. "Misters first." He gestured towards them, since Kalo had officially branded them as the girls.

"Fine," Kalo snorted, turning towards Fiona and Rani. "We ready?"

"Ready," Rani confidently agreed. Fiona nodded as well.

"Great. Bring in the judges then!"

Adam grinned, but then put his fingers in his mouth and whistles loudly. "Judges!"

And with that, a flood of other dancers, students and teachers came into the studio, gathering along the walls of the studio to take part in their dance-off. Now that they had their cheering audience and thus their judges, all that was left to do was turn on the music.

"Hit it!" Kalo shouted, just as Rani had run up to the stereo and plugged her phone in. She quickly ran back to Fiona and Kalo, who had both taken their place on the dance floor. They turned towards the boys who had all taken a seat in a chair, ready to watch them.

And then, the music hit them.

– The second the music started booming, Kalo, Rani and Fiona all moved in sync, turning around as the trumpet counted down the beat. Then, as the baseline of Ain't No Other Man hit, they all moved together.

The crowd around them broke into cheers, and even though Fiona was blushing her way through it all, she worked with the vibe the crowd was giving her and followed the steps, trying not to focus on the nerves that still bit her stomach every time she had to perform.

– But instead focused on the jungly eyes that was watching her.

As the beat switched, Fiona followed Rani and Kalo's lead and walked forward, hips swinging, before stopping up in front of the three boys that were watching them. Their eyes all followed when the girls sent them mischievous grins and continued to walk towards them.

Sitting in their row of chairs, all the boys then howled excitedly as the three girls killed it on the dance floor before them, before walking in a circle around them, teasing them. All the boys followed them with their eyes, grinning so widely it was contagious. When Fiona walked behind Adam and grazed his shoulder, his wagged his eyebrows mischievously back at her. She nearly lost her step.

Quickly doing as they had rehearsed for weeks though, Fiona followed Kalo and Rani again as they then all slung their legs over their man. Fiona slid herself over Adam's thighs and then wrapped her arms around his neck, watching his surprised laugh and saw him shake his head. She couldn't help but laugh back, sliding her hands down to his chest, before leaning backwards on the chair, letting herself drop down, twisting her head as she went.

Whipping up again, hair following, all the boys got a mouthful of it before the girls swiftly stood up and left them again. Then, just as the big note came, all three girls lined up and raised their hands to the sky; in unison, they slowly slid down on the floor in a split.

The crowd went wild as they continued, the boys howling and whistling as well. The girls all spun around on the floor, before getting up and continuing their routine. Fiona almost couldn't concentrate as her eyes found Adam's again, seeing him watch her so enthralled. Even after seven years, he still looked at her like the day they fell in love.

On the cue, all three girls then suddenly flung themselves across the guys who instinctively caught them, just as the music ended. Sitting astride their laps, one leg kicked up, and arms around their necks, the music came to an end and the crowd around them exploded; Everyone cheered as the boys hollered, holding each their girl. Adam grinned as well and lifted Fiona to his lips, pressing a quick, but deep kiss to her mouth, before helping her sit up and bask in her applause.

All of the girls joined hands and made a bow to the audience, before all three boys behind them seemed to have the same idea; they all grabbed their girl and dragged them into their arms.

"Not bad," Adam chuckled hoarsely in her ear, just as Fiona turned in his arms and met him with a bright smile. "I'll score you a 7 out of 10. Could've done more with your feet."

"Save your teaching for your classes," Fiona snipped, to which Adam laughed and dipped down to steal her lips. Cupping her cheek, he planted a good kiss on them.

Adam had been teaching for about five years now. It took him some time to actually find a sponsor who would support him starting classes at the DanceDec for the kids who came in from the street. He and Dimitri had then finally managed to book some classes for all who wanted to learn how to throw down on the floor. Along with Fiona, who had been studying nutrition and health for years now, they had managed to scrape together enough money to be able to pay for their own apartment. Adam's grams had moved into the senior care center and was spending her final days with all of her friends. They still stopped by on Saturdays to visit and dance with them all.

Seven years of going strong, not a day had gone by where they hadn't loved each other. But today, they were enemies.

"Alright!" Kalo suddenly burst into the cheering crowd and shouted above them. "Now for the boys! Don't forget to boo!"

When Fiona giggled up at Adam, he rolled his eyes, but then looked down at her with a mysterious grin. Then, pushing her back on the very seats that they had just been in, he whispered near her mouth; "You're going to lose, baby. Trust me."

Fiona shook her head with a pursed lip, but then sat down with Kalo and Rani as the boys walked into the center of the room. They pulled their hoodies up over their heads and then took their mark. Fiona held her breath and waited for the music to start.

– But then, very anti-climatically, the lights in the room cut out instead.

The crowd gave a surprised gasp, and in the darkness, Fiona could tell both Rani and Kalo were looking around confused as well. Someone even yelled "who turned off the lights?" when suddenly, it happened.

The music started playing and Fiona froze up.

Single Ladies by Beyoncé started blasting through the speakers, and with knowing Adam for more than seven years, Fiona could do nothing but whisper as she knew what was coming; "Oh God, no."

The lights cut on, and it only took a moment for her eyes to adjust, but sadly not to the light. No.

It was to the fact that a smirking Adam was standing in a tight pair of leggings and a black leotard, alongside Dimitri and Twitch who wore the same. Oh, no, he wouldn't...

But he was. All the boys were moving along to the song, doing the Single Ladies dance, wiggling their hips and waving their hands – exactly as Fiona had anticipated as soon as she heard the music.

Fiona couldn't stop herself; She burst into laughter as all the boys kicked their leg out and spun around, wiggling their asses.

"What the fuck!" Kalo screamed, just as breathless from laughter as Fiona. Rani was wheezing as well, watching the three fully-grown men swing around on the floor in tight and very revealing leotards. Kalo started howling and whistled loudly. "Woo! Yeah, baby! Shake it!"

Fiona couldn't even focus as the boys continued dancing, looking about as ridiculous as was even possible, but the fact of the matter was, they were nailing it. Every step, every swing, every sassy hand wave and whip of the head. They trotted around on the floor and delivered the perfect reen-actment of Beyoncé's masterpiece.

– Right up until the end.

Instead of freezing in the classic pose, only Dimitri and Twitch froze up, while Adam kept moving. Letting himself slide across the floor, he slid up on his knees to Fiona who widened her eyes when got up in her face, panting hard with a stupid smile on his face. Then, grabbing her hand, he lifted it to his lips and then suddenly reached for something tucked inside his leotard. Fiona's heart froze to a complete halt.

"Fiona Torrence," Adam then breathlessly panted, lifting himself up on one knee. With a broad, but also cheeky smile, he lifted his hand and presented her a ring; "You better fucking marry me."

Everyone screamed and broke into shocked gasps as they watched Fiona cup her mouth and let out a hopeless sob. What the actual fuck?

"Oh my G-God, Adam," She sobbed, shaking everywhere as she reached for him. She pulled him tightly against her and sobbed against his lips as she kissed him. "I l-love y-you—" She was such a mess, she wasn't even sure the words translated as she tried to kiss him while speaking.

Adam kissed her back and chuckled against her lips as she kept blubbering. "So yes?"

Fiona nodded wildly, hiccuping as she choked on her tears. "Yes! Yes, yes, yes!"

The room burst into an ear-piercing cheer and seemed to explode with tumult. The boys who had helped Adam with his little number whistled and howled, clapping loudly as he got his yes. Fiona couldn't believe it.

However, none of that was compared to the look on Adam's face as fireworks seemed to explode in his eyes. He nearly cracked his face from smiling so much.

"Yes? You said yes?" He laughed, standing up and lifting her to the floor as well. "She said yes? SHE SAID YES!"

Fiona screeched and had to catch herself as Adam without warning then lifted her off the floor and spun her around, looking up at her mesmerized.

"SHE SAID FUCKING YES! SHES MINE, GUYS! I GOT HER!"

Fiona burst into laughter, but then had to brace herself again when he suddenly flung her over his shoulder. She let out a screech when he then bolted off, smacking her ass as he ran out of the room and down the hall.

"SHE SAID YESSS! SHE SAID YES! I FUCKING GOT HER! SHE SAID YES, GUYS!"

The whole of the DanceDec got to know the news as Adam ran around with Fiona bouncing helplessly over his shoulder, no intention of putting her down. She couldn't stop laughing and crying at the same time as Adam screamed the news at the top of his lungs.

"I GOT MYSELF A WIFEY!"

"Okay, put me down!" Fiona finally laughed when this had gone on for long enough. He stopped at studio 13, the very same studio where they had first met seven years ago – where he had first peeped on her feet.

Setting her down, he captured her in his arms and held her closely. Cupping her cheek, he then leaned his forehead against hers and panted heavily after having run around, screaming. "You said yes, baby."

"Of course I did," Fiona cried, shaking her head with a stupid smile on her lips that she couldn't wipe off. "What the hell took you so long?"

Adam stared at her for a moment, then burst into a laughter. Then, shaking his head, he took her hand and finally placed the ring on her finger. Looking down at it, more tears filled her eyes when she saw the rock. She knew that thing had to have cost him nearly everything.

"There," He said, kissing her hand. "Now you can't run away from me anymore."

Fiona rolled her eyes, but still couldn't stop smiling. "Whatever. You were wrong, though."

Adam frowned a little, looking confused at her. "Wrong how?"

Fiona grinned a little. "I didn't lose today; I think I won."

Adam let out a laugh, but then pulled her to his chest and poked her nose. "Baby, I've been winning ever since that day you pirouetted right into my arms."

And to that, Fiona couldn't agree more.

The very hardest thing she had ever had to do had ironically led her to the best thing that ever happened to her.

– And now, thanks to the man in her arms, her heart would never stop pirouetting.